PRAISE FOR *BEA*

"Informative and engaging, with solid pacing and engaging dialogue that keep the plot moving steadily over its half-century timeline. Foster has a deep knowledge of the history of both the region and the era, and his well-developed characters transform a timeline of events into a captivating tale. An epic novel."

—*Kirkus Reviews*

"At times tragic and at times triumphant, *Beardstown* serves as both cautionary tale and blueprint for any would-be city builder. In this literary tour de force and part two of an American trilogy about western frontier expansion, Foster pens a novel so wrought with ambition, grief, exultation, and relief that the sheer weight of emotion overwhelms the reader while reminding us that the grueling work of placemaking is never done. Foster brings all of this to life in rich detail, with just the right amounts of detachment and sympathy. He's a master at his craft and one who's fun to read. I can't wait for part three."

—Ron Starner, executive vice president of Conway Data, Inc.

"Sam Foster's tale of life on the midwestern frontier relates very well with current issues facing industrial development.... [an] amazingly entertaining story."

—Ron L. Frierson, director of economic policy, City of Los Angeles

"Once again Sam Foster has delivered an incredibly delightful novel. As a man setting out to build a modern American city two hundred years after Tom Beard showed up on the banks of the Illinois River, I really identified with the characters. Especially Tom Beard, who is asked, 'Who will build the churches and schools?' by his business partner. 'We will,' he says, 'because we are empire builders, the others are just in it for the money.'"

—Randy Kendrick, developer of Hayden,
Texas, America's city of the future

"A wonderfully done historical novel on the battle for the Midwest. I can't wait to read the third book in the American Trilogy series . . . and anything else Sam Foster writes."

—Catraphoenix, book blogger

PRAISE FOR *A PANTHER CROSSES OVER*, BOOK 1 OF THE AMERICAN TRILOGY

"Absolutely stunning. *A Panther Crosses Over* is either time travel or reincarnation, a tactile trip of immense believability."

—Charlie Newton, award-winning author of
Traitor's Gate, Privateers, and *Canaryville*

"A solid tale with a firm historical grounding that examines early American conflicts."

—*Kirkus Reviews*

"Foster has written a work of fiction that brings the history to life and enriches and fills in the gaps with the novelist's art and insight. The tale he tells is Homeric, not just in the savage grandeur of the subject and complex nobility of the heroes, but in the poetry of the smallest details and hidden mysteries of the hearts of its great cast of (real) characters."

—Chris Flannery, host of *The American Story* podcast,
senior fellow at the Claremont Institute

"[Foster is] a brilliant storyteller and weaver of historical fact and fiction; I was so deeply involved from the first pages that I stayed up all weekend to consume this wonderful tale of the Midwest's founding."

—Jay Weston, film producer of *Buddy Buddy* and the Academy Award–nominated *Lady Sings the Blues.*

"[A] compelling read . . . The first installment of a trilogy captures the fierce splendor of the time. With meticulous attention to detail, Foster transports his readers to eighteenth- and nineteenth-century America and then into the hearts and minds of the novel's protagonists. A master storyteller, he weaves together historical facts with a fertile imagination. The result is a thought-provoking novel that is a must-read not only for history enthusiasts but for readers of all ages."

—Readers' Favorite

BEARDSTOWN

Rooney,
   The entire
book is one big
development project.
Right up your alley.

[signature]

[signature]

BEARDSTOWN

~ The ~
**AMERICAN
TRILOGY
BOOK 2**

A NOVEL

SAM FOSTER

Agave
Americana
Books

This book is a work of fiction based on historical facts. Names, characters, places and organizations are either products of the author's imagination or used fictitiously. Research materials that have been used to direct the narrative include the 1965 "Mile Eighty-Eight: The History of Frontier Beardstown, 1818–1860," a graduate research thesis by Judith E. Hager; *History of Cass County, Illinois*, edited by William Henry Perrin; the 1915 *Historical Encyclopedia of Illinois*, edited by Newton Bateman and Paul Selby, and *History of Cass County*, edited by Charles A. E. Martin; the 1907 *Historical Sketches of Cass County, Illinois*, by J. N. Gridley; *Beardstown Yesterday and Today 1829–1979* by *Beardstown Gazette*; *The Potawatomi, Conquerors of Illinois*, by James Scott; "Mascouten History," an online article by Lee Sultzman (http://www.dickshovel.com/mas. html); "Abraham Lincoln: In His Own Words," a lecture by Professor David Zarefsky, PhD, presented by The Great Courses; and the 2002 edition of *Prairie Smoke* by Melvin R. Gilmore. Also, newspapers of various issues from Beardstown and Cass County, Illinois, from 1834–1870 have been consulted, including *Beardstown Chronicle and Illinois Military Bounty Land Advertiser*; *Beardstown Gazette*; *Beardstown and Petersburg Gazette*; *Central Illinoian*; *Beardstown Democrat*; *Cass County Messenger*; *Beardstown Enterprise*; *Beardstown Star of the West*; *Illinoian-Star*; *Cass County Star Gazette*; and finally, Google.

Published by Agave Americana Books, Redondo Beach, CA
samfosterbooks.com

Cover design: Rachel Marek
Project management: Emilie Sandoz-Voyer

Cover image credits: © Rita Asia Chow (illustration)
and © W. Phokin/Shutterstock (texture)

ISBN (hardcover): 978-1-7372601-6-5
ISBN (paperback): 978-1-7372601-3-4
ISBN (ebook): 978-1-7372601-9-6

Library of Congress Control Number: 2022912296

This book is dedicated, with very special thanks, to the research staff and librarians of the Abraham Lincoln Presidential Library.

"The test of a first-rate intelligence is the ability to hold two opposed ideas in the mind at the same time."

—F. Scott Fitzgerald

PROLOGUE

OCTOBER 4, 1818

Edwardsville, Illinois Territory

Enos Marsh stood behind his bar, wiping a shot glass. Even at midday the room was dim, the only light in the log building coming from one unshuttered window and the flicker of a low fire in the hearth. He'd debated lighting the fire at all. The weather this mild October day didn't yet require it, but he'd had fifteen cords of wood chopped and put away, so he had plenty to last through the winter. He also liked the smell and the light, as well as the warmth, of a first fall fire, so he'd lit it.

Marsh saw the explosion of light before he heard the door burst open. He turned to it, looking at a figure that almost filled the space. Backlit as the man was, Marsh could not make out much except that he was tall, more than six feet, wearing a wide-brimmed felt hat with a low crown, shoulders broad enough to block most of the light, and waist and hips thin enough to suggest youth. As the stranger stepped into the room and closed the door behind him, he removed his hat. That and the ambient light gave Marsh a better vision of the man's face. He was in his early twenties. His hair was light brown, thick and grown oddly inward from his temples, giving the sense of a low, narrow forehead. He wore long side whiskers that shone with a reddish tint, but he had no mustache or beard. His lips seemed thin and his nose long and robust. His buckskin jacket was festooned with foot-long cords of fringe across the chest and down the length of the sleeves, many of them missing, obviously cut off for some use. His pants were rough-finish homespun wool brushed smooth in the wearing. His collarless shirt was of unbleached linen. In the dim light, Marsh could not make out his eye color, but his whole face and being gave a sense of great vitality and warmth. He was a complete stranger, in a new place, and nonetheless his face beamed joy and goodwill. His broad smile was not one of a man who was uncertain and wore it to announce he presented no danger. It was the smile of a man who genuinely enjoyed his life and felt very much in command of it.

He strode straight to Marsh and extended his hand across the bar. "Name's Beard, Thomas Beard. Call me Tom. I'd like a beer, a warm meal, and a room—in that order. And I need a place to stable my horses."

Beard was tall enough that Marsh was forced to move his hand up to accept the offered one. And his smile was infectious. Marsh could finally make out the color of the stranger's eyes. They were a light, almost ice, blue, and they twinkled delight with the world. Marsh could not help but be infected by the young man's mood. "We can do all of that, Tom. Edwardsville is an orderly town, but on the frontier, you never know. Unhitch your horses and lead them around back. We've a stable there where they can get rubbed down and fed. I'll bring one of my men to help with the gear."

By the time Beard got his mount and packhorse around back, Marsh and a middle-aged black man were there to greet him. Marsh pointed the helper to the horses. "Jim, lead them on in and get the saddle off Mr. . . ." And then quizzically he said, "Beard? It was Beard, wasn't it?"

"That's right, but make it Tom." And there was that smile again.

"Take Mr. Beard's horses, Jim, and get the trap off his mount once you get it in the stall." Marsh then moved his glance to Beard. "Tom, would you like us to store those things on the packhorse," he said as he pointed to the beast whose burden was covered in white canvas, the three legs to a surveyor's transit tripod sticking out the back, "or would you like to have it all taken to your room? Room's small, but it will fit."

"I'll take the transit myself, and the musket," Beard said and, now looking at Jim, added, "but would you be so kind as to bring those trade goods up to my room. I'm going to need them soon."

Marsh nodded to Jim, confirming he was to do as requested, turned to Beard, and said, "I believe a beer was the next thing on your list. When you come back in, there will be a cool one on the counter." And with that he walked away.

* * * *

Beard ran his hand over the flank of his mount as he stepped by, took the lead of the packhorse from Jim's hand, and led the horse into a stall. "Jim, you slave or free?"

The black man turned to face Beard and looked directly at him, his face opening to a smile that showed pride. "Free. Complicated, though."

As Beard untied the transit from the horse's back, he said, without looking back, "Complicated? How's that?"

Jim picked up a large piece of burlap and began to rub the roan. "I was born slave. In Tennessee. When I was 'bout ten years old the Cherokee raided the little settlement my masser started. Killed the men but took women and children captive. Me, too. So, I was a slave to the Cherokee for a while. I was traded around a few times and ended up with the Shawnee. Didn't none of them treat me no worse than my white masters, so it didn't much matter to me. Maybe five years ago, Mr. Marsh was trading with the Shawnee along the Wabash. He stopped to talk to me. Was tough 'memberin' my English, but as we talked it come back. He told me that in the end the Shawnee was gonna get whupped. Real soon. Mr. Marsh said if I wanted to come back to a white world, he'd buy me from the Shawnee."

"And Marsh freed you?" Beard asked.

"Yes, sir. Mr. Marsh made me the damnedest offer. Said if I went with him, he'd give me papers, and I could work for him if I wanted or not. That'd be up to me. No one never done nuttin' like that fur me. So, I took him up on it and he made good. I got ma papers right here."

Jim touched his hip pocket.

"I can leave anytime. But why? Got no place to go. Here I got a room of ma own to sleep, and he pays me 'nuff wages to keep maself and set a little aside. Maybe wun day I meet a nice woman. . . ."

Even the garrulous Beard seemed to have nothing to say in reply, but he was smiling. "Jim, hand me the musket that was in the saddle scabbard if you please."

Jim did as directed. Beard, with his transit thrown over one shoulder and the musket dangling from his other hand, turned to walk toward the stable entrance, the smile still on his face.

"Mr. Beard!" Jim called after him. "Mr. Marsh's a good man. You kin trust 'im."

* * * *

When Beard came down for dinner that night, he sat quietly in the corner, surveying the crowd. As he sopped the last of the venison gravy with his corn bread, Marsh approached him from across the room, a shot glass in either hand. He set them both down on the table and said, "I thought a corn whiskey might top off that meal better than a beer. May I join you?"

Beard smiled broadly and said, "I'd enjoy the company. Haven't had much the last couple of weeks."

Marsh pushed one shot glass across the table toward Beard, sipped from his own, looked directly into Beard's twinkling blue eyes, and said, "So, if I'm not prying, want to tell me what you and that transit are up to?"

Beard killed his whiskey in one quick swallow, set the empty glass down gently, and looked intently into Marsh's eyes. "Me and my transit are here to build a town, maybe a city." He said nothing more, leaving time for the audacity of his statement to soak in.

"And just where do you plan for this vision to bloom?"

"That, Mr. Marsh, I do not know, but I'll know the place. . . ."

"No. No 'Mr. Marsh.' Call me Enos. Most folks do."

"Fair 'nough. Enos it is.

"Enos, I like your metaphor of blooming a city. It's apt."

"How so, apt?" Marsh asked.

"It may be fall, but it's the season for planting here. The St. Louis Treaty gave America rights over everything in Illinois north and west of the river. Even though the Potawatomi haven't signed on, neither have they made a peep since Thames River. I think they will sign soon, maybe even this year. If there has been lingering trouble, it's been the Kickapoo. But since Colonel Howard marched up the Illinois River and roughed up a couple of their villages, they may still grumble, but they haven't taken any scalps. And President Monroe has made it clear he wants them to move west of the Mississippi. That will happen soon, Mr. Mar . . . Enos."

"You do keep up on politics, Tom."

Again, Beard broke into a broad open-faced smile. "It's my business to, Enos. I've been wandering the frontier for going on two years now, doing nothing but a little trading to live and learning all I need to know to make this biggest decision of my life the right one. All those soldiers who fought in the second war are going to accept their mustering-out bonus of 160 or 320 acres in the Illinois land north of the river as soon as the survey is complete. And then they will be coming in the thousands, maybe tens of thousands. And I'll be there to greet them."

Marsh took another sip of his whiskey. "So, if now is the season to grow your garden, where is the place to plant it?"

Beard composed his thoughts for a moment before answering. "Let me tell you what I do know. It has to be a place with a few Indians left because I've got to make enough to live on until these settlers come. Trading is the only way I know to do it. Second, and most important, it must be on the Illinois River. If my town is to be a center of commerce, it will have to fulfill two requirements. First, the land must be rich so farmers will be prosperous enough to have surpluses to sell. Second, it must be near transportation so those surpluses can get to markets—St. Louis, New Orleans, or on to the east coast. And that means river transportation. It's the only way. So, on the river and with good anchorage for a port and surrounded by rich land."

Beard laughed, a deep rumbling laugh. "Bold enough plan for a young man, Enos?"

Before Marsh could respond, Beard added, "Two more things, Enos. It's going to have to be on the south side of the river because everything north is reserved for all the bounties that are mustering-out bonuses for those veterans. But they'll all be coming from the south, from this direction. And because they will all want to get to the north side, I'll have to provide ferry service. I need to be able to get them to their land, as they come looking to plant. And they'll need to get to me, as they come looking to sell their surpluses. For that I'll need a ferry. If I can create a ferry, that will create the town. And if my little transit and I can lay out a town, in a spot like that, we'll have lots to sell and places for merchants and city dwellers to build.

"That's the plan, Enos."

"You seem like just the kind of man to pull this off, Tom. But the one thing you'll need to build this town of yours is money. When the time comes to buy the land, you'll need a money man. Come to me then."

"I will. But I need to find the right spot first," Tom replied. "You know a place where I can plant my garden?"

Marsh finished the last of his whiskey and smiled a slow, easy smile. "No, Tom, I don't. But I know a man who does."

PART I

A SQUATTER'S PARADISE

CHAPTER 1

NOVEMBER 12, 1818

Mascouten Bay, Illinois Territory

Young as Thomas Beard was, Murray McConnel was even younger, just twenty-one. But he was an experienced woodsman and trader who had wandered the continent's frontiers since he was fourteen years old and was one of the few men who knew the Illinois River Valley for more than a few miles north of its confluence with the Mississippi.

Marsh had introduced the two young adventurers over dinner, thinking McConnel might be able to serve as Beard's guide. When Beard told his story to McConnel, he'd added that he planned to pole his ferry across the river, so it would have to be a place where the bottom was shallow. At this, Murray's long, red bushy eyebrows immediately shot up into a knowing arch, and his high-pitched tenor voice filled the room. He shouted, "I know just the place!"

Every head at the bar turned toward them, and McConnel looked down, embarrassed to have brought attention to their

conversation. By the time he looked back, others in the tav-
ern had realized nothing of interest was happening and had
gone back to their own talk. McConnel, now in control of himself, but with blue eyes still twinkling, said, "There's a small
Potawatomi village at mile eighty-eight. Us boys with Howard
in '13 marched there to revenge the Fort Dearborn massacre.
But the Potawatomi had all gone. Every last one of 'em went
and hid. They eventually came back, but that was after Thames
River, and they have been quiet as church mice since their
defeat there. The place is just below Mascouten Bay. That's the
entrance to the swamp formed where the Sangamon runs into
the Illinois. Water is deep enough for easy navigation to that
point, but right in front of the village, the alluvial flow from
the Sangamon forms a bar clear across the Illinois. I can take
you there."

That had been just six days ago, and now here they were,
final supplies of grub and trading goods purchased, horses well
fed and rested, last kitchen-cooked breakfast either would have
for a long while in their bellies, morning sun on their faces, the
eagerness of youth in their hearts, and ready for whatever the
world had to hurl at them.

The two men, each mounted and with one packhorse
behind, rode straight and steady across the prairie through
grass tall enough to brush across their stirrups and boots and
along the horses' bellies. McConnel, taciturn man that he was,
led without conversation in a straight line headed due north.

"Murray, I've never seen anything like this," Beard said to
the back of McConnel's head. "Does this grass never end?"

"Not used to this, are ya'. Where're you from, Tom?"

"From a world of forests, Mo. May I call you that?"

McConnel tipped his hat in a small nod.

"Born in Upstate New York, but my folks moved to the
Connecticut Western Reserve when I was five," Tom continued. "I may have been very young, but I remember it vividly.

Storm in January. Why would a man move his family into the wilderness in January? Was the coldest I've ever been. My kid sister was just three and almost froze to death. There were five of us on two horses. That's it, just two horses. Ma held the baby with me behind. My kid sister rode in front of Pa. We'd have all froze, had my uncle—he'd gone there first—not come back and found us. Uncle had convinced my dad that the Reserve would explode with army vets from the Revolution coming for their mustering-out land bounty. And he was right. It will be no different here. Just different vets from a different war but same signing bonus paid at mustering out. Paid in land."

McConnel turned to look at Beard, but said nothing.

"Anyhow, my uncle had found a stream that would push a grinding mill. Figured all the incoming farmers would need one. He was right. Dad was big on education. Us kids labored all day, but every night after dinner he became the teacher. Eventually, the mill got enough work that he had to hire men. They got included in night class. Dad insisted. Finally, the mill made enough money to send my sister and me to school for a couple of years. Kid brother stayed home to help on the farm. I got a little education." Beard jerked his thumb toward the transit tripod legs sticking out from under the canvas covering his goods on the packhorse. "Learned to do that. That's what I got. Surveying skills and a transit. Kid brother will get the family farm and half the mill one day."

"That why you started wandering?" McConnel asked, finally breaking his silence.

"Sorta but not quite. Men in my family always been soldiers. Grandpa fought in the Revolution. When the Brits wanted a second shot at us, my dad, Jedediah, thought it was his turn. So, I came back from school to run the farm and help with the mill. He came home in '14. I stayed around for a few years but left home two years ago and wandered down through Ohio and Indiana before I got here. It's all trees back that way,

Mo. Never seen nothing like this. A man wouldn't even have to clear it. Just put a plow in the ground and start farming."

McConnel suddenly stopped his horse and turned back to face Beard. His thin, pale, freckled face showed no more expression, but his blue eyes twinkled with excitement. "Some Frenchman, guy named Jolliet who was about the second white man to see this territory, said somethin' very much like that. Don't remember it exactly, but it was somethin' like 'Illinois River Valley is most beautiful and suitable for settlement. A settler would not have to spend ten years cutting down and burning trees. On the very day of his arrival, he could put a plow into the ground.'"

They rode silently for a few moments before Beard spoke again. "America is going to get rich here, Mo. Very rich. You and me should find a spot to get rich with it."

McConnel stopped his horse and waited for Beard to come up beside him, looked over at him, and cracked his face into the first smile Beard had seen there since he'd shouted, "I know just the place."

* * * *

The two men camped in a grove of hardwood trees along a stream that seemed to feed them. The wood was mainly oak and elm, but there was one large black walnut. McConnel allowed as how he had enough of a taste for walnuts to get the black stain on his hands. Stains that would come from removing the soft outer husk. So, after they'd pulled into the trees and unloaded the horses and hobbled and released them to eat to their contentment of the tall grass, McConnel went collecting walnuts, and Beard took his musket to provide a turkey for dinner. It took neither of them long to collect what they wanted.

McConnel used his hands to rub the outer husk off the walnuts and two rocks to split the hard inner shell. He had two full cups of rich walnut meat before Tom got the feathers off the bird.

"Do wish I had a pot of boiling water to dip this beast into and make pluckin' these feathers easier."

"Just keep plucking, Tom, you'll get there." He handed him a cup of walnut meat. "Nibble these. They'll give you strength for the task. Meantime I'll get a fire going and set up something to roast that bird on. When you finally get it ready."

Two hours later, they both sat with their backs against trees and close enough to the glowing coals to collect some warmth as the cool of a fall evening fell upon them. They'd consumed most of the turkey, and McConnel pulled a bottle from the gear and poured three fingers of whiskey into both their cups. Theirs was the silence of shared contentment. But silence was something Beard could tolerate for just so long.

"Mo, I told you my story already. Your turn now. How'd you get here? How'd you come to know this valley?"

McConnel looked into the glowing coals as though for inspiration, sipped at his whiskey, and in his pitchy tenor voice, still full of an Irish lilt, if not an accent, started. "Like you, I'm from Upstate New York originally. Like your father, mine's a farmer, though no other trade. And like you, I had a couple of years of schoolin'. Mine was subscription school, not boarding. But I learned to read and write easily and do figures. Maybe it's that my ancestors are Irish, but I have a great love of words."

Beard interrupted from across the fire. "Well, for a man who loves words, you don't bother to use many of them."

McConnel barked back, but with twinkling eyes illuminated by the firelight, "Well, maybe it's because you talk enough for both of us. Hush and I'll see if I can't spin a few together."

McConnel sat up a bit and began his tale.

"I left home at only fourteen and afoot. Walked to Fort Pitt, doing day labor here and there along the way for room and board. When I got to Fort Pitt, I found work on a barge and floated to Lexington. I labored there for a year. When Governor Edwards called for men to join Colonel Howard in a march up the Illinois to punish the Potawatomi and Kickapoo for the Fort Dearborn massacre, I volunteered. Some fourteen hundred of us from Kentucky were going to go. For reasons I still don't understand, the regiment fell apart. In the end, we weren't going to go. Well, maybe not 1,399 others, but I was. I found a job poling a flatboat downriver, and when it got to the Mississippi, I hopped off and walked north to Edwardsville. I arrived just before Howard left."

He paused for a moment, then continued. "Mascouten Bay was the first place we thought we'd fight. But the Potawatomi village was entirely deserted. They knew we were coming. But the Kickapoo were not so smart. They had a village just a few miles away back from the river, near the bluff. We killed a bunch of them and burned their village. Then we walked a bit farther up the river, found another Kickapoo village, and did it again. That's how I learned this territory."

McConnel took another sip of his corn whiskey and stared back into the flames.

"Mo, that was four or five years ago. What you been doing since?" Beard asked.

"Oh, Jefferson bought all that land from Little Boney when I was about five. I've always wanted to see it. Still do. But I've managed to see some of it. I worked on a boat down to New Orleans and then wandered to Tejas. Not many white people there. A few Mexicans and a very few Americans. They do have some of the biggest Indians you've ever seen. All of them big as you. Name is Karankawa. Americans just call 'em Kroncs. Also got the meanest Indians you've ever seen. They're called Comanches. They live by stealing other Indians' stuff. Only business they practice is slavin'. I wandered a bit with groups of traders I could find. Not a place for a man to wander alone."

McConnel was silent again. Beard decided he was through talking and ready for sleep. So, Beard moved away from the tree, threw his saddle close to the fire, laid his head on it, and pulled a blanket over himself as a little protection from the frost he knew would come tonight. McConnel did the same.

Just as Beard's eyes were blinking closed, McConnel added, "I'm home now. Not as certain as you what my future is, but it will be here."

* * * *

The next morning, they reached it. Below them, the river ran in a straight line across the land. Straight save that it seemed to flow out of a slough that covered the valley floor as far north and east as they could see. The river was some three or four miles in front of them. For two miles the trail ran down a hill sloping toward the water. The third and fourth seemed almost at grade with the riverbank. On the other side the valley extended for what they guessed to be five miles before a bluff shot up sharply. Both men sat just taking in the majesty of it all. Without comment, Murray nudged his mount and started slowly along an old trail that wound downward. As they moved down the grade, the soil, which had been rich loam for three days, became ever sandier. The plants were lower with few patches of real green.

"Mo, you ever been on the other side of this river?"

"Yep," came the taciturn response.

"We're riding through the poorest soil I've seen in this state. Loam has given way to sand."

"Seems so," McConnel acknowledged.

"But on the other side of the river what soil I see—the soil that isn't covered with tall grass—seems so rich it looks black."

McConnel answered the question before it was asked. "Don't know where all this sand came from. But I know about the soil on the other side. You're right. It's rich. Take a handful, hold it up to the light, let it crumble through your fingers, and it still looks black. Richest soil I've ever seen. But the river floods every spring. Been doing it for all of time, I suppose. Maybe thousands of years. Try to farm it now, you'll just get flooded out."

He was silent for a moment before he added, "That's why the Indians put their villages on this side. But get some Dutchman here, who knows how to build dikes, and that will be the richest farmland in America."

They rode the last mile to the river in silence. Theirs was the silence of men pondering: pondering whether Indians would be here, and if so, would they bring trade or would they bring trouble; pondering the wonder of this entire river valley; pondering the future of the life they were choosing.

They knew they were close because they could see the black richness of the north side very clearly now. The terrain was flat but high enough above the river to cut off any vision of water. And then there it was. Their horses stood on a low bluff, a tall riverbank really, no more than twenty feet above the water level.

McConnel nodded to it. "The French loved this place. Called it Beautiful Mound Village."

"Mound Village? Why?"

"You'll see 'em," McConnel explained. "Don't know what they are, but they're man made for certain. Though by what men, no one seems to know. Biggest one is maybe eighty feet tall and five hundred feet in diameter. Down there a mile or so." McConnel pointed downriver.

Then he turned to look upriver at a crumbling log structure some fifty yards upstream. It was nearly covered by the brush and small trees thriving along the riverbank. "That was the last French traders' place. They had to give all this up after the Brits took over Canada. So that building's just been decaying for more than fifty years now."

The two men sat on their horses, taking in the valley—upriver a great meandering swamp of a wetland, from which the river seemed to flow, almost as though it were the source. The wide river flowed gently along, separating them from the richest soil either of them had ever seen covering the valley beyond the north shore.

McConnel turned and looked at Beard. When the bigger man's focus came back toward him, he spoke. "Tom, you're going to stay, aren't you?"

This time the loquacious Beard was laconic. "Yep."

"Winter's coming. The first thing we'll have to do is keep you from freezing to death. Let's spend what's left of the day looking for a place to build a cabin. Got to be high enough not to flood."

"How about here?"

McConnel pointed downriver five hundred yards to a copse of hardwood. "You and your horses may want to drag fifty to sixty trees a quarter mile, but me and my horse would kinda like to find a place where we can drag them just a few feet. Let's wander down that way."

McConnel turned his horse downriver, riding along the top of the bluff. It didn't take long to find what they sought—a wooded knoll that stood on the riverbank but high above it. The knoll was flat on top and treeless, offering a clear view upriver, downriver, and across the river as well as behind them to the south. At the foot of the knoll grew a copse of straight timbers. They would be just the right diameter for the cabin wall and close enough to drag up the knoll without a great deal of effort. This would be Thomas Beard's new home.

* * * *

Dinner was fresh venison and bread they'd packed for the trip. After, McConnel broke the bottle of corn liquor out of his pack, poured three fingers into a mug, and handed it to Beard.

"Mo, the stain from those walnut hulls ever going to wash off? Your fingers look like they belong to a black field hand."

"Nope. Won't wash off. Have to wear off. Be a week or so. Man wants to eat walnuts, that's the price." He froze as he said it.

Beard saw him motionless save his eyes darting about with a franticness that Beard knew meant he was locating his musket. Beard whirled to look at whatever it was that had frozen McConnel. An Indian, still but for the fluttering of his long hair in the evening breeze, stood at the top of the knoll. He was no more than twenty yards away.

The Indian was a big man, or at least wide—Beard guessed maybe five foot eight and well over two hundred twenty pounds. He wasn't holding a musket and had no other visible weapon, but the blanket that covered his upper torso from his huge shoulders to his broad hips could have concealed almost any weapon—a tomahawk, war club, or knife. His legs were covered in fringed buckskin trousers and his feet in moccasins. His hair, heavily streaked with grey, was unadorned, hanging long to his shoulders. He appeared to be alone.

Without moving, the Indian said in very clear English, "My name is Chaubenee. I've been expecting you."

CHAPTER 2

DECEMBER 2, 1818

Mascouten Bay, Illinois Territory

"You ever built one of these things?" McConnel asked Beard.

"When I was a boy, Mo, my dad and I helped several new settlers in Ohio. We cut a bunch of trees down, maybe a foot or bigger in diameter and more or less twenty feet long. About fifteen inches from each end, we hacked notches in them. Every log had four notches, two at each end. Then we just stacked them one on top of the other. The notches fit into one another and held the logs in place. Simple. Lots of work but simple."

McConnel's look suggested he was not eager to start. "How about the chimney. We got no bricks, and I don't even see any flagstone around here to stack."

Beard smiled. "But we have clay, Mo. We got lots of clay."

"You gonna try to make bricks?"

"Nope. Say the hearth is four feet wide. OK?"

McConnel nodded agreement.

"We decide which wall we want the hearth against. We build two log walls perpendicular to that exterior wall, about eight feet apart, and five feet out into the room. Then we build a second set of walls inside the first two. That and the exterior cabin wall will make a U-shaped space. We pack that whole space with clay. Got it?"

"Let's get to work, Thomas. We got a lot to do before the real cold gets here."

Despite the fall chill, both men had stripped to the waist and had rivulets of sweat running down their foreheads and backs by the time they stopped for lunch. Beard was starting to develop a blister from swinging the ax. Each was young and strong and used to living outdoors, but this was backbreaking labor.

They sat against the two logs they'd managed to get in place on the north wall of the cabin, accepting what support it would give their weary backs. McConnel took a long drink from his leather-wrapped water bottle and then poured some over his head.

"Tom, you ever seen slaves work?"

"Saw a couple in Louisville but just domestic labor. But I didn't have to see much to know that a man, a human being, shouldn't be forced, under the lash or not, to work as hard as we are for any reason but his own benefit."

"I've seen lots. Seen work crews in the cotton fields. Seen men and women on the auction block in New Orleans. Humans stripped for inspection of muscles. Saw a buyer once examine a woman by using his riding crop to lift her breasts. Makes men nothing but beasts. And God said men, all men, were made in his image. No, it ain't right."

Beard took his face from the river and looked directly at the man sitting beside him. It was the face of a man holding his anger in check.

"I never told you why I left home, Tom."

"You just said you were fourteen. Thought that was a bit early but didn't feel like it was for me to ask. But I'd like to hear if you're willing to tell."

"I am. Unlike your dad, mine never had a craft. No mill to bring in cash money. We got what we could make if we had surplus production to sell. That's all. Sold any grain or meat we could get by without. And it was the price we got for that surplus that made the difference in whether Mom got any store-bought cloth, or whether we could buy a metal plow instead of the board we drug behind that ox, or whether I got another year of subscription school. It was the price of our surplus production that made our lives better or worse. And you know what controlled the price?"

Beard shook his head.

"It was the market. Not complicated. How much how many people want to buy and how much how many people want to sell. And you know what controlled how much there was to sell?"

Again, Beard shook his head.

"I promise it wasn't us dirt farmers in Upstate New York. It was those damn aristocrats from the South." He paused for a moment and took another drink of water. "Those bastard Southern aristocrats with their slaves. They grow a hundred times more crops than a dirt farmer in Upstate New York, and they sell it all. How much of that do they need? Very little. It's all for sale. It drives prices down to nothing."

McConnel's head snapped toward Beard, and his dazzling blue eyes blazed with hate. "That's why I left home at fourteen. My folks had plenty enough kids to do the work and too many mouths to feed because the prices were too low to buy enough to feed them all. A man can't compete with that system. Only when those damn rich aristocrats have to pay for labor like everyone else in the market will free farmers prosper."

He looked away, and Beard could see him letting the hate drift away. Beard said nothing and waited.

When McConnel looked back at him, he was calm. Both men stood and, having not only cooled from their labors but also having been cooled to chill by the fall weather, pulled their shirts back on. They knew that soon they'd get hot and remove them again, but for now the shirts were protection from the dropping temperature. As they mounted their horses, riding stock turned into draft animals, Beard looked over his shoulder and saw men coming up the knoll behind them.

"Mo, would you look at that? We got company."

One foot in the stirrup, McConnel rose up to standing but did not mount. He just looked behind him at one of the oddest sights he'd ever seen. A broad, silver-haired Chaubenee was riding slowly up the knoll, four other Indians following behind, each mounted and each of their horses pulling a log. Both men stepped off their horses and walked the few yards to the top of the knoll to greet the new arrivals. They still knew little about the Indian, except that he was apparently the leader of the small Potawatomi village not far away.

Chaubenee dismounted and extended his hand in the conventional American greeting. He wore a broad smile, exposing a complete set of amazingly white teeth. "In my culture, we help each other do these things. And you two are going to need a lot of help."

A stunned Beard finally gained control of himself and threw his arms around the aging bear of a Potawatomi warrior. "I promise, you and your men are more than welcome. This cabin is a lot of work for just two."

The other Indians pulled up beside their leader and dismounted. None of the faces carried Chaubenee's enthusiastic grin, but neither were they hostile or even glum, just stoic. Introductions were made around. All four spoke enough English for that. Two seemed to be almost fluent.

The work started immediately. The four accompanying Chaubenee knew what they were doing and needed very little direction. Chaubenee contented himself translating where needed, which wasn't often. By the time the sun was getting low, all four cabin walls were up to shoulder height.

As the Potawatomi prepared to depart, Chaubenee offered, "We'll be back tomorrow morning. Two more days, we may have this done."

Five days later, the cabin was complete. Five days instead of two because at Chaubenee's suggestion they had expanded the original plan by adding on a trading room creating two tidy rooms with a large fireplace between. There was a small door out the rear for Beard to look out over the river. The Indian work crew had even built a small log porch in front with an awning extending out about five feet in front of the door. It was hearth and home in the wilderness.

Beard stood looking with great joy at his new abode and business. Chaubenee stood next to him, his joy almost as obvious as Beard's. Even the laconic faces of McConnel and the four Indians showed smiles.

"Chaubenee, I need to thank you somehow. I want you to bring your entire village to this cabin for a feast. Give me a little time to hunt enough meat for all. And I've got a little whiskey among my trade goods. Let me sponsor a feast by way of thanks?"

"My small village will be pleased for your offer. There are only about thirty of us. We'll all be here. But don't start preparing until after tomorrow."

"If that's what you want, certainly. But why?"

"Because tomorrow I don't want you to work. I want you and McConnel to come with me."

"Why?"

Chaubenee let his lips open into a full-toothed smile but said nothing as he turned to his horse and mounted. Looking down, he finally answered. "To look at things you should see."

* * * *

The three men sat on horseback, staring up at the huge mound of earth. It started at the river and ran back almost two hundred yards. It was round and stood the height of over a dozen men at the top.

"What is it, Chaubenee?" McConnel asked, his thin face arched upward until his long red eyebrows looked almost like little wings on his forehead.

"A tribe called the Mascouten lived here. Well over one hundred years ago. They buried their dead in these places. I think the word in English is sepulchres."

"Did they bury all their dead in this spot?"

"No. You'll find eight of these. But this is the biggest. Biggest by far."

The mound was covered with tall prairie grasses blowing gently and vivid green in the full sun. It was a very odd contrast to the low scrubby plants growing in the sandy soil all around. Beard got off his horse and walked to the edge of the mound where he kicked at the grass until he'd loosened the dirt below. He bent and picked up a handful and held it to the light. It sprinkled out of his hand, a rich reddish black.

"It's clay, loam and clay, Chaubenee. Not like the sandy soil around here. Where did they get it?"

"You are an observant man, Beard."

"Tom, Chaubenee. Call me Tom."

"You are an observant man, Tom. One day you will get to the Kickapoo village along the bluff." Chaubenee pointed away from the river to the south. "That bluff is this same soil. They must have carried it."

Beard looked toward McConnel in surprise. "Basketful at a time?" He allowed a long pause and then pointed his finger to the mound and made a circle with his arm to encompass the mass of it. "That's a lot of burying."

And then he looked back to Chaubenee. "Where did they go?"

"Most of them are still here, or their bones are but not all in the mound. There was no one left to put the last ones here. Legend says you'll find the bones of the last in a pit up by the bluff." He again pointed to the south. "The story is that the Kickapoo took the last of them in and we hear buried them there. But I don't really know."

"Disease?"

"Iroquois."

Beard looked up in surprise. "Iroquois are from the area where I was born. Other side of the mountains in Upstate New York. What were they doing here and in what must have been a huge war party to wipe out a people big enough to do this?" He pointed again to the mound.

Chaubenee smiled. "It all had to do with you white men and your taste for beaver hats. The French traded for beaver pelts and made them into hats. They traded mostly with the Illini, including the Mascouten. Trade with the French brought the Illini many wonderful things—blankets, iron pots, knives, and tomahawks. Oh, and most important of all, muskets and gunpowder. The Mascouten and other Illini septs got rich on the trade. Much richer than the other tribes.

"Eventually, the Illini made deals with the other tribes. You bring us your furs. We'll give you the manufactured things you want. Then the Illini traded the furs they got from the other tribes to the French. But, of course, they kept a little for themselves in the process. Everybody got better, but the Illinois most of all. But east of the mountains it wasn't the French who controlled trade. It was first the Dutch and then the English."

Chaubenee looked straight at Beard. "And the Iroquois had the good fortune to live on some river in New York named after some Dutchman."

"Hudson," Beard filled in.

"The Iroquois had the same relationship with the Dutch as the Illini had with the French. And after the English threw the Dutch out, the Iroquois continued to trade with the English. But the Iroquois were even greedier than the Illini. They wanted to stop the Illini trade with the French and make even the Illini come to them for European goods. They made war on the Illini to make it so. They came a thousand miles to do it, but they came."

"All five tribes of the Iroquois came here?" McConnel asked. "The whole confederacy?"

Chaubenee smiled an easy and pleased smile. "Good for you, McConnel. Not all you whites are so ignorant of our ways. Yes, the Iroquois were five until they let the Tuscarora in. Then it was six. That was in my grandfather's time. And they all sent warriors to snuff out the Illini."

Chaubenee looked down.

"The Mascouten tombs are here, but the village was upriver by the slough. There was an island there with the river on one side and the slough on the other sides. You couldn't get to it on foot. Every time the Iroquois tried, they were beaten back. They tried three times, and each time they lost many warriors. But eventually, they started cutting logs to fill in the swamp. It took a month, but they did it. And when they did, they slaughtered all but a very few of the Mascouten who got away in canoes. But it was the end of the Mascouten. A few that were left got upriver to the closest Illini tribe, the Peoria. A few others may have joined the Kickapoo. The Kickapoo still have a village on the bluff, but all that is left of the Mascouten are these sepulchres. They are sacred places of the dead."

Chaubenee looked sternly at Beard. "The Kickapoo treaty with Clark is almost finalized. Next year the Kickapoo, they will go west of the Mississippi. The Potawatomi will follow a few years after. Then all this will be yours. It will belong to the whites.

"But when it is yours, Tom, remember: it is a sacred place. Remember!"

* * * *

The coals glowed warm along the length of the firepit. Deer were being turned on long wooden spits by Indian girls. Most of their guests hovered close to the warmth. Snow covered the ground at any distance farther than six or eight feet from it. An adolescent Indian tossed a snowball into the back of one of the girls. She screamed and raised her fist over her head but didn't even turn to give her young suitor the benefit of a pouting frown.

Beard, McConnel, Chaubenee, and most of his dozen warriors stood inside the cabin, warming against the hearth. Beard had opened a keg of corn whiskey. It seemed to impart warmth and goodwill to the company.

"Chaubenee, there are some gifts I want to give to you and your people. I want you not to consider it payment for labor. That I know you did from goodwill. But I hope you will allow a new trader to show his appreciation to all his future clients?" Beard said as he ladled a bit more liquid warmth into his guest's cup.

"That we will accept. And thank you for it."

Chaubenee invited the rest of his tribe to crowd in. Beard nodded to McConnel who stepped from the trading room into the bedroom and returned with a blanket with the corners pulled together and bulging at the bottom. Beard stepped up onto a small three-legged stool McConnel had built. The crowd noisily pushed into the small room.

When he thought they were all in, Beard held up his hands for silence. He looked at Chaubenee and asked, "Would you translate if necessary?"

Chaubenee nodded.

"My friends," Beard started, "you and your leader have accepted McConnel and me as though we were relatives. We would not be in this safe, warm place without you. And for that I am grateful. I have no way to thank you for what you have done except to give you each a small gift."

That most understood was obvious from the crowd's murmur even as Chaubenee translated.

"For the men, I have some things I think you will find useful." With that, he stuck his hand into the bottom of the blanket fold and pulled out a small packet wrapped in burlap and held together at the top with twine. He pulled the twine string and let the packet fall open in his palm. "In each of these there are ten musket balls and three iron fishhooks. These I offer to each of the men so they may more easily provide for their families as they have provided for me."

A chorus of shouts filled the room as Beard pulled more of the packets out of the blanket and threw one to each of the men.

"And for the women, I have something that it's best I not throw to you but which I think will also help you provide." And with that he pulled a thin skinning knife out of the blanket and held it up. This time the chorus of appreciation was in a higher tone. "Ladies, would each of you come to me so I can hand you one of these?" The ladies obliged, and Beard did as he had promised.

"Now, there is one more thing left here. It is for the entire village, and so let me give it to Chaubenee so he can distribute it as he thinks best. Chaubenee, would you work your way to me?"

Chaubenee made his way through the small crowd. Beard stepped down from the stool as Chaubenee approached him and then rose again, holding a small wooden keg in both hands. "Chaubenee, those lead musket balls I gave out won't do a bit of good without powder. Hopefully, this keg will get you through the winter." And with that, Beard held the keg over his head for all to see and then gave it to Chaubenee.

Again, there was a chorus of approving shouts. Chaubenee, displaying still prodigious strength, balanced the keg on the palm of one hand, wrapped his other arm around Beard, and pulled him in with a crushing hug.

When Beard managed to get his breath back, he said, "I'm glad the man had only one arm to do that with. He'd have crushed me with two. Now let's go eat."

The three men sat together on stumps pulled onto the porch, each balancing a plate of roasted venison and ears of corn the Potawatomi had contributed.

It was Chaubenee who spoke first. "I presume the news has come to you. The Kickapoo have signed William Clark's paper. They must now cross the Mississippi."

"I knew it was coming, but I'd not heard it was done." And then with a smile, Beard added, "How do you hear these things before I do?"

Chaubenee let a small grin turn up the corners of his mouth and shrugged. "There is more. Clark was very clever in the way he will get them all to leave."

Both Beard and McConnel stopped chewing and looked directly at him.

"How?" McConnel finally asked.

"They are given land in Missouri near Council Bluffs, and they get paid every year for twelve years. In cash money so they can buy whatever they want rather than merely in trade goods"—Chaubenee arched one eyebrow and turned from one to the other—"the quality of which is always suspect. But here's the clever part. The money will be issued at Council Bluffs. If you're not there, you don't get your share.

"They will be gone in the spring."

McConnel set down his empty plate, picked up his mug, and took a sip. "For Meriwether Lewis's junior partner, that man turned out to be awfully smart."

"Now, Chaubenee, let me see if I have a piece of news you don't know."

The burly Indian turned rapt attention as Beard continued.

"We got the news two days ago from a horseman coming through, as of a week ago Illinois is no longer a territory. It is a state. The twenty-first such."

Sadness momentarily flickered across the big Indian's face. But he almost instantly regained himself and replaced the expression with a wan smile. "So now there are twenty-one fires. When we started fighting you there were only thirteen. We never really had a chance, did we?"

Then he regained himself and said with what appeared to be genuine cheerfulness, "We've spent one hundred fifty years fighting the Iroquois, and there are only six of them."

Not knowing what to say, Beard ladled a bit more corn whiskey out of the cask and refilled Chaubenee's cup.

"No thank you, Tom." Chaubenee shook his head, declining. "Indians seem to have a weakness for that stuff. And this is a night of joy and celebration. Not one in which I wish to be anything but a joyous friend."

There was silence for a moment, and then McConnel spoke.

"Chaubenee, you have made yourself a very good friend. Tom, you too. But unfortunately, I have to go. Tomorrow I, like the Kickapoo, will leave for Missouri. So this is goodbye from me."

Beard looked stunned. "Why, Mo? Why are you leaving?"

"I'm going to Missouri. It's going to be a state soon. And it may come into the Union slave or it may come in free. I'm going to do what I can to influence that decision."

"Then may Moneto ride with you, my friend," Chaubenee said. "Perhaps I will see you there. The Potawatomi have not signed with Clark yet, but we will. We are the next to go."

CHAPTER 3

APRIL 8, 1819

Mascouten Bay, State of Illinois

"You have news," Beard said as he saw Chaubenee approaching. "Is it good or bad?"

"Just news." Chaubenee was silent for a moment, a pensive expression on his face. "No, it's bad for me, I think. Like a winter storm. Inevitable and known to be coming but saddening when it finally arrives."

Beard's face took on the look of a deeply concerned friend. "What happened?"

"The last of the Potawatomi, the Peoria band to which my little village is a part, have signed Clark's paper. The one all the other Potawatomi signed before. It says we agree to the 1803 treaty Harrison signed with the last remaining Illinois. We will have to go now."

"When, Chaubenee? When do you have to go?"

"Clark did it the same way with us as he did with the Kickapoo. The Peoria get $2,000 plus $300 per year for twelve years. But the money will be paid at Ste. Genevieve, Missouri. That's the land we've been given in return. And if we are not there, we don't get our share. That's up to us. We don't have to go until the twelve years are up."

"Is it good land?"

"I was through there once with Tecumseh. It's on the other side of the Mississippi and just above Kaskaskia. Good land." And then he was silent, his focus far away beyond the horizon. "A good land, but not my home."

"So, you can stay here for another twelve years?"

"No. Clark dated the Peoria signing back to the date when all the other Potawatomi signed. I must be gone before the end of 1828."

Again, there was a long silence. Beard did not speak. He offered the silence of friendship.

It was Chaubenee who broke it. "I always wanted to die here. Perhaps I will before that time comes."

CHAPTER 4

DECEMBER 22, 1821

Mascouten Bay, Sangamon County, Illinois

Beard watched the rider as he came across the treeless sand to the south of the river. It was cloudy and bleak and bitter cold. There was no snow falling, but the snow already on the ground was being whipped around by the wind so hard the rider had the brim of his hat pulled low and a scarf wrapped around the lower half of his face, his only visible feature his eyes. His shoulders and upper body were wrapped in a buffalo robe. Beard was standing on his porch, dressed in no more than the buckskin shirt and homespun woolen trousers he'd had on when he first heard the whinny of a horse on the wind and stepped out to look. He was torn between stepping back in and pulling on a coat or waiting the few minutes dressed as he was. In the end he opted for the latter.

When he was within hearing, Beard barked into the wind, "Pull your horse into the leeward side of the building. There's a hitching post there. I'll get a couple of horse blankets." When he stepped inside, he pulled on a heavy coat before he grabbed the blankets and a feed bag with some oats and stepped back outside.

"Let me get that saddle while you cover and feed the beast." Beard handed the blankets and oats to the rider who had spoken not a word.

Beard stripped the saddle and stepped back inside where he threw it before the fire and then scooped a bucket of water from the barrel and went back out. As he set the bucket on the ground, Beard said, "Come on in when you're done here."

Two minutes later, the stranger burst through the door and slammed it behind him. He still had his hat low, and Beard couldn't make much of him save that he was tall, lean, and had very well-worn boots.

The man pulled off his gloves and extended his hands to the fire, rubbing them the whole time. He shucked the buffalo robe and coat underneath it and presented his entire body as close to the fire as he could get it without ducking under the mantel.

When the stranger turned around, Beard had a cup of rum in his hand extended handle first. The stranger took it with a nod of appreciation. Now Beard could make him out, midthirties with hair already receding on either side of his forehead. His face was red, but Beard assumed that was from the cold. His brown eyes were dull, but Beard thought that might be from the cold as well. His nose was hatchet straight and seemed to stop in eyebrows so grown together they appeared as one long brow instead of two individual ones. After he pulled at the rum, he finally looked at Beard through a smile full of yellowed and irregularly spaced teeth.

"Damn, that was good and warm. Thought I'd freeze before I got here." He took another long pull at the rum. "Gets any colder, we might have to bring that horse in here. Don't want to be left on foot."

"After we get you warm, we can walk him down the knoll. There's a grove down below. The hill and the trees stop the wind. It never gets cold enough to freeze the animals in that grove. I have my two down there."

The stranger nodded and licked his lips to catch a drop of rum. "You Beard?" he asked.

Beard stuck his hand forward. "Tom Beard. Who are you, and what brings you all this way in such inhospitable weather?"

"Peabody. Just call me Peabody; everybody else does. And I came for you."

Beard arched an eyebrow in surprise.

"I'm traveling from Jacksonville to Springfield. Farmer down there asked me to come straight upriver instead of cross-country so I could deliver a letter to you. Just said Beard's Trading Post at mile eighty-eight."

"Farmer? Who?"

"Guy named McConnel. Murray McConnel."

"Mo! He's living in Jacksonville? I've heard of it. Little village on the prairie 'bout halfway from here to Edwardsville. Kinda out of your way coming here, isn't it?"

"Yep, that's the place, and yep, it's out of my way. But he asked, and I said I would."

"Well, I'm grateful, Peabody. How about a bit of dinner? You warm enough to take your horse to the bottom of the knoll? Only a hundred yards and even with the snow blowing, you can't miss it. You'll see my two. Hobble yours near them. There was good grass there before the snow. He'll kick it up. I'll have a hot meal on when you get back."

Peabody drained his cup, pulled on his coat, gloves, and hat, and opened the door.

"You want venison or duck?"

"I'll take the duck." Peabody closed the door behind him.

* * * *

From the moment Peabody had handed him the letter, Beard had wanted nothing more than to read it. But simple courtesy had caused him to defer his desire until now. Peabody was wrapped in a blanket and lay in front of the fire on the trading-room side. And while the fire on this side gave almost enough light to read, Beard had used some precious whale oil in the reading lamp for extra light. He opened the folded-and-sealed paper slowly and then read with relish.

> Dear Tom,
> So much has changed. So much to tell. First, you know Missouri has come into the Union, and much to my dismay came in a slave state. The compromise to let Maine in as a free state and Missouri as slave distressed me sorely, but it is done. I will not live in a place that allows such a stain on the dignity of the republic, so Mary and I have returned to Illinois. Yes, Mary. Mary Mapes. She is the most wonderful girl. We met in Missouri. She not only has my heart but shares my sentiments on the morality of the compromise. I didn't want to leave without her, and so we married last summer and returned.
> Managed to buy a truly rich eighty-acre piece here and am farming. But that is not my true love. You always teased me about being laconic despite my protestation that I'm a man who loves words. I'm studying law. I spend all the surplus of the farm on books. Despite my having only three years of schooling, the reading is easy. Sometimes understanding how it all relates is difficult, but with enough thought (it's amazing how clearly a man can think while

walking behind a plow), it all makes sense. It
will take a few years, but as soon as I'm ready to
stand examination before the bar, I will.

Anytime you decide you want a three-day
ride through the prairie, come see us. Ask anyone in the village. I look forward to introducing you to Mary.

Ever your friend,
Murray McConnel

CHAPTER 5

SEPTEMBER 4, 1822

Mascouten Bay, Sangamon County, Illinois

The sound of Beard's hammer rang loud in the quiet of the hot summer day. He smiled at the sign he'd tacked on his front door. "Gone for a couple of days. Back at the end of the week. Signed T. Beard."

"You don't read English, do you?" Beard asked Chaubenee.

"No. Tecumseh was the only one of us who did," the burly Potawatomi standing beside him answered.

"Well, it says I'm going to be gone for a couple of days. That's why I asked you to come. Would you mind the store while I'm gone?"

"Certainly. How do I do it?"

"If anyone white comes along, just tell them I'm gone until the end of the week. If you or any of yours need anything, keep track and we'll square up when I get back. I want to meet some of the new neighbors. I know squatters have been coming into the area. I'd like to know them and maybe sell them a few goods."

"What's a squatter?"

"US government owns all this now." Beard let his arm describe an arch of all he saw before him. "Soon as they get it surveyed, the state will sell it. Anyone who lives on it now doesn't own it. They're just 'squatting' on it."

"Humph," the big man snorted. "Still don't understand how a man can own a piece of land." Then he gave a rumbling chuckle. "But we lost that battle, didn't we?

"So, what happens to these 'squatters' when the land is sold?"

"They'll buy it. Or at least that's what they—and I—presume."

"Can anyone buy it?"

Beard nodded.

"Then what if some other man buys it first?"

Now it was Beard's turn to chuckle. "Then they go to a court of law and the judge decides."

"They never fight over it?"

"Sometimes," Beard admitted with a smile.

"Anyone ever get killed?"

"Sometimes," Beard admitted.

He stepped off the porch to his mount standing before him, put his left foot into the stirrup, and swung into the saddle. He looked down at Chaubenee with a final thought. "The system's not perfect, but it works." And with that he turned the horse and headed south.

* * * *

The sun was getting low as Beard rode toward the cabin that had been visible across the flat prairie for the last fifteen minutes. It was situated at the bottom of a low hill that was covered with hardwood. He presumed he'd find a stream running down that hill and cutting into the prairie close to the house. As he got near, Beard could see the silhouettes of three men backlit by the lowering sun. They all had stopped working and were standing erect, watching him come. Some two hundred yards before he reached the house, the prairie grass opened, and he found himself crossing ground that had been broken with a plow. The crop had been harvested, and his horse was walking across a stubble of cornstalks. Now he could also make out a woman and two children standing by the house in the shade of a very large oak at the edge of the wood. He was right. A small stream ran between the field and the house.

The men he approached said nothing. When they were within easy distance of conversation, he stopped, dismounted, and, horse reins in hand, continued walking forward. "Afternoon, gentlemen. I'm Tom Beard, and I think I may be your closest neighbor."

The oldest of the men stepped toward him and extended his hand. "Afternoon, Mr. Beard. My name's Lindsley, Martin Lindsley."

Lindsley was dressed as Beard expected—homespun woolen pants and short boots. He had a wide-brimmed leather hat on his head. He was stripped to the waist, sweat glistening on his chest and dripping from his forehead. He was a thin man of medium height and powerful arms. His smile was friendly but cautious.

"Hard work you're at, Mr. Lindsley."

"Indeed. We planted corn this spring. And we got some, but I know this soil. It'll grow cotton. That'll grow more cash than this corn." At the last statement he smiled.

Lindsley turned, picked up a rough, long-sleeved cotton shirt from the ground, and pulled it on over his head. "Mr. Beard, this is Tim Harris and John Cettrough." He pointed to the two men beside him. "We all came up from Kentucky together last winter."

There were handshakes all around, and then Lindsley said, "Your timing is good. Day's work is over. Ma and the kids will have supper on. Join us."

As the four men walked together toward the cabin, Beard could see between him and the house a woman in a linen smock setting out a large table under the massive oak. A barefoot boy of about eight was sitting under the oak, a large pile of corn ears to his right, a smaller pile of shelled corncobs to his left, and an even smaller, but growing, pile of corn kernels on a blanket before him. He was shelling them by hand. A girl, perhaps a year younger, was also working in front of the house. She was standing behind two large iron pots, each about eighteen inches in diameter and equally deep. One was propped on iron legs over a small fire. The legs of the other pot were planted on nothing but the ground. The girl was holding a thin limb about two feet long with as many as eight strings tied to it and dangling down. These she would alternately dip in the heated pot and then into the second, which Beard knew to be filled with cool water. He watched fascinated as the candles she was making grew thicker each time she dipped the strings into the pot of melted tallow and then cooled firm in the waterpot.

"Mr. Lindsley, if your daughter makes any more candles than you need, I'd trade for them. Or even buy them for cash."

The thin, hard man smiled over at him. "We can talk some over dinner, Mr. Beard. But right now, why don't you take that roan of yours behind the cabin. After you've put her up, I'll introduce you to my wife and kids."

As Beard walked past the oak, both the children looked up at him, but neither spoke and both continued their work. Behind the cabin he found more than a corral. A large heavy wagon, which he presumed had brought the Lindsleys and everything they owned to this place, was pulled in behind the cabin as well. And lying beside it, propped against the cabin wall, was a plow with a wooden moldboard. Beard knew from painful experience how difficult it was to get that wooden board to cut through the soil, especially the first cut into prairie soil laced with decades of grass roots. It must have taken those three men two months of dawn-to-dusk labor to cut open the forty acres of prairie they were farming, even with the brace of oxen he noticed in the corral pulling the plow.

He examined the corral. It was split-rail construction and, in addition to the oxen, contained two cows and three horses. He could also see several pigs at the edge of the forest rooting for acorns. Between them stood a smokehouse with hickory smoke rising above and next to it a smoldering pit of ashes. After Beard unsaddled the mare, he put her into the corral and threw his saddle over the rail. He pulled his musket from the scabbard, flung his saddlebags over his shoulder, and walked back around front.

By the time he returned, both the boy and the girl had abandoned their work and were helping their mother lay out dinner. He could tell from the smell it was pork and corn on the cob. But it was the smell of freshly baked bread just out of the oven that made his mouth water.

Lindsley greeted him with the smile of a contented man, saying, "Mr. Beard, let me introduce you to my wife, Patricia, and my children. Billy and Jessica you've seen workin'. The little one in her arms is Benjamin."

"Mr. Lindsley, call me Tom if you would." With that he turned to greet the family.

Patricia Lindsley was a small woman, her face and arms, below her sleeves, sunned to a rich brown that made her blue eyes the more noticeable. Her dark hair was pulled back and tied into a bun. Her smile was shy but vibrant.

She extended her hand. "Pleased to meet you, Mr. Beard. These are my children. Children, say hello to our guest."

Jessica made an ever-so-proper curtsy and said, "So pleased to meet you, Mr. Beard," in a friendly, almost precocious, way.

Billy was the shy one. He kept his eyes almost to the ground. "Hello" seemed all he could manage.

"Billy," scolded his mother, yanking his ear, "offer Mr. Beard your hand."

Beard extended his and said, very formally, "It is my pleasure to meet you, Billy."

This seemed to please the boy, who took the offered hand and looked momentarily into Beard's eyes before dropping his own.

Lindsley spoke up. "Mr. Bea . . . Tom, take any seat you want while we all help Ma get the hot food onto the table."

As Lindsley turned to go inside, he barked over his shoulder, "Billy, you go get the butter."

As the boy started to walk off, Beard said, "Let me help you with the butter, Billy," and walked after him.

Beard followed the boy to the well. There were two ropes anchored to the stone sides. Beard put his hand on the crank. "I don't know which rope, Billy. If you'll attach the correct one, I'll crank."

Without response, the boy took one of the ropes and attached it to the crank. Once it was secured, Beard began the task of cranking up the surprisingly heavy bucket. When it appeared out of the depths of the well, Beard was not surprised to see the bucket was completely full. It contained a large stone crock full of milk and a smaller crock he took to be cream as well as the one they sought, a large tub of butter. Billy took the butter tub out of the bucket, which Beard then let slowly back down. When the rope played out, Billy unhooked it from the crank and anchored it again to the stone wall of the well. The two walked in silence back to the table, which, by now, was heaped with steaming platters of pork chops, roasted corn on the cob, and bread baked to a golden crust, the insides of one broken piece a golden yellow.

After all had settled onto stumps that served as chairs, Lindsley looked at Beard and said, "Tom, will you offer a blessing, or shall I?"

"Please, Mr. Lindsley, you. It's your table."

After looking to ensure all had folded their hands and bowed their heads, Lindsley began. "Dear Lord, who has delivered us from all the threats and evils through which we have passed, and heaped upon us the bounty of this good land, bless this table and all present."

And all joined him saying, "Amen."

Lindsley picked up the platter of pork chops and handed it toward Beard. "Dig in, Tom."

"Thank you, I will." As he picked up the large two-tined, wooden serving fork to stab a chop, Beard looked to Mrs. Lindsley. "Smells delicious, ma'am."

As Beard laid the thick chop on his plate and returned the serving fork to the platter, Lindsley offered, "It's a bit early, but we had a hankering for pork, so last week me and Cettrough built that little smokehouse you saw out back. Harris found some dry hickory sticks in the brush, and we slaughtered one of the hogs."

Beard inhaled as though to respond, but Lindsley cut him off. "And no more 'Mr. Lindsley.' I'm Martin to you from now on."

"Thanks, Martin, for the friendship and for the unexpected pork. I'm so tired of venison and turkey, I can't even begin to tell how good this tastes." And with a smile across the table, he said, "Thank you again, Mrs. Lindsley." With that, he reached to the platter of bread and took a piece, broke it open to the golden yellow of the center, and slathered it with butter. Then he looked up and added to the shy young Billy, "And thanks for the butter, Billy."

Lindsley spoke again. "Tom, you'd asked about buying candles. May I ask what your business is?"

"Martin, I got here in '18 and opened up a trading post at Mascouten Bay on the river, just north of you maybe seven miles. I'm always looking for things people want and trying to supply them."

"You mostly traded with that little bunch of Kicks up by the bluff? And I hear there are still some Pots by the river," Lindsley said.

"Yes, sir, I do."

"Well, the Kicks are all gone and the Pots soon. What'll ya' do then?"

Beard's face broke into a wide smile, and his blue eyes twinkled. "Why, Martin, I'm going to buy that cotton from you and ship it downriver. This place is gonna grow, not get smaller."

Lindsley sopped the pork fat molten in the bottom of his plate with a larger square of bread and crowed with satisfaction. "Maybe the cotton, Tom, but not the candles."

Beard stared into Lindsley's open eyes but said nothing, knowing more would come.

"When we slaughtered that hog, we were glad for the fat. Melted it to tallow as you've seen. We'll make just enough candles for the winter. The rest of that tallow we'll mix with our cooking grease. When Jessica is done makin' candles, we'll rinse the ash from the smokehouse in those iron pots and leach out the lye. Then Patricia will mix in all the tallow and grease with the lye and make soap."

Beard's face reflected reverie. "I remember it well. When I was a kid, whenever we'd slaughter a fat pig we'd make our soap the same way. Then if not this year—next fall after you've harvested the cotton. I'll have gunpowder and shot for you gentlemen and a bolt of cloth or two for you, Mrs. Lindsley." He smiled toward the small, sunburned woman across the table.

"That's not what I'll be wanting, Tom."

Beard turned back to the head of the table. "And what is it you will be wanting, Martin?"

"A steel moldboard for that plow."

"I'm guessing that will take a lot of cotton."

"Told you, Tom. I know the ground; I know the weather. I'll have a lot of cotton to offer. But it might take time."

CHAPTER 6

JUNE 18, 1825

Mascouten Bay, Morgan County, Illinois

He could see it coming down the hill more than two miles away. It started as no more than a vivid white speck. The speck grew larger as it grew closer. Beard stood stunned. It was a sail. Someone or something was sailing down the hill from the bluff. That whoever, or whatever, it was, was coming straight toward him was clear. His feeling that the pistol at his right hand might not be enough caused him to turn back into his cabin where he slid a tomahawk through the belt loop by his left hand and picked up his musket, powder horn, and shot bag before stepping back outside. By then the speck of white had disappeared, but the cloud of dust along the flat ground a mile away told him whatever it was, was still coming. When it finally hove into view above the rolling terrain, the mystery became a wagon, one of the biggest wagons he'd ever seen. It was covered in a large white canvas. Not just covered but it appeared the covering was held six feet above the wagon bed by hoops of some sort.

As it got closer Beard could see it was pulled by four oxen harnessed in twos. One man was walking next to the lead oxen, a long stick in his hand. Another was sitting on a high lazy board, a woman and child beside him. Beard exhaled and set his musket against the cabin wall.

The wagon, still facing the river, pulled to a stop. The man on the lazy board pulled hard at the brake lever and stepped down. His wide-brimmed felt hat cast a shadow over his eyes and nose, but from there down to his neck the face was burned brown by the sun. The man's shirt was of good woven cotton and his pants machine-woven wool. The boots were dirty but appeared to be well made. The owners of this ship crossing the prairie were not poor.

As the stranger turned to help the woman and the girl down from the high lazy board, two more children of eight to ten years of age came scrambling around from the back of the wagon. Upon close inspection the man walking with the oxen appeared to be a boy of perhaps sixteen. The boy was thin, rail thin, with almost no hips. His pants would have fallen to the ground were it not for the leather belt around his waist. He was perhaps the driver's son, but if so, he was two inches taller than his father. The boy joined his family, and the six of them walked together toward Beard.

Beard stepped out from under his porch awning and strode toward them. "Afternoon, strangers. And welcome." With that he extended his hand to the sunburned man with the large hat. "I'm Beard, Thomas Beard, and this"—he gestured behind him—"is my trading post."

The stranger took off his hat, revealing a head of rich, thick black hair; a thin, almost patrician, nose; pronounced cheekbones; and deep and sober brown eyes. He transferred his hat to his left hand and extended his right to Beard. "Name's

Briney, Nathan Briney. And this"—he put one arm around the shoulder of the woman next to him and extended the other behind the line of his children—"is my family."

Before Beard could respond, Briney took his arm from around his wife and pointed across the river. "That Schuyler County?"

"Sure is. Now, answer a question for me?"

Briney nodded.

"What is this 'schooner' you're sailing across the prairie?"

Briney let his sober eyes relax into a smile and gave a short laugh. His wife joined him in the smile, and the youngest girl laughed out loud.

"Mr. Beard, you have hit it about right. We needed a wagon big enough to carry our whole world on our backs. We're out of Pennsylvania and bought this from the Conestoga Wagon Company there. But you're not the first to think of it as sailing across the prairie."

"Mr. Briney, why don't you bring your family into the shade and the cool inside."

The children all looked up into their father's eyes, hoping they would find agreement.

"Thank you, Mr. Beard. We'd like that. But before we do, is there a place I can tend to my team and the horse tied on behind?"

Beard pointed off to his right and down the knoll. "In the grove right down there. You'll find my horses hobbled in the cool and feasting on the grass."

Briney pointed to the boy. "John, take it down there. Make sure you've got room to turn it wherever you stop. You can hobble the horses but picket the oxen."

"Yes, Father," was John's only comment as he turned to the assigned work.

"Come on inside. I don't have but four chairs, so one of the children will have to sit on the floor." Beard turned and led the way. As all entered behind him, he said, "Water bucket is to your right. Let me get a few mugs.

"Mr. Briney, I've got some smoked venison, got bread and a pail of blackberries one of the Potawatomi brought. Will you accept an offer of lunch?"

In the ten minutes it took Beard to prepare the meal, the Brineys made themselves at ease save for Mrs. Briney, who tried to insist she be allowed to help lay out the table. She was a woman of no more than midthirties and, despite the four children, maintained a figure that showed a very small waist inside the gingham dress. Once she'd removed her bonnet and shaken out her rich blond hair, she showed the face of a woman in full bloom.

When three Brineys were seated at the small table, having left the fourth chair for John when he returned from his chores, and Beard and Briney were standing over the bar, plates before them, Mr. Briney asked Beard if he'd like to offer a blessing. Once that was complete, the eating began, and after the first two hungry bites, chatter started among the children.

Briney wiped a crumb of golden-yellow bread off the corner of his mouth with the back of his hand and looked across the bar at Beard. "Is there a ferry along here large enough to get that wagon on it?"

"No, I'll build one, one day, but I need to get a sawmill here first to cut the planks. We're at mile eighty-eight here, and there's not a ferry between us and the confluence with the Mississippi."

"Flatboats come by?" Briney asked.

"In the fall, St. Louis merchants have crews pole up here to collect the little cotton, corn, and pork surpluses our local farmers produce. That will be a two-month wait."

Briney shook his head, causing the rich black hair to fall into his eyes. He used his fingers to brush it back as he said, "No. We'll do it the hard way."

"How's that?" Beard asked.

"We've had to do it before. Last time was crossing the Wabash. John and I know how."

"How's that?" Beard asked again.

"We take it apart. Get everything out, take off the tongue and the wheels and axles, and float it across. We'll swim the oxen over first and bring a rope along, with one end still fixed here. You can see it's shaped like a boat. High sides, prow, and stern. It's built nearly watertight as well for just that purpose. We'll have to pull it back and forth several times. First to get the axles and wheels and tongue across, then all our supplies and possessions. It will take John and me a week or so, but it will beat waiting."

"What's the rush?"

Briney took a long drink, set his mug on the bar, and inhaled deeply before he started. "Mr. Beard, Nan and I got married a couple of years before the war. Had John pretty quick thereafter; he's sixteen now. War came along, and I wasn't excited about joining. Had a prosperous little farm around Lancaster. But when Madison really needed men, he upped the bounty to 320 acres—four times what I was farming there. So I took it. Was away for three years." Briney's face took on an almost-secret smile. "Nan and I didn't start having the others until I got back."

The smile left the corners of his lips, and he sobered again. "I admit it; I joined for the bounty. And it's here now. We are almost there. In fact, it's right there." Briney put great emphasis on the last word and pointed toward the wall behind Beard's head in the direction of the river. "We sold the farm and put every dollar we had into that wagon and the tools with which it's loaded. And we came. Timed it just so. Bounty lands have been surveyed and made available this year. I need to get to the county seat in Rushville to stake my claim. So we can't stay here any longer than we have to."

Beard considered what Briney had said, then looked him in the eyes. When he had thoroughly sized him up, he said, "Step outside with me, Mr. Briney." Then he looked over at the tall boy. "John, join your dad and me. There's something I want to show him. You should see it, too."

Beard walked down the porch until it ended and then turned toward the river, followed by Briney and John. He stopped at the edge of the knoll overlooking the river and the bottomland beyond.

"Mr. Briney, John." Beard pointed across the river. "That bottomland there, all covered in grass, is the richest land you will ever see. It is black, solid black, as far down as I've ever dug. It's made so by flooding almost every year since the beginning of time. Some years it floods all the way to those hills. Even in the summer, the land between here and there will be a bit moist and soft, sometimes a hard pull for a wagon. Once you get there, it's a gentle two-mile rise to the top, where it flattens out into prairie. After you reach the top, Rushville is no more than five miles."

"So close." Briney's face was that of a man seeing his dream. "John, all we have to do is get the wagon across this river, and then we're one day, two at the most, to the book where I can record our future, your future." His smile was pleased and very paternal as he looked at the rail-thin boy beside him.

He paused and then turned to Beard. "And I don't plan to wait here two months while other veterans record all the best land." There was a firmness in his voice that would brook no interference.

"One thing, Mr. Briney, if I may?"

Briney nodded.

"I'll help you and John get across, but once you get to Rushville, bear in mind that, rich as that soil is, you won't be able to get a crop in the ground with all that flooding. Until some Dutchman who knows how to build dikes comes along, it will be more heartache than heaven. Look closely at the land between the top of the hill and Rushville before you decide where to take your bounty."

* * * *

The following night, mosquitoes buzzed around. Lots of mosquitoes. He wanted to shut out the bugs, but he needed the light to work on his books. He finally picked the least worst alternative. He put logs in the fire, added some kindling under it, and with flint and steel got it going. He stepped outside and cut an armful of small green limbs from the closest tree, went back inside, and threw them on top of the now-blazing fire. It would be even harder for the bugs to breathe than it was for him. They'd leave him alone as he choked his way through the task at hand.

"I raced the last half mile. Looked like the cabin was on fire. Thought you'd need help."

Beard looked up to see a tall man with an angular face whose most prominent feature was the wavy hair hanging down to his shoulders and, even in the smoke, glimmering silver against the solid black of his worsted coat cut to hang down to his knees. The pants were black worsted as well, and the boots black polished leather. The only things not dark about the man were his silver hair, his blue eyes, and the bleached white of his cotton shirt with the Roman collar. His stern visage showed no teeth.

Despite the stern, almost hostile expression of his guest, Beard beamed his usual good-natured smile. "Wouldn't be the first time a man of the cloth had tried to save me. But unless you can incant away these mosquitoes, we'll both have to live with the smoke."

"Close to blasphemy, young man."

An undaunted Beard toned down the smile only slightly. "Close but not quite, Reverend. And I assure you none was intended."

His unsmiling guest made his way from the door through the smoke to the bar behind which Beard stood. "You're Beard, aren't you?"

Beard extended his hand. "Yes, Reverend, I am. Tom Beard. How may I help you?"

"You have it wrong, Mr. Beard. I've come to help you."

Beard felt a shiver of caution run through him with the ominous undertone of the man's voice and the fact that he'd not accepted Beard's offered hand. Beard held it there. The stranger dropped his piercing gaze from Beard's eyes and looked down, and then, as though seeing the offered hand for the first time, extended his own toward it.

"I am Reverend Reddick Horn, Mr. Beard." And with the first hint of a smile, he offered, "It is my pleasure to meet you. And I do have something for you."

So saying, he removed his hand from Beard's, reached into one of the inside pockets of his coat, retrieved a paper, and extended his hand back to Beard. "A letter for you. From Mr. Murray McConnel."

"Thank you, Reverend Horn. What can I do for you in return, Reverend? If I can, I will."

The distinguished and severe man of the cloth reached, this time, into one of the large, deep pockets along the outside of his coat and pulled from it a roll of paper some twenty sheets deep. He unrolled the bundle, licked his index finger, and stroked one sheet off the top, which he handed to Beard. "Please post this on your door."

Beard held the paper close enough he could read in the smoke.

> The Reverend Reddick Horn of the Method-
> ist Episcopal Church of Savannah, Georgia,
> invites you and all of yours to come celebrate
> the glory of the Lord, to be renewed if you
> are saved and saved if you are not. He will be
> speaking several times at a camp meeting to
> be held along Indian Creek, ten miles south of
> Mascouten Bay, the days of August 17 and 18,
> 1825. There will be no liquor allowed in the
> campsite.

The thin man's coattails swirled as he turned to leave. Upon reaching the door, he stopped and looked over his shoulder at Beard. "Young man, I expect to see you there as well. You may have been saved, but you need a reminder."

And he disappeared through the smoke as suddenly as he'd appeared.

Beard stepped outside and watched Reverend Horn ride away on a Tennessee walking horse that he guessed must have been sixteen hands high. Beard sat down on the stump that served as his porch chair, rapidly pulled open McConnel's letter, and read with relish.

> Dear Tom,
> This is to share great good news. I have sat
> before the bar of the State of Illinois (why
> do they say "sat"? I promise, I stood and was
> grilled all afternoon) and been accepted. We
> have sold the farm and moved into Jacksonville.
> Jacksonville has, as I'm sure you know, just
> been chartered by the state as a town. And
> I'm guessing you also know it will now be the
> county seat of Morgan County, formed just
> eighteen months ago. A county, which I might

add, you and I now share, the south side of the
river, up almost to the Sangamon River, being
included. I have opened a law office. In addition, I plan to enter politics as a Democrat as
soon as possible. Morgan is, for now at least, a
Whig county, but my time will come. I hope
you will visit us here. I look forward to seeing
you and introducing you to my Mary.

I am at your service as your friend and/or
lawyer.

Murray (Mo) McConnel

CHAPTER 7

AUGUST 17, 1825

Indian Creek, Morgan County, Illinois

"My friend, how does this compare to the way you Potawatomi celebrate to your god?" Beard said it with the smile of a man enjoying the irreverence of his own jest.

The two men sat on horseback, looking into the circle of some forty wagons pulled into the grove. Each was loaded with a family that seemed to include mother, father, and a dozen children of various ages running around the grove and giggling, screaming, playing games of tag, hide-and-seek, and all the other methods children turned loose use to amuse themselves. Mothers were laying out meals on the tailgates of the wagons or doing the other chores required of them to put a whole family into a wagon and, like turtles, move their shelters with them. Only the men seemed quiet, gathered in small groups around the circle, some smoking, some chewing and spitting, and all holding themselves with the stern rigidity men require of themselves at public meetings.

Chaubenee answered the question with a small smile on his lips but a surprising sense of seriousness in his eyes. "People are pretty much the same everywhere, Beard. The more I come to know you whites, the more I realize it is so."

As they rode from the shadow of the trees into the circle, conversations ceased as eyes turned to inspect the new arrivals. They seemed especially focused on the unusual, but not unknown, specter of an Indian calmly riding into their midst. Chaubenee was known to perhaps half of the men here from times they and he had been together at Beard's store. But his appearance at this camp meeting was outside the context in which they were used to seeing the big Indian. It took a moment or two for calming recognition to come to those who knew him and for those who didn't know him to have his presence acknowledged by those who did. All here were used to seeing Potawatomi. They had been good neighbors from the beginning. He was no cause for threat or alarm, and they knew it. Besides, he was Beard's companion, and that was enough acceptance for all.

"Beard! Tom Beard!" a tenor voice bellowed from one edge of the circle.

Both men stopped their horses and looked toward the voice. It came from the thin, muscular form of Martin Lindsley standing on a wagon bed to their left.

"Martin Lindsley. It's been a very long time," Beard bellowed back.

Beard and Chaubenee dismounted and walked their horses around the outer edge of the circle, common etiquette being to keep horses, their bulk, and their droppings out of the middle of the circle. Lindsley, coming toward them, met them halfway and with a bold welcome that showed none of the reserve Beard expected from him.

After introductions Lindsley asked, "You had lunch? Patricia brought enough food to last the pack of us for a week instead of two days. Come on over and sit for a spell."

The two men followed along and, after tying their horses to the rear of Lindsley's wagon, walked forward to be reintroduced to Patricia and the children.

Patricia had her dark hair pulled back in a bun, the same as Beard had remembered it. She had her bonnet off and, like her husband, showed pale skin from the forehead to the nose and skin burned deep brown from the nose to the neck. There remained about her that same shy but vibrant quality that struck Beard when they had first met.

Upon introduction she extended a small hand to Chaubenee. "Pleased to meet you, Mr. Chaubenee. Let me introduce my children as well."

Billy was the first. He had grown taller but still showed reserve. However, his reserve no longer held the quality of shyness he'd displayed as an eight-year-old. Like his father and mother, Billy extended a hand of greeting to the Potawatomi. Jessica appeared around the corner of the wagon. She, like her mother, was dressed in gingham. Unlike the others when introduced, she offered a heart-stopping curtsy and then raised her eyes to the large dark man with the flowing black-and-grey hair and offered the same words as her mother. "Pleased to meet you, Mr. Chaubenee."

With the formalities almost complete Beard asked, "Where is young, was it . . . Benjamin? He'd be about three by now."

That brought the biggest smile onto Lindsley's face Beard had ever seen there. "That scamp?" Lindsley ran his arm in an arch around the camp circle. "He's out there somewhere causing a ruckus. You'll see him later. But there are other introductions. You've not met Patricia's pride and joy."

"Introductions—plural?"

Lindsley actually blushed, his cheeks below the tan line glowing pink. "Twins. Boys. Sound asleep here in the back of the wagon. They ain't got much to say, but you can meet 'em later, over dinner, after they're up."

"And your help, Martin?" Beard inquired. "They along as well?"

"Nope. Harris is watching the farm. Cettrough is gone."

"Where'd he go?"

"He's a war veteran with a 160-acre bounty owed him. He went off to collect. 'Spect we won't hear much from him. Now you and Chaubenee have a bite of lunch. I've got a bit of business I want to talk with you, but let's do that after."

* * * *

The fire was huge—more than a bonfire but well contained and theatrically placed. The Reverend Reddick Horn had parked his wagon at the open end of the grove with the prairie to the horizon behind it. But he'd not left it that way. Reverend Horn had created a platform of freshly chopped green trees cut and formed into an open square some three feet deep. He'd had the square filled with packed clay and then laid a deep pile of dried timber on top. It was that timber which now blazed in the dark behind him. Reverend Horn, standing on a wagon bed at the edge of the circle, Bible tucked into the crook of his arm and with a backdrop of blazing flames behind him, appeared an avenging angel.

"The man does know how to put on a show," Beard whispered to Chaubenee.

"Tecumseh did exactly the same thing the night he got Tensk named Prophet of the Shawnee," Chaubenee whispered back.

Horn had thundered on for well over an hour, his rhetoric as compelling as his theology. His long silver hair now lay damp against his face and neck.

"Brothers and Sisters, this fire"—he extended his arm behind his back, pointing into the flame—"may be the fire of eternal damnation or the fire that burns away sin. The fire and power of Jesus Christ to those who will be saved."

And now his voice rose to a scream. "WHO AMONG YOU WILL BE SAVED?"

A man's voice from the rear thundered back at him, "I will, Reverend Horn. I would be washed clean."

"Come to me, Brother. Come now and confess your commitment to Jesus Christ!"

And from the rear a man in homespun came staggering forward. Staggering as though drunk.

"Who will join this man in salvation?" Horn bellowed.

"Praise Jesus!" blasted a soprano voice, high and clear, and a woman in a fine woven cotton dress with a ruffled mandarin collar strode purposely forward. As she caught up with her staggering fellow in salvation, she thrust her arm under his and almost as though by the force of her conviction pulled him erect. The crowd parted to make way for them both to come to Horn's feet at the bed of his wagon.

Horn continued. "Brothers, Sisters, now is your moment to confess your belief in Christ and redeem your soul for eternity."

And they came forward. By the time Horn finished his rail call, there were eight people lined up at the church rail that was his wagon bed. Horn had placed a makeshift ramp at the back of his wagon and invited the group to walk up the slope. Once they were with him, he produced a low silver pan of water, and dipping his palm into the water, he baptized each "In the name of the Father, the Son, and the Holy Ghost."

And to the thunderous approval of all assembled, the converted stood and beamed love back at the gathered. Horn stood in the middle of the group, the stern countenance of a dedicated soldier of the God he served.

After a prayer of dismissal, those in the crowd milled about, enjoying the last moments of this fellowship before they slowly dissolved into the dark.

As Beard and Chaubenee made their way back to the Lindsleys' wagon where they would lay out their bedrolls for the night, Beard looked at his friend and asked, "So, what did you think?"

After a moment's reflection, he gave his answer. "Just what I said this morning, people are pretty much the same everywhere." He paused, his countenance reflecting a man pondering. "But I do have one question."

"Ask."

"I thought you whites believed in just one god."

A puzzled Beard responded, "We do."

"I'm confused. The preacher mentioned three at the end."

Beard kept his head down and took two or three steps before answering. "You're right, Chaubenee. It is confusing." He had no more to say on the subject.

By the time they reached the wagon, the Lindsleys, all seven of them, were gathered. The smallest three were already asleep in the bed of the wagon. Lindsley and his wife were sitting on the tailgate, legs swinging slowly.

"Tom, you going to stay tomorrow as well?"

"No, I've got a long ride ahead of me, and Chaubenee has agreed to mind the store while I'm gone. Why?"

"Then walk with me for a moment. A little business."

Lindsley steered toward the wood lining the grove, a place where the men would not be disturbed. When they had strolled past the noise of the crowd, he finally asked his question. "We've had good years since you were at our place. Two good crops and I think this year another. We've kept twenty-five acres in corn. That and a vegetable garden Patricia cleared and a little pork and a lot of venison and turkey . . ." He paused mid-sentence. "That little Billy has become one heck of a shot. Got a turkey, on the wing, and with solid shot, not scatter, just last week." And then another pause. "Anyhow, we've made do with that. And the other fifteen acres, the part you saw us turning the day we met. That we did just what I told you. Planted cotton. And I was right. Soil and weather were good. We've harvested three bales and kept them dry and the varmints away. This year we'll get at least one more, maybe two."

"How big is a bale of cotton, Martin?"

"Not from the South, are you?"

"Nope."

"A bale will be the width of my wagon and half as deep. So, two bales fit on the bed. They'll stand four feet high. We can stack them in twos. So, we'll have cleaned cotton, meaning no seeds, stacked five feet by ten feet and eight feet high. Will that be enough to buy that steel moldboard plow?"

Beard couldn't help but smile in the dark at the thought of a man working years to make his dreams reality. "Should be, Martin. When I leave here, I'm going to Edwardsville. If I can't find out there, I'll cross to St. Louis. I'll be back in two weeks. Soon as I'm back, I'll come out and tell you or send someone with the word. You've done good, Martin. You've done good."

CHAPTER 8

AUGUST 23, 1825

Edwardsville, Madison County, Illinois

"Hello, Jim."

The lean, muscular black man stopped mucking the stall, stood up balanced against his pitchfork, and squinted into the light filling the barn door. He could not make out enough of the tall and broad silhouette to recognize the face, but he knew the voice immediately.

"Mr. Beard, that you?"

"It is indeed, Jim. It is indeed. What a memory you have. Been seven years since I've seen you, and you know me right off."

"A man don't get all too many friends in the world, Mr. Beard. Ought not to forget the ones he's given."

Beard closed the distance between them, leading the roan behind him. When he got close enough, he extended his hand.

"I see you still got that roan mare. She's getting on."

"You're no one to talk, Jim. Your beard was salt and pepper last I saw you. Now it's all salt."

The older man gave a warm smile as Beard chuckled at his own joke.

"What brings you back to us, Mr. Beard?"

"Your wisdom."

Jim's expression was startled and then puzzled. "How's that, Mr. Beard?"

"You told me Marsh was a good man. That I could trust him. I'm about to. You take care of the horse, and we'll see how it works out."

* * * *

"I'll take a beer, a warm meal, and a room in that order," Beard loudly commanded out as soon as he opened the door to Marsh's public house.

A very well-dressed Enos Marsh slowly looked up from behind the bar. His expression was one of a man who wasn't used to being ordered about and didn't take kindly to it. It changed almost instantly to one of joy. He wiped his hands on the rag at his belt and rushed out from behind the bar and across the floor to embrace the man tall enough that he had to stand on his toes to do it.

"Tom Beard, what a pleasure. Wasn't certain I was ever going to see you again. Beer first. Right?"

Beard threw a leg over a stool at the bar, pulled it in under him, and slid it toward the counter. The beer was there waiting for him. He drained it like the very thirsty man he was. "Hot day for a long ride," he said.

"Where'd you come from?" Marsh asked.

"Mascouten Bay. Same place I've been these seven years. Much to tell, Enos. Much to tell."

* * * *

"Jim's cookin' gotten a lot better," Beard said as he bit into another piece of tender, spicy pork.

"Ain't Jim's," Marsh responded.

"Whose then? Not yours."

"Cook's name is Amanda. She's Jim's wife."

"Wife! I'll be damned. How'd they meet?"

"Few years back some of those underground railway people smuggled her here. Don't know where they got her. They stopped here while taking her north. While they were here, her owner came after her. Big ruckus. The owner and his field boss found her and the abolitionist in the loft of my barn. They were fixin' to whip them both when I got there with my shotgun. People gathered all around, and tensions were running high on both sides. Don't know what would have happened were it not for Jim."

"Why? What did he do?"

Marsh got a huge smile on his face and sipped his whiskey to draw the moment of drama out just a bit.

"Jim comes walking out pretty as you please and goes straight by me. He looks at the owner and says, 'What you want for her?'

"Owner sputters and fumes a bit, and the field boss comes marching toward Jim. I take a step forward and point that big double-barreled scattergun right at his belly and say, 'Don't!' He doesn't. And then Jim asks again. Same very calm tone he always uses. 'How much you want for her?' Southerner don't believe Jim has a dollar but finally answers, '$100!'

"Jim takes a step or two back until he's beside me, reaches in his pocket, and takes twenty half eagles out of his pocket and hands them to me and says, 'Mr. Marsh, may I ask you to pay this man and get a bill of sale from him?' And then he turns around and goes back inside."

"Damnedest story I ever heard. So Jim took her in then?" Beard asked.

"Not quite. When I finished the business with the Southerner, Amanda goes to Jim's room and knocks. He opens the door but doesn't make way for her. She says something to the effect that she's his now and tries to step in. Jim don't move. He just says, 'Tomorrow have Mr. Marsh make a place for me to put my X on your papers. I'm giving you to you.' And he won't let her in. After she was free, he insisted on courting her. For maybe a month she slept in the loft. Eventually, they both started coming out of Jim's door in the morning. I don't know any more than that save that I offered her a job as cook and maid. And you're right—she's a lot better cook than he is."

Beard chuckled and cut another piece of pork.

"Let me introduce you. You stay put. I'll bring Amanda." Marsh rose and walked back to the kitchen and returned momentarily, followed by the biggest woman Tom had ever seen.

Amanda was tall, as tall as Tom, and weighed enough that she almost rolled when she walked. Her hair was covered in a kerchief and her body in a shapeless multicolored cotton frock that hung from her shoulders to the middle of her shins. As Beard watched her coming, he decided that if she was a hundred pounds lighter, she'd be a pretty woman with regular features. But the rolls of skin under her chin and along her neck made that vision almost impossible to imagine. But as she stood over him, Amanda's smile lit up the room.

Beard rose. "Amanda, I know your husband, and I just heard your story. Mr. Marsh is right fond of you, and I'm right fond of your cooking."

Without a word, Amanda threw her arms around him and crushed him to her. Her pendulous breasts pushed against his diaphragm. By the time she let go, he was ready to collapse. "Mr. Beard. My husband like you. That's all I needs to know."

And with that she turned with amazing grace for a person her size and went back to her kitchen.

"So, what's your story, Tom?" Marsh asked when they were alone again. "Why are you here?"

"Seven years ago, the last thing you said to me was, 'When the time comes to buy the land, you'll need a money man. Come see me then.' I've come."

* * * *

The sun was just coming over the horizon when Beard walked into the barn. Jim was already up and at work.

"Thought you might be leaving us this morning. Got up early to make sure that old roan of yours got a few oats before you put her to work."

"Thanks, Jim. I'm grateful."

Jim unhooked the feed bag and led the roan out of the stall, grabbed the saddle blanket with one hand, and threw it over her back. Beard pulled the saddle off the stall rail and landed that on top of the blanket.

As he slipped the bit into her mouth, he looked at Jim who was bent tightening the cinch. "Met your wife last night, Jim. She's a lot better cook than you are."

Jim looked up over the mare's withers, a large smile showing teeth that gleamed white against the black face.

"Lot better," was all he said.

"Heard the story, too."

Jim continued to tighten the cinch without comment.

"Got a question if I may," Beard continued.

Jim looked up again and nodded.

"Was she worth it?"

Again, Jim's face beamed the magnitude of his smile. "Every dime and more, Mr. Beard. She makes everything in life better."

"Maybe I should try," Beard said as he swung into the saddle and turned the roan to ride out.

Before he reached the door, Jim spoke again. "You heard the story, Mr. Beard."

Beard stopped, turned his head, and nodded.

"Good thing the man didn't ask $110. He asked for everything I had, and everything I had was enough."

CHAPTER 9

AUGUST 31, 1825

Jacksonville, Morgan County, Illinois

Beard stood stunned, almost in awe, by the house before him. It was two stories and of milled lumber rather than split logs. The entirety of it was whitewashed save the shutters on each of the six windows facing the street, three on each floor, which were painted a deep green. The roof was wood shingles. A tall chimney extended above the roofline at each end of the house. To the right, the kitchen was a small single-story building of the same architectural style and connected to the house by a covered walkway. Beard tied his horse to the white picket fence running in front of the house, swung open the gate, and strolled along the slate walk crossing the manicured front lawn to the small portico, the roof of which was held up by two Greek columns with Ionic capitals. He raised the large brass knocker on the front door and simply let it fall. The sound rang out loudly.

Murray McConnel's clothing was as stunning as his house. Even in the heat of an August afternoon he wore a coat with a high collar, a double row of buttons down the front and ending at the waist but cut so that it extended down from the hips into a long tail. His pants were tight fitting, ending at his calves with hose below. His shoes were low cut and with buckles. His shirtfront above the coat was ruffled white silk.

Neither man spoke for a moment, Beard stunned into silence by the transition in his old companion and McConnel apparently dazed at the sudden appearance of a friend, not seen for six years, suddenly standing at his door. The silence was broken when both men, moved at the same instance from shock to joy, threw their arms around one another, shouting gleefully.

"Tom, Tom Beard. The last man I expected to see at my door and the one whose presence would please me more than that of any other. Come in, man. Come in out of the heat and into the cool."

As he ushered Beard toward a room off the entry, McConnel paused to stick his head up the staircase and shout, "Mary, come down. Please do come down. Such a wonderful surprise." And with that he opened the double doors leading to what was obviously his office.

Beard stood inside the doors, looking at a room with a large window in the front through which sunlight flooded. The far wall was a fireplace with a large desk before it. The floor between was covered with an ornate red Oriental rug and two matching wingback chairs facing the desk. The rear wall was a floor-to-ceiling bookcase with a rolling ladder. It was only partially filled.

As he took it all in, a commotion behind him caused Beard to turn back to the door. A woman, presumably Mary McConnel, came rushing in.

Mary McConnel was short, petite, and clearly a dervish of energy. Her attire was as elegant as her husband's, her dress cinched tight at the waist and buttoned up to the neck with wide sleeves and skirts so flowing they had to be held out with hoops. She was pale and, like her husband, had vivid red hair, which was pulled back tight into a bun.

"Mary, this is my friend Tom Beard. Tom, this is my wife, Mary, who did me the great honor of returning from Missouri with me these five years ago."

She extended her hand. "Mr. Beard, I have heard so much about you. Sometimes I think Murray wishes he were you."

Beard finally seemed to collect himself from the unexpected world that his frontier guide had created for himself and the consuming energy that was his wife. "Mrs. McConnel, my friend, your husband, has written me about you, but he never hinted what a marvelous and beautiful woman he managed to capture."

Turning his head to McConnel, he said, "You always did say too little." And then back to Mrs. McConnel, added, "May I ask you to call me Tom?"

With a birdlike smile and a small curtsy, she answered, "Only if you will call me Mary." And before he could respond asked, "How long will you be staying with us, Mr. Beard?" And then she chirped, "And you will be staying with us, Tom."

"That is most gracious of you, Mary. I fear I am in a rush to get back to my store. But I need your husband's wisdom and counsel first."

"Then you will stay the night. Let me go and start to prepare a nice dinner and make certain your room is tidy. And I will learn more of your adventures over dinner. Now, let me leave you two men to your plans." And with that she turned abruptly and, head erect, strode out the doors, closing them behind her.

"She is a whirlwind, a beautiful whirlwind, of a woman." Beard's face beamed his usually big smile. "Perhaps I will get as lucky one day," he added wistfully.

Mo McConnel's face showed that he was proud. "I did better than I should have? Now sit and tell me all."

For the next hour the two men enjoyed themselves catching up on the details of life that friends want to know concerning those for whom they care and with whom they have lost touch. But when the conversation finally wound down into a moment of silence, Beard turned the conversation to his purpose.

"Mo, I've come to you because I need the help of an attorney," and then he gestured at the bookcase, seeming to take in the elegance of the whole room and the life McConnel had created, and added, "And you seem to be a very good one, at least one with clients who pay their bills."

McConnel snorted. "That's not really true, Tom. I've been in practice for just months. We spent every penny we got for the farm to build this," and he matched Beard's same gesture. "But we talked and agreed that a good attorney, who expects to be well paid, should look like one. So here we are, house poor and hopeful."

Beard smiled and settled back into his chair. For the first time since he had hitched his horse outside, he was completely comfortable. His friend was at the same place in life as he was, still poor but gambling all. "Then let me be one of the first to help pay for all this," he said, making the gesture for a final time. "I want to buy some land."

"Where?"

"Give me a minute and I'll explain all. The federal government has given the state the land on the south side of the river."

McConnel nodded understanding and agreement.

"And the state is in the process of getting the land to the counties for sale," Beard continued.

"Tom, that's set to happen in Morgan County next month."

Beard sat up a bit in his chair, a very excited look on his face. "I knew it was soon but not that soon. Good. I want to buy the piece I'm squatting on. It's Section 15, Township 18, Range 12. I want the whole section. That one and no other."

"Has to be that one? Why?" McConnel asked.

"It's a mile of frontage on the Illinois River at Mascouten Bay. It's the site of my town. No other will do. I've got to have it, Mo."

"You know that will be $800 for the section. Cash! You got it?"

Beard moved to the edge of his chair, put his hand into the deep pocket of his deerskin jacket, and pulled out a bulging leather pouch that he placed on McConnel's desk. "Yep. Mo, I'm not certain anyone else will try to buy it. I've been squatting there since you left. Everyone knows it. But you never know. So, I need you to do two things for me."

"What?"

"First is a partnership agreement between me and Enos Marsh."

"So that's where you got it?" McConnel's face was sober, but his eyes twinkled.

"And I need you to buy that section for me the instant the book opens. Can you do it?"

McConnel eased deeply into his chair, looked up until his eyes were pointed to the ceiling, and closed them. He was silent for several moments, and when he brought his eyes back to Beard's, there was a very satisfied look on his face.

"I told you in my letter that I'm a Democrat with the intention to go into law. I've not kept that a secret around here, and Morgan County is currently a Whig county. So, while I know all the politicians, I'm not positioned to get political favors from them. But this is not a political issue; it is merely an administrative one. I know all the people in the courthouse including the recorder. Nonpolitical favors I can get from him.

"So you'll get your section."

"Mind telling me how you're so certain?" Beard asked.

"The recorder's office will open at 8:00 a.m. There will, no doubt, be a line outside going from the lobby to his second-floor office."

"And you'll be first in line?"

"I'll be in the Morgan County recorder's office before the door opens that day," McConnel replied with a self-satisfied smile. "That's what friends are for, Tom. That's what friends are for."

"Is that ethical, Mo? Sounds a bit crooked."

"You want your section or not?"

* * * *

Mary's dinner was superb and made of things Beard wasn't used to feeding himself. The meat was roast beef with abundant ground horseradish to slather on top and roasted carrots all around. Beard couldn't remember when he'd last had carrots. And he had also forgotten how much he enjoyed fresh salad. That Mary had a very good kitchen garden was made obvious by it. A small chandelier with eight burning candles hung over the table and not only gave light enough to enjoy the meal but also to appreciate the china and silverware.

Mary's company was also unique. While she was polite, she certainly was not deferential to the men. She was part of the conversation. And it was from her that Beard heard of the perils of life in a border state where the question of slavery was still being hotly debated in the marketplace of ideas. Beard found her not only charming but very thoughtful and even more aware of national politics than he.

"Tell me of your plans for your town. Murray tells me you will build one," Mary said.

So, Beard had the pleasure of telling the whole tale from beginning to end, his vision of developing the port that would provide goods for Springfield, Rushville, and all the rest of the center of the state as well as providing a path to export farm surpluses and bring in wealth.

"What you make me see, Tom, is prosperity. But not just prosperity for yourself but for hundreds, even thousands, around you. A better life for many thanks to the vision and labor of one."

For not the first time today, Beard found himself very surprised. "Ma'am . . . Mary, you say that so clearly."

"Because I see it through your eyes, I see it clearly." The small pale face beamed back at him.

Mary stood, collected the plates, and disappeared out the door onto the walkway leading to the kitchen.

"What are the next steps, Tom?" Murray asked.

"I'll lay out a quarter section in city lots. That will include some residential, some commercial, a couple of wide streets, and a town square. And we'll put them up for sale. I'll need you to record the plat as soon as I'm done."

McConnel merely nodded.

"The first thing we're going to need is a sawmill."

"And a distillery," McConnel added.

Beard laughed.

"Not teasing, Tom. Men are thirsty. No place is gonna get men to stay when whiskey is hard to come by."

The door rattled as Mary's foot pushed it open. She stood holding a bowl with vapor rising off the top. "When's the last time you had ice cream, Tom?" With a glow of pride, she laid on the table a bowl full of vanilla ice cream covered in strawberries.

"Oh, Mary, do you have a sister at home?" Beard asked.

As they ate dessert, Mary spoke up. "Tom, Murray tells me you picked the Mascouten Bay in part because there is a bar in the river that makes it shallow enough to pole a ferry across. Have you done it yet?"

Beard set his spoon down before responding. "No, Mary, I have not. There are wagons of families coming to claim their bounty land north of the river. I will have clients the moment I do."

"What are you waiting for?" she asked.

"A sawmill. I want that ferry to be plank, not timber. Timber will be far too heavy and hard to pole. Especially with a wagon on top. A wagon, two horses or oxen, a man, his family, and all they own."

"When do you get a sawmill?" she asked.

"Mo . . . er, Murray and I were just talking about that. It will be the first lot I sell. I plan to sell it really cheap to any man who will open a steam mill."

Before his wife could speak McConnel set his spoon down into the saucer with enough clank to get their attention. "Tom, I've given that some thought, and I think you want my help with that ferry."

"Why, how?" Beard turned curious eyes toward his friend.

"Well, suppose you open a ferry. And suppose it's wildly successful. What's to keep another man from opening another, competing with you?"

"Nothing, I suppose. But even if that happens, there will be business enough for both."

"Maybe," McConnel said. "But maybe not. But even if there is business enough for both, the competition will drive rates down. Wouldn't you make more money if you were the only one?"

"Fair enough. But how do I, or you, stop competition from happening?"

McConnel's face took on the look a man sprouts when he is proud of a devious thought. "Suppose you had a license to run that ferry. An exclusive license."

"But no license is required," Beard objected.

McConnel's expression stayed the same. "A license isn't required . . . until it is. So, what if a law was passed requiring a license?" McConnel picked up his cup, took a drink, and set it back down before answering. "And you got the license, the only license."

Beard pondered a moment. He was trying to think like the political beast he was not. "Even if this were so, it would take a political act to create it. Am I correct?"

"You are."

"And you are a politician, but you are a politician of the wrong party in Morgan County. You're a Democrat. The county is run by Whigs. How could you get it done?"

"You're starting to think like a politician, my friend. You're correct; I could not do that in Morgan County. But there are two sides of the river. The other side is Schuyler County. And Democrats run the show there."

Tom sat quietly for a moment, seeming to stare at nothing but the spoonful of ice cream waiting to be lifted to his lips. After what was obviously serious reflection, he set the spoon down in the bowl and looked unblinking across the table at his attorney. "Murray, is it right to exploit the system for personal benefit like that? Isn't there another way?"

McConnel's eyebrows arched up into the image of red bat wings, his stare almost a glare. "Do you want the money to build your town or not, Tom?"

CHAPTER 10

MARCH 27, 1827

Mascouten Bay, Morgan County, Illinois

Beard had inserted the steel wedge into the split he'd made in the log. The sledge was extended over his shoulders and he was in the process of swinging it mightily when a cracking sound, so sharp it thundered through the sky, caused him to drop the sledge in midswing and jump forward. He looked toward the sound, coming from the river, just in time to see a crack in the ice separate a huge downstream mass of ice from the rest of the river.

"Next time you'll drop that on yourself if you don't watch out."

He turned to see a very amused Chaubenee making his way up the icy knoll. He was holding a folded white paper.

"I'll trade this for a hot cup of coffee."

"Trade what?" a still-embarrassed Beard grumbled back.

"Don't know. Not in the habit of reading your mail. Might but I don't know how." Chaubenee grinned mischievously. "A rider dropped it off yesterday afternoon while you were out."

"You're right. I'll trade." Beard walked inside and came back out momentarily with two steaming mugs of coffee, offering one to Chaubenee. "Two lumps as usual. Now, sit and sip while I read."

> Dear Tom,
> All good news. You and Marsh have your title recorded on Section 15, Township 18, Range 12. You're the owner. Now, go build your town. Your dreams are becoming reality. Both of them. You have been issued a license by Schuyler County to run a ferry across the river. It is an exclusive license. In theory, other ferry services could leave the Morgan County side but have no right to land on the Schuyler County side. So it effectively gives you exclusive rights. It cost $6.00, which I paid and will add to your next bill for legal services. I look forward to hearing from you when you need me next.
>
> Mary sends a fond "Hello."
> Murray (Mo) McConnel

* * * *

Beard didn't wait for the snow to melt before starting to create the plat of his city. The twelve-year-old Indian that Chaubenee sent to help had been befuddled as to why he had to hold a pole in the ground at a specific spot, even if there was a rock in the way. Why not next to the rock? Why did he have to move the rock, even dig it up, no matter how large, and put the little stake in the exact spot? But Chaubenee had told him to do it, and he always did as Chaubenee said. Everyone did what Chaubenee said.

The boy was doing exactly that when a Potawatomi warrior came racing toward them, his horse throwing up clods of dirt softened under the melting snow. He brought his horse to such an abrupt stop that its hocks ended up touching the ground.

"Mr. Beard, Chaubenee says to come, now. Said to leave the tools with the boy and come now."

"What is it?"

"Something none of us have ever seen. Please jump up behind me."

Beard handed the transit to his helper and did as instructed. He'd never known Chaubenee to be urgent and could not imagine what it was but feared it would not be good.

As soon as the horse crested the knoll by the store, Beard saw Chaubenee, and half the villagers, standing, staring downriver. Beard ran to join them. For the only time since he'd known him, Chaubenee had a look of concern on his face.

"What is it?" Chaubenee asked as he pointed downriver.

Beard, his jaw gone slack with wonder, found himself staring at a large, strange, wide-prowed boat, the keel cut low and square in the water, pushing its way through the remaining ice. It had a two-story superstructure with large twin stacks rising high above, billowing black smoke. It appeared to be propelled by a large wheel turning wide blades along its starboard side.

As the beast bellowed the long deep blast of a steam whistle, Beard, waving his hat frantically and with a smile even more radiant than usual, answered, "It's progress, Chaubenee. It's progress."

* * * *

A deckhand, stripped to his shirt even in the cold March air, threw a rope that Beard deftly plucked from the air. Beard nodded to Chaubenee, who in turn nodded to the small group of Potawatomi, who each grabbed hold of the line and pulled until the square prow of the vessel rested gently against the bank. Two deckhands extended a gangplank over the edge of the deck and onto the river's bank.

A tall man in heavy navy-blue serge trousers, a peacoat, and a jaunty white cap bellowed, "Captain John Clark of the good ship *Mechanic* at your service, gentlemen. Is one of you Thomas Beard?"

Beard took three steps up the gangplank toward Clark and extended his hand. "That would be me, Captain."

Clark held his eyes with an expression that was either an expression of mock solemnity or an excess of self-importance—Beard could not tell which. "I have a steel plow for you, Mr. Beard, and I'm ordered to pick up four bales of cotton from you."

Beard opted for the former explanation for Captain Clark's demeanor and responded in kind. "Captain, that is an exchange I'll gladly make. May I offer you the meager hospitality of my firm's headquarters for dinner to celebrate this event?"

Clark's expression gave way to cordiality as he responded, "Indeed you may."

Beard stepped back down the ramp and said softly to Chaubenee, "Would you ask one of your men to get out to Lindsley's before we lose the sun and tell him he and his four bales of cotton need to be here as quickly as he can make his oxen move."

* * * *

Lindsley, Beard, Chaubenee, and several of his young warriors stood on the knoll, watching the *Mechanic* steam away. They watched until it disappeared round the first curve in the course of the Illinois River.

"Gentlemen, we have just witnessed a moment that represents the passing of one era and the beginning of another," Beard commented without looking away from the disappearing trail of smoke rising above the trees downriver.

"I fear," Chaubenee responded, "that I and my people are part of the era that's just passed."

Beard was struck dumb, as a man is when he has spoken words without realizing the pain they impart to others. "I'm sorry, Chaubenee, I . . ." The face he saw looking back at him showed none of Chaubenee's usual goodwill. It bore the deepest sadness Beard had ever seen.

"Be at peace, my friend. These things are beyond the control of either of us. Of any man, really. It does sadden me to see that the lives of these"—Chaubenee swept his arm to take in the young men behind him—"may be lived to no purpose. The will of Moneto is the will of Moneto, but it is hard for me to accept the white race as the instrument of his will."

Lindsley, realizing he was caught in an uncomfortable place, spoke into the silence. "Well, Beard, I've got what I wanted, what I came for. I'll be getting gone to bring this home before dark." He turned and walked toward the oxen chewing placidly in harness before his wagon.

Beard left Chaubenee looking downriver and walked Lindsley to his wagon.

As Lindsley stepped up into the wagon and sat on the lazy board, he looked down at Beard. "Tom, I'm grateful. You got this done for me, just in time."

"Why just in time?"

Lindsley looked behind him at the plow tied firmly into the bed of the wagon and then back to Beard. "Harris has left me. Billy is getting stronger but is not yet a man. I'd have been able to plant very little without it. Now I'll get in a full crop."

And with a smile added, "Maybe next year Billy and I can break some new ground."

With a whistle and a sharp "Gee," he pulled the oxen in a hard right turn to head back toward home.

Beard shouted after him, "My best to Patricia and all five children."

Lindsley stopped the beast, looked over his shoulder with a smile, and said, "Six now, Beard. As of November, it became six. 'Nother boy. Five boys and one girl. Gonna have lots of help."

CHAPTER 11

SEPTEMBER 2, 1827

Mascouten Bay, Morgan County, Illinois

Dear Murray,

Enos and I have made our first sale, and it is just the one we wanted. I need to ask you to prepare a deed and bill of sale. It is slightly complicated. We've sold twelve acres along the riverfront to a gentleman named Charles Knapp. The price is $100 but includes other obligations on the part of the buyers. First, they have agreed to open a steam-driven mill to make barrel staves as well as lumber, and they have also agreed to create a distillery for corn whiskey. They will have these open within six months, or the property reverts back to Enos and me. Additionally, within two months of the mill opening, they will provide me lumber adequate to build a ferry large enough to hold a Conestoga wagon and a team of two horses. Further, they will provide lumber enough for me to construct a two-story public house with no less than ten rental rooms upstairs. That, however, they do not have to provide until September 1828. All of the lumber will be part of the purchase price and at no additional cost. Please create the appropriate documents. Once they are fully executed, we'll get them back to you for recording.

Please offer my best wishes to Mary as well.

Tom

Beard looked up into the sober brown eyes of Enos Marsh, who seemed unable to stop his full lips from thinning out into a contented smile. "We are in business, Enos. It's no longer just your money and my work going out. We now have money coming in."

Enos stepped behind the counter of Beard's store, found the jug of whiskey he knew was there, poured some into two glasses, and handed one to Beard. "To wealth," he said, holding his glass up to Beard.

Beard didn't tap Marsh's glass but held his in place as he added, "And to the progress and our town. May it be a moral as well as prosperous light in the wilderness."

Marsh lowered his glass but held Beard's eyes. "Not our town, Tom. To your town. To Beardstown."

PART II

RIVER RATS

CHAPTER 12

APRIL 20, 1828

Beardstown, Morgan County, Illinois

The spring air was cool and the day cloudless, but Beard was stripped to the waist, muscles on his arms and chest glistening and covered with sweat as he poled the ferry back toward land on the Morgan County side. He'd been at it since sunrise, and this was his third trip. He couldn't feel the three half eagles in his trouser pocket, but he knew they were there, and the knowing made him smile.

Two wagons waited for him, but they'd have to wait a bit while he took a drink. The wagon in front was a large buckboard, sturdy but old, and drawn by a team of mules. The contents of the wagon were piled high and covered with a canvas stretched tight. A middle-aged woman sat on the lazy board. Beard couldn't make out her face, covered as it was by the shadow of her bonnet. But he could see the younger woman beside her. Late teens he guessed. Her bonnet was corded at her neck, but she'd allowed it to slip onto the back of her head and release her golden-blond hair to flow freely around her face in the breeze. And what a face it was, alabaster in color, not burned brown below the nose as that of most prairie women. The billowing hair caused light to glow as a halo around it, the pale amber-green of her eyes and vivid pink of her lips beaming through. Her gingham dress was worn and a bit faded, but its reflected blue gave more life to her eyes. Even though she was sitting, he could see the lovely swell of her breasts above the thin waist, accented by her belt drawn tight.

The man standing beside the wagon was big, very big. Not tall but with a chest as large as Chaubenee's. He wore a pullover red cotton shirt, the sleeves of which he'd pushed up to his elbows, revealing bulging forearms that even from this distance looked as big as oak limbs. Wide suspenders held up the homespun trousers he wore covering his short, almost stumpy legs. He was hatless, the sweat of his bald skull glimmering in the sunshine. The smile he wore was reassuring in a man of such stupefying strength.

"Howdy, mister," Beard bellowed as he poled onto shore. Pulling his shirt on as he stepped to land, he added, "You'll have to wait a bit for me to take you across. Gotta step up to the store and get a drink." Beard nodded in the direction of the building at the top of the riverbank.

The stranger strode down the slope toward him in short but purposeful strides. "Not goin' across."

Beard turned toward the bull of a man, a surprised look on his face. Two more strides and the man was down to him and extending a meaty hand with short but hugely thick fingers. As Beard took it, he could feel the horny calluses developed on every pad of every finger.

"You Beard?" the stranger asked. "This your town?"

"Yep. I'm Beard, Tom Beard. And people here do me the honor of calling this place after me."

"I'm Bell, Dan Bell. I'm a smith. Your town need one?"

For the first time since the short bull of a man said, "Not goin' across," Beard was comfortable. Now he understood. "Mr. Bell, we need a blacksmith. You are very welcome here. I'm going to have to work this ferry until they stop coming or the sun goes down. We can talk then. Meantime, if you'll turn your team downriver and down the back of the knoll, you'll find a grove where you can unhitch and leave them in a shaded place with grass to graze. You and your family spend the day on the porch of the store. If Chaubenee is there, just tell him I invited you. If not, let yourself in. We'll talk this evening."

Bell walked back up the knoll, stepped up and took a seat on the lazy board, and turned his wagon. Beard thought he noticed the girl looking over her shoulder and smiling as she did.

As Bell turned, the wagon behind him, a proud new Conestoga, rolled down the bank toward him. It stopped, and a tall, thin, and unsmiling man stepped down and toward him. "Mr.? How much to float this wagon and team across the river?"

"Five dollars," Beard said with a smile.

The man's face turned to a scowl. "Fi' dallar one hell of a lot for thirty minutes' work."

"It is, isn't it?" Beard responded, the smile still in place. "But you see, sir; you're not paying for the thirty minutes of labor. What you're paying for is the labor it saves you, three, maybe four days probably, and a lot of risk avoided."

"Meaning?" The scowl was still in place.

"Meaning, sir, that before I was here, what men like you had to do was take everything out of their wagons, remove the tongue, wheels, and axles, and then float it all across the river. Took three or four trips. Not all of them made it with all their things intact. Possessions fell out, oxen drowned, ropes broke, and once an entire wagon floated downstream to God knows where. But, of course, you can still do that if you'd like."

Beard's smile grew even larger. "And save yourself 'fi' dallar.' Your choice."

Without a word the man reached into his trousers, pulled out a half eagle, slapped it into Beard's outstretched palm, got back up onto his wagon, and pulled it onto the ferry.

* * * *

It was midafternoon when Beard moored the ferry tight and walked back up the high bank to his store and home. Chaubenee had brought chairs out onto the porch where he sat with Dan Bell, his wife, and daughter. Beard was just tucking in his shirttail as he rounded the corner and saw the four of them. Bell had his head thrown back and was bellowing a deep laugh. Mrs. Bell was giving forth a slight giggle. Miss Bell, Beard couldn't help but notice, either hadn't joined in the laughter or had stopped because her eyes lay silently upon him from the moment he came into her view.

"Beard, your friend Chaubenee was just regaling us with the greatest tale of a fellow named Blue Jacket who hoodwinked some Kentuckian into buying a legendary, but nonexistent, silver mine."

Beard quickly, and with some embarrassment, pulled his hand out of his pants and with force of will pulled his vision away from the young woman and to her father. He felt his face flush, knowing her father interpreted his gaze, probably correctly.

When he got control of his thoughts, he stammered, "Tom . . . please make it Tom, Mr. Bell."

"Tom it is," came the response, projecting both vitality and goodwill. "But then, I'm Dan." And rising, he said, "And let me introduce my family. My wife, Charlotte"—he nodded toward the plump blond woman sitting in the one upholstered chair Beard owned and then shifted his direction to the beautiful

young woman sitting in the straight wooden chair beside her—
"and my daughter, Sara."

As the young woman rose, Beard was surprised at the
height of the girl compared to her father. She was tall and slender, but her breasts swelled proudly. She was still a teenager,
perhaps late teens but he guessed not yet twenty, and she was
beautiful—stunningly beautiful. Beard, ever in control of himself, realized that just now he was not.

Sara Bell neither curtsied nor offered her hand. Nor did
she smile. She looked directly into his eyes, her expression
enigmatic, and said simply, "Mr. Beard."

Beard fought to regain control of himself. A small nod was
all he could muster. He forced his eyes from the face, and as he
turned back to Mrs. Bell, "Ma'am," he said, coughing out of his
dry throat.

As his head swung back toward Dan Bell, he couldn't help
but notice Chaubenee's ill-concealed look of wry amusement.
His composure completely gone, he offered meekly, "I need to
wash up. As soon as I get back, we can talk a little business."
And with that he turned into the cabin.

Upon returning, his hands washed, wet hair pulled back,
and wearing a clean shirt, composed if still uncomfortable,
Beard joined his company. He pulled a stool into the group but
positioned it so he was looking at Dan Bell with Sara outside
his field of vision. "Dan, we need a man like you here. A man
with skills and a family." As he said "family," Beard thought
of her again, whether he could see her or not. "And the skills
you have are needed. Do you know that just downriver from
here"—Beard turned to point and, as he did, could not help but
see Sara Bell; she was still looking at him, just looking—"we
have a steam mill making boards and staves. Same folks are
distilling whiskey as well. Lumber and whiskey, those are the
first two things men need most in the wilderness. Next thing
is a smith. You see; it's not just horseshoes and plow blades that

need fixing. We have manufacturers with no one to build tools and improvements or fix what's broken.

"Tomorrow morning, how about you and I ride together, and I'll show you plots available for you to set up on."

* * * *

When the Bells had gone off to their camp, Chaubenee looked at his friend but said nothing.

Beard let his head dangle until it was hanging almost between his knees. "Damn it, Chaubenee, just say it," he commanded without looking up.

"Say what?" The big Indian was clearly enjoying his discomfort.

"Was it that obvious?" Without picking up his shoulders, Beard twisted his head and eyes upward.

Chaubenee was silent for a long moment. "I seem to keep saying it, but it's true."

"What's true?"

"People are pretty much the same everywhere."

Beard sat up now and brought his concentration with him. "Did they see it?"

"The father? Don't think so, but we men are always the last to know."

"So she knows? And her mother?"

"Both of them. Yes. Women always know," Chaubenee said.

Beard finally smiled. "Well, it's perhaps time I found a woman."

Chaubenee was silent for a long time, letting the dark of the night settle in around them. Finally, it was time for him to walk back to his village, and he rose to go.

As he stepped off the porch, he turned, looking toward the face it was too dark to read, and said, "Beauty is often not the best quality in a wife."

* * * *

Beard rode out of the grove at the bottom of the knoll with Dan Bell on one of his mules riding beside him. Once they cleared the grove, nothing in the sandy soil grew tall enough to impede their view. Looking just a few hundred yards downriver they could see the burgeoning operation of Charles Knapp & Co. Knapp had built a small dock into the river both to receive logs floated to them and to ship out boards, barrel staves, and the barrels being delivered downriver to Jacksonville by way of Meredosia.

"Dan, by the end of the year they'll be making staves enough to produce seventy-five barrels a day," Beard said, starting his observations on the development of his city.

"And how many barrels of whiskey? I can smell the mash from here," Bell responded with a grin. And then more soberly, "May I ask what you sold them that land for?"

"Well, there was more than money involved, but the cash was only $100," Beard answered.

"What else?" It was clear Bell wanted to know what this would cost.

"I was going to save this for later, but you've pounced," Beard said, his smile never flagging. "You want a lot to build a home for your family. That's $100 to $200 depending on just where. Commercial lots are $10 a front foot. Most are fifty by one hundred feet, so $500."

Bell took off his hat and wiped the sweat off the top of his head with a rag he carried in his pocket. His big shoulders drooped low, and his voice became subdued. "I thought I liked your town, Beard, but $600 I haven't got."

Beard turned left, away from the river, and continued to ride. "Would you like to hear the deal I made with Charlie?" He pointed back over his shoulder at the mill.

"Yep." Bell seemed to perk up a bit.

"I needed them. Some businesses a place has just gotta have to even get a shot at growing into a town. A lumber mill is one of them. In fact, I needed lumber. I needed it for two things. First to build that ferry of mine. I knew once I got my ferry going this would be the place where every bounty veteran coming for his land would cross the river. I'd not only make money on the ferry but create a place people come to. And to build the ferry, I needed lumber. Couldn't get the one without the other. So, my deal with Knapp was that in addition to the money, I got lumber to build the ferry. That's how I got it."

"You said two things, Tom. What was the other?"

"I'm opening a hotel. Need lumber for that, too."

Bell gave out a low whistle. "How big?" he asked.

"Two-story with a public room downstairs, ten rooms upstairs to rent, and a stable out back. He owes me that lumber by September, and then I'll start building. But you know what else I need to build?" Beard looked directly at the big man on the mule beside him.

For the first time since he'd asked the price, Bell smiled. Suddenly a big smile. "Nails."

Beard just returned the smile and nodded. "And hinges and latches."

"And you need them by September?"

Beard nodded again.

"I'll be wanting a commercial lot near Charlie Knapp's place. I'm guessing he'll need a lot of stuff as well."

They rode in silence. The quiet was broken when Bell pointed to a mound so large and green it stood out distinctly against the sparse background of the flat sand-based scrub around it. "What's those? I've seen more than one."

"Old Indian burial mounds. There are eleven of them around here."

"I'd like to live near one. I'm thinking that rich soil would make a better lawn than this sand."

The two men took the rest of the morning riding the 160 acres studded with pegs whipping little red pennants bravely in the breeze, Beard explaining them to Dan Bell. There was a peg at the corner of every lot, both home and business lots. Beard was proud to point out that even the smallest streets were sixty feet wide. Wide enough for wagons to stop along both sides and still leave room for two wagons to pass going in opposite directions in the middle. He was especially proud to show a town square where he hoped eventually to see a bandstand. He also pointed out nine cabins under construction and one store, a general merchandise store, going up on the main street in town, Washington Street.

"I'm surprised you sold to that general merchandise store, Tom."

"Why?" Beard responded.

"Why would a man bring in competition to his own business right off?"

Beard chuckled. "Promised him I'd close when he opens."

Now it was Bell's turn to be confused. "Why would ya' do that?"

"It never was my plan to run a store. That was just a way to make a living these last eight, going on nine, years, waiting for the likes of you to show up. I plan to run a ferry and a hotel, and maybe sell a few lots. To make a town." Beard's face nearly glowed. "That's why I came here, Dan. To make a town."

By the time they got back they had come to an agreement on both a commercial and a residential lot, the prices heavily subsidized by a trade in nails and other hardware.

* * * *

"Chaubenee, it has been a very good day. I've sold two lots, got a business in town we need and a source of nails for building the hotel. And I've got five shiny half eagles in my pocket."

The big Indian sat quietly in the dark of the porch awning, looking up at Beard but saying nothing. Beard walked past him, and in the door, before he realized Chaubenee had not spoken. He stopped and, without turning, walked backward the three steps he'd taken into the cabin and, standing beside him, looked down at his friend.

"Cat got your tongue?"

Chaubenee looked up at him, his face a blank. "What's that mean?"

"Just an expression meaning why are you not talking?"

"I'll tell you, but first go in and pour us both a little of that whiskey you keep behind the counter and come back."

Beard did exactly as he was told and quickly. He'd never seen his friend like this and wanted to know why. But he knew Chaubenee well enough to let him roll it out in his own way and his own time.

"Here you go." Beard handed him the mug, pulled a stump up before him, and sat down. "Now tell me."

"It is time, Beard. It is time for the last of the Potawatomi to go. And me among them."

"Jesus, I'd forgotten. Or maybe I just didn't want to remember."

That brought a wan smile from his friend. "Gomo, and the remainder of the Peoria band, and I and my little village will meet outside of Edwardsville in two weeks. We will ferry across the Mississippi and walk to our land at Ste. Genevieve and claim it and our money."

Chaubenee took a small sip of his whiskey. "It is a sad task, but I must lead my people one last time."

Beard sipped his as well but didn't speak.

"I was nineteen when I took leadership of this band. I'd joined Tecumseh and a small band of Shawnee for three years of raids into Tennessee. We'd just come back. My father died while we were away. His friend Spotka, who was our chief, was very old and wanted to set his burdens down. I had a warrior's reputation, my father's blood, and was married to Spotka's daughter. I was selected to replace him. That was thirty-five years ago. From that moment to this I have never been called upon to do a sadder thing."

For once, Tom Beard had no idea what he should say. So he sat sipping as the evening shadows grew longer, and said nothing.

When Chaubenee spoke again, that his heart was lighter was obvious in his tone. "Tom, I said something to you once, and you said something to me once, and I want to see if they go together."

Beard was puzzled by the mysterious suggestion, but his heart lifted a bit because his friend's had. "Tell me."

"I once told you I wanted to die here."

Beard nodded.

"And you once told me that any man could buy land."

Beard lifted his head, a small smile slowly growing across his face. "That is true as well."

"Does 'any man' include your defeated enemy, an Indian? Will you sell me a piece of land?"

Beard burst up off his stump. "Chaubenee, I will *give* you a piece of land."

Chaubenee's expression did not change. "No. That will not do. It must be all legal so no man may challenge it. You have been good to me, but you are not all white men. Many would cut out my heart with a smile. I need the protection only a white man's bill of sale can give me. I will not have this plot stolen from me the way the rest of this land has been taken from my brothers."

Chaubenee reached behind him and brought forth an object he had obviously placed against the wall of the porch. It was a sword. Even as he passed it forward Beard could see it was a sword in a scabbard with a regally crafted handle and guard. He passed it to Beard. "What will this buy?" he asked without expression.

Beard pulled the sword mostly from the scabbard and stared at both. It was well polished with the shine of a blade well cared for and loved. "What is it? Where did it come from? How did you get it?" His questions ran together in erratic excitement.

Chaubenee remained calm, almost remote. "The night before Tecumseh died at the Battle of Thames River, he gave it to me. It had been a gift to him from the governor and commanding general of His Majesty's forces in Upper Canada, Major General Isaac Brock."

Then his voice became sad and very remote. "The day Brock was killed, our world ended. His replacement, General Henry Procter, was as incompetent as Brock was brilliant. It was the end of the war and all our hopes as a people. But we did not know it then."

"Hey, Beard, you coming to supper?" came the bellow from the edge of the knoll as Bell rose above it.

Beard rose and stepped to the edge of the porch, not realizing he was still holding the sword. "Sorry, Dan, I've gotten involved in a rather deep conversation."

As Bell approached, his eyes came to rest on the object in Beard's hands. "What you got there, Tom?"

A somewhat flustered Beard suddenly realized how awkward he must look standing on the porch of a log cabin holding a relic, a beautiful relic, but a relic all the same, of a bygone time. "Chaubenee and I were just looking at . . ." And he stopped midsentence. "Dan, you're a man of metal. Know anything about swords?"

Bell's curiosity piqued, he extended his hand. "A little. Mind if I look?"

Beard glanced at Chaubenee who nodded his head, giving permission. Beard handed the blade and scabbard to Bell.

Bell held both sword and scabbard momentarily and then, removing the blade from the scabbard, handed the covering back to Beard. He studied long and hard. He turned slightly so what was left of the sun shone on the blade. He looked at the handle, guard, and mostly the blade. After several minutes he reached into his pocket and took out a pair of wire-framed spectacles.

With an embarrassed look he said, "I'd be grateful if you didn't tell people I need these." And then cast his attention back to the blade, repeating the examination exactly as before.

Finally, he said, "Is it yours, Chaubenee?"

The Indian gave a nod. The blacksmith turned the sword handle toward Chaubenee and gave it back to him.

"It is perhaps the finest piece of steel I've ever seen. If smithing were alchemy, then I'd call this magic."

"What's so special about it?" Beard asked.

"Let me show you. See on the butt of the blade where it is fitted into the hilt. Look closely and you will see that it says, in English, 'Bend to my will.' It is a metallurgist's play on words. A weapon makes opponents do just that. But this message is not its owner's command to his opponent. It is the maker's command to the blade."

"What do you mean?" asked a startled Beard.

"There are two ways to make steel," Bell explained, "strong or flexible. Each has inherent flaws. If steel is so strong it is inflexible, then it will break under brute force. But if steel is too flexible, it can be snapped like a twig. The trick is to make the steel both. Metallurgists have been trying to solve that problem for a thousand years. This is as close as they've ever come."

"How do you know that inscription is not merely the egotistical fantasy of a smith who is a better poet than craftsman?" Beard asked again.

Bell smiled and then proved his point. "Look on the middle of the blade just above that command. Do you see the runic markings? They are called a cartouche. They are the mark of the maker. That particular cartouche is the mark of the Royal Sword Factory in Toledo, Spain. Some long-ago king of Spain turned his mint in Toledo into a sword factory and commanded that the best metallurgist in the world learn the perfect blend of strength and flexibility."

"Why would a Spaniard write his command in English?" Chaubenee asked.

Bell took off his glasses, putting them back in his pocket. "I'm not certain, Chaubenee, but I can guess."

"So, guess," Beard directed.

"They do accept private orders at Toledo. I would guess this was commissioned by an Englishman. A very rich Englishman."

Bell's face molded into an expression that was part longing and part humility. "If, before I die, I could make just one piece of steel like that, my life would have had purpose."

His usual joviality returned with his smile. "But I make a pretty good nail.

"Now, gentlemen, come to dinner. My women are expecting you, and they are not ones to be kept waiting, as you will find out."

As he turned to go, Beard stopped him. "Dan, wait."

Bell stopped and turned back.

"One question. Just one."

Bell nodded.

"What is it worth?"

Without hesitation Bell said, "It's priceless."

All stood still and no one spoke for a moment, waiting for more words from Bell.

Bell finally offered some. "If you could buy priceless, I'd guess it would cost one thousand dollars. Now come to dinner."

* * * *

"Hope you men are hungry," a jovial Charlotte Bell greeted them as she threw her arms around her husband and gave him a small kiss of welcome. Then with an unexpected exuberance, she performed the same ritual on a startled Chaubenee.

"I'm starved," said Chaubenee. "I hope the food is as abundant as the welcome." He looked at Beard with a smile that said, "There. Did I give you time to recover?"

A small crockery jug appeared in Bell's hand as if by magic. "Charlotte, get out four cups. We've got much to celebrate tonight." And then with a look toward his daughter, he added, "No, make it five."

The cups were produced and placed on the tailgate of the buckboard that was currently serving as a kitchen counter. Bell poured a little from the jug into each cup, passed them out, and insisted all stand and clink the cups together. Then he said, "To our health, friendship, and the prosperity of all we venture together."

After everyone had sipped, he said, "Momma, pull some chairs out of that wagon and let us make our guests comfortable as well as welcome."

Charlotte Bell hopped up into the wagon with a spryness that belied her weight. The chairs were quickly handed down to her husband who set them around the fire. The men sat talking as the ladies tended to dinner, Charlotte Bell at the tailgate pulling all together and Sara hunkering low by the fire, turning steaks in a large frying pan propped up by rocks along the edge.

Tom Beard struggled hard to contribute to the conversation and not cast his eyes toward her where he feared they would be hopelessly lost.

"Mr. Beard." The soft but perfectly clear voice came from somewhere below his knees.

He knew who it was and where she was. He allowed his head to bend slowly downward toward Sara at the edge of the fire. His willpower aside, when her eyes took in his, he seemed powerless to talk, think, or look away.

"Do you want your steak black . . . sir?" The last word slid off her tongue almost as a tease.

It seemed moments before he could respond. "Yes . . . thank you." And momentarily he gained control again. "Miss Bell . . . Sara, if I may. If we can drink together, surely your parents would not object if you call me by my Christian name. It is Thomas, but I prefer Tom."

"Sara," Charlotte's voice boomed across the campfire, "I agree with Tom. If your father thinks you are old enough to drink corn liquor, then you're old enough to call our friend by his Christian name."

Sara raised herself slowly to her full height, pulling the frying pan, a towel wrapped around its handle, with her. For the first time he could remember, she smiled at him. "If that is what you want, Tom, that is what I will do." And then she turned and carried the panful of steaks to her mother at the tailgate.

Beard struggled to keep his mind on the conversation, but Chaubenee and Dan Bell seemed to be doing fine without him. For the next five minutes, he merely stared into the fire before him.

"Tom?"

Nothing followed until he looked up from the fire. Sara Bell was standing beside him, a large metal plate in her hand.

"I have your dinner here. If you'll take the plate, I'll get something to set it on."

She bent slowly forward as she handed him the plate. He finally found the antidote to her eyes. The moon flooded down the front of her dress, giving the skin from her collarbones to the tops of her breasts a silver glow. He was unable to look away. The sway of the full skirt of her dress twirled as she turned and departed.

He looked back up at Dan Bell. The man held a stump between his hands, which he set before Beard.

"That's all we've got for a dinner table for the moment, but thanks to you, we'll soon have something more civilized for you to eat on."

Beard just looked up and nodded.

Bell looked down, smiling. "Careful of that first bite. Sara may have served it too hot."

Beard was daft most of the rest of the evening. Eventually, Chaubenee rose to walk back to his village. Beard, realizing the evening had passed, rose and let the moon, high overhead, lead him to his cabin. As he reached it, he heard the voice of an angel call out behind him.

"Mr. Beard . . . Tom."

He turned to see Sara Bell scampering on light feet up the path toward him. He stood on his porch, waiting for her to come to him.

When she reached the porch, Sara Bell stepped lightly onto it and handed him a small package. "Momma sent me to bring this to you. She said bachelors were no good at taking care of themselves."

Tom Beard reached out, took her wrist, and pulled her toward him.

CHAPTER 13

MAY 1, 1828

Beardstown, Morgan County, Illinois

The Reverend Reddick Horn looked the soul of resplendent authority, a man who speaks for God without hesitation. He was hatless, his pronounced cheekbones casting shadows down his cheeks in the noonday May sunshine. He had planned to stand in the shade of the porch at Beard's store, but he hadn't counted on a crowd of well over one hundred gathering. Even allowing for two dozen of them being Indians, he'd not seen this large a crowd since his camp meeting of almost three years ago. He now stood on a stump above them, high enough that his mane of silver hair and the brilliance of his ruffled silk scarf were visible even in the back of the crowd.

Directly before him stood Tom Beard and Sara Bell. Reverend Horn had never seen Beard in a cloth coat and thought he looked almost statesmanlike. Sara Bell, Horn guessed, must be fifteen years younger than Beard or almost so. But that was not unusual here, where young men were still making their way and could not afford a wife. Especially one as beautiful as she. Dressed in no more than a clean blue gingham frock, which was tight enough in the waist and bodice to suggest Venus-like curves, Sara Bell was the most beautiful woman Horn had seen during his four years in Illinois. And like him, she was vain enough of her hair to stand in the sun without a bonnet. And Horn had to give her that she had caught the most eligible man between Springfield and Jacksonville.

There was little formality here. Reverend Horn had them captured for a few minutes, and he'd use the opportunity to preach a little righteousness to them. He would save no souls that day, but he might get one or two to think a bit, go home and read that Bible collecting dust on the shelf, and maybe come to one of his services. And most of all, when this place, this Beardstown, got large enough for a settled congregation, perhaps the city—or Thomas Beard himself—would donate a prime lot to build a sanctuary.

So, he would pray, offer a short homily, say the vows of matrimony, pronounce them man and wife, receive his small payment, and then get out so they could drink, his departure saving him from besmirching his own reputation by appearing to condone their drunken frivolity.

And that was just what he did. After a half hour of ceremony and light proselytizing, he uttered the words everyone had been waiting for: "In the name of the Methodist Episcopal Church and with the right conferred upon me to do so by the State of Illinois, I pronounce you, Thomas Beard, and you, Sara Bell, man and wife. You may kiss your bride."

* * * *

Almost instantly, as Horn stepped off his stump, a tall, angular man with extraordinarily long arms and legs stepped up on the vacated platform and shouted to the crowd. No one paid him much attention, so he tried again with the same result. This time he reached in his belt, pulled out a huge, old horse pistol, and fired it into the air. All conversation stopped, and all eyes turned to him, the result he'd wanted.

"Most of you know me; some don't. I'm Charlie Knapp. I own that sawmill down on the river. I also own the distillery next to it."

At this he got a huge chorus of "Hurray!"

"As a small present to Tom and Sara Beard, and an introduction of my sour mash whiskey to those of you who don't know it, which would be damn few"—

Again, a chorus of loud whistles and catcalls.

—"I've put a keg of my best on the edge of the porch. Y'all gonna have to supply your own cups, but it's yours. Enjoy. And if you like it, you know where to come buy more."

And with that, there were hoots and hollers as the celebration of the first wedding in Beardstown started.

* * * *

The moon had set by the time Knapp's keg was emptied and the final revelers had wandered home, including Dan and Charlotte Bell. Beard stood on the porch and listened to the last of the laughter, filled with final ribald words that drunken men had offered on wedding nights for as long as anyone remembered. He didn't bother to clean up. He just stood with his hand on the support post holding the roof over the porch. With the moon down, the stars were vibrant in their full glory.

He stood not because he was fearful. He stood because he didn't know what to do. How did a man approach his wife, especially for the first time, when what he wanted, and what was expected of him, was to take her? What if she didn't want it? She wouldn't have any idea. She would be fearful; of that he was certain. And much as he wanted her, he didn't want to scare her or hurt her. Would it hurt the first time? He just stood, not knowing.

He hadn't heard a sound, but he felt her arm come around his back. Her head slid under his arm and pushed against his ribs. And he could feel the mass of her breasts pressed into his back. She said nothing, just stood holding him. When he finally looked down, he could see her hair hanging along the front of one of his shirts, her legs extending out below.

"Tom, come to me." She took his hand and turned to lead him into the store. She led him through the store and into the back bedroom. She turned to him in the dark and, using her fingers to feel the way, unbuttoned his shirt. When it fell open, she reached down and undid the buckle on his belt and then the buttons on his trousers. Without a sound, she put her hand in the middle of his chest and pushed backward. He fell into the bed. Then he felt, more than saw, her kneel down beside the bed and pull off his boots. A moment later he heard the cloth of his shirt sliding off her shoulders. She got onto the bed on her hands and knees and, feeling her way up his body, crawled forward until her face was above his. She lowered herself just enough for him to feel her breasts swaying across his chest.

She dropped her face close to his but did not kiss him. "I married you, Tom, because you can give me the life I want. I grew up with Father working and Mother laboring and me laboring with her. I know how to work. I don't like it only because it's dull. The same ordinary routine every day. Life with you won't be like that. Life with you will be exciting. You are a man making things change.

"Don't bore me, Tom Beard. Don't you dare bore me."

CHAPTER 14

SEPTEMBER 28, 1828

Beardstown, Morgan County, Illinois

He was conscious of the morning voice of a mockingbird before he knew he was awake. His eyes fluttered open to the complete darkness of the room, but he knew there would be a grey hint of light showing along the far edge of the slough. It was time to start the day, but his desire to do so was suffocated by the warmth of Sara's butt buried into his belly. Her head still lay on his arm, exactly where it had been when he fell asleep last night. He allowed his hand to drop below her collarbone and cup her breast. Then he pulled his arm out from under her neck with the fluid ease of practice and rolled away, trying not to disturb the covers or her sleep. It was time to get to work.

"Tommy, don't go away. Stay here with me awhile." It came out as a soft murmur almost indistinguishable as words.

He rolled back toward her and kissed the only part of her uncovered by either the quilt or her hair. It was her ear.

"I'd love to, but there is work to do."

He slid out of bed, walking, on the feet of a man who wanted not to disturb his woman, toward the chair where he'd left his pants. It was a step closer than he'd thought. "Ouch!" he exploded as he barked his shin on its edge.

He heard a giggle and the rustle of covers and then her voice in the dark.

"Did I pull you too close to bed last night when I peeled your trousers?"

No longer needing stealth, he plopped down in the chair and began the ritual he could easily perform in the dark. His foot located the pants, which he pulled on first. His shirt was on the back of the chair and went on. Next, locating the boots with his foot as he pulled them toward him. One sock neatly tucked into each boot where he'd methodically put them before she'd attacked him to get his trousers off.

"Honey, I'll get a fire started and water on if you want to get up and join me before I go."

He was just turning the bacon and the kettle was starting to steam when she stepped into what had been the trading room, now a kitchen. Beard looked at her. She liked wearing his shirts. Always had since that first night she dragged him to bed wearing nothing else.

Sara stood, her hip pressed against one side of the doorjamb, her hand against the other. Her blond crown was a bird's nest of languid sensuality, her long bare legs extending below the tail of the shirt. She'd only buttoned the bottom three buttons of the shirt. Her nipples were the only part of her breasts that the shirtfront covered. She smiled, that enigmatic smile she'd worn when they first met on the porch just outside that door. Only now it wasn't enigmatic. Now he knew what she was thinking.

"You sure I can't entice you to come back to bed?"

Beard just smiled, picked up the steaming kettle, and poured its hot contents into a cup, which he then handed to her.

Sara removed her hand from the doorjamb to accept it. She took a sip and looked back at him. "There are parts of you that haven't been kissed in a few days."

"That's the hardest offer I've ever had to say 'no' to, but I must. There is work to do, and I must do it."

She walked soundlessly to the table, turned a chair so its back was next to the table, and, straddling the seat with her bare legs, slid down. Beard set two plates of fried eggs and bacon on the table and joined her. They ate in silence. As they finished Sara spoke. "Go on. I'll clean up."

As he started to rise, she spoke again. Beard stood, knees half-bent, his body half-erect. "Tom, you come home exhausted; you rise in the dark and you work."

He stood and looked at her, sheepish at this small scolding.

"You must find more time for me."

He nodded and turned to go.

When he reached the door the still-sitting goddess added, "Remember what I told you the night we married, Tom." It was not a question. It was a command.

* * * *

The early-morning sun was clear of the horizon as he walked the few yards to the old French trading post. Behind him he heard the sounds of a wagon, heavy tread of draft horses, slap of leather reins, encouraging command of the driver, and growl of wooden wheels on wooden axles. He turned to see Charlie Knapp's tall, thin figure encouraging the team up the knoll from the bank below.

"I wanted to bring the first delivery myself, and here it is." Knapp pointed behind him to the wagon piled high with cut lumber. "More coming today; more coming tomorrow; more coming until our account is settled and I'm free and clear on my twelve acres." Just saying it brought joy to the thin face.

He pulled the wagon to a halt and stepped down. "I'll help you unload all this, but who's gonna do the other work for you?"

"Pardon?"

"Beard, you gonna build a two-story structure big enough for ten rooms upstairs and a public room down. All that plus a stable and, I presume, corral behind. You gonna build it yourself?"

Beard laughed aloud. "Charlie, see that path beside you, between my place and where we stand? It leads down to the river, doesn't it?"

Charlie Knapp looked confused and said nothing, just nodded.

"You know how many men with wagons come down that path? And you know how many of them complain about the $5 I charge them to carry them across to the Schuyler side? An awful lot of them will be more than willing to labor for a dollar a day. I'm counting on it."

CHAPTER 15

MARCH 10, 1829

Beardstown, Morgan County, Illinois

The temperature was only just above freezing, and it was raining hard. His old buckskin coat was more than enough to keep his body dry and warm, but his heart was chilled, fearful really. His fear was not for his partially completed hotel. The frame was up on both stories as well as the roof and siding. The coming rains wouldn't trouble that. But they would trouble the rising river. The ice had broken and was floating down in large chunks, some big enough to come together and form temporary dams. And the rain was early and constant. The river was rising. It always rose this time of year, but this year it was higher than usual. And the rains just kept coming. If it was raining this hard or harder upriver, and he presumed it was, the rains would pour into the river, behind those ice dams, and come down in rushing walls as they broke. Even after they broke, if it kept raining the river would continue to rise.

McConnel had told him the land on the Schuyler side flooded all the way to the hills, five miles distant. It flooded every year, but he'd never seen it flood that far or that deep in the almost ten years he'd been its observer. If this were the year, what would he do with the new settlers? He'd had McConnel record some dozen land titles of pieces he'd sold. Knapp and Bell had businesses on the river. Others had homes and businesses a bit farther back but still on low ground. He was certain both his cabin and the hotel were safe. The river wouldn't rise this high. Here they were at least thirty feet above the waterline, but what of the others? What would they do? What could they do? What would he do for them? What could he do for them?

* * * *

Two days later, Beard stood behind his cabin, looking across the Illinois River. He couldn't see more than half a mile through the steady rain. In his entire field of vision there was no shoreline to mark the Schuyler side. It was all water. On his side he could tell the water had risen a foot overnight.

He had to untie his ferry and let it rise up with the river, or the craft would come to the end of its tether and become inundated by water pouring over its sides. Beard walked back inside the cabin and picked a long coil of rope off a peg on the wall.

"Tom, are you going out there?" she asked.

"Gotta. The ferry's mooring rope is too short. It will soon be pulled under."

"You'll get sucked into that river and killed!" Sara's face showed the same concern her words did.

Beard leaned toward her and kissed her lips. "You said you liked excitement."

With a frown, Sara stepped into the front room and pulled on a pair of boots and a buckskin jacket of her own.

"Where do you think you're going?" he asked.

"You do what you need to do with that boat. I'll go down to the grove and bring the horses up and tie them here."

Beard smiled and nodded. When he walked out, he went straight to an ancient oak standing on top of the knoll and overlooking the river. He wrapped the rope around the tree and tied it securely. Then he started slowly down the bank, uncoiling the rope as he went. The bank was steep and slick. The dirt gave out below him, and he slid down, seemingly unable to stop his slide. He grabbed at the rope trailing from his shoulder and hung on until it jarred him to a stop. Muddy and wet, he regained his feet and keeping a firm hold on the rope, he played out just enough at a time to keep it taut as he descended the slope. When he'd last left the ferry, he'd tied the bowline to a large rock on the bank. The bow of the ferry was by now tilted dangerously toward the water, its tail rising high out of the water.

Beard could not reach his arms in the water deep enough to find the end of the rope where it knotted to the rock. He threaded the rope he was carrying through the ferry's bow ring and then struggled back up the hill a few feet, where he formed a loop in the section of rope coming down from the oak. He slid the end of the rope through the loop and tied it off. He worked his way back to the ferry using both the heels of his boots and the rope beside him to keep from sliding into the water. The nose of the ferry was now underwater and its tail completely above the river.

Beard took the knife from his belt, reached underwater, and sliced the old bowline, holding the ferry to the rock. The boat's bow immediately popped back up, and the tail came back down until the craft was floating level. Almost as quickly, the current swept the ferry downstream until it came to the end of its rope and then pushed it gently against the shore ten feet downstream.

Beard gingerly worked his way the ten feet down the bank until he again had contact with the bow rope and, using that to steady and secure his steps, pulled and struggled his way back uphill.

She was standing at the top, as wet as he was muddy, her long golden hair plastered against her head and shoulders. "I wasn't sure you were going to make it for a moment."

A very muddy, wet, and exhausted Tom stared at her as she threw open the buckskin jacket. "Ever seen a woman soaked to the skin?" She turned and ran to the cabin.

Beard plodded through the mud behind her. The two horses were tied at the hitching post in front of the cabin, and Sara was standing barefoot and coatless in the front door. The smock she had on was so wet it was plastered to her body as though painted to the curves of her breasts, the pink of her nipples vivid through the cloth. The thin fabric clung to her belly and thighs, accentuating the shadow of her mons. She was giggling.

Beard stood under the roof of the porch, stamping the mud off his boots, a sad look on his face. "That," he said leering at her nakedness, "is the best offer I've ever had to refuse."

The expression on her face went cold and straightened rigidly.

"Sara," he explained, "this water won't wait. It's rising, and I've got the only boat to lift Knapp, and your father," he added with a hopeful smile, "to high ground."

Her expression warmed from cold to cool, and her voice matched it when she spoke. "Go do your work." And with that, she turned into the doorway and closed it behind her.

Beard picked up a saddle blanket where it lay on the porch and threw it over the three-year-old black gelding. Today he needed strength, and he wasn't sure his old roan mare had it to offer any longer. He picked up the saddle and threw it over the blanket. When the saddle cinched up and the bridle was in place, Beard screwed the wide-brimmed felt hat onto his head, turned the horse, and rode away from the river. When he was far enough away from the water to make certain no low, wet ground would block his progress, he turned the gelding downriver. He stayed in that direction for a quarter of a mile and then turned back to the river, hoping it had not already risen beyond his ability to get to Knapp or Bell.

He got to Dan Bell's shop first. Bell had managed to get up a crude roof over his forge by now. When Beard arrived, Bell, shovel in hand, was building a small dike around his operation. In the rain and with the softened soil he'd not heard Beard coming until he bellowed, "Need some help?"

Dan Bell stopped his work, stood against his shovel and looked up with a big smile. "Not sure there's much you can do to help. I'm guessing Noah must have felt the same way."

Beard led his horse under the roof, ducking as he entered. He dismounted, took off his hat and shook it, and then accepted the huge but stubby fingers offered to him by the hand of his father-in-law.

"Dan, I'm not sure that little dike you're building will hold much, but I do have the same help Noah did, an ark."

Bell looked puzzled, so Tom continued. "What do you have in here you can't carry by hand or horseback to your higher lot?"

"I can't get anything out. I tried to bring the wagon down to get the big things—forge and anvil—but the soil's too soft. Horses couldn't pull through it. I'll make multiple trips and carry the hand tools out myself, but I'm afraid the forge and anvil may be buried too deep to find even after the water goes down."

"No, we'll get it all. Here's what we're gonna do," Beard instructed. "You and I will stay in constant touch." He looked out to the rising water before him. "Another foot and it will be here. When that happens, I'll float the ferry down here. We'll put those things on and either keep them onboard or float them to higher ground."

"If I'd known you were smart, I'd have let her marry you sooner," Bell teased.

"Sooner than ten days?" Beard teased back. He kept his head low as he remounted. "I don't think it will get to you before tomorrow, so I'm going to go on over to Knapp's and see what I can do to help."

"If it happens before then, I'll come get you."

Beard put his hat back on and rode out from under the shelter. "Dan, when the time comes, I'm going to need your help to do it. Meantime, you might want to get Charlotte up to the cabin. Gotta be drier at my place than yours." And he rode back out into the rain.

When Beard got to Knapp's, the rain had stopped, but no reassuring sun had forced its way through. The decking of Knapp's dock was just at the surface of the water, giving it the appearance of floating. Knapp had his entire crew loading everything movable into a wagon.

"Bell wasn't able to get his team to pull through the mud. He had to do it on foot and horseback," Beard offered.

"Dan Bell was pulling with two mules. I've got four oxen in harness. We'll get this stuff out. It's the steam engine I'll have to leave behind that worries me. I can get the rest," Knapp responded.

"Can you get that contraption free from its moorings and out onto your dock?" Beard asked.

Knapp looked confused. "That's how I got it here, but why?"

"Because if I can float up to that dock and we can hoist it onto the ferry, that will keep it out of the water."

"Damn it, why didn't I think of that?"

"Charlie, I'm going to come down now, before dark. If we get a surge from some ice dam breaking upstream or the rains start again, that dock will be underwater. Not sure we can do it after that."

"Much obliged, Tom. Much obliged."

Beard smiled. "Charlie, I told you last year to make a town. I need a sawmill. I got one, and I ain't gonna let it go."

* * * *

Tom Beard and Dan Bell had scrambled and slid down the bank and were standing by the ferry.

"You see the problem." Beard made it a statement. "The minute I cut this ferry loose and start to pole downriver, the current is going to sweep me into the middle of the river, and I'm adrift until I get to New Orleans or an ice jam. I've got to keep it here, close to the shoreline. I can, and will, pole from the outboard side, but that's just not going to be enough torque to keep it along the shore. I'd tie to the horses and have them hold me in, but the bank is too steep in some places for them to maintain footing."

Dan Bell smiled. "I've been pounding iron and steel all my life just to prepare for this."

"OK, then. When I get onboard and get the pole in my hand, you untie from the tree, and God save me if you're not strong enough to hold me in," Beard said.

The moment Dan Bell untied from the tree, the current tried to force the boat outward. Beard honestly felt his poling efforts were almost useless. But between them they kept the craft along the edge and moving downstream, until Bell slipped in the mud and fell down the bank. Beard watched in horror as the line went slack and the ferry whipped away from the shore instantly. He could see Bell hanging on to the rope with Herculean effort, unable to get his feet under him.

But Beard saw the bull of a man right himself, with unimaginable strength, against the force of nature and bring the line taut, his heels underwater but apparently dug deep into the mud. The raft curved slowly into shore again, and Bell regained his footing on the bank as though nothing had happened.

As the ferry followed the short quarter-mile course that turned slowly to their left, the vision of Knapp's flooding sawmill came into view.

"Charlie! Charlie!" Beard bellowed. Knapp was not visible, but one of his men was and heard the call. He disappeared for an instant and then came rushing back, Charlie Knapp running before him.

"Get some of your men out here to catch this thing and tie it to the dock." Beard only had to say it once. Whether Knapp heard him, or merely saw the obvious, he didn't know, but within a minute five men were standing on the dock, one of the latecomers rushing up with a ten-foot length of two-by-four lumber in his hand.

Bell now had the rope around his shoulder like a harness and pulled backward with his bull's strength to keep the ferry from ramming the dock. Beard, standing in the front of the ferry, extended his fifteen-foot pole and held strong against the dock for the same purpose. Two men put the two-by-four against the ferry rail and held. Between them they brought the ferry almost to a stop and drifted it into place, letting the current turn it against the dock.

An hour before dark they had the steam engine securely tied into the middle of the ferry. Charlie Knapp had a very satisfied look on his face.

"We got one more thing to do, Charlie." Beard's voice was a command.

"What?" snapped an exhausted Knapp.

Beard pointed to the oxen hooked to the wagon. "You're going to unhitch that four-up from the wagon and hitch them to this ferry. And then they are going to pull it one hundred yards upstream to Bell's shop, and you and your crew are going to help get his anvil and forge on here as well."

Exhausted or not, Knapp understood and nodded.

"And, Charlie, when we're done with that, I want your crew to move all Dan's hand tools onto that wagon and take them out of here with your stuff."

Knapp started to bark objection, but Beard cut him off. "Charlie, weren't for Dan Bell and his strength of Hercules, this boat would have never made it here, and you and I would both be out of business."

* * * *

It was well after dark when two very exhausted men pushed their way up the knoll toward Tom Beard's cabin. The first thing they saw was Bell's mules hitched beside Beard's horses. Tired as they were, their efforts to climb the little knoll created noise, and as they crested, Charlotte Bell opened the door.

Her presence brought a smile to Bell's face. "I thought you might come here to get out of the rain."

Charlotte smiled. "It was dry enough there in the tent, but Sara insisted. Rode Tom's roan over to get me. I thought it best to keep the mules with me, so I rode one and led the other behind." She had a slightly worried look on her face. She stepped off the porch and came to him, her arms outstretched. "I'm glad to see you. I worried," Charlotte said as she reached her arms to enfold her man. Just as her hand went to his shoulders, she jumped back. "Dan Bell, look at you. What a muddy mess." It was a scream, but there was joy and teasing in its tone. "You are not coming in this house like that," she commanded. "Sara!" she screamed.

The young woman appeared at the door to the cabin, her face showing no expression. "Sara, bring me a bucket of water, some soap, a towel, and those clean clothes I brought for your father."

Sara returned in moments, listing toward the side where she carried the water-filled bucket, her other arm wrapped around a bundle of clothes and towels, all of which she handed to her mother.

"You come around the back of this cabin with me," Charlotte commanded her husband. Then with a smile, she looked at her daughter. "We won't be back until I have this man fit to appear in public." And then she stormed off, her huge husband in tow.

Beard looked up at his wife standing on the porch, her face placid. He walked toward her. As he stepped up onto the porch, she barked, "Stop right there. You're not coming in my house like that either." And then she turned to go inside but left the door open and shouted back out to him, "Strip. I'll be right back with what I need to fix you."

Sara Beard's hands on his belly made the only warm spot on his entire body. The cold rain washed over him, rinsing the soap from his skin almost as soon as her hands applied it. Cold or not, he could not help but look down at his wife and enjoy her rain-soaked shift clinging to every curve of her body. Tom spoke loud enough she could hear him over the rain. "Sometimes having a woman is a wonderful thing."

Sara, kneeling in the dirt, stopped her work and looked up. He was surprised at the sobriety in her eyes.

"The day we met, you said the dumbest thing I've ever heard."

Now it was Tom's turn to look sober. "What was that?"

Sara pointed over her shoulder at the porch. "We sat right there. You looked at my father and said, 'Lumber and whiskey are the two things men need most in the wilderness.' What a fool you are sometimes, Tom Beard. The thing men need most anywhere, especially in the wilderness, is women."

Tom gave his wife a dismissive look. "When prosperity comes, the men in this town will find good wives easily." Then Tom's face broke into a broad smile. "I certainly did."

Sara's expression did not change. "I said that men need women, Tom. I didn't say they need wives."

CHAPTER 16

AUGUST 10, 1829

Beardstown, Morgan County, Illinois

Tom and Sara Beard stood in front of the just-completed hotel, the afternoon sun still shining hot and bright even though it was low enough to partially blind their view of the trail coming off the bluff from the south. They could see the two large wagons heading toward them, but they could not yet distinguish the features of those sitting high up on the lazy board of either. But they knew. They knew who they were, and the Beards were here to greet them. By the time the lead wagon pulled into the yard before them, the jet-black hair of a hatless Enos Marsh gleamed in the sunlight.

Marsh's deep voice bellowed a "Whoa" to the team of large draft horses as he pulled hard to set the brake and jumped down without using the step board, landed gracefully on the balls of his feet, and shouted, "Hello, Beard." As he strode toward them, his eyes moved from Beard to the beautiful blond woman standing beside him. He threw his arms around

Beard, who stooped low and wrapped the man in a most affectionate hug.

"Enos. You're here. Now we truly start."

The instant the two men let go of one another, Beard turned slightly toward Sara. "Enos, this is my wife, Sara," and then added, "Sara, this is Enos Marsh, the man without whom I don't believe any of this"—he gestured grandly toward the very large two-story building to his left—"would have happened."

Marsh made a small bow and, with the manners of the gentleman his dress portrayed him to be, said, "Mrs. Beard, Tom said in his letters that you were lovely, but his description did not do your beauty justice."

If he expected her to blush, Marsh had the wrong woman. She extended her hand in a somewhat formal way and said, "Mr. Marsh, I have heard so much. It is my great pleasure to meet you." And while saying, she took in all of the little man. Tom had been apt and correct in his description. The face was thin, almost pinched, but so offset by the oddly large ears and lips as to remove from it any hint of cunning.

As they spoke, the second wagon pulled up beside the first, and a thin black man with short hair and a grey beard stepped down, walked around before the team, and extended his hand up to one of the largest women Sara had ever seen. Sara watched her climb down, stumbling as she reached from the step board to the ground. Sara was taken not so much with her clumsiness as with the evident and surprising strength of the thin man supporting her.

"Jim, Amanda," Beard bellowed. "Welcome to your new home."

Jim turned toward them, still holding the big woman's elbow, and walked slowly, standing very erect, toward them. A slow and easy smile crossed his face. "Mr. Beard, it is nice to see you again."

Sara could see the big woman's face now and couldn't help but observe that the rolls of fat beneath her chin seemed not to rob her face of its beauty.

Before any of them could speak the big woman rolled her eyes toward the big house and almost exploded. "Jim, this is home. Oh, I'm gonna like it here."

All, even Sara, could not help but laugh at her charm.

"Well, we're going to like having you here," Beard responded.

There were introductions around, and then Beard said, "Enos, we've been waiting these last two weeks since it was finished to open. I wanted you to see it brand new and be the first to sleep here. Let me show it to you all."

There was a row of hitching posts between them and the veranda that swept across the front of the building and, in the middle, a set of three wide steps leading to it. The double entry doors were locked. Beard took a large brass key from his pocket, and with the audible snap of a brass bolt being released, the lock opened. Beard pulled open both of the doors and stepped back to allow Marsh and Sara to step through, followed by Jim and Amanda.

To their right was a large open room in which a dozen round tables, with four chairs each, were placed. The floor of polished oak gleamed in the light coming in from the glass window all along the front of the building. A large stone hearth sat in the far wall. To the left was a bar with a service board extending almost to the top of the nine-foot-high wall behind. Directly in front of them, dividing the floor, stood a stairway. It was six feet wide, with banisters up both sides, and extended straight up to the second story. Underneath the staircase a set of half-high doors led elsewhere.

"Amanda," Beard called. "All behind those swinging doors is your domain. You can look at it later, but now we should go upstairs." And he pointed them up.

At the top of the stairs an open hallway, only ten feet long, ended in a hallway crossing it and extending both to the left and the right.

"Turn either way you want," directed a trailing Beard. "It's the same in both directions. Rooms on both sides of the hall and all open for your inspection. Enos, the hallway to the right ends at your door. That is a two-room suite extending the width of the building. All of the others are pretty much the same, large bed, dresser, and chair. There is one right here at the top of the stairs that's a little bigger than the others. Big enough for an armoire, which is already put in place along with all the other furniture."

Beard walked slowly back down the stairs, leaving the four to wander to their hearts' content. Fifteen minutes later they were all downstairs again.

"Amanda," Beard said, "you go wandering back through those swinging doors"—he pointed behind the stairs—"while I show Enos and Jim the barn." Then realizing he'd left out his wife, Beard added, "You want to see the stable or the kitchen?"

"I think I'll stay here and just enjoy this room," Sara said in that expressionless way of hers that always left him not knowing if he was in trouble with her or not.

So he did what he always did to hide his ignorance and confusion; he changed the subject. "Gentlemen, let me show you the barn. There is a back door behind Amanda's kitchen."

It took no more than half an hour to show the ten-stall stable with hayloft above, corral and watering trough outside.

Jim wandered off for a moment, giving minute inspection to the rear wall, and caught the other two as they walked into the back door of the hotel.

As they passed through the kitchen, Amanda seemed gleeful. "I ain't seen a kitchen this big since those underground-railway saviors smuggled me off."

When they got back to the main room, they found Sara sitting at a table in the bar, a glass tumbler of amber-colored liquid before her. The men walked to her table and, as Beard sat beside her, Jim pulled out the chair across the table and seated himself, but Marsh walked past them to the bar and came back with three more shot glasses and an already-opened bottle of brandy. "A good idea, Sara. I think we should all join you."

Sara smiled up. "Mr. Marsh, I've never had brandy before. It is certainly easier on the throat than corn whiskey."

Marsh poured the three glasses full and refilled Sara's saying, "Will you do me the friendly honor of calling me Enos and allowing me to call you Sara?"

Her amber-green eyes twinkled in the rays of the setting sun coming in the window. "Deal, Enos," she agreed.

Marsh raised his glass and said, "I propose a small toast."

They all raised their glasses, and Marsh said, "To a long and prosperous friendship," and held his glass in place for each to clink theirs against it and then swallow the brandy down.

Sara looked pensively at her glass. "Why did these sound so clear and pleasant when we knocked them together?" she asked of no one in particular.

Marsh laughed a deep, rumbling laugh. "Sara, this glass is leaded. Sounds better."

She turned to hold hers to the light, watching the glass separate the light into beautiful colors. "Prettier, too," she added. Then looking at Amanda, a genuine smile filling her face, she said, "I'm with you, Amanda; I'm gonna like it here. I'll need to change a few things, but I'm gonna like it here."

Tom gave his wife a quizzical look out of the corner of his eye. It was a look that said, "What changes?" but he remained silent. All remained silent for a moment. Then for the first time since hellos, Jim spoke. "Mr. Beard, I think you may have forgotten one thing."

"What's that?"

"You didn't put no room at the back of the barn for Amanda and me."

Beard broke into a huge smile and looked to Marsh whose look mimicked Beard's. "You're not going to need one, Jim. The room at the top of the stairs. The larger one with the armoire. That's for you and Amanda. We, Enos and me, thought you'd like it better inside."

Jim was silent for a long moment and then looked straight at Sara. "It seems you and Amanda spoke for all of us, Mrs. Beard. I think we're gonna like it here."

* * * *

Tom and Sara sat quietly sipping the last of the bottle, watching the others trudge up the stairs loaded with personal possessions. Tom seemed wholly content, oblivious to the furrowed brow on his wife's face. Then, Sara finally broke the silence.

"It's all happening for you, isn't it? You are building an empire. That's what you came here for, and that's just what you are doing. But what do I do, Tom?"

That he was dumbfounded by her words was obvious even to him. Again he paused, stalled really, trying to figure out what it was she wanted, was after. But he had to speak, and he knew it.

"You run our lives, Sara. You run our home. You make certain all the clean comfort is there that is available." He paused, a long pause, and finally added, "And you love me. Isn't that enough?"

Sara's face was that same blank expression Tom had never been able to figure out. It was a cipher. She stayed just that way long enough to be certain Tom was uncomfortable. Only then did she speak, slowly and without emotion. "No. It's not." She looked into his eyes, unblinking and without looking away, and sipped at the last of her glass. "Put yourself in my place,

Tom. Would that be enough for you? I warned you the night we married—don't you dare bore me."

Tom was more composed now, more sure of himself. He knew where he was. He was in a negotiation of some sort. He did not know the stakes as yet, but they would appear. He exhaled, and the exhale took his fear and apprehension with it. "What is it you want, Sara?"

"This room and two bedrooms upstairs."

"And what is it you plan to do with them, Sara?"

"Solve the one problem you've missed in building your town and make money doing it."

"Keep talking."

"This room will be for gambling. A couple of card tables to start, and when it's made enough money to afford one, we'll get a roulette wheel. We'll make money on the gambling and sell more whiskey across the bar." She stopped and stared at him, looking for a hint of response.

But Tom was on ground he understood now.

"And the rooms upstairs?"

"For the girls."

Tom rolled toward her in his chair, his jaw clamped tight. "What girls?"

"We'll have barmaids."

"And why will these barmaids need rooms?"

Sara's eyes twinkled. "To take care of the thing men need most on the frontier. The one thing you haven't bothered to give them yet."

Tom stood, turned, looked out the big glass window toward the river, and stretched into a long, leisurely reach with his fingertips to the ceiling and his back curved into an arch. He relaxed into this normal posture and turned to look at his wife. And in a flat, almost atonal, voice said, "Not a chance in hell, Sara." Then he calmly walked out of the room.

CHAPTER 17

SEPTEMBER 15, 1829

Beardstown, Morgan County, Illinois

Chaubenee sat astride his horse, looking down at the Illinois River Valley below him. It had changed so much in such a short time. Even from this distance he could see the cloud of vapor rising from Knapp's steam engine, and he could see the black dots of at least two dozen buildings sprinkled between Knapp's lumber mill and the huge structure outlined just about where the old French trading post would have been. But the biggest change of all was on the river itself. Just coming into view at the bend in the river, south of Knapp's, were floating twin towers, each of which exhaled the same jet of white vapor, rising high, expanding as it rose, until it disappeared like early-morning fog, assaulted by the sunshine. Just now, on the wind, he heard the vague mournful wail those floating palaces seemed to make just for the joy of announcing their own presence. He'd seen one before. *Mechanic?* Was that the name of the one he'd seen? The one that came to deliver the steel plow and take away bales of cotton. He made a clicking sound in his cheek, and the old horse started down the hill to home.

* * * *

Francis Arenz stood on the bridge of the stern-wheeler making its way up the Illinois River Valley to what he presumed, hoped really, would be his new home. In the three days of travel from St. Louis, the ship's captain, also a German immigrant, had befriended him and allowed him access to the bridge. He'd been glad for the privilege because it had been beautiful and pleasant, standing this high, watching the valley unfold before him. So, he'd stood here often beside his new friend, the captain, watching him read this almost-unfathomable river with its treacherous sandbars and waterlogged fallen timbers floating just below the surface, hidden like Nile crocodiles, only their noses extended; but unlike the crocs that hunted fish or fishermen, these submerged timbers hunted ships. If he hit one head-on, it would puncture the hull, and the river, the beautiful, placid, deadly river would come pouring in. It seemed that, like everything on this lovely and serene-appearing place, this river would kill with ease and indifference. And the captain, standing behind the wheel, almost as tall as he, was tasked with guiding around all those dangers. It was a task he accomplished with seemingly the same ease and indifference with which the river hunted him and his boat. They were a well-matched pair.

Francis Arenz would miss this perch when he left it. And this stop before him, this place so small it was a long stretch of the English word "town" to call it such, was the place where that would happen. It was his destination, and he had picked it carefully.

Francis Arenz was from a river town in Germany. He had known from birth what it meant to be from a river town. It meant trade. And trade meant just one thing: prosperity. Upon arriving in America two years ago, he had immediately come west seeking just that. He wanted to go where money was to be made, and he wanted to get there before others. And that meant not staying in Boston or New York or Philadelphia but to go where America was going and to get there before America did. To do that, he had to figure out where America was going. And anyone who did not know America was going west did not have his finger high enough in the air to feel the breeze. A breeze that had become a wind and might well become a storm. So, figuring out the direction was easy. Figuring out the place took a bit of study.

Philadelphia to Fort Pitt and then down the Ohio River, that was easy. Just follow the throng. And that led him down the Ohio River to the state of Kentucky. Two years there taught him the American economy and ways of doing business. But once he was schooled in uniquely American practices, they were practices that essentially said it helped a man to be political, but the political order was not, as in his native land, a top-down hierarchy. There was no royal upper class. The upper class here was self-made. Anybody could join. And the specie of wealth in America was land. Land more than trade. George Washington was a land surveyor and speculator before he was a general or president. Every president in the history of this shiny new republic had been a man of land save the Adamses, father and son, and they were the only two who hadn't been or become rich.

But he left Kentucky because he hadn't come to follow the throng. He'd come to get in front of the throng, to be there where and when the throng arrived. So, he'd come to Illinois and first gone to Galena. Oh, there was wealth in Galena, but it wasn't based on land or trade; it was based on mining, lead mining. That was not his route, not his path. Mining was not the way.

Arenz knew his way was on a river; on a river port; a port on a river that would be the center of trade; a port surrounded by land, land not yet taken. And so here he was, Beardstown, Illinois. Here not just to make his fortune, but to make a city in the wilderness, to bring the things he knew from Germany—civic institutions, education, literature, arts, and religion. He had come to do the things his Protestant upbringing had taught him: that works would not give him redemption but works would show him to be among the chosen of God on Earth. Francis Arenz had come to Beardstown, Illinois, to meet his destiny.

"Captain Schumann"—Arenz looked at the man standing feet planted shoulder width and hands directly above, holding the large wheel—"those large boxes stacked on the foredeck." He pointed to the wide and open space below them packed with cargo. "Where are they going?"

"Wagons will meet them all." He took one hand off the wheel and pointed to the wide sloping bank at which he was aimed. There were no less than five teams hitched to empty freight wagons standing just up the bank. "Do look forward to the day they get a dock in this place. Would make it easier." Then he looked back to Arenz. "I don't think any are for Beardstown this trip. One is for Rushville." He nodded up the hill. "Beard owns that two-story hotel. A nice place. I recommend it to you. He also owns the ferry. The cargo for Rushville will get loaded onto one of those wagons. The wagon will get loaded onto Beard's ferry. He'll take the loaded wagon across, and some teamster will take it the ten or so miles to Rushville."

"He owns the ferry and the hotel?"

Schumann rolled his eyes and added, "And the town. He bought the section and surveyed it into lots." And then a big smile. "Your kind of man, I think, Mr. Arenz."

"The other boxes?"

The captain continued. "Springfield. It's maybe fifty miles up the Sangamon River."

"Where is the Sangamon?" Arenz asked.

The captain pointed grandly before them. "About two miles upstream."

"Then why drop them here? Why don't you carry the freight? Springfield's river connects to this river. Just keep going."

Schumann kept his eye on the approaching shore but took one hand off the wheel and pointed upriver. "See that swamp before you? The Sangamon forms it. Gotta get through that swamp to get to the river channel again, and neither this nor any other sizable craft will make it. And one other change. Your eyes sharp enough to see the river change color about two hundred yards upstream? Just above our landing spot."

Arenz squinted but wasn't certain he could see the change and said so.

Schumann guffawed. "That's why they pay me to captain this ship and not you. I see it clear as day. And that color change is caused by the bottom. It goes shallow right in front of us. I think that's why Beard picked this place. Bottom is shallow enough he can pole his ferry across. When water is high it's no problem, but some seasons it's too shallow to get over that bar. So all the freight for the middle of the state gets off here." The captain then reached up and pulled the lanyard hanging by his right hand, and the steam engine, again, gave a mighty blast on the whistle.

"You've taught me all I need to know, Captain. I've been grateful for the freedom of your bridge these last days." So saying, he reached down, collected his valise, and stepped toward the companionway leading down to the main deck and his exit. Stopping to look toward the captain one more time, Arenz asked, "Would you have one of your stevedores bring my trunks up to that hotel? I'm going to accept your recommendation."

* * * *

Chaubenee tethered his horse to the post in front of the hotel. He stepped up the porch stairs just as a small but very dapperly dressed man did as well. His coat was a dark blue, double lapelled, fitted tightly at the waist and flared over the hips to extend in a wide loop to his calves. His pants were long and ended in shoes rather than boots. He wore a waistcoat with a white silk shirt showing beneath. His head was topped with a tall black beaver hat. He carried a canvas valise in one hand and a cane in the other. He fairly skipped past Chaubenee rising the three steps and threw one of the doors open before him. Chaubenee caught the door before it was fully closed and stepped in behind him.

The two stood inside the door waiting for their eyes to adjust to the dimmer light. The smaller man stood in front, his tall beaver hat blocking Chaubenee's view of the room. Once it was removed, Chaubenee could see over the top of the small man's head. He stood, taking in all that Beard had wrought since he left. It was a lot, he decided.

As the small man stood waiting to be received, his eyes fell on the most gorgeous young blond woman. She wore a collarless cotton dress of a bright yellow cloth decorated with small brown figures. It had sleeves that billowed from her shoulders to her wrists where it was gathered in tight cuffs. That it was gathered tight at her waist gave a hint of a well-formed figure. Like the sleeves, the dress billowed from her waist and out over her hips, but, unlike the sleeves, it continued to expand all the way to the floor.

She turned to him, her eyes appearing focused just above his head. He was used to that. Her lips formed into a smile that grew to cover her whole face, and she came running to him, her pace accelerating as she came. Just as she reached him, she threw her arms open. His rapture at the greeting was brought down as she whirled about him and screamed, "Chaubenee," and threw herself at the Indian who had come in behind him.

The big man held her back at arm's length, the gesture pushing the small man forward and causing a brief stumble from which he recovered.

"You are lovelier than ever, Sara. Marriage seems to suit you."

"Chaubenee, if you could get him to pay a little more attention to what I say, it would suit me even more." She frowned slightly. "I've got some great ideas for this place, but Tom insists on ignoring them."

The big Indian chuckled, and they stood smiling and talking with joy.

"Ammmm," the small man coughed to get her attention.

Sara whirled gracefully. "You see he is an old friend, long not seen, but do accept my apologies. May I help you?"

"You could get the proprietor for me. I'd like to see about a room."

"I'm she," Sara said in her flat, expressionless way. "And, yes, we have a room for you, Mr.?"

"Arenz, Francis Arenz."

"Will you be staying long, Mr. Arenz?"

Arenz, looking up at her with a smile containing real warmth, said, "For the rest of my life, I believe."

For the first time Sara seemed to take him in, to credit his presence in any sort of meaningful way. "Mr. Arenz, may I ask you to give me just a moment? When did you last eat? Perhaps you would like a meal. I think Amanda has some corned beef she's slicing for lunch." She pointed to the tables to his right. "If not that, perhaps a drink." She pointed to his left. "Mostly it's corn whiskey, but we also have some Madeira or a brandy. Give me just a minute to get my friend settled, and I'll be right with you."

Arenz said, "I think I'll accept that corned beef," bowed slightly, and walked to the right.

Sara turned back to Chaubenee. "Do you know Jim? Marsh's man?"

Chaubenee shook his head.

"You can't miss him. Only black man in the stable. It's behind. Take your horse to him. I'm sorry to be the one to deliver the bad news, but the flood this spring slowed everything. Your house isn't done, so you'll stay with us until it is." She pointed up the stairs. "Top of the stairs to the left. Yours is at the end of the hall. When you're all put away, come back to me and we can talk, or I'll send for Tom if I can get him away from the ferry. Now let me go deal with Mr. Arenz."

Chaubenee nodded and started to turn away.

She grabbed him, turned his shoulders back toward her, and kissed his cheek. "Welcome home." And then walked to the dining room.

As she walked by Arenz, she said, "Would you like a coffee with your lunch?"

Arenz nodded, and she kept walking straight toward the kitchen door. "Amanda, a late lunch. Wants corned beef and coffee." And without seeing the woman, turned and walked back to the small elegant man sitting in the dining room.

"Mr. Arenz, my name is Sara Beard. May I sit with you for a moment?" Sara asked when she reached his table.

"Of course, you may, Mrs. Beard."

She sat and for the first time observed this man. His eyes were a color she'd not seen before. They were a deep color that was neither black nor blue but almost purple, the color so dark that it had the effect of making her feel there was depth behind them. The feeling was perhaps created, she thought, by the deep brow ridges that made his eyes seem to be far back in his head. The heavy dark brows and long lashes and sculpted cheekbones all enhanced the effect, almost as though his entire face were designed to draw you into those eyes. A dark widow's peak, pointing down to his eyes, made it almost impossible not to stare into them. Sara, who had never been shy about quietly studying faces, took it all in before she spoke.

Arenz appeared unphased by her study.

"You will be staying the rest of your life. I hope that is a very long stay, Mr. Arenz," she said finally. "But may I ask what brings you to that conclusion so quickly?"

He received her comments with a very modest grin. "Mrs. Beard, I come from a town on a river. I know about trade, and I have discovered that in America wealth is created with land. This place, your town, named for your family, I presume, appears to have an abundance of the latter and soon, I assure you if you don't already know, will also have an abundance of the former."

"Mr. Arenz, I think you and my husband should meet."

CHAPTER 18

SEPTEMBER 4, 1830

Beardstown, Morgan County, Illinois

Enos Marsh and Tom Beard sat alone at a table by the front window of the hotel, needing the light to review their books. Marsh, his coat removed and sleeves held up by garters, opened a black-leather-bound journal and spread it across the table. He peered momentarily, and then his plump lips pursed into a frown. He reached behind to the coat hanging on his chair, fumbled for a moment, and then produced, from the coat's large side pocket, a pair of wire-rimmed spectacles that he proceeded to twist into place behind his overlarge ears.

"Enos Marsh, I'll be damned." Beard exploded in laughter. "You're getting old."

Marsh's lips formed into an embarrassed smile that changed almost instantly into a defiant one. "Not too old to be the best partner you'll ever have." He slid the journal toward Beard, spinning it around as it crossed the table. "I've been here one year and, in that year, we have sold exactly one hundred lots of which sixteen are commercial and the remainder residential. We have a population I estimate at over four hundred as well as the commerce to support them: three freight-forwarding firms, two separate folks buying and shipping agriculture products, including your friend Francis Arenz, two general merchandise stores, two stables—one besides ours, a livery stable—another smith to give your father-in-law a little competition, and a saloon to compete with this, the finest hotel between Springfield and St. Louis. And all of that is supported by regular steamboat traffic. Since the river opened at the end of February, we've averaged almost a boat a week. Two years ago, when the *Mechanic* came up, it was not only the first boat up the river but the only one that year."

"Your vision is coming to pass."

"And let me add one you left out. We have a ferry. A ferry that on some days grosses $100. That's twenty trips across the river and back. If Arenz hadn't suggested we change from poling power to horsepower, we wouldn't be able to do half that with me working dawn to dusk," Beard added to the summary.

"That Arenz," Marsh said, in a tone that left Beard wondering if it was a compliment or complaint. "Where the hell did he come up with one thousand yards of heavy rope to do it?" And then in a tone that clearly was complaint, he said, "And sold it to you for twice what it cost him."

Beard pushed back from the table, extended his legs, and placed both heels on the floor. "Enos, you ever hear what I tell people who protest paying a half eagle for a thirty-minute ride?"

"Yeah, yeah, yeah," Marsh muttered. "They pay because the option is even more unappealing. Something like that. Still, that ferry is one of our businesses that worries me."

"Why, Enos?"

"Bounty land will all be taken soon. And when it's gone, yeah, we'll have traffic and freight going across but nothing like now."

"Enos, you just said you are the best partner I'll ever have. You can figure out how to make things happen and make money doing it. But you're not a visionary, Enos. You need me for that." For the first time in the conversation Beard's huge smile spread across his face.

"Meaning?"

"Meaning, that ferry is not just the gateway to bounty land in Illinois. It is also the gateway west. To Iowa."

"Iowa!" Marsh almost exploded as he leaned across the table toward Beard, his eyes dancing. "We just pushed the Sauk over there. And they are nothing but trouble. Settlers not going to go have Sauk arrows put in their backs."

"Wrong, Enos," Beard answered. "It is the Sauk's own aggression that will do them in."

"How?" Marsh asked, interested now.

"There are always those pioneers who take too many risks. They will go. And you're right. They will end up with Sauk and Fox arrows in their backs, and the backs of their women and children as well. What do you think will happen then?"

By now Enos Marsh was settled all the way into his chair, a look of understanding on his face. "We will destroy them," he answered.

"As we always do, Enos. As we always do. And then what will happen?" Beard asked.

"When the Sauk and the Fox are gone, the settlers will come. They will follow the set path and cross the Illinois River here." Marsh nodded understanding.

"Our ferry may have a slow period in between the last of the bounty land and the first of the Iowa land, but we won't give up on it, Enos. It is a cow that gives half eagles instead of milk."

"So even you admit, Tom, that the cow may go dry for a while. There are a couple of ways to keep it flowing, obvious ways."

Tom's eyebrows pulled together, giving way to his perplexity. "What ways?"

"The bar. It would sell more whiskey if we had a couple of gambling tables. Maybe a roulette wheel."

Tom interrupted. "And that would create a need for a couple of barmaids. Maybe we could get extra money out of them by putting them up for hire in a couple of rooms upstairs." His tone barely concealed his revulsion. But his partner didn't seem to hear it.

"Great idea, Tom."

"Not my idea. It was Sara's." His disgust was obvious now.

Marsh pulled the wire rim of his glass frames off his big ears. "Sara! I'll be damned. More to that woman than I'd guessed."

"Me either. And I'll tell you the same damn thing I told her. No! That is not going to happen in any business I own." He stared defiantly at his partner, sparks flying out of his eyes.

"Even if your partner disagrees?" Marsh fired back.

"Even if my partner disagrees. Not happening!"

"Tom Beard, as long as I've known you, I've never realized you were a prude."

"Call me what you want. Say what you want. I'm not a pimp and my wife won't be a madam, and that is the end of the discussion."

Beard rose, turned abruptly, and looked out the window at a large freight wagon pulling up in front. The wagon was loaded with bales of cotton and driven by a slim young man of maybe sixteen. He had a leather hat pulled low over his face, and Beard could not recognize him. But he did recognize the wagon. It was Martin Lindsley's wagon. The first wagon to ever bring crop to a steamboat on the Illinois River.

"Excuse me, Enos. I have business to attend to." He turned and walked out the door.

Enos Marsh watched as Beard strode directly to the wagon. He looked up and spoke to the young driver who stepped down off the wagon. The two shook hands and after a moment turned and walked back into the hotel and back to his table.

Beard seemed to have cooled. He looked down at his partner, saying, "Billy, I don't believe you know my partner, Enos Marsh."

Marsh rose, a smile on his face looking at a person who elsewhere would be a boy, but here on the frontier was a man expecting, and expected, to do a man's work. His hair was white blond, and his complexion matched down to his nose. Below that it was baked a dark brown. The deep-blue eyes carried a sadness.

"Enos, this is Billy Lindsley. He's Martin and Patricia Lindsley's oldest."

Marsh extended his hand. When the young man took it, Marsh felt strength in the grip.

"Billy, please, sit. Join us. Would you like a meal? How's your family doing?"

The limbs seemed disjointed, almost disconnected as Billy Lindsley fell into the chair. "Thank you for the offer, sir, but no. Mom packed me a lunch this morning."

Billy Lindsley dropped his eyes and seemed to study the hat in his hands that he was fingering in a way that made it turn slowly in his lap. "Mr. Beard, Mom's fine and most of the younger are all right. But—"

Billy halted and swallowed and while still looking at his hat said, "Dad and the baby died three weeks back."

"What?" Beard came bolt upright. "What happened?"

"Disease, Mr. Beard," Billy explained. "Baby came down with it one night and was dead by morning. Dad took sick that night and lasted only two days. They both shat themselves to death, Mr. Beard. Nothing left inside."

"Cholera," Marsh muttered.

Beard nodded.

Billy finally raised his head. "Awful way to die, Mr. Beard. Awful."

There was complete silence around the table.

It was Billy who broke it. "Mr. Beard, I need your help."

"Anything, Billy."

The white-blond shock of hair nodded out the window to the freight wagon. "Most of the cotton was in when Dad died. Ben's nine now, and he and I and Jessica and Mom got the rest in." A small smile came to his face. "Twins still too small to do much, but they wandered along behind us, trying to pick any cotton we may have left on the bolls.

"I came to you to sell it. Went to your old store and the woman there . . ."

"My wife," Beard inserted.

"She said you were not in that business anymore, but said I could find you here. So I came. Can you help me sell it, Mr. Beard?"

"You bet. Two buyers in town now. Both honest far as I know. One of them's a friend. Be delighted to take you to his place and introduce you."

Billy got up on the lazy board and released the brake. Beard walked around and stepped up on the other side. He had Billy turn the team tightly and drive them down the street, the one block to Francis Arenz's business.

Arenz had purchased lumber from Knapp and hired workmen to build a small frame building a block from the river. He'd had to pay Beard $350 for the lot. He'd wanted to be near the river and paid for the privilege. His building was two steps up from the street and consisted of one room with a glass front window. There was a back door leading to a barn taking up most of the lot with a small corral of split-rail fence between the two. The room inside was sparse with Arenz's desk, two chairs in front, a chair and three wooden file cabinets behind.

Billy and Beard walked in to find Arenz at his desk. After introductions and obligatory handshakes Beard explained to Arenz who Billy was and what was needed. Arenz offered a sober condolence.

"'Blessed are they that mourn, for they shall be comforted.' I wish I were able to offer more comfort than mere words, but it will come to you, Billy. I promise." Arenz's deep-set eyes seemed to project real emotion beyond the mere words.

"Thank you, sir," Billy replied.

"And about the immediate problem—I can offer an immediate solution. Two really," Arenz responded. "First option, what I would normally do, and will do if you want, is simply buy the cotton. I'll need to examine it for quality, but the last steamboat brought news of the price being paid in St. Louis last week. Price goes up and down daily, but I can guess the price I'll get within a range when I sell in St. Louis. To buy it from you now, I have to assume the low in that range, reduce it a bit for possible risk, adjust for my cost of shipment to the market and St. Louis and selling costs. That gives me a basic price that I reduce by twenty-five percent. That's my profit."

Billy, who had not spoken during the entire lesson—a lesson his pa had never taught him—offered only a question. "And the other option?"

Arenz's dark eyes showed a lighter shade of purple for a moment, expressing some appreciation of the workings of such a young man's mind.

"I take the cotton from you now. I ship it to St. Louis and sell it and pay costs. I reduce the net price by only ten percent because you have reduced the risk I take to almost nothing."

"How much more do I get doing it that way?"

"I'd guess you'll make somewhere between twenty-five and thirty-five percent more, but it's much riskier. The market is unpredictable."

"I'll take it," Billy said without any change in expression.

Arenz held up his hand. "I want to make certain you understand the risk here. If the bottom falls out of the price of cotton between now and then, you suffer."

"Is that likely?" asked the unsmiling young man.

"No," answered Arenz.

Billy turned in his chair to look at Beard, seeking assurance.

"I'm not the trader, Billy. But I trust Arenz."

"Stop. Don't answer yet, Billy," Arenz commanded. "There is one other issue. If you do this, you won't get your money now. It will come later."

"How much later?" the unsmiling lips spoke again.

"Boat next week takes it to market. Auction days in St. Louis are Wednesday. So, it will be sold within ten days. But the market in St. Louis is slow to close transactions. May be as much as a month before they do so. Then a week for the boat back upriver. All that is six or seven weeks. So sometime the first half of November. Unless of course the river freezes early. Then it will be next spring."

Billy looked at Beard again.

"Your mom got money to get you through the winter?" Beard asked.

Billy nodded at Beard and looked back to Arenz. "Where do you want me to unload the cotton?"

It was almost dark. Tom Beard and Francis Arenz stood on the porch of his building, watching the slim boy head his team south out of town.

"That boy going to be all right going home in the dark?" Arenz pondered out loud.

"That boy, Francis, is a man. And those horses know the way home," Beard responded. "Now come on up to the hotel and have dinner with me."

Arenz shook his head. "Love the pleasure of your company, but there's a lot of work to do between now and bedtime. Another night."

As the two men parted Beard offered, "Thanks for doing that for me. You were good to him."

"He's your friend and he needs help. Of course, I was good to him. Besides, there are things I want from you."

"From me, what?"

Arenz smiled a secret smile that Beard could barely read in the gathering dark. "We'll talk over dinner," Arenz insisted.

"OK," Beard conceded, "but give me a clue."

"About things this town of yours needs," the small man offered.

Beard's face took on a tone of caution. "Like?"

"Like a dock instead of a muddy bank. And speaking of banks, we need one of those as well."

Beard's face lightened as he turned and walked away. "You're right. We'll talk over dinner."

As Beard started to walk back to the hotel, Arenz shot after him, "And a newspaper, Tom. We need a newspaper."

Tom Beard just waved a hand over his head and kept walking.

He walked to his cabin. The door was open with smoke coming from the inside. The light smoke that filled the inside, he instantly realized, was from the green leaves Sara had put in the hearth. "Bugs eating you tonight?"

A very unhappy Sara Beard peered at him through the smoke. "And every night. I want out of here, Tom."

"To where?" He waved a hand in front of his face to clear the smoke.

"To the hotel with everyone else."

"Sara, the hotel is to make money."

She stormed across the room toward him and when she was within a foot, pushed herself up on her toes so her eyes were only a few inches below his. "Yeah! Well, I offered to use it to make a lot more money, and you turned me down flat. But your partner lives there; your help lives there. Make any money off them?"

Beard walked into the bedroom, sat down on the bed, and pulled off his boots. Sara came in after him, taking a position directly over him, her hands on her hips. Beard rubbed his feet.

"And I'm bored living here!" she shouted.

"Jim takes care of the stable and maintenance. Amanda runs the kitchen and cleans the rooms. Are you willing to run the bar and the hotel?"

"Even if I don't get to run it my way!" Her eyes shouted defiance; her voice did not.

"OK," he said. "We'll move."

Without a word she jumped on top of him and threw him back into the bed.

CHAPTER 19

FEBRUARY 2, 1831

Beardstown, Morgan County, Illinois

It had been the hardest winter anyone on the frontier could remember. By mid-November the river was frozen solid. The first snow arrived before December. It snowed thirty inches in three cold days, leaving drifts that covered the roads until it was impossible to tell what was road and what was prairie.

The bitterly cold months that followed hardened the snowbanks to ice and made the roads impassable. No one could travel. There had not been a single guest in the hotel for weeks.

That February night, the hotel residents all sat by the hearth very content. Even Jim was able to relax and do nothing for an hour. Amanda kept bringing food and Sara drinks. Chaubenee and Marsh pulled chairs to the hearth. Jim and Beard pitched wood into the fireplace until it was roaring. Both hands in the small of his back, Arenz stood by the window, looking at the purity of the town, and dreamed.

"Francis, I poured brandy into two of those large crystal snifters you bought and insist you use one."

Moving his hands to his side, Arenz turned to see a rare smile on one of the loveliest faces he had ever known. She extended an arm toward him, holding his snifter with her fingers around the top rim so he could place the stem between his middle and ring finger, palm up. She held hers the same way in the other hand.

"Your husband is a very lucky man." The purple eyes twinkled mirth at her.

"I'm not sure Tom would always agree, Francis. I can be difficult at times."

"It is a trap beautiful women often fall into." His smile didn't fade. "But I'm sure Tom has adjusted to your ways."

Her smile was gone. Replaced by that penetrating and unreadable expression he was so used to seeing on her face. "Maybe."

"If the brandy is just for you and me, what have you poured the others?"

"The men seem never to have found anything they like better than corn whiskey. That is except Jim. Somewhere he picked up a fondness for Madeira wine, and he's taught the habit to Amanda as well. I simply left a bottle of each on the table." She pointed to the group by the fire. "Now come to the fire and join us, Francis. You're like Chaubenee. You speak so little, but it's always of interest when you do."

The two walked across the room together. Arenz offered Sara the vacant chair by the fire, but she shook her head and sat in a chair behind the others. Arenz took the chair Sara had refused and sat down.

Enos looked at the new arrival. "Is there winter like this in Germany?"

"Sometimes," came the terse response. He looked back out the window.

Breaking the silence, Chaubenee turned to the ever-quiet Jim. "Jim, someone told me you were a slave in Tennessee. It was warm there?"

"Yes."

"And I also heard it was the Shawnee who brought you north."

"Well, not quite. A Cherokee war party, and some Shawnee running with them, burned my master's village. Cherokee got me but eventually traded me north of the Ohio."

Chaubenee did something no one had ever seen him do. He looked excited and moved forward until his elbows were on his knees. "You remember anything about the Indian party?"

"Oh, a little bit. Mostly, I was scared to death."

"Would you tell me anything you remember?"

"Thing I remember most is some Cherokee warrior hit one of the women and then ripped the front of her dress off. One of the Shawnee, a young warrior, knocked him down. The young warrior then took off his shirt and gave it to the half-naked woman. In English, better than mine, he told her to cover her nakedness. We captives were all stunned."

Chaubenee sank deep into his overstuffed chair, his face going back to its usual sense of repose. "But you were north of the Ohio in the winter of 1789? It was the coldest winter I ever remember. Honestly thought I'd freeze to death when I had to cross the river."

"Don't remember the year, but the winter after I was traded north was the coldest I ever remember. More than the cold I remember the snow. How deep it was. It just kept coming. By the time March arrived we were out of firewood and food, too. Can't hunt or cut timber in snowdrifts that deep."

They were all silent again and everyone grateful to be warmed inside by the liquor and outside by the fire.

After two full minutes of quiet contemplation by all, Chaubenee's voice broke the silence. "You had that story about the Indian raid in Tennessee wrong in one little particular, Jim."

Jim and all other eyes turned to him.

"The raiding party was composed of Cherokee, Shawnee, and one Potawatomi."

* * * *

A week later, it was still grey outside the window when Beard woke, the kind of grey sky that made him shiver just to look at it even though he was perfectly warm and toasty covered by quilts and Sara's arms and legs. She liked to sleep that way, her arms and legs wrapped around him. He didn't always like going to sleep that way, but she seemed never to move during the night, and there was nothing he liked more than to wake with the warmth of her breasts pushed into his rib cage and of the inside of her thigh lying on his belly. He would like to stay here all day, forever perhaps, but he couldn't. So he tried to slide his legs from under her naked thigh and his belly away from the hand lying on top of it. He almost never managed, and today was not an exception.

"Where're you going?" It was a mumble that came out of a mass of blond hair.

"To the Lindsleys'. Remember?"

She sat up, looking at him, the quilt fallen away, one breast now lying beautifully on top of it. She gave him the sort of smile she only offered when she was trying to coax him back into bed. "If you come back, I'll let you do anything with that you want." She stroked her naked breast from collarbone to nipple as she spoke.

Tom's naked penis instantly rose to attention.

"I see part of you wants to take me up on that suggestion."

He looked serious. "Part of me does. But the better part doesn't want me to be self-indulgent. The better part knows

I need to go check on a widow and her five kids to make certain they neither starve nor freeze. I would've done it earlier, but Chaubenee said he'd come with me if I waited until today. Don't know why."

"Fine, damn it. Go take care of your city. Your wife is used to playing second fiddle in this particular orchestra."

"Sara. Don't. Please don't."

By way of response, she merely pulled the cover over her head. "Pull the curtains on your way out," came muffled from underneath.

Heat and delicious smells were already wafting from the kitchen when he walked down the stairs. He pushed the double swinging doors with one hand. His other was full with the heaviest coat and gloves he owned, two mufflers, and his large felt hat. As soon as he stepped in, he set down his burdens, but he was still warm. The old buckskin shirt and trousers along with heavy socks and boots made it very warm in the space shared with Amanda's stove. Chaubenee was already there.

"Morning, Mr. Beard," Amanda's perpetual goodwill rang in the near dark. "I've got a warm breakfast for you and Chaubenee and, as you told me, a half side of beef—when you take this, what we got left is the other half plus one more side. After that we're down to shooting that old roan of yours."

"Don't you worry about my old roan. I like that horse. And that three-fourths of a cow will hold us for three or four more weeks. Morning, Chaubenee."

The Indian nodded. "Tom, how you gonna carry that quarter of a cow and a rifle?"

"I'm not."

"How long you think before some starved pack of wolves smells that beef?"

Beard smiled his usual confident smile. "Well, you got that old musket of yours, and I've got this horse pistol." He touched the handle sticking out of his belt. "Neither one of us miss and they can feed on each other."

They sat silently, warming and filling on Amanda's corn cakes and butter, bacon, and coffee so thick Beard felt like he could stand his spoon up in it.

"Now why did you ask me to wait until today?" Beard asked.

"You'll see outside."

Both men threw on their heavy coats and went to the back door. They did not step down from the back door; they stepped up. They had, with each successive snow, been forced to cut steps up to get on top of the fallen and drifted snow. As soon as he got to the top of the snow steps, Beard saw very strange contraptions stuck into the snowbank. There were four of them, and they seemed identical. Each was about three feet long and almost circular. No, Beard decided, more elliptical than round. Elliptical save for the back where they came to a point some six inches long. At the middle they were perhaps two feet wide. On closer examination each was a frame of willow with inch-wide strips of tendon, from some large beast, strung across it.

"See the loop in the middle?" Chaubenee asked, pointing. "Stick the toe of your boot in there and walk."

"Walk?" Beard asked. "How do I walk with that on my foot?"

Chaubenee laughed. "A lot easier than without it on your foot."

For the first hundred yards it was awkward, but even then, Beard had to admit, it kept him above the snow. His right foot came out just once and buried instantly in the snow up to his midthigh. By the time they passed the last cabin in town he'd learned to balance the half side of beef across his shoulders and make a regular pace with the snowshoes. But the going was slow. This was not like walking on dirt or turf. This was slow going. Small steps made with precision seemed to be the only way.

For the entire morning the only animals they saw were birds. The sun came out briefly. Low as the sun was—and it stayed low and south before them—the glare coming off the snow required him to squint. Once he saw a rabbit dart across the snow. A small hawk swooped at it, but the rabbit made a 180-degree turn in midstride and dove under the snow.

"No lunch for the birdie," Chaubenee said, making a rare attempt at humor.

Thirty minutes later, they heard it. A howl coming from the woods to their right.

Chaubenee stopped cold. "Tom, hear wisdom from a man who has spent his entire life outdoors. Do not run. Not now or ever."

Beard nodded. He knew better, but that howl, that sound a harbinger of death, tempted him to.

"And Beard."

It had been a long time since Chaubenee had called him that. It got his attention.

"What has attracted them, what they want, is what you're carrying. They have smelled it long before they would have smelled us. If you give it to them, they will not pursue. A predator will never pick a fight he can avoid. Give it to them if you have to."

Beard didn't say a word.

The first wolf came out of the woods, now perhaps two hundred yards distant. The grey of the beast was beautiful against the white snow. He did not come on. He stood looking. And then another came out of the woods and came to stand beside the first. And then a third. When the fifth appeared, the pack started slowly across the snow, fanning out as they came. By the time they were within fifty yards, the fan was thirty yards wide. The big one, the one in the middle who had first come out, was huge, but he was thin, very thin. He stood still while both ends of the fan came forward. When the two at the ends of the fan were within twenty yards, the big brute in the middle started forward again.

"We only have two shots, Tom," Chaubenee said in a low voice. "The one we need to bring down is the brute. I've never seen one that big. They may run if he goes down. But he knows it. He won't come first. Oh, he'll be quick at the kill, but he'll use these outer two first. They'll charge us. It may be a feint, or they may actually come. You got a knife, Tom?"

"Yes."

"Take it out. That pistol only takes one hand, and you may need the knife. And drop that beef now. This may end up hand to claw."

By now the leader in the middle, his head hung low and drooling, had stopped again, his growl the most ominous sound Beard had ever heard. The two at the ends of the fan were now behind them. Beard dropped the quarter of beef, fumbled up the tail of his coat until he could get to the handle of the big knife. He pulled the pistol from his belt and cocked it. Knowing Chaubenee had to face the big one, Tom turned to watch the ballet of death closing behind him. He could see them both, the two who had come around.

The one to his left came at him. Beard wasn't sure it was a feint, but out of the corner of his eye he could see the one on his right coming as well. She growled as she came and when, within five feet, lunged. The retort of the pistol covered all sounds of the charge, and the cloud of black powder made it impossible to see clearly. Beard spun to his right. If the one on the left was still up and got to him, well, it was his fault. He'd missed. The powder cloud cleared as the second one lunged. Then he heard the much louder sound of Chaubenee's musket. Beard dropped into a low crouch, knife pointed to where he thought her throat would come.

But it didn't.

She had turned and run almost as quickly and athletically as the rabbit of earlier in the day. Not five feet before him lay a limp grey form, the head encased in a halo of vivid red.

He whirled to Chaubenee to see if there was danger there. The big man was crouched with the barrel of the musket in his hand. Fifteen yards away lay the biggest wolf Beard had ever seen. He was lying on his side, the upside shoulder shattered beyond recognition of form. The beast growled low, even when down making the most menacing sound Beard had ever heard. The other three had run to the edge of the wood and sat watching.

"Kill him, Tom."

Beard opened his coat and pulled a powder horn off his shoulder. He loaded the powder and then took a ball from the pouch at his belt. Once it was loaded, he stepped toward the beast.

"Tom, not too close. He'll kill you if he can."

From less than five yards he aimed and pulled the trigger. The pistol roared; the wolf went silent. When the gunpowder cloud disappeared, the remaining three had disappeared as well.

Chaubenee finished reloading his musket and adjusted his coat. "I'd love to skin that brute, but we haven't got time." He walked to the beast and extended its head and tail straight. Then standing beside the top of the spine, he placed one foot so the tail of the snowshoe was exactly even with the nose of the wolf. Methodically he placed his other foot so the tail of that snowshoe just touched the mark in the snow left by the front curve of the other. And then did it again. The third snowshoe track ended at about half a foot short of the tip of the tail.

"Three tracks at three feet apiece each, plus a few inches. No one will ever believe this killer was over nine feet tip to tail. Let's go, Tom. We've got another hour to walk before dark."

Finally, they reached their destination. The only part of the cabin that was visible was the roof. All else appeared to be below ground, really below snow. And there was not a sound. All was still, desolate, save the periodic whirl of snow across the barren landscape and a periodic wisp of smoke from the chimney, so light that it looked almost the same as the whirls of snow coming off the chimney top.

And with heads down, they just continued trudging along in the big, awkward shoes that kept them afloat on the crest of the snow.

Once they reached the cabin, the snowbank that surrounded it represented nothing so much as a dry moat with a door visible somewhere below them. Toward the bottom were the remains of steps cut into the snow but now half-blown away. The two men studied their access and how to obtain it, pondering a problem neither of them had ever faced before.

Beard stood above the remains of the blown-in steps, took off his snowshoes, and turning his back to them, started kicking new steps, toeholds really, into the snow. Halfway down, his path intersected the remains of the earlier steps someone had cut in the snowbank, making the end of his descent as simple as walking backward down a crumbling staircase. He finally stood in the open space between the snowbank and the cabin.

Chaubenee threw Beard's abandoned snowshoes down to him and then his own and followed down the crude steps backward. Once both men were at the bottom they walked to the door. Beard banged on it with his gloved hand. There was no response. He banged again. After his third attempt there was the sound of a latch being lifted and the scrape of ice breaking. The door swung open slowly.

It revealed the shrunken visage of a small woman with no expression showing on her face. The only part of her face that even showed life was her blue eyes that now seemed shrunken into her skull, a skull with skin drawn tight across it. She was wearing a heavy coat that seemed to fall from her shoulders as though it were not hers but that of a much larger woman.

The room behind her was dark. It would have been black as a mine shaft had it not been for the dim glow of a small fire in the hearth, a fire that looked as though it were as bravely clinging to life as the woman before him.

She did not speak.

"Patricia?" It came out of Beard's mouth as a question.

The woman said nothing but finally nodded her head and then swooned. She would have collapsed had Beard not caught her. Beard carried her in his arms to the very little light seeming distant across the room.

In front of the fire, or what was left of it, lay a pile of quilts with only lumps of human forms showing in the deep shadows. Beard counted. There were five of them, and three had turned their faces toward the door, their eyes showing life. The largest of them lifted his head to look up at Beard and spoke in a voice that came out a whispered croak.

"I tried, Mr. Beard." And then the eyes closed and the head fell back down.

Chaubenee spoke. "We need to get heat into them even more than food. There is no wood left in the kindling box."

"Break furniture. Start with a chair. That fire is too low to catch anything big. I'll go break up a fence rail in the back. As soon as you get the fire going, put some snow in that big kettle." Beard nodded to the kettle hanging on the crane inside the hearth. "You'll find some tea here somewhere. They may not be strong enough to chew, so give them this." He reached in the large pocket of his coat and tossed Chaubenee a small package. "It's the bread Amanda packed for us. Warm it and get it into them as quick as you can."

Chaubenee nodded understanding. Beard looked around the cabin for a shovel and saw one sitting where he expected, beside the door. He picked it up and stepped outside. Once there, he followed the moat between the cabin and the snow around to the south side, where he knew the Lindsleys had built a corral for their animals. When he turned the corner, he felt a rush of relief. Young Billy had used this shovel well. On this, the leeward, side of the building it seemed that he had fought a regular fight with snowfall and drift and won or at least fought nature to a draw. He had kept a space the width of the cabin and extending ten feet from the wall entirely open. In it stood two of the most emaciated oxen he'd ever seen.

The split-rail fences forming the corral were visible at either end of the cabin. Those were the boundaries he'd maintained for the area he'd kept clear for the oxen. Beard went back inside and replaced the shovel with an ax. In ten minutes, he'd broken up a section of rail fence and forced it free of the snow. It took seven trips to get it all inside and stacked by the hearth.

Chaubenee had the fire going and must have filled the kettle with snow because the crane holding it was swung back over the fire. And evidently it was his second kettleful because he had all six Lindsleys sitting up and drinking.

Thankfully, all of them were alive and eating bread. Chaubenee was holding one of the twins in his lap, feeding him. The others were all managing to eat on their own. The room was bright again. In just fifteen minutes the men had converted what had appeared a morgue back into a life-sustaining place.

Billy had some expression back in his face as did his fifteen-year-old sister, Jessica. She looked as starved as her mother, but there was beauty even now.

"Billy, how'd you keep the wolves from the oxen?"

Billy turned to him, just the hint of a smile forming on the sunken face. "Sat on the roof a lot of days. Killed a couple, and mostly they went away. The few nights the wolves announced themselves, I brought both the oxen inside."

Beard's face allowed a big smile, and he tousled the young man's hair.

After all the Lindsleys had fallen back to sleep, Beard and Chaubenee planned.

"Chaubenee, there is a rail fence extending from the far wall of the cabin. Extends some forty feet out on both sides and then joins across at the end. That rail is plenty of wood for the rest of the winter, but it will be hell to pay getting to it out from under the snow."

"How'd you get to this so quickly?" the big Indian asked.

Beard pointed to the sleeping form of Billy Lindsley. "Kid did one hell of a job. That rail extends off the south wall, which happens to be the lee. He must have shoveled every day, even when it was snowing, because he kept it cleared for ten feet from the cabin wall."

"Why?"

"He was protecting his oxen."

"They still there?"

"Both of them," answered Beard. "Skinniest beasts you ever saw, but he's kept them alive."

"Should have killed at least one before they came to this." Chaubenee grunted his disgust.

"May have been the kid's one mistake. But come spring, he can't plow without them, and he knows it." And then Beard continued. "That brace of oxen is the biggest problem you and I have."

"How so?"

"We gotta keep them alive four more weeks, maybe six."

Chaubenee didn't look up from the fire. "Only one thing will keep them alive. Grass. And that's all covered in six feet of snow."

"Not all of it."

Now Chaubenee looked at him. He didn't speak, just looked.

"They built this cabin twenty feet from the woods. Did it on purpose to make it easy to drag the logs here. So just twenty feet from here the snow is only two, maybe three, feet deep. Trees have sheltered it all from drift."

"So how we gonna get those two beasts through twenty feet of six-foot-deep snow to a place where they can manage to use their hooves to dig down and get their own?"

"I don't know," said Beard.

"I'll dig a trench," came the muffled voice of Billy Lindsley.

* * * *

Three days later, Chaubenee had dug up enough rail fence to keep the fire going until spring, and Beard and Billy Lindsley had managed to dig a trench through the snow wide enough for the oxen to go through one at a time. He had even cleared a patch of snow in the forest to get the starving beasts started at regaining strength. There was also life and vitality in the still-thin faces of all the Lindsleys. It was a cold, clear morning when Beard and Chaubenee picked up their snowshoes to leave.

"Patricia, that quarter of beef will feed the six of you until it warms up. Soon as I can get a wagon down that road, I'll come back with more food for you and some hay for the oxen."

"Thank you, Tom Beard. You, and your friend Chaubenee, have been our salvation. Literally." And with that, the spritely little woman reached up on tiptoes and gave him a kiss on the cheek. And then she turned to Chaubenee and, to his complete embarrassment, did the same to him.

The two men turned to the cabin door, and Billy spoke. His tone of voice was subdued, that of an awkward teenaged boy, but the look in his eye was that of a man. "Mr. Beard, I don't mean to look a gift horse in the mouth. Mom's right. You've saved us. All of us. But there is something I need to ask." There was a long pause, and every eye in the cabin seemed focused on Billy Lindsley. "When will I get my money? For the cotton?"

"I should have it when I come back," Beard answered. "Arenz got note of the sale and the price." Beard paused, his face covered in the smile of success. "You got a good price. Your gamble paid off. But the river closed early. Before the money came up. It should be on the first boat. Soon as the ice breaks."

Billy didn't smile, but his face was relaxed. "Good. You know, Mr. Beard, Harris left last year. Dad and I"—then he turned his head to look at his nine-year-old brother—"and Benjamin, did the work ourselves. Ben and I finished the harvest after Dad died. But we're going to need help planting. I'll need to hire a man."

Beard just nodded. He and Chaubenee walked out and toe pointed their way up the snow staircase. At the top they slipped into their snowshoes and started walking. They'd gotten no more than twenty feet when they heard Billy calling. He was standing on top of the snow.

"That's why I took the risk, Mr. Beard."

Beard said nothing for a moment and then said gently with great respect, "Ya' done good, Billy." And then he waved one arm to encompass the cabin and all around. "Ya' done real good."

CHAPTER 20

MAY 12, 1832

Beardstown, Morgan County, Illinois

Brigadier General Murray McConnel was not comfortable in his uniform. For one thing it was only three days old and still stiff. But even more than that, he thought he might look like he was on his way to a costume ball. While he was used to the knee-high boots and the coat cutaway and the tail split from waist to hem to allow the long back to fold out over his saddle, he thought the two-inch-wide yellow stripe down the pants and the bright blue of the coat looked clownish as did the shoulder boards with the single silver star in the middle. But oddest of all he thought was this big hat that looked like nothing so much as a half-moon sitting on his head with one point down in the front and the other in the back. He knew everyone was looking at him as he rode down the street toward the river.

He dismounted and tied his horse to the post before the grand hotel overlooking the river, walked up the stairs to the front porch, crossed it, and threw open the door, trying to hide his embarrassment with the hardest look he could muster.

The bar was half-full as was the dining room to his right. All turned to study this new man and his uniform. As he took off his hat and put it under his arm, he panned the room, looking for Beard. He didn't see him. But what he did see was one of the most beautiful women he'd ever laid his eyes on. Had he not been a man of self-control, he would have gawked. She was standing behind the bar, looking directly at him, her expression revealing not a single thought. Just taking him in. She did not look away as he walked to her.

"Ma'am, I am General"—he stumbled over that word but continued hurriedly—"General Murray McConnel, and I am here to see Tom Beard. I presumed I'd find him here. This is his hotel, is it not?"

She had a towel in one hand and in the other a wet glass that she was in the process of drying. She finished her task, draped the towel over a hook he could not see behind the bar, and bent slightly to put the cleaned and dried glass in its place, also apparently behind the bar. She didn't look away from him the entire time.

"General, I am Sara Beard, Mr. Beard's wife. And yes, this is his hotel. He is often here." She nodded her head toward an empty table by the window in the dining room. "That is pretty much his office. But he's out now. If you'd like to wait, I can pour you a drink. Or if you prefer, you can wait at his table, and I can have Amanda bring you a meal."

"I'll go into the dining room and have lunch. I've not eaten since early this morning."

"Tom's table is by the window. If you'll seat yourself, I'll tell Amanda she has a guest."

McConnel nodded and turned to the dining room.

"General."

McConnel turned back to her voice.

"He speaks of you frequently. He just never told me it was 'General.'"

McConnel could feel his face turn red. "That's new." He finally smiled.

"That blue coat goes well with your red hair," spoke a very lighthearted Beard as he slipped into his favorite chair. "You obviously have much to tell."

General Murray McConnel let his face slide into an uncharacteristic smile. "And from the look of *Beards*town," he said, putting heavy emphasis on the first syllable, "so do you."

Beard looked out the window, not trying to control the pride glowing on his face. "Over two hundred residential lots sold. So many of them to Germans you hear that tongue almost as often as English around here. We've sold more than a few commercial lots as well. We have some significant businesses, the newest of which is a slaughterhouse."

McConnel used the last cube of his bread to sop up the remainder of pork pie on his plate. "Fine cook you found yourself."

"Jim's wife."

McConnel looked up from his plate. His face showed enough curiosity that one eyebrow shot up into a vivid red arch.

"You remember Jim, don't you? Enos's stableman."

McConnel nodded, the confusion gone from his face as he licked the last golden crumb of bread off his finger.

"Great story on how he found her, but that's for another time," Beard said. "The story for now is what are you doing in that uniform and with that star on your epaulet?"

"I'll tell all, but then I have two questions for you."

Beard nodded agreement.

"Four days ago, Governor Reynolds made me a brigadier general in the Illinois Militia."

"But you know nothing of . . ."

McConnel held his hand out palm up to cut off the comment.

"Let me tell this my way, Tom. You just hush for now."

Beard grinned embarrassment and again nodded his head.

"My job, Tom, is not to lead an army in combat. My job is to assemble the army and make it, as Boney famously said, able to 'travel on its belly.' As well as a few other things like making sure they have guns to shoot and things to get them where they're going to shoot them."

"And what army will this be and where is it going?" Beard asked.

"The army will be the Illinois State Militia." McConnel paused for a moment and then digressed. "You know it is an Illinois state law that every able-bodied man is subject to militia call?"

Beard nodded but said nothing.

"And where they will be going is north."

Beard interrupted excitedly. "Mo, didn't we already send one thousand men north last summer to escort Black Hawk and his Sauk and Fox friends back across the Mississippi?"

McConnel nodded. "I know, Tom, but, apparently, we didn't get Mr. Black Hawk's attention. He and his friends came back this spring. Haven't killed anyone yet, far as I know, but they're trying to scare the settlers off. Tearing down fences, killing livestock, and burning barns. So we'll have to do it all over again."

"And they're going to assemble here again just like last year?" Beard asked.

McConnel nodded. "Reynolds is merely waiting for Black Hawk to overplay his hand. Soon as he takes a scalp or does anything to truly enrage public opinion, Reynolds will make the call. But we all know Black Hawk well enough to know he will overplay his hand, eventually. And my job is to prepare for eventually."

"Is that Murray McConnel, hiding in that outrageous getup?" Enos Marsh bellowed from the kitchen door.

Every head in the restaurant turned as Marsh's small but purposeful strides marched him across the room. McConnel stood to greet his old friend, a big smile on his usually taciturn face. Marsh, dark with black hair, and McConnel, fair with red, threw their arms around each other. McConnel eventually pushed away and held the smaller man at arm's length.

"You look just the same as you did fourteen years ago, only richer," McConnel said.

"And you, Murray McConnel, look completely different."

"Enos, sit down and join us. What Mo is saying will affect all of us," Beard said, and the three men sat back down.

"Enos, the short version is Black Hawk is acting up again, and Reynolds is going to have to do something about it. He's sent me here to prepare. Reynolds seems to think he's going to call seven hundred. It will be no less. They will gather here and form companies and marshal supplies. Then they'll march north, so all have to cross the river. And eventually come back. We're going to need your ferry, and we're going to command exclusive use of it. How many trips to get seven hundred soldiers, supplies, wagons, and horses across?"

Beard pondered. He looked out the window and cast his gaze upward as though calculating in his head. "We can take one large wagon and a two-up team at a time. Men standing maybe thirty-five a trip. Horses standing twenty. Presume each company is one hundred men and they have four wagons of supplies and maybe half mounted. So, seven trips per company. Make it eight for safety. Then quartermaster stuff, I'd guess another ten trips. That gets us to ninety trips. Round it to one hundred."

"How many trips can you make a day, and what do you charge?" McConnel asked.

"Working sunup to dark, twenty trips is maximum. So five days to get them all across. The ferry rate is $5 each way," Beard answered.

"So that's $1,000," Mo said to no one in particular.

Beard gave a little laugh. "I like your calculation, but you never were much good at math. One hundred trips at $5 a trip is $500, Mo."

"We all expect to come home, Tom." McConnel's eyes twinkled. "Then we are agreed you'll transport our army of seven hundred across and back for $1,250."

Beard looked startled. "What's the extra $250 for?"

"The army will have exclusive use on those days. We'll piss off a lot of civilians who want to cross, and they'll take it out on you. The $250 is for aggravation."

Tom nodded and extended his hand, which Brigadier Murray McConnel accepted and then added, "Tom, while you're doing this, you can carry whoever you want if we're not using you. I just expect you to be at the ready anytime I call.

"OK, that's item one. Item two is space."

"What space?" Beard asked.

"I've got seven hundred men with gear and horses who need space to bivouac. They need space for sleeping tents, mess halls, latrines, corrals. They need it laid out in advance with camp areas and streets marked," McConnel answered. "How long will it take you to mark off ten five-acre plots for the camp?"

"Not much work. Not like I'm getting correct survey lines. No more than three days," Beard answered.

"If you get $100 a day for poling that ferry, how about $50 a day for this?"

"More than enough."

"OK, then $250 a month, guessing no more than two months beginning to end, plus $150 for staking it."

Beard and Marsh nodded agreement.

"OK, that's item two. Now let's talk about the tough one. Feeding these men. Tom, when we started you mentioned a slaughterhouse opened in town. Tell me about it," McConnel directed.

"You remember the winter of '31? Worst winter in anyone's memory," Beard started.

"And the winter your friend Beard killed the biggest wolf I've ever seen." The deep rumbling words came from a figure so big that it put much of the table in shadow.

McConnel looked up to see the smiling face of a huge Indian blocking out the sunlight. For a moment he was perplexed, and then recognition came to him, and the warmth of it spread across his face. He bolted to his feet, stepped behind Beard, and extended his hand to take the largest, strongest one he'd ever known. "Chaubenee!" he almost yelled. And again, the room turned toward them to see the old friends meet.

Chaubenee reached down and took McConnel's hat off the table. "Harrison used to wear a hat like this. You look a lot better in that uniform than he did. Sit back down, Mo. I'll go get a beer from Sara and come back."

"What's this about a wolf?" McConnel asked Beard.

"Later, Mo. Too long to tell now. But you asked about the slaughterhouse. It's run by a guy named Gallagher, Bill Gallagher. After the cotton crop failed in '31, Gallagher decided to grow corn for the local farmers so their pigs wouldn't have to live on acorns. He came here and opened a slaughterhouse so he could slaughter, butcher, salt, and ship. And like all of us before him, he figured that last part meant he had to be on the river. So he came here. Just opened up this year. He's probably your guy. When we're done here, I'll take you over and introduce you."

Chaubenee, beer mug in hand, pulled out the last remaining chair and sat down. "Mo, why are you in uniform?"

"Tom can tell you the details later, but Governor Reynolds thinks there will be another war with Black Hawk. So he's enlisted me to come set this place up as base camp for the trip north."

"Black Hawk?" Chaubenee said quizzically. "Sauk and Fox. My people have fought with them over the area north of the river for as long as anyone remembers. How about I ride along, out front, and keep you pale ones out of trouble? They're very good at ambush, you know."

There were smiles around the table.

"I'll arrange that, Chaubenee. We'll be damn glad for your wisdom and knowledge."

"And maybe even my club." Chaubenee smiled widely.

"Mo, before we go talk to Gallagher, what more you gonna need we can help with?" Marsh asked.

"List goes on and on, Enos. Wagons to carry everything, every horse we can get, a smith to shoe them, powder, ball, and guns. Some of these boys will show up with squirrel guns and some with none at all."

"I can help you with all of that, Mo. All of that and more. If it's to be had in this part of Illinois, I can find it."

Mo McConnel's friendly expression suddenly changed. His face transformed into Brigadier General Murray McConnel. "Enos, I have many responsibilities—gathering the men, signing them, paying them, confirming supplies along the way. What I need is a good quartermaster. A man who can concentrate solely on gathering supplies. How'd you like to become quartermaster of this army? Pay may be sporadic, but I'm sure the governor would make you a major or maybe a light colonel. Your grandchildren would like it."

"So would I." Enos Marsh looked very pleased.

"Mo, early on you said you had two questions to ask of me. Is now the time?"

"One you've answered. That was about the slaughterhouse."

"The other?" Beard asked.

McConnel's face lit into a very satisfied smile. He pointed across the dining room toward the bar. "That stunningly beautiful woman behind the bar introduced herself as Mrs. Beard. Wherever did you find her?"

Beard smiled. "She came to me on a wagon."

"Well, however you got her, she must make you very happy."

Beard's smile was replaced by a solemn look. "Most of the time."

* * * *

Bill Gallagher was a shrewd man. Perhaps his one failing in that regard was that his face showed it. It was the face of a fox; his chin, nose, and ears were all pointed. His tendency to scowl forced his lips down and then pulled thin brows to arch upward into inverted *V*s. His skin was very light where it was not touched by the sun. But on his face the result was a profusion of freckles that, while they made him look youthful, also gave his face a reddish cast. His red hair, which grew forward into a widow's peak and seemed trying to come down to touch the peaks of his arched brows, enhanced the reddish cast. He was tall, very tall, and seemed to use his height as advantage to loom over others especially when bargaining.

The two red-faced men, the tall and the short, seemed to dislike one another instantly, like Celtic warriors come from opposite clans.

"So, you want fifteen hundred barrels of salt pork, and you want part in two weeks and part by the middle of July, mister?" The tall man's voice had the quality of a wood rasp being dragged along a board.

"Mr. Gallagher," McConnel said, his tenor making the name sound like an insult, "I have two things to say to you.

First, it is 'General,' not 'mister.' And second, 'want' was not the word I used. The word I used was 'need.'"

Gallagher glowered back, not the least daunted. "Well, General!" the wood rasp spat back. "First, I only have about one hundred barrels left from last winter's kill."

"What's the asking price of those." McConnel's question came out as a command.

"For you, General," he said, again spitting out the word, "I can let you have half of them at $50 a barrel."

"Bill," Marsh's voice almost crooned, "you shipped as many to St. Louis last week at $40."

Gallagher shot him a harsh look but didn't respond. Instead, he spoke to McConnel again. "General, let me explain my business to you." His tone was hectoring. "Farmers farm corn in the summer; they harvest it in the fall and fatten their pigs, which get slaughtered in the winter. So, in the summer I don't expect much supply of hogs to slaughter." He paused the lecture and then added, "You understand that?"

McConnel seemed in complete control of himself when he spoke. "Then you'll have to increase your supply."

"How, General, do you propose I do that?"

"Same way you buy more of anything, Mr. Gallagher. You increase the offering price," McConnel seemed to be explaining as to a slow student.

"Why would I do that?"

"Because, Mr. Gallagher, farmers sell in the fall only because their hogs are fat. They weigh more, and you, and other men in your business, buy by the pound. Am I correct?"

"You are correct, sir," Gallagher answered, and then added hastily, "General."

"Hogs gain about twenty percent of weight on that fall grain. So, you buy now at twenty percent above market. Farmer gets the same price for his hogs and also has grain to sell in the fall. Who would say no to that?"

Gallagher's wood rasp of a tone seemed to mellow. "I can do that." He paused to calculate. "And I'll sell to you at $60 a barrel."

"No, Mr. Gallagher, you won't. You'll sell the State of Illinois Militia fifteen hundred barrels of salt pork between now and mid-July at the following pricing. Mr. Marsh will pick up the hundred barrels you have now tomorrow and pay you $40 a barrel. The other fourteen hundred barrels will be delivered in regular increments of two hundred barrels per week for the next seven weeks. For those, you will receive $48 a barrel. And you will be paid by the State of Illinois from war funds as available."

Gallagher leaned down over McConnel like a heron about to stab a frog. "No, that I won't do. The price will be $50 a barrel for fifty that I will deliver now and $65 a barrel for all future deliveries, and I will be paid cash upon delivery."

McConnel said nothing for a long moment. He removed the double-peaked hat from his head, took a handkerchief from his pocket, and wiped the sweat from his forehead. He then sat his haunch on the bench beside him. Once firmly established on his perch, he looked up into Gallagher's hostile eyes. "Mr. Gallagher, are you aware that every able-bodied man in the State of Illinois is subject to military call? And if so, perhaps you are further aware that in wartime all required goods are subject to conscription for military use."

Gallagher leaned back, a look of sullen skepticism on his face.

"Governor Reynolds is about to put out a call for soldiers. In two weeks' time, Mr. Gallagher, you will find yourself Private Gallagher in the service of the State of Illinois Militia and your business run by Mr. Marsh or whoever I choose to appoint for the duration. The choice is yours." And he turned and walked away.

A stunned Enos Marsh stood flat-footed, watching General Murray McConnel's back. An equally stunned Bill Gallagher also stood flat-footed and mouth agape. Gallagher recovered before Marsh.

"McConnel! General McConnel! Stop. Please, sir, stop!" It was a plea, not a shout.

McConnel took two more strides before he turned. When he did, he said nothing but just looked at Bill Gallagher.

"You win, General," Gallagher said, defeated.

CHAPTER 21

MAY 25, 1832

Beardstown, Morgan County, Illinois

Dr. Charles Chandler was a tall man of aristocratic bearing. His dark hair had a natural curl to it that gave his already handsome face an almost pretty aspect that, for the moment, was distorted by the red color of his complexion and forward thrust of his already long jaw brought on by his anger. It was only his normally gentle demeanor that precluded his anger from becoming rage. "Captain," he commanded, "I did not pay for passage to this small village"—his arm swept across the open windows of the bridge to encompass the muddy village before them—"of . . . of Beardstown." His voice dropped to a tone that made the single word an insult. "I paid passage to Fort Clark, and that is where I intend you take me."

The captain of the steamboat *Talisman* was a man who had originally learned his craft in New Orleans and was far more comfortable with the sophistication and comforts of that city and its people than he was with the crude frontiersmen of Memphis and Cincinnati and other western river ports. He had enjoyed Dr. Chandler's companionship since picking him up in St. Louis, so he was not predisposed to be swept into Chandler's upset. "Charles . . ." He paused. "May I still call you Charles, or is Dr. Chandler required again?" He said it with a knowing smile, hoping to remind his passenger that they had become almost friends and that such a reminder might calm him.

Chandler exhaled as though the reminder had taken some of the hot wind from his sails.

"Charles," the captain continued, "I can and will take you to Fort Clark, but not now. I know Black Hawk is suspected to be north, but Reynolds has effectively declared war. All upriver between here and Fort Clark is country through which the Sauk and the Fox roamed. They will be familiar with it."

"And from their ponies along the bank they can do exactly what to this boat?" Chandler demanded.

The skipper nodded understanding. "If we were on the Mississippi or even the Ohio, you'd be right. Or even the Illinois below us. But the river narrows above us. Not only that but see that fork in the river?" He pointed upriver, and Chandler's gaze followed his arm. "Tell me which channel is the river and which leads into the Sangamon slough behind this bay."

Chandler looked upriver and studied for a moment. Both left and right forks looked almost the same. "I'd guess the left fork," Chandler finally said. His voice calmed almost to his normal baritone.

"And you'd be right, Charles. You'd be right. But you know why it's so hard to tell? Because that slough—that's our polite word for swamp—is so damn big that the water draining out of it looks like its own river channel to the untrained eye." He brought his eyes back to Chandler's and risked a smile. "You were guessing, weren't you?"

Chandler returned the smile, calm again.

"Charles, as the river channel runs beside the slough, it gets narrow and sometimes crowded with debris flowing in. If there's anywhere on America's western river system for an ambush, that's it. And I'm not going there. At least until Reynolds gets that pesky Black Hawk back on the west side of the Mississippi."

Chandler's complexion was back to its normal pale color and the doctor clearly back in control of his disappointment.

"See that building on top of the knoll by the landing?" The ship's captain pointed. "This 'small village,' is that what you called it?"—the skipper again offered a hopeful smile—"is a village of huge pretentions. And that hotel is the finest you'll find between Louisville and St. Louis." And then the captain's smile grew huge. "And the proprietress is said to be the most beautiful woman between the two as well. Her name, Sara Beard, is mentioned wistfully by riverboat gamblers from time to time."

Chandler smiled and responded smoothly. "I'm married, Captain. Happily married. And as soon as I get to Fort Clark, set up a practice, and get a suitable house built, I will go back to Rhode Island and return with my wife and family."

"Nevertheless, the Beard Hotel is the place for you. You stay there until this is over, and then I'll collect you and take you to Fort Clark as planned."

* * * *

Sara Beard sat propped up, the two large pillows pushed into the headboard. As was her custom in warm weather, she was naked. She had brushed out her long blond hair that now hung loose, sweeping inward around her collarbones to give a whisper of covering to her breasts. Beard could not decide whether the glow of yellow light from the hurricane lamp beside her suggested a halo of heaven or the fire of hell.

"Tom, let's spend the day together tomorrow. When the militia gets here, you won't have time. Let's take a ride out of the valley and onto the prairie. I'll have Amanda pack lunch for just the two of us."

"I'd love to, Sara, but I'm taking out our new guest, the doctor, to look at property tomorrow."

Sara looked at her husband, her smile still hopeful. "It won't take you more than two hours to show him every lot you've laid out."

"It appears, Sara, that our Dr. Chandler is not a man of the city. He wants a more pastoral . . . that was his word, 'pastoral' . . . setting for his new home. So, I'm going to take him up along the bluff and see if we can't find a suitable place for him."

Her face turned cold.

"You can join us if you'd like," he added.

She rolled her back to him and turned off the lamp. The room went dark.

* * * *

Tom Beard and Charles Chandler sat at Beard's window table, watching the long shadows shorten as the sun rose behind the building.

"Mr. Beard, your cook does a marvelous job. Best breakfast I've had since Louisville. Do offer her my compliments."

"I will, Dr. Chandler. But would you call me Tom? I'd prefer it."

Chandler's long jaw seemed to retract to make room on his face for the wide grin. "Delighted, Tom. And call me Charles, then."

The door burst open, and an excited General Murray McConnel rushed into the room and straight to Beard's table. "He's done it!" McConnel exclaimed, slapping his hand on the table. "He's overplayed his hand, and now it's our turn!" The excitement in his face caused a flush that made the color in his cheeks almost match that of his eyebrows.

With no response to his friend's excitement, Beard said, "General Murray McConnel, allow me to present Dr. Charles Chandler, ex of Rhode Island and soon to be a citizen of Illinois." And then with a conspiratorial smile directed toward Chandler, "And of Beardstown, or at least Morgan County, if I have anything to say in the matter. Dr. Chandler, General McConnel is not only a general in the Illinois State Militia; he is also the finest attorney in Central Illinois and most of all my longtime and dear friend."

Beard's long introduction allowed McConnel to regain his composure. Chandler stood, and the two men shook hands. As they sat back down Beard asked, "Who overplayed his hand, and what is it we get to do about it?"

"Black Hawk. Fulton County put together a militia of a couple of hundred farmers and selected a guy named Israel Stillman to lead them. And he led them into one of Black Hawk's ambushes. They got cut up pretty bad. The governor put out the call two days ago. Seven hundred will assemble right here by June 10."

"Well, Doctor"—Beard grinned at his guest—"you think Beardstown is a bit small. It's about to get a lot bigger, and you get to watch. But not today. Today, I will show you some of the most beautiful land you have ever seen."

* * * *

Beard and Chandler sat under the shade of a small grove of dogwood trees, their large flowers still in bloom causing the light filtering through to flash bursts of white. The men picked slowly at the pieces of chicken Amanda had fried and packed for them. They lay in silence, not talking, just absorbing the wonder of it all. Immediately below them the slope was the solid green of grapevines growing up and over the edges of a raspberry briar. As the slope flattened out below, the sway of grasses waving was dotted with patches of color from late-spring flowers. In the far distance, a pencil-thin ribbon of dark water meandered across their visible universe.

"God was having a very special moment when he created this place," Chandler said.

"It's yours for the taking, Charles."

"How much will having this cost me?"

"Depends on how much you want, Charles. State sells it for $1.25 an acre. They'll sell you up to 640 acres," Beard said.

"How much pressure to buy is there?"

"If you mean are there other buyers, yes, always."

Chandler rose off his elbow and sat up, looking intently at Beard. "Meaning?"

"America is moving here, Charles. Mostly those moving are still veterans collecting their bounties, and bounty land is north of the river." Beard used his chin to point to the far horizon across the river. "But not everyone coming west is a veteran. And those, like me and my partner and McConnel and everyone who has bought in Beardstown, are on this side of the river. This side of the river because land on this side is available for purchase by nonveterans. Most of those are farmers and want the flatland below, but this place is stunning, and you are not the only man taken with the beauty of it. Are you still interested in Fort Clark?"

"It cannot possibly be better than this," Chandler replied. "I'll stay here."

Beard sat up, smiling. "We could use a doctor here. Even if he does want to be a three-hour ride from the rest of us."

* * * *

"Jesus Christ, the place is in chaos!" McConnel sat on horseback, staring at the thousands forcing their way into the campground. Men, wagons, horses all pushing and shoving to claim ground, some of which had already been claimed. "Enos, you're going to have to get me more land, and you're going to have to do it now."

Enos Marsh sat calmly watching the scene of volunteers packing the marked streets in the campground, their officers having no idea where to put them. "Well, General, I gotta say this: whoever ends up leading this bunch is gonna be happy to have three times what was called for. Black Hawk never had much of a chance. Now it appears he has none.

"And, OK, I'll get Beard out here to mark off another dozen five-acre tracts and streets to them. And I'll be seeing Bill Gallagher as well. He may have to up the ante on the hog offer. The ferry will be easy enough. Just take more days. I'll get on it, but you're going to have to push these men back out of here and onto the prairie. I'm guessing Tom can work by moonlight." He laughed. "If it doesn't have to be very exact."

"Fight!" It was one scream and then a chorus. "Fight! Fight! Fight!"

McConnel kicked his horse and dashed forward toward the sound, forcing men to dive out of his way as he went by. When he and Marsh reached the five-acre lot neatly marked "Parcel 10," two men in the middle of the crowd were stripped to the waist and circling one another warily. One was awkwardly tall, perhaps the tallest man McConnel had ever seen. That he was rapier thin seemed to add to his height and make his arms and legs resemble spiderlike attachments. But his biceps were surprisingly large, giving evidence he was a man used to hard labor. His opponent was almost his physical opposite, medium height but with the width of a bull and a neck as thick.

McConnel drove his horse to the middle of the ring, pulling it to a hard stop and throwing dirt clods up behind it. Without dismounting he screamed, "Stop! Stop now!" Instantly the two men stopped circling and stood facing the clearly exasperated general. "Officers. Where are your company officers? I want them now." McConnel's high tenor pierced the air to bring attention to all around.

No one spoke for a moment. Then the two combatants looked to one another, and both faces became sheepish grins. And then a chuckle started with the assembled troops and rolled to a full laugh.

"That will do!" McConnel commanded more firmly but with less volume this time.

The taller of the two combatants took a step forward to stand directly before McConnel. "General, I fear to say, but you are looking at the company officers," said the tall, awkward figure, pointing first to himself and then to the muscular beast of a man behind him.

A shocked McConnel sat quietly collecting himself and then, peering down with a look of contempt, asked, "What is the meaning of your conduct, Captain?"

"Well, sir," the very tall man continued, "I've been elected captain of a company gathered from in and around New Salem. When we arrived, we were directed to camp at 'Parcel 10,' and so we came here. This gentleman is Captain Roberts. He was elected leader of a company up from Belleville. They arrived about that same time, and they were also directed to 'Parcel 10.' That is, we both arrived here at the same time with the same orders. There being no superior military authority to resolve our conflicting orders, we decided to resolve it ourselves, two out of three falls being the agreed method. Captain Roberts seems to have been elected to lead his company for the same reason I was. We were the best wraslers in town. When our companies appointed us to represent them, it seemed appropriate. We were in the process of the resolution when you arrived."

General McConnel sat very still for a moment, and all watched as a smile slowly formed and then took over his entire face. "What is your name, Captain?" he asked the man before him.

"Lincoln, sir. Abraham Lincoln."

McConnel nodded first toward Captain Roberts and then the tall officer before him. "Carry on, gentlemen.

"Within an hour I'll have men here to lay out quarters for the loser's company." And with that he wheeled his horse and exited the entire encampment.

* * * *

The moon was well up by the time Beard drug himself from the stable into the back door of the hotel. Amanda was in the kitchen, warming his dinner when he arrived.

"You're working too hard, Mr. Beard. Even for you, honey. It's too much," she offered.

A weary but happy Beard rewarded her concern with a warm smile. "I might say the same for you, Amanda. But it's appreciated."

"You've still got company," she added.

"Who?" Beard asked.

"Mr. Marsh and Mr. Arenz are at the table. I fed them, and they've been sippin' for an hour."

Beard nodded thanks and walked into the dining room now lit by hurricane lamps on the tables and moonlight in the window. "Hello, gentlemen." His voice carried across the nearly empty dining room.

"Long day, Tom," Marsh offered.

"What's up that keeps you two this late?" he asked.

"A little business, Tom. Not complicated but necessary." So saying, he spread two papers before Beard's chair. "Contract changes, Tom. One for the ferry and one for the land rental and surveying."

Beard looked at them for a moment, then looked up without reading either. "Tell me what they say."

"One on top is for the ferry. Same terms but it extends from seven hundred to two thousand. That's what it looks like the size of this army will be."

"And the other?"

"It's for the land expansion. I'd have signed it, but it might be a conflict if I, as landowner, signed a contract that I, as quartermaster, had drawn up. Thought it was better if my partner signed."

Beard scrawled his name on both and pushed them back just as Amanda showed up with a steaming bowl of pork simmered in early tomatoes. "Smells so good, Amanda. And might be the last I taste for a while."

"How's that, Mr. Beard?"

Beard nodded with his head toward Marsh. "This man is buying every hog in Morgan County and then some."

Amanda's white teeth gleamed in the moonlight. "Oh, don't worry. Mr. Marsh is a friend of mine. I'm guessing he'll find a little piggy for a friend every now and again." She turned and walked back to the kitchen.

"That what kept you here this late?"

"That and a couple of other things," Marsh answered. "First, I want to know who won the wraslin' match."

Beard pushed his spoon into the bowl and pulled it out, carrying a steaming hunk of long-simmered pork. "I heard the lanky guy gave a good match, but the 'Bull from Belleville' took two out of three. I gave the lanky one and his New Salem guys first lot I laid out. Hard not to like that young captain of theirs. Wish we had more like him." He chewed slowly on his pork. After he'd swallowed, Beard asked, "And?"

This time it was Francis Arenz's thinly accented German voice that spoke. "Tom, you spent the entire afternoon and evening with those boys. I'm guessing they filled the lots as soon as you laid them out."

Beard nodded.

"And you saw each company move into its space?"

Beard nodded again.

"So you've seen most of them up close."

Beard nodded a third time. "What is it you want to know, Francis?"

"Are they all armed?"

Beard looked across the table directly into the face of his German friend. The moon out the window backlit the small face, creating shadows so deep Beard could not tell if the eyes were now purple or black. But even so he could see they were filled with an intelligent shrewdness. "Some with nothing but tomahawks and knives."

"Most?"

Beard took another bite of his dinner before he spoke. "Most? No, most, I'd say eight or nine out of ten, carried muskets. Why?"

This time it was Marsh who spoke. "My job is to supply these men, and an army armed with tomahawks and knives is just a mob."

Beard kept his head down, deep in thought. He took a long sniff of Amanda's pork and looked up, satisfaction showing on his face. "And Francis might be able to help?"

Both men nodded agreement.

CHAPTER 22

JUNE 1, 1832

Beardstown, Morgan County, Illinois

Tom Beard stood on the front of the ferry, watching the taut line drawing them across. He saw no weakness in the line. The horse on the north bank was pulling steady; a glance upstream revealed no debris floating toward them, at least none he'd need to fend off. It was a clear, cloudless, if hot, late-spring day. He could see no threat coming against which he would need to take action. He exhaled.

He was being especially watchful as the ferry was full of militiamen standing, if not shoulder to shoulder, then closely packed. The last thing he needed was one of them to get knocked overboard. Today would be a long day even without having to stop to rescue some reckless young soldier. He turned to look into their ranks. They were a nervous lot and as high strung as he'd expect of young bravados going off to war. His eyes were drawn to a short, stocky young man who was standing beside him and studying him intently. He had a head full of dark hair lying neatly directed by an orderly combing. The nose was straight and broad, the chin square, and brown eyes penetrating. But the thing that drew Beard's attention was the shiny new musket he was holding at his side. That it was brand new was made obvious by the blotches of creosote still visible on the barrel.

"Ever fire that thing, son?" he asked as he moved his glance from the gun to the soldier.

"No, sir," came the embarrassed reply.

"Might want to make sure that creosote is well out of the inside of that barrel first." He ran his finger along the dark-brown resin still showing on the outside of the barrel. "This won't hurt much, but if there is still some inside the barrel, it will be hell to load and may even blow up on you."

"Thank you, sir. I'll make sure I do that."

"May I examine it more closely?" Beard asked.

The stocky young man beside him immediately raised the musket up and handed it to him. Beard inspected it closely. That it was cheaply made was clear from the simplicity of the model and the fact that it was entirely unadorned and the wood in the stock was soft, wide-grained pine. But the thing that struck his attention was the bore in the barrel. It was a small bore. Built for small game not anything larger than a fox. Certainly not designed to knock down a man.

Beard handed it back. "Where did you get it?"

"Just yesterday, from the quartermaster," came the happy response.

"You didn't bring your own weapon?"

Again, the response was delivered with an embarrassed tone. "No, sir." There was momentary silence. "I've never owned a gun." Again, momentary silence. "Until now." The last words were spoken with a voice of chipper pride.

"Where you from, son?" Beard asked.

"Jacksonville, sir."

Beard looked down somewhat askance. "And you don't own a musket?"

There was a slight flush of red on the wide and already florid cheeks. "Only recently came to Jacksonville. I'm from the East."

"And what are you doing here?"

"Studying law."

Beard smiled. "I meant what are you doing here. On this ferry. With this militia."

The young man studied the toes of his boots for a moment, swallowed, and looked up, an expression of determination on his face. "Truth is, sir, I have political ambitions. And a military history, however small, helps in those pursuits."

The ferry slowed and slid up onto the Schuyler County bank. As Beard lowered the loading ramp to allow the militia to step off, he spoke one last time to the young private in the State of Illinois Militia. "In case I am offered the chance to vote for you one day, what's your name?"

With short, determined steps he moved down the plank, shouting over his shoulder, "Douglas, Stephen A. Douglas."

When all the infantry was off the ferry, Beard's attempt to raise the loading ramp for the return trip was halted by a barked command. "Hold up!"

Beard looked up from his task to see a tall, thin young man in the impeccably displayed uniform of a lieutenant in the United States Army standing beside an equally elegant dapple-grey stallion.

"If you'll drop that ramp back down, I'll join you on your trip across." It all came out in a deep Southern drawl.

Beard did as requested, and the lieutenant and his horse stepped onboard, his only companions for the return trip. "Going the wrong way, aren't you, Lieutenant?"

Beard received a small smile and an explanation. "I've been dispatched from Fort Crawford to meet Governor Reynolds and escort him and the state militia north."

Beard openly appraised the man and his face. He was well over six feet, with a very angular face. The cheekbones were so high they cast shadows toward his ears. The nose was long and straight and the lips thin. The jaw very square and long. The eyes were somewhat deep set, the jaw and chin covered with a rich thatch of light-brown hair. He had seen that face, or one very like it, before, and he pondered where. When it came to him, his face broke into a smile. "Lieutenant, you got any kin in this militia you're meeting?"

"Not that I know of. Why?"

"Just curious. Saw a fellow looks very much like you, enough to be a cousin at least, in one of the volunteer companies. He's captain of the company from New Salem."

"What's his name?" the officer asked.

"Lincoln it was. Let me think. Abe Lincoln, I believe."

"Can't say he's any kin of mine by the name." And then the polished and proper young officer presented his hand. "My name is Davis, sir. Lieutenant Jefferson Davis of Mississippi."

Beard took the offered hand. "Tom Beard, Lieutenant Davis. My pleasure to meet such a fine representative of the United States. May I ask a question, Lieutenant?"

"Please, sir. Feel free."

"What do you think of this war that you're leading all these men to?"

"Well, sir, it won't be much of a war. I know the Indians in the north pretty well, having served here for three years now. I can usually get along with them and have found it easier to be polite and respectful of them than to kill them. But, sir, this country"—the young lieutenant swept an arm to encompass all before them—"is for white men. God made it for us as surely as he made the Promised Land for the Jews. And like Joshua, it ıs merely for us to take it. If they won't go, we will escort them out. If they won't be escorted, we'll have to kill them."

* * * *

"Francis, did you see those muskets you sold to the militia?" It was a bark more than a question, and before Arenz could answer, Beard barked another. "How many of them were there anyhow?"

Francis Arenz had never seen his friend angry before, and as much as he wished to reassure him, he also was fascinated to see how deep the streak of anger ran in him. So he didn't respond quickly. He knew what he would say, but he wanted to give Tom Beard time to get it all out.

"And how much Goddamn money did you make doing it?"

Arenz had to work to suppress a smile. He'd never heard Beard swear before. These were two new experiences with his friend in one conversation. He waited until he was certain there was no more to come out.

"Thomas," he finally said, "I sold the militia two hundred thirty-five muskets. Yes, they were fowling pieces and cheap ones at that. But think for a moment. Would you rather those men were armed with hatchets and knives? Angry farmers used pitchforks in Germany. Didn't work so well. Lot of them died. No one else had arms for this militia. I found them. Do you think those young and inexperienced militiamen felt better with a musket in their hands? Of course they did, Tom. You know it's true."

Beard said nothing but sat in the quiet of the empty, and almost dark, dining room, barely able to see into the deep eyes of Francis Arenz. "Hard to stay angry at you, Francis." There was no smile, but neither was there bitterness in the voice. "But for all your good intentions, you did make a lot of money doing it, didn't you?"

Arenz set his brandy snifter down and leaned forward, just a little, into the dark toward his friend. "Tom, I am a merchant. I know people and things others don't. It is the nature of success in my business. And yes, I knew a man in New Orleans who had purchased some cheap arms in Europe, thinking to sell them to Simón Bolívar for his South American adventures. But Bolívar died, and he couldn't get rid of them. He's been stuck with them for three years. And yes, he sold them to me cheap, what he paid for them plus shipping costs here—expedited shipping costs. And yes, Tom, I sold them to the militia for three times what I paid for them."

"Three times!" Beard coughed up the swallow of beer before it could get all the way down.

"Tom, we all make money here. That's one of the reasons we came. You know that better than any of us."

Beard inhaled to get his breath back, took a handkerchief out of his pocket to wipe the beer from the table, and exhaled.

"Tom, let me tell you what I expect to do with the money," Arenz continued. "I've told you there are things this town needs to be more than a village. We need a schoolhouse. We could use a church building as well. And we need a newspaper. It will lose money, but we need one. All of that costs money. You and I, Tom, we are empire builders. We are here to build a city of prosperity and refinement. So, who will spend this money it costs? The answer is you and me. Marsh won't do it. He's here for the money. He'll pitch in now and again when he has to, but building this dream is for you and me to do. And it takes money. Lots of money."

CHAPTER 23

AUGUST 3, 1832

Bluff Above the Illinois River Valley, Morgan County, Illinois

Charles Chandler sat under his favorite dogwood tree, enjoying his moment in quiet contemplation of what would be. In his three months here, camping under a tent, he had managed to figure it all out. He could look along the ridge and know that he owned this middle portion and once he purchased the eighty acres on either side, he would own all the high ground along the bluff, before it fell away on either side. His house would be here. Well, not exactly here. This dogwood grove would remain in front of the house. The house would be just uphill where he could walk across the lawn and sit under this tree. Off to the right he would plant an apple orchard and perhaps peaches, once he decided whether it was warm enough to grow them in abundance. Behind them he'd plant berries, maybe just move these raspberries below the grove. Oh, he'd bring some order to them to make harvesting an experience that didn't require wearing a buckskin coat with the sleeves buttoned down, but still keeping a berry bramble. Between the fruit and berries, the harvest might be enough to allow him to give up medical practice and all those late-night and stormy-weather calls that went with it.

To his left, he planned to do no more than thin the brush and some of the trees and create a deer park of over one hundred acres where he and his beloved Martha, his bride of twenty-five years, could ride and enjoy the leisure and beauty of this place.

The plans for the house had been drawn up years ago. He'd brought them along and now had Charlie Knapp cutting the lumber to size. He wouldn't get the house finished by winter, but if he got the roof on, he could finish it all in the spring. As soon as it was complete and ready for her, he'd go back to Rhode Island and bring her home, to her new and beautiful home in this wilderness Garden of Eden.

As he looked out below, a small stream of dust rose along the trail. Company was coming. That was still a rare treat that he always enjoyed.

Rising up over the top of the bluff, the horse and rider came into view. The horse was one of those tall, lean Tennessee walking horses like the one Reverend Horn rode. The rider, at this distance, appeared a large man. All he could make of him was a wide-brimmed black felt hat and a black duster. The stranger pulled his big horse to a stop just outside the canopy of the dogwood. Chandler stepped from the shade into the sunlight to greet him.

"Welcome, stranger. I can't offer much, but there is cool water and a little bread and ham."

"Thank you, sir," the big man said as he swung out of the saddle. "The water would be good." And then he asked, "All this yours, or are you like me, just considering?"

Chandler immediately recognized the sharp nasal sound of a New England accent. *Perhaps much like my own.* "A little of each," he offered with a smile. "I own the one hundred sixty acres we stand on, but the eighty on either side of me I'll purchase in the future."

"Sure is pleasant up here on this ridge." The big man in black turned to look into the valley below. "Magnificent, really." And then he extended his hand. "My name is Thompson, Bart Thompson."

The two men exchanged greetings. Charles Chandler pulled a water jug, as well as food, out of the tent and served his guest the humble fare. After he'd finished, Chandler offered, "If you'd like to see more, let me saddle up and show you."

Chandler stepped behind his temporary canvas home, threw a saddle over the small mare he'd purchased, and pulled up beside Thompson's big walking horse. Chandler couldn't help but chuckle as he did. "Usually, in this world, Mr. Thompson, I feel tall, but on my little mare next to that big stallion of yours I feel downright short."

The two men rode mostly in silence for the next hour along the bluff from one end of the knoll to the other. When they were done and back to his tent, Thompson offered, "I like it here, Mr. Chandler. Best view I've seen of the Illinois River Valley, and based on the fact that this high spot along the bluff is less than a mile long, there probably is no other like it." He was all smiles. "I think I'll be your neighbor."

"I'd like that, Mr. Thompson. It's Massachusetts I hear in your voice, and it rings like home to me." He pointed down the slope. "All that below me is available."

"Mr. Chandler, I think I want this view. I'll buy the eighty to the right, I'm thinkin'."

"Yes, it is lovely, isn't it?" Chandler offered. "But it's mine and not available."

"Mr. Chandler, forgive me, but did I not hear you say you owned this one hundred sixty but not the eighty on either side of you?"

Chandler nodded agreement and then said, "You're new to Illinois, aren't you?"

"Arrived in St. Louis last week, crossed the river and been riding north since."

"There is a custom here, Mr. Thompson, you've obviously not come to know. A man has the right to buy the eighty acres on either side of his land. No other man takes it as long as he wants it."

Thompson stood silent for a moment, his head down. When he looked back up, any hint of a smile had left his face. "You said 'custom,' Mr. Chandler. Did you mean 'custom,' or did you mean 'law'?"

"'Custom.'" Chandler's face went hard. "But it is a custom universally abided in these parts."

Bart Thompson put one leg in a stirrup and lifted himself into his saddle. Once there he looked down. "I'm a Yankee, Mr. Chandler, as are you. Where you and I are from, men abide by laws. I'll buy the eighty. I'll go to Springfield now to make it so." With that he turned his horse and trotted down the slope.

Charles Chandler watched the man disappear down the hill and wondered if his dreams had disappeared with him. What he needed to keep them from evaporating was $200 cash and a fast horse. He had neither. He had $110 and a slow mare.

* * * *

Tom Beard had never seen Dr. Charles Chandler excited before. But the man leaning forward over the sweaty mare's neck and continuing to kick at her flanks was certainly a very excited Charles Chandler. He raced to the corral gate and pulled the little beast up so hard she almost came over backward. He threw his right leg over her flank and leaped to the ground before she was even back to standing. Then he raced to his waiting friend.

"Tom," he choked, gasping for air, "I need to borrow $100 cash and a very fast horse."

"Whoa, Doc. Tell me more."

As Chandler stood telling his story, Amanda peered out the kitchen door to see the commotion. Beard pantomimed drinking a beer to her, and within two minutes she was out offering a mug to Chandler. Beard understood at once not only the story but the urgency. "It's fifty miles to Springfield. The kind of fast horse you need is one that can cover a lot of ground at a trot and keep it up."

As Chandler pulled at the mug of beer, Beard whistled to Jim who appeared very quickly. "Jim, put Dr. Chandler on that gaited little mare and stuff one of his saddlebags with corn. Amanda"—he turned to the cook—"whatever you've got that will stay in a saddlebag and be enough for the doc for dinner and breakfast, get it now and be back by the time your Jim gets that horse. Doc, you just exhale in the shade of the barn, and I'll be back before Amanda is."

Chandler strode purposefully into the barn. Beard was back in less than three minutes, Amanda on his heels. Jim came out of the rear stall, leading a small, thin mare of no more than thirteen hands. Beard took the paper-wrapped parcel from Amanda and stuffed it in one saddlebag and looked over at the other to see it bulging. Jim, sensing what was needed, had tied a blanket behind the saddle.

"That little thing will never catch him, Tom." Chandler looked disappointed, almost despondent.

Beard handed him a small leather pouch. "This 'little thing' will trot all night long. It's fifty miles to Springfield. This is not a sprint, Doc.

"There are twenty half eagles in the pouch. If you're lucky, the Yankee will underestimate you and stop for the night. Don't go back home. Take the cutoff through Virginia. It will get you back to the main road at Ashland. I'm guessing the Yankee doesn't know that."

Chandler looked heartened as he turned the mare to the corral gate.

Beard shouted after him. "Don't kill her, Doc. No matter how rushed you feel, trot out of here, trot down the main street, trot to Virginia, and trot to Springfield. She may not make it without rest. You may have to stop for a few hours, but if you don't and you kill her . . ." Beard paused for a moment. "If you kill her, I've only lost a horse, but you've lost a dream."

* * * *

The first rays of sun were rising before him. He was exhausted. So was the mare, but they still had fifteen miles to go. He'd not seen Thompson or his walking horse, and Beard had been right. The mare had trotted most of the night. He'd stopped to water and feed her several times and once to give them both two hours' rest. He hoped Beard was right about Thompson's underestimation of his opponent. Maybe he had stopped for the night. Or maybe not. Maybe they got in front of him using the Virginia cutoff. Or maybe, *God, let it not be so,* he was still in front. About that he could not know. But what he did know was there was not much left in this mare and still fifteen miles to go.

For a few minutes the rising sun was so low in his eyes it blinded him. Now it was rising, and he could see the road again. Ahead he could barely see the outline of a big man on a big horse, or perhaps two men. One big and on a big horse. Could it be Thompson?

"Little mare," he said, "you got any trot left in you, it's time to use it."

He asked for it, and she gave him what she had left. In ten minutes, he'd caught them. At first, he'd thought his worst fears were realized. The horse was big, and so was the man and dressed in black. But when he got within fifty yards of them, he knew it wasn't Thompson.

When he got within beckoning distance Chandler let forth a "Hallowww!"

The two stopped and turned slowly to see a traveler, up even earlier than they and catching them from behind. Their horses stood in the middle of the road, waiting. When Chandler got within twenty feet the tall man sitting ungainly in the saddle said, "Stranger, you are in a mighty hurry. That horse of yours is almost blown."

Chandler drew her to a stop and ran his hand over her withers. Even in the morning cool it came back dripping with sweat. Without responding Chandler asked, "You two seen a big man in black riding a tall Tennessee walking horse?"

"No, but we spent the night in a grove, back a mile or so, and only got on the road just a bit ago."

Chandler smiled. "Save a few hours' sleep, she and I"—he patted her withers again—"have been on the road all night. And you're right; she may well be close to blown, but I must get to Springfield. Killing her is a risk I have to take."

"Mind telling me what's the hurry?" the smaller of the two men asked.

"She needs a rest. If you're curious enough to hear, let's dismount and I'll tell you while I rest her." And he did and they did. And he told his story. All of it.

When he got to the part about the Yankee saying he'd abide by the law and damn local custom, the big man spat. Chandler finished the story with comments of Beard's help and generosity and then started to remount.

"Don't do that, mister." The tall, awkwardly jointed fellow spoke his command with soft goodwill.

Chandler just looked at him, and the man continued.

"If you do, you'll never make it to the recorder's office in Springfield, and you'll have a dead horse. Take mine."

Chandler looked at him in startled disbelief. He finally choked out, "You don't even know me."

"Yes. Yes, I do. You're a man who came west to make a life. And to fit in. We want you here. Now trade me saddles and be gone."

An unbelieving Charles Chandler stripped his saddle from the mare. By then the big man had taken his off as well. Chandler had to reach up to throw it onto the plow horse. The big fellow had thrown his saddle over the mare but didn't bother to cinch it.

Chandler stepped into the stirrup and rose into the saddle. He looked down at the tall man still just standing by the mare, holding her reins in one hand. "Where will I return your horse?"

"On your way home, divert to New Salem and ask anyone there for Abe Lincoln. I'll walk yours home and have her rested by then."

CHAPTER 24

AUGUST 29, 1834

Beardstown, Morgan County, Illinois

Tom and Sara Beard, along with her parents, Chaubenee, Enos Marsh, Francis Arenz, Jim and Amanda, and almost everybody else in Beardstown sat in contemplative silence on the rock-hard maple pews, looking up at Reverend Reddick Horn, his stern visage having softened only a little with time, glowering down at them. But Beard couldn't help but think the passage of these fifteen years showed on his thin face. His jaw seemed even longer and his cheekbones even more pronounced. His long silver hair, ever his defining feature, even all those years ago, was thinner and receding back along his forehead just a bit. His blue eyes were not as clear, showing some red against the whites near his nose. And the lids appeared just a bit baggy above and puffy below.

But the biggest change was in his clothing. He was still wearing the black worsted suit, the coat cut to his knees, and a white shirt with a Roman collar. His boots were black leather and still polished but worn at the toes and the heels. The worsted of his suit was threadbare at the knees, and the white shirt no longer of fine Sea Island cotton but rough woven linen.

Horn thundered to the climax of his fiery sermon and received a universal "Amen!" from the hundred in the room. He paused to allow silence to fill the church and then did something that surprised them all. Reverend Reddick Horn smiled.

"Before you depart, I have a personal thought I would like to share with you. You all know that I am from Savannah, perhaps the original home of civilization on this continent.

"'It used to make my heart sick, in the early years of my ministry, to dismiss my charges to churches in distant regions, as our brothers and sisters, our neighbors, left us for the new settlements in the opening territories. But as I have grown older, and followed these migrants to their new homes, I have found them far more useful to church and state in these new territories than they ever could have been in the regions they have left behind, where others held the places of influence—as I have seen them giving a healthy and vigorous tone to society, while the separation causes a pang of sorrow, the good accomplishments more than compensate for pleasures lost.'"[1]

Horn looked down at all, a smile of loving brotherhood on his face. He stepped down from the podium and walked the length of the middle aisle until he reached the opened front doors where he turned to face them. He stood, arms spread, the morning sun filling the doors with light and making his tall, thin figure look like nothing so much as the crucified Christ.

"Go in peace, Brothers and Sisters, and do the Lord's work."

---

1. Quoted from an unnamed minister of the Gospel in Newton Bateman and Paul Selby, eds., *Historical Encyclopedia of Illinois*, and Charles A. E. Martin, ed., History of Cass County (Chicago: Munsell, 1915).

The members of his congregation stood and slowly filled the middle aisle, shuffling to the church door where they would, one at a time, shake the minister's hand, offering thanks and congratulations and sometimes a donation, perhaps a bill or a coin tucked into the palm with a handshake. Those in the first pew now being the last out made small conversation as they waited their turn.

"Chaubenee, I hear you've been to a tent meeting, but is this your first Sunday service?" asked the cheery voice of Charlotte Bell.

"Yes, ma'am, it is."

Dan Bell, shoulder to shoulder with Chaubenee, turned slightly to look him in the eye. Neither man had to look up or down. They were the same height, and standing as they were, their combined width took up the entire aisle. "How does what you hear here compare to Indian beliefs?" the ever-thoughtful blacksmith inquired.

The question caused Arenz to turn and take them both in. "Listen to you two." That he was startled was clear from his tone. "You two are huge men, the largest, strongest men of your race, and you talk of things of the spirit. It is a wonder."

"Mr. Arenz, our strength is no more than that of an ant beside that of our creator. I suppose that is most obvious to big men like us," Bell said, and put his arm around Chaubenee's shoulders and pulled him toward him. "But please, Chaubenee"—Bell looked up to check the progress of the line—"there is time. Answer me please."

"I have told my friend Tom Beard that I find all people very much alike. But our gods are a bit different. From what I've heard from Reverend Horn, your God is very like the Shawnee Moneto. He commands the same of you in terms of honesty and care of the community and honor in your speech and conduct. But there is one huge difference."

Now all in the line that could hear were turned to the conversation.

"And that is what, Chaubenee?" Dan Bell asked.

"Moneto commands those rules for Shawnee in dealing only with other Shawnee. Your God's rules apply to all."

There was silence as they approached their moment with Horn. Finally, Beard broke it. He tapped Francis Arenz on the shoulder. When he had his attention, Beard said, "Francis, come back to the end with me. There are words I'd say to Reverend Horn when you are near."

Arenz stepped into the space between the rows of pews and let Chaubenee and Bell walk by. He stepped back into the aisle to join Sara and Tom Beard.

"Tom, I'll offer my courtesies first and then wait for you and Francis in the courtyard."

Beard nodded. They had reached the door. Sara thanked and congratulated the reverend, pulled on her bonnet, and stepped into the yard.

Beard was always disconcerted that he had to look up at Reddick Horn, even if just a bit. Not because he disliked looking up at other men but because he harbored the suspicion that Horn enjoyed looking down at them.

"Reverend Horn, accept my congratulations on the first sermon ever preached in a church building in Beardstown." He offered the good wishes with a genuine smile and an extended hand.

And Horn's response seemed, for almost the first time since Beard had known him, to carry not even the slightest hint of condescension.

Horn's hand reached forward and accepted his. He continued to hold it as he spoke. "It was truly good of you gentlemen"—he looked from Beard to Arenz—"to offer this land and building for my church and school."

Horn's face suddenly reflected an emotion Beard had never seen there, embarrassment, and the minister pulled his hand from the grip he seemed to realize he was holding overlong.

Beard smiled and pointed to the stack of bags behind Horn. "Your parishioners seemed to have appreciated your work, Reverend. There's enough food there to last a month. This keeps up, you'll be selling the surplus."

Horn smiled benignly, his dignity recovered. "I think gifts to those more needy even than a servant of God rather than the market."

"Good enough, Reverend Horn. I'm just glad to see they appreciate you."

Arenz extended his hand, and they shook briefly. Then Arenz said, "Reverend, it is my pleasure to be part of building the community here, and without you, and others like you, there would be no community. And there will be others. Methodists are not the only religionists here. I think my Germans will want Lutheran services here as well. When they come to us, we will come to you and schedule times on Sunday for each. During the week, the building is yours to use as a school. Another civic institution we desperately need and that you provide. You are a blessing to us all, Reverend."

"And I am grateful to you as well, as I've previously said. When it is time to talk other services, other religions, we'll have that discussion. But I do hope you'll not let Papists profane the building."

Arenz's face tightened, and he stood up just a little straighter. "Reverend, I am a follower of Martin Luther. I come from a place that spent over a century trying to commit suicide over the answer to questions similar to that. And do you know what we learned?"

A somewhat startled Reddick Horn looked down into the deep-set purple eyes that revealed nothing. "What did you learn, Mr. Arenz?"

"That God loves all his children." It was said with a flat, even tone that reflected unshakable belief. "For now, the land and building belong to Thomas and me. Who has use of the property and when is up to us. We are, however, in the process of gifting it to the city. Once that process is complete those decisions will be up to others. Good day, Reverend Horn."

Beard and Arenz stepped into a courtyard abandoned by all save Sara Beard who stood in the shade of a large elm.

"You were angry, Francis. Not certain I've ever seen you that way."

"Tom, sometime we can talk more over a drink, but for now ask yourself why so many of those coming to this uncivilized place we are trying to tame are German.

"But now I have to go fawn over my printing press and write some words for the typesetter. You know the first edition of the *Beardstown Chronicle and Illinois Military Bounty Land Advertiser* will be out this week, and its editor and publisher is too busy even to talk to his best friend." With a nod of his head, he pointed toward Sara waiting patiently under the tree. "And you, dear Thomas, have a very pretty lady waiting for you."

* * * *

Sara Beard always looked her best in the sunlight, and she knew it. Direct sunlight made her hair more than golden blond; it made her hair into a halo and she the angel beneath it. She was standing with her bonnet in her hand and her hair flashing the light bursting between the shimmering leaves of the elm. As he came within a step, she pushed up on tiptoes and pointed her full pink lips up, inviting them to be kissed.

"Even in front of the church?" he teased.

"Especially in front of the church," she responded.

He bent down and gave her a small peck of a kiss. She took his arm, and they strolled out onto the street.

"Tom, may we have a religious discussion?" She was trying to hide an impish smile.

He couldn't tell what was coming, but he knew something was. "Sure," he said hesitantly.

"I never remember if it's the fourth or fifth commandment, but one of them says we must 'honor the Sabbath and keep it holy.'"

He nodded, still not able to figure out where she was leading him.

"Most people think that means 'don't work.' So how about you spend the day, not working, with me."

"Ah, Sara, I'd love to, but . . ."

"But what?" Her happy face immediately became a pout.

"See that line of wagons on the street? Now that the bounty lands are all taken and Indians in Iowa are quiet, everyone is going there. And the best way to get there is to give Tom Beard a half eagle to get you across the river. Those people"— he pointed at the line of Conestoga wagons at the end of the block—"are waiting to give me . . . and you, Sara, money."

"Damn it, Tom. We have plenty of money. I don't want their money. I hoped to be one of the builders of this empire of yours, but you only want to do things your way. So if I can't have your empire, then I want attention. Your attention."

Beard tried to jolly her. "That, I believe, is the third one."

"Third what?" she demanded, not looking up.

"Commandment." His voice was still teasing. "The one about not taking the Lord's name in vain."

She stopped, planted her feet firmly, and looked directly up at him. Her expression was no longer petulant or even defiant. "Tom"—she pointed down the street toward the river—"there are three wagons parked there. It will take you half an hour to set up the horses, another hour and a half to take those three wagons across, and a half hour to put the horses away. It's noon now, so you'll be done about two thirty or three o'clock. Tell me. What will you do then?"

Beard found himself staring at his boots, feeling like a small boy being scolded. He couldn't answer.

"You don't need to tell me, Tom. I know." He looked into eyes that conveyed a very deep sadness. "You'll find some other task that *needs* doing today, won't you?"

It was an accusation he could not deny. He didn't try.

Sara pulled her bonnet onto her head. "Don't need to walk me home. I know the way." She turned and, head down, walked away.

Tom Beard was shaken, angry, and at his core, uncertain. He just stared at the back of a departing angel.

CHAPTER 25

SEPTEMBER 1, 1834

*On the Illinois River, Downriver from
Beardstown, Morgan County, Illinois*

The only sound in the salon of the *Illinois Queen* was the steady
throbbing of the big wheel digging into the river. Even with the
breeze provided by the open doors onto the deck, this, the largest room on the riverboat, was stuffy from heat and humidity
provided in part by the still August night and in part by the
bodies pressed together. The chandelier, hanging low over the
card table, gave soft focus and deep shadow to the faces pushing to lean toward the drama of the cards unfolding before
them. This was the moment that seemed not always to happen
and, when it did, happened only once a night. This was the big
hand. Six of the eight players sat back, their cards thrown face-
down in the middle of the table, some of their money having
joined them there. Two men were still close to the table. Still
in it.

A lean, handsome man in his midthirties, his face the picture of studied calm, pondered the last cards he had just dealt. He was a man who gave the appearance he was never perturbed about anything. Certainly not poker. He was the only man in the room with his coat still on, the heat seeming a matter of total indifference to him. As though to confirm it so, not a drop of moisture showed on his tanned face. Even his neatly parted but abundant auburn curls stayed where he'd ordered them rather than hanging down his forehead. His green eyes didn't twitch, didn't even blink, as he pushed two neat stacks of ten half eagles each onto the table. In a drawl, smooth as Tennessee whiskey, he said, "My Yankee friend, it will cost you $100 to see if I've got it."

Bart Thompson stared, as though sending bolts of fire into his opponent's eyes. But he was trying to intimidate a man upon whom the effort appeared wasted. Thompson's sheer size intimidated most men. He'd learned to dress in black to enhance that power. His harsh New England accent and bullying demeanor frequently, usually, made the effort successful. He looked down and studied the green felt table.

Both men had one card down. Neither had looked at it except immediately after it was dealt. Both men had four cards showing before them. Bart Thompson had a pair of eights showing. He had another eight as his "hole" card. The ace of diamonds and three of spades that he was also showing were irrelevant to him, and he knew to his opponent as well. The opponent's cards, showing in mixed suits, were a ten, a nine, a seven, and a six. His opponent had bet cautiously throughout the hand, just staying in. It was only after he received his last and final card, the ten, that he bet big. Thompson's three of a kind could beat any pair the Southerner might have. The only thing he could possibly have that would beat Thompson was an eight. That would give the opponent a straight, which would beat Thompson's three of a kind. The cool man with the

Tennessee accent had played the whole hand like he was waiting to finish a straight and now like he'd gotten it.

But he needed an eight in the hole to fill it, and Thompson had three of them. There was only one card left in the deck of fifty-two that would fill that straight. One card that could beat him. One chance in fifty-two.

Thompson pushed $100 onto the table. "Colonel? You introduced yourself as Colonel Fulks, I believe. Well, Colonel, your bluff is called," he announced proudly, and reached to sweep in his winnings.

"Not quite so fast, my Yankee friend," the sensuous lips drawled out of the handsome face. "You paid to see it. Would you not like to?"

Thompson eased his big frame back into his chair. "Show it," he commanded.

The long fingers of the Southerner's left hand reached out onto the table. He slipped one manicured nail under his hole card and turned it over for all the world, including Bart Thompson, to see.

It was an eight.

The crowd gasped and then guffawed and then whooped. Thompson sat glowering. Colonel Fulks never moved. He didn't even reach to scrape in his winnings. He sat, left hand still on the table, his right hand low at his side, his green eyes studying Thompson.

Thompson exploded as a bull out a gate but backward, pushing his chair forcefully away from the table. Plainly visible in his belt was a repeating pistol. "You cheating son of a bitch! You dealt yourself the one card that could possibly beat me! From the bottom, I'm thinking."

Fulks's gaze penetrated the glare above the chandelier, glued unblinking to Thompson's black eyes spitting fire. "I believe, my Yankee friend, that weapon in your belt is one of Samuel Colt's new invention. I would very much admire to see it, but if you move to pull it from your belt, I will kill you. I would prefer not to do that. It would be inconvenient and spoil an otherwise pleasant evening. If you would care to apologize for the unkind thing you've just said of me, I will understand your words were spoken in disappointment and haste, and you and I may remain friends. Otherwise, go ahead and draw that fancy gun, and we'll get this over with."

Thompson's face was a battle of self-control with rage. Rage won. He dropped his butt low as his hand flew up to his belt.

The blast exploded into the room, covering the sounds of shattering wood and of glass tinkling down from the bursting chandelier, as the big man screamed and was thrown backward. Every voice in the room went silent as the colonel stood slowly to his feet, not a hair out of place, the only sign of his disquiet being the smoldering coming from his coat pocket as he removed his right hand, smoke still rising from the short-barreled flintlock pistol he held. He walked slowly around the table to see the fallen figure of the big man who was on his back, his legs spread, his right hand holding a heavily bleeding left shoulder. He was moaning. The floor next to his wounded shoulder was red. The Colt was still in his belt.

"You've ruined my shoulder, you son of a bitch," Thompson groaned.

"Yes, I have," Fulks agreed, "and a perfectly good coat of mine as well, I fear." He looked down at the fabric of his coat pocket shredded by the exit of the pistol ball.

Fulks stepped to the fallen man's right side and slipped the Colt from his belt. He held it to the still-swaying light, cocking the hammer but holding it down tight, to prevent it falling forward, as he pulled the trigger. He then laid the hammer gently down.

Fulks looked down at an agonizing Thompson. "What did this cost you, sir?"

It took a moment for the answer to form. Thompson finally stuttered through his pain, "Seventy dollars."

Fulks placed the Colt in his pocket, turned to the table, swept up his winnings, neatly counted fourteen of the half eagles, and while holding them in one hand, put the remainder in his pocket. He stepped back toward Thompson, reached down, and put the fourteen gold coins into his vest pocket. "I think it's better I keep the Colt." And then to the room in general announced, "I presume the captain of the *Illinois Queen* will be here shortly. If he wants to talk with me, please tell him I can be found in my suite."

* * * *

Colonel John Fulks sat idling with the Colt, trying to learn its assembly, when the expected knock on the door came. He presumed it was the ship's captain, Hannibal Percy, but caution being the father of safety for a gambler, he cocked the flintlock and held it at his side as he opened the door.

"Colonel, I fear I shall have to ask you to leave my boat at the next stop," said Captain Percy as he stepped into Fulks's suite.

"Why, may I ask?" was John Fulks's calm reply as he motioned for Percy to enter.

"Don't misunderstand, Colonel," said Captain Percy, taking a seat. "I'm not suggesting you have done anything wrong. All the voices seem to agree you conducted yourself with calm and aplomb throughout the unfortunate affair. But I will not have a killing on my boat. Bad for business and my reputation."

"I did not kill him, Captain. I did not try."

Percy chuckled. "To shoot a man from under the table with what amounts to an unaimed wing shot shows remarkable skill with a gun or remarkable luck. If you say it is the former, I will believe you. But it is not his current condition that worries me."

"I assure you, Captain, I can care for my own well-being," Fulks responded.

Again, Percy chuckled. "As before, I certainly believe you. But he is a bully of a man. He will try. And no matter how that comes out, it will not be good for the boat, the line, or me personally. So one of you must go. And he can't."

Now it was Fulks's turn to chuckle. "Your point is made and taken. But where will I stay while I'm in the hole of river rats we are approaching, and how shall I get out?"

"As for the latter, I'll take you out. The *Illinois Queen* will be a short day getting to Fort Clark, where Thompson can be tended to, and a then a short day back. We will be back to Beardstown about noon two days from now. There will be no freight to deliver or load, so as soon as I collect you, we will be gone. Then I will return you to St. Louis or anywhere south to New Orleans. That's where we're bound, downriver. And as for the former question, it happens that Beardstown has the finest hotel north of St. Louis. And while I have no personal knowledge, the proprietress is said to be the most beautiful woman in Illinois."

* * * *

Sara Beard had finished her work for the evening. The bottles were sealed and tucked away; the glasses were washed and put away and the cash drawer locked when he came in. He opened the door, looked around, and seeing only her, turned and walked toward her. It gave her pleasure to watch him coming. He was of middle height and lean, but what interested her most was the way he carried himself. It was more a glide than a stride. Neither his hips nor his shoulders moved much. He came toward her, hips forward, shoulders back, chin down and smiling. A small smile, a self-satisfied smile, a feline smile.

He removed his hat, revealing a mass of auburn curls. His face was almost feminine. He was only saved from being pretty by the nose that was slightly too large for the face and bent at a sharp angle at the top.

She watched him come and said not a word of greeting.

He set his panama hat on the bar, dropped his valise on the floor, pulled out a stool, and sat down. "Ma'am," he said, the softness of his drawl hypnotic with the first syllable, "I have just been removed from the *Illinois Queen* and am seeking a warm and comfortable place to spend two nights." And then he smiled, a smile that revealed a mouthful of perfect teeth. "I'd like it if it were here."

"As would I," she said without smiling.

She had given him the key and directions to his room. She had also told him the hours of kitchen operation and had one shot of whiskey with him before he left the bar to head upstairs. She watched him walk. She liked watching him walk.

As he reached the stairs, he turned to her and spoke softly but in a voice she could hear across the room. "I believe your eyes are greener than mine."

"We'll see in the daylight; won't we?"

* * * *

Sara floated down the staircase as though her toes were bouncing across clouds. There was just enough light coming in from the windows to illuminate the chairs and tables as she skipped between, making her way to the swinging kitchen doors.

Amanda looked up with surprise and then delight. "My, my, young lady, what did your husband do to put you in such a pretty state of mind? Bet I can guess."

"Hush, Amanda. I'm too old for you to make me blush. And no, he did nothing." She looked around the kitchen for him and, not seeing him, said, "I presume he's already eaten and gone."

"Out of here ten minutes ago."

Amanda cocked one eye toward her. "Have I seen this dress before? Green. When you wear green, you know what it does to your eyes." And then Amanda playfully wagged her finger at Sara. "What has gotten into you?"

"I've told you, Amanda. Nothing. I just woke up when Tom left and felt in a very gay mood. Thought rather than waste my good mood on myself, I'd come down here and help you." And then she caught herself. "No, I'm not going to cook. You do that, and I'll see to serving the guests."

* * * *

It was ten thirty before he came to breakfast. She was just cleaning off the last table when she heard a chair scrape on the floor behind her. She'd had heard no footsteps, so knew it was him before she turned. He was dressed as he had been last night, long, black fine-worsted trousers, a double-buttoned vest, and long frock coat. He was also wearing a white silk shirt open at the collar. That the shirt was clean and fresh was obvious, but otherwise he was dressed as last night save that the woven panama hat was not with him. Sara turned to him, smoothing her long white apron as she did.

"Good morning, Colonel. I trust you slept well."

"Madam, the only thing here that exceeds the comfort of the hotel's accommodations is the beauty of its proprietress."

Sara's expression did not change save the small twinkle in her eyes. "Colonel, this is not Tennessee. Here a simple 'Good morning, Mrs. Beard' will do."

The handsome face with the Roman nose smiled easily, appearing to take neither offense nor interest in her correction. As he slipped into the chair he responded, "I had been prepared for the abruptness of manners and the roughness of the frontier, but no one had warned me of the rose to be found among those particular thorns." He stared into her eyes with a long pause and then added, "Mrs. Beard."

She rewarded him with a smile. A small smile but a reward for his victory of language all the same. "Colonel, this morning Amanda has made some corned-beef hash and fried potatoes. If you'd like, I'll have her put an egg or two on top. And she made some wonderful biscuits. Tell me what you'd like."

John Fulks looked at her, his green eyes glimmering the morning sunshine at their edges. His expression was not a leer, but neither was it without innuendo. It told her of the response he was contemplating, and would suppress, but let her hear it as clearly as though he'd mouthed the word, *You*. "I'll have it all. One egg over easy and enough butter on those biscuits that I can watch it roll down the sides as it melts. And hot coffee . . . Mrs. Beard." Again, he strung it out. "Lots of hot coffee."

In less than ten minutes she returned balancing a large tray over her shoulder. She set the tray down on the adjacent table. It contained his entire order and two cups of coffee. As she served him, he studied her every move, enjoying the watching. When she had put everything before him, she said, "Colonel Fulks, I've brought a cup of coffee for myself, too. May I sit with you, or would you prefer to eat alone?"

Without a word he stood and walked around and pulled her chair away from the table. "It would be my joy to have the company of a woman such as you."

She untied the long white apron, slipped it over her head, and laid it across next to the serving tray. She took a moment to brush the green cloth of her skirt down smooth, a gesture that tightened the top of the dress and emphasized her breasts. Only then did she sit. Looking down at the square-cut bodice of the dress, he pushed her chair toward the table. When she was seated, he reached back to the serving tray and got her coffee, which he set before her. Then he walked back around to his own chair.

"Mrs. Beard, last night when I said I thought your eyes are greener than mine, you said we would have to wait to judge in the daylight. It is now daylight. What do you think?"

"Colonel Fulks . . ."

"Please, Mrs. Beard, will you call me John? Colonel is so formal."

She gave him the flat look that always kept men guessing. "Yes, John, I will. But then you must call me Sara."

He merely nodded.

Sara continued. "While I don't see my eyes as clearly as I see yours, I am fairly certain yours are greener. The green of yours is pure."

"Perhaps that is true, Sara. But yours are of emeralds and amber. Like emeralds we find here in America."

"Georgia, I have heard."

"Yes, and do you know where amber comes from?"

She shook her head.

"It is from Poland and Russia. They find it in the sand along the shores of the Baltic Sea. And do you know how it was formed?"

Again, she shook her head.

"It is said to be sap from pine trees from millions of years ago, saved from decay by the salt and then pressed to hardness by the sea. It is like your eyes, Sara; the mysteries of a million years are hidden there. I will accept that mine are greener, but yours are far more mysterious."

Sara said nothing, and John Fulks went back to eating his meal. She watched him. As with his walk, it seemed there was a delicate precision to all he did.

"Sara, the *Illinois Queen* will be here about noon tomorrow, and I will board her and ride south. But between now and then I have a day to spend. How shall I spend it in Beardstown, Illinois?"

Sara said nothing as she contemplated. And then with suddenness and resolution she spoke. "There is nothing in this town of interest, but what is of interest is the country around— the beautiful, if treacherous, slough upriver to the east and the bluff at the south of the river valley. That is what you should spend your day seeing, the beauty of this place."

"And where shall I find a horse for this adventure?"

She looked startled and then laughed. "We have a livery as part of the hotel."

"And where shall I find a guide for this adventure into this beauty and treachery?"

Sara Beard said nothing but just looked into his clear green eyes until he finally spoke again.

"Will you show me, then, Sara?"

"I thought you would never ask."

* * * *

Sara knew the path was there and had to be followed closely. One small misstep and her horse would get a hoof caught deep in the mud and go down. The worst outcome was horse and rider would both drown. The best outcome was her new green dress ruined. There was danger here but such beauty and joy if one navigated the trail surely, a trail of which she was not entirely sure. In fact, she suspected the horse knew it better than she.

The tall swamp grasses were still wet and glistening with dew. The morning mist was rising enough to offer vision of all immediately before but concealing, at least intermittently, the path, the rushes, the water, even the trees more than a few yards ahead. She stopped suddenly, motioning him to a stop and to silence in the same gesture. Then she pointed. A three-foot-tall gunmetal-grey heron stood rigid, its long bill held high. And then with a swiftness that exceeded the eye's ability to follow went into the water and came back up with a small fish, almost the shape and size of a coffee saucer, glimmering yellow and blue in the beam of sunlight, wriggling manically, pierced through by the slim bill. The heron tossed its head upward sharply, the wiggling fish thrown into the air and swallowed on its way down before it fell back to the safety of the water.

They proceeded without a word.

Soon the mist was lifted, and the sun, the sun that would be brutally hot in just three hours, brought warm contentment to their shoulders. It also brought turtles up to sit silent as statues on logs anchored somehow in the muck of the bottom.

And again, she stopped and held up her hand, but this time she spoke. "See it?" Sara's voice was very calm even though her finger pointed toward death. Curled not three feet from the edge of the trail, warming, as all other swamp creatures were, lay a jet-black snake no more than four feet long but thick. "That thing is thicker than my father's forearms."

As she spoke, the snake, completely lacking the ability to hear, flipped itself into a coil, raised its head toward them, opened its mouth, a mouth white as cotton, and hissed at them, an evil and vile sound that caused her horse to shiver along its spine from the flank to the withers. Sara stroked the horse calmly and said, "Shuuuu. It's all right."

Fulks pulled the Colt from his belt and said, "It's time for me to try out my new toy."

Sara turned to look and spoke in the same tone with which she'd reassured her horse. "Don't, John. It's a beautiful creature. And like so much God has made, the beauty of it carries risk. Let it be beautiful, and it will let us walk past."

The snake stayed coiled but lowered its head as they went by.

Lunchtime found them out of the slough and up on the hill along the top of the valley. They lay side by side on a blanket, the lunch hamper Amanda had prepared between them.

She studied him slowly, starting with his auburn hair and running her appraising gaze downward. Suddenly she propped herself up. "John, I'm surprised."

"At what?"

"You seem meticulous, almost fastidious, in your dress, and you have such a ragged hole in the pocket of your frock coat. You must let me have Amanda fix it when we get back."

"I do believe, Sara Beard, you have embarrassed me. But it just happened last evening, and I've not had time to get it fixed or buy another."

"What happened?"

Fulks was silent for a moment and then shrugged as if deciding to tell her. "It's a bullet hole." He expected her to gasp or at least inquire further. She did neither.

"And that's why you came to me?" She needed no more, it seemed. "If you give me the coat when we get back, I'll have it fixed by the morning."

They were silent for a while, the only noise the rustle of the leaves. It was very hot even in the shade.

"Sara, you said that water moccasin was as large as your father's forearms. What is it your father does that makes his forearms so large?"

"Blacksmith. Dad's a blacksmith. What are you, John?"

John Fulks rose up on one elbow and got high enough to study her. She didn't move or change expression. Just looked back at him, waiting.

"I gamble, Sara. I'm a gambler."

Neither her posture nor expression changed. "And you're good at it?"

"Good enough to buy good whiskey and cigars, nice clothes, and live in suites on riverboats. That is good enough for me."

She rose up on her elbow now. High enough that she could look eye to eye. "And expensive women, John. Do you make enough to buy them, too?"

Fulks looked at her, eye to eye across the space of the hamper. "I very seldom have to buy women, Sara."

She nodded. "That's what the bullet hole was about. A woman?"

He smiled now. It was a mischievous smile. "Nothing so important as a woman, Sara. Just a little money and a small point of honor.

"Now it's my turn to ask again, Sara. What is it you do?"

Sara lay back down and rolled from her side onto her back, looking up at the sky's twinkly patches of blue through the large maple canopy. She didn't answer for a long time. "I watch my husband build an empire," she finally said, and then spoke no more.

John Fulks sat up. He picked up the hamper and set it behind him and then studied her lying before him.

For a long time, Sara Beard continued to study the sky. Finally, she turned ever so slightly until their eyes met. "Colonel John Fulks, if you want me, you can have me. But not here. If you want me, you'll have me when we get to your suite on the *Illinois Queen*."

* * * *

The midday air was pierced by the penetrating and demanding steam whistle of the *Illinois Queen*. It was a demand that those coming along do so now or be left behind.

Sara Beard finished writing her note, folded it, and put it in an envelope. She rose, pushed away from her dresser, picked up her valise off the bed, and, valise in one hand and note in the other, walked down the hall and then down the stairs. At the bottom of the stairs stood a smiling John Fulks who extended his hand to take her valise and started to the door.

"John, give me just a minute, please."

He nodded and watched her walk into the dining room to the table by the window occupied by a very large and aging Indian and a small and very dapperly dressed man with a continental air.

She said a few words to the Indian, handed him a small envelope, turned and came back to Fulks. "I'm ready to go now," was all she said. He opened the door with one hand and held it for her and then, with his foot holding it open, reached back to pick up the bags.

And they walked down the knoll and up the gangplank to the *Illinois Queen*.

* * * *

The moon was well up by the time a very tired Tom Beard came in the back door of the hotel. Amanda had closed the kitchen but left a heaping plate of dinner warming in the oven. He knew it would be there, picked it up, and pushed the door open to the dining room with his shoulders. He was surprised to see Chaubenee and Francis Arenz illuminated in the glow of a hurricane lamp on the table by the front window.

Beard walked to them and with a voice both exhausted and full of goodwill asked, "What keeps you two here so late? Not just to keep an old friend company at dinner, I'm sure."

Neither man responded as he sat down. When he had, it was Chaubenee who spoke. "Truth is, Tom, that is the reason we stayed." He said it with absolute sincerity.

Beard, now understanding the sobriety of both friends, looked from one to the other and said nothing.

Chaubenee handed him an envelope. "This is for you."

Beard's eyes shone with the anxiety of knowing something was wrong but no idea what. Neither man spoke, and both looked at him with immense sadness.

Tom Beard opened the envelope, unfolded the paper, and held it in the light of the lamp and read.

> Dear Tom,
> I hope you get all you want in life. Those things, obviously, do not include me. So I have gone to seek my own. I hope you will wish the same for me.
> Sara

PART III

THE FOUNDER'S EMPIRE

CHAPTER 26

JANUARY 31, 1836

Beardstown, Morgan County, Illinois

The two men riding side by side were bundled against the cold, their mufflers drawn up tight around the collars of their winter greatcoats, their breath, and the breath of their horses, showing long streams of rapidly disappearing water vapor with each exhale. The cold aside, it was a beautiful winter's day, a clear powder-blue sky with not a hint of a cloud to be seen or wind felt.

"Tom, I appreciate your letting me pull you from the warmth of that big fire, but I wanted to have you look at something. Some things really."

"What things, Enos?" Beard asked.

"Just ride beside me and look around. In an hour or so, tell me what you've seen."

And for the next two hours they rode all the streets in the city they had built. They rode the riverfront, the main street, and most of the residential streets, doing just as Marsh had mysteriously requested, letting their eyes take it in without one word of comment. Eventually, Marsh led them back to the place where they had started, to the place it had all started, the knoll above the river. They sat looking at the frozen river before them.

"Now tell me what you saw?" Marsh asked.

Beard looked at him with the anxious expression of a student being queried by his master. He exhaled and started his recitation. "Before me, I see two large floating docks spaced widely enough apart for a riverboat to moor on either side and wide enough to roll big wagons off and onto those boats, docks that have handled as many as seven boats a day taking our produce and goods to America and even the rest of the world. I see a mooring for the only ferry across the Illinois River between here to its mouth. The month before the river froze, that ferry handled over one hundred fifty teams going to or from this little city as well as one hundred seventy mounted travelers."

He looked up to his right. "And I see the finest hotel and public house in the center of the state."

He turned slightly until he was looking downriver, inviting Marsh to look with him. "I see businesses, large and prosperous businesses. A steam mill to make staves and boards, a distillery, a cooperage, a cabinetmaker, a tannery newly arrived but opening next year, a simple blacksmith become a manufacturer of plows and hand implements. I see a grain mill with large silos to transfer Illinois crops to river barges. I see a livery stable with hacks available for transport."

Beard turned his horse to look back down Main Street. Marsh swung his horse with him. "I see businesses that provide hardware, dry goods, paint, and tools. I see a drugstore, a bakery, a dress shop. I see offices of doctors and grain merchants and even a newspaper. And I see a city with a population of over one thousand about to run out of plats for building."

Beard turned to look at Marsh. Beard's face beamed with pride. "That's what I see, Enos. I see great prosperity, and you and I built it."

Marsh nodded slowly but did not return the smile. "You know what I see, Tom?"

"What?"

"I see civilization." His expression remained unchanged.

"Enos, you say that like it's a bad thing."

"Oh no, Tom, not bad. Just not for me."

Beard's brows pulled together in a perplexed frown. "Not for you? I don't understand."

"Tom, you were the one who wanted to bring civilization to the wilderness. I just wanted to make money. Personally, I like the frontier."

Beard sat in stunned silence. The breathing of the horses the only sound between them. Marsh continued. "Tom, when I came to Edwardsville, it was the edge of the frontier. I came here with you partly because Edwardsville had grown large and somewhat civilized. I wanted to come back to the frontier, and you gave me that opportunity. But success has changed what I love. Ruined it for me. I wanted a place where I was free to make money with no rules or my own rules. You wanted to build structure, civilization. I wanted liberty and money. There is still frontier somewhere. That's where I belong and where I will be. I'm telling you this because as soon as the ice breaks I will get on the first boat going downriver, sell my stake in this place, and be gone. I wanted you to know first so you would have the chance to buy me out rather than have a partner you didn't choose."

"Where will you go, Enos?"

"There's a guy who took over Mexico a couple of years back. Some generalissimo named Santa Anna. He's been inviting Americans to Tejas. Offering land for free. I'll go there."

Both men sat quietly, taking in what there was of the cool winter sunshine and pondering all that they had done together.

After a moment Beard nodded understanding and then spoke. "I'm grateful that you told me, Enos. Without selling the hotel, though, I don't have the money to buy you out. But I think I know someone who does, someone with whom I think I could comfortably partner."

* * * *

The house Charles Chandler had built for his wife reminded Beard very much of Murray McConnel's. But stunning as McConnel's was, Chandler's, situated by itself at the edge of the wilderness, was more so. Even in the winter landscape, bereft of the softening effect of green foliage, it was magical. And the smoke rising from chimneys at either end of the structure made it seem like enchantment was welcoming them, pulling them in.

"I've not seen anything like it since I crossed the Allegheny Mountains," Francis Arenz commented as he and Beard encouraged their mounts up the last few yards to the top of the bluff. "What an extraordinary man this must be to build such a mansion on the edge of the frontier."

"He told me he was building it for his wife and daughters to have when they arrived," Beard said to his friend. "Must be an extraordinary family as well."

The front door swung open, and the tall figure of Charles Chandler stood welcoming them. "Tom Beard, what a very pleasant surprise."

Both men dismounted and tied their horses. Introductions were made around. "Come into the warmth, gentlemen," the rich baritone welcomed.

Just inside the front door stood an attractive woman of middle age, her abundant black hair swept straight back, a reserved but welcoming smile on her lips and a very erect carriage. She was flanked by two girls, both in their early teens. Both appeared to reflect the beauty of their mother's youth, one blessed with her mother's straight black hair and the other her father's dark brown curls.

"Gentlemen, allow me to present my wife, Martha, and our daughters, Angela and Candice."

The formality of introduction was followed by an invitation to join them at the table. It was a meal that seemed abundantly prepared. Lunch was followed by the young ladies and their mother proceeding to clean up while Chandler invited Arenz and Beard into the sitting room for coffee and cigars.

"Civilized companionship is always a pleasure, especially in our wilderness abode, but may I ask if there is any purpose to your visit save visiting a remote neighbor?" Chandler asked.

Arenz nodded in response to Beard's conspiratorial glance.

"Charles, we'd like you to join us," Beard said.

"In what endeavor?"

"We are making a trip to Springfield, and we think you should come along," Beard answered.

"To what purpose? Both the trip and my joining," Chandler asked cautiously.

"Two really," Beard answered again. "Let me explain. As you may know, the legislature is considering dividing Morgan County in two. If they do, Beardstown and its surroundings will become its own county. We favor that. It'll bring government power closer to home. Gives us more control than having to reach to Jacksonville."

"May I guess that you would like to make Beardstown the new county seat?" Cigar smoke came out of Chandler's mouth in small puffs as he spoke.

"That will be put to a vote of the people, but Beardstown, having the largest population, seems logical." It was Arenz who responded.

"And the second purpose?" Chandler asked.

"We'd like the state to build a plank road from Beardstown to Springfield," Beard answered. "We've always been the port of access for Springfield's goods. Now that the state capital is moving from Vandalia to Springfield, that traffic will get heavier, and the wagon rut of a road that now connects us to Springfield will become a choke point. We thought that might particularly interest you, as the choice for the path of such a road will either be below the bluff, near you, or through Virginia. We thought you'd prefer the former and might speak to it."

Chandler nodded. "May I ask what connections you have now with the legislature?"

Beard took the cigar from his mouth and laid it on the ashtray. "There is an attorney in Jacksonville named Murray McConnel, a Democrat, who has just been elected to the state legislature. He is a very long-term friend of mine. In truth, he was the man who guided me to Mascouten Bay these eighteen years ago. He and the governor are close, and he has asked to be put on the Committee on Internal Improvements."

Chandler took a long pull on his cigar, rolled the smoke in his mouth for a moment, and exhaled. "I may not always agree with you, you know?"

It was the philosophical Arenz who spoke. "Dr. Chandler, none of us agree all the time. What we need, what the county will need, in truth what the entire state needs, is educated, thoughtful men of goodwill. From all Tom has told of you and from all I have observed today, you are among them."

He then, like Chandler, enjoyed his cigar for just a moment. "Will you join us?"

CHAPTER 27

FEBRUARY 5, 1836

Springfield, Sangamon County, Illinois

The wrought-iron fence surrounding the new capitol building was complete. It was one of the few parts of the building that was. The three men tied their horses to the fence, opened the gate, and walked the fifty yards to the building, admiring it as they did.

"We have clay and sand for brickmaking and limestone to grind for mortar. In fact, a brickmaker is the next business we need."

"No, it's not, Tom. The next business we need is a bank. I've been saying that for years," Arenz interrupted.

Beard just grinned down at him and finished his thought. "But where do they get these huge granite stones? Where is the quarry?"

No one answered. They walked up the stairs and pulled open the nine-foot-tall, but thankfully well-balanced, doors. It was as cold inside as out, the open, unfinished dome seeming to pull cold air in from the sky.

They all looked down the vacant corridor. "Do you know where your friend's office is, Tom?" Chandler asked.

"No, let's just wander." And they did.

"Dr. Chandler, isn't it?" The voice boomed from behind them.

They turned to see an awkwardly tall, thin man with a scruffy black beard who, dressed in a black suit and wearing a tall black stovepipe hat, was coming in the door behind them.

Beard knew he'd seen him but could not remember where, but Chandler immediately left both his friends, and his customary patrician manner, and strode, almost running, his hand extended. "The man who saved my dream," his baritone boomed, almost a scream.

They stood with a long warm handshake, the stunned Beard and Arenz slowly coming behind.

"Tom, Francis, this is the man who, like you, Tom, helped save my land from that damn Thompson fellow. Abraham Lincoln, may I introduce my friends Tom Beard and Francis Arenz of Beardstown?"

After handshakes and hellos all around, Lincoln looked at Arenz. "Unless there are two Francis Arenzes in Beardstown, I owe you a debt of thanks."

Arenz looked even more stunned.

"You are the publisher of the *Beardstown Chronicle*, are you not?" asked Lincoln. "A Whig paper."

"That is my privilege, Mr. Lincoln. And now I understand. You are newly elected to the state legislature."

"Indeed." Lincoln smiled. "Do you gentlemen have a moment to come to my office to talk?"

It was still cold in Lincoln's small office but at least not a tunnel for cold wind when the door was shut.

"What brings you three to our new, and unfinished, state capitol building?" Lincoln asked as he hung his hat on the coat tree in the corner.

"We're politicking, Mr. Lincoln," Arenz responded.

"What is it you'd like to see happen and what help do you need?" the tall man asked.

Chandler and Arenz nodded to Beard who started. "Two things, sir. We're drumming up support for the new county. Cass County I believe it's being tentatively called."

"You want it?" Lincoln asked.

"Very much, sir."

"That one is easy," Lincoln responded. "Even as a freshman here I can tell you, you'll get what you want on that score. Newer and smaller counties have overwhelmingly favorable sentiment here. What's the other one?"

"A road, sir."

Now it was Lincoln's turn to look quizzical. "What road?"

"Mr. Lincoln, most of the deliveries of goods to Springfield come through our river port. That has been substantial traffic and means a lot to Beardstown as well as Springfield. Once this building is finished and the capital is officially moved, that traffic will increase a great deal. We'd like what is now a dirt track turned into a corduroy timber road."

"That is a measure I would support. But that committee is, I believe, about to go to a new Democrat, Murray McConnel from Jacksonville. He will be powerful, and I don't really know the man yet. Don't know what his position will be."

Beard beamed his conventional face-widening smile. "I know General McConnel very well, Mr. Lincoln. He and I traveled across the prairie together in '18. We were on our way to see him when you hailed Dr. Chandler here."

"If you can convince him, I will support a bill," Lincoln said.

"There is one other favor I would like to ask, Abe, if I may?" It was Chandler who spoke.

"Of course, Charles. What is it?"

Chandler passed a long smile to his friends. "I'm not sure you've figured this out yet, Tom, but when I borrowed your money and your mare to race to Springfield and buy the contiguous pieces, it was Abe who saved me. When I'd about killed your mare, it was he who loaned a complete stranger his fresh horse to race to the recorder's office. I already owe you more than I can ever repay, but what I'd like to ask is, Can you make that road run below the river bluff instead of through Virginia?"

Lincoln nodded. "That won't be up to me, but in so far as I have influence, I can't see why not. Now I have a question for you gentlemen. What do you think of railroads?"

Beard responded immediately. "Mr. Lincoln, the river and river traffic have made our town, little city now. We tend to see water as the best, and most reliable, method of moving goods in this country. We don't see that changing."

Lincoln watched Beard the entire time, his face expressionless and his eyes appearing to take in Beard's thoughts as well as his words. "I understand your position, Mr. Beard. And you are right, of course; our river systems are what has given life to everything west of the Appalachians. But the railroads are the future. They will open even more of the world. I don't expect to change your mind on the issue, though. You're what is called, sometimes with affection and sometimes without, 'river rats.'" He turned and looked at Francis Arenz and winked. "But maybe one day I can convince the Whig paper in Central Illinois to support this Whig legislator in expanding the modernity of railroads to other places in the state.

"Now let me point you to General McConnel's office. I'd be grateful if you'd let me know how that conversation goes."

* * * *

"OK, gentlemen," McConnel told the three men. "You have my vote on the formation of Cass County, but you won't need it. The bill has overwhelming support. But about the road we have issues."

"What issues?" Beard asked his old friend.

McConnel's face suddenly went hard, and the eyebrows peaked into red butterflies, a sign Beard knew to mean he would be combative. "I will not only tell you what, but I will be brutally candid. I hate to disappoint an old friend, Tom. It's not personal; it's politics."

All sat quiet with attention concentrated on the brilliant blue eyes. When he spoke McConnel's tenor was shrill.

"I like my new job. I plan to keep it. I'm a Democrat"—he swiveled to make direct and intense eye contact with Francis Arenz—"and you, Mr. Arenz, are a Whig. I don't give a damn that you, personally, are a Whig, but I do care that you are the publisher of a Whig newspaper, the only newspaper between Jacksonville and Springfield. I care very much. In two years, I will run again. And someone will run against me. And whoever that is, you will support—not me. I care about that very much."

Silence fell over the room and hung there like the humidity of a hot August afternoon, going nowhere, just hanging there. Arenz's expression never changed nor did his posture. His eyes seemed to have sunken so far as to become unfathomable and even in the well-lit room appeared black rather than purple. And then a small smile formed.

"General, you are correct. I am a Whig. When I came to America, I found the positions of that party more inclined to my own than those of the other party. The newspaper for which I am editor and publisher naturally follows my inclination. And I am a man of integrity, not one to change public position just for my own convenience. So the paper would, as you say, support your opponent in two years." He paused in a full stop. When he spoke it was to say, "If it were still in operation."

McConnel's expression didn't change, but both Beard and Chandler turned to look directly at their friend.

"If I close the *Beardstown Chronicle*, General McConnel, will you give us our road?" Arenz asked in a quiet monotone.

* * * *

They walked out of McConnel's office and back down the drafty, cold corridor toward Lincoln's.

"Francis, you don't need to do this for me or Beardstown," Beard pleaded.

Francis Arenz's eyes twinkled purple from their depths. "I'm not doing it for you or Beardstown, Tom."

"Then why are you doing it?"

"I told you long ago; Beardstown was not large enough to support a newspaper. That it would lose money and I needed money to let that happen. Well, I don't have the money to both buy Enos Marsh out and run a money-losing newspaper. I'd rather be your new partner."

CHAPTER 28

NOVEMBER 23, 1838

Beardstown, Cass County, Illinois

Almost one hundred souls were packed into the dining room. Thomas Beard had invited them all. The tables had been pushed together to form one long one. But it wasn't enough. Martha Chandler had allowed him to have her banquet table brought down, and Charlotte Bell had added hers. Other friends had loaned smaller tables. They had all been strung together to form three long rows extending the length of the room. Amanda had ordered long linen tablecloths and one hundred settings of china and silver plate last summer. All had arrived before the river froze. Beard had also instructed her to buy two chandeliers and enough candles to fill them and keep them lit the entire evening and into the night. The fire was roaring the warmth and light of greeting before the first guest arrived. Arenz had managed to assemble a small orchestra of German musicians. Beard would have rather had a banjo player, but Francis had insisted that for a soiree this large, classical music was required. On the frontier, everyone knew only the German community could provide that.

Charlotte, grown huge with time, had remained a woman of boundless energy. Since her daughter had left Beard, Charlotte insisted on being his hostess when one was required. She had spent most of the week decorating the entire room, boughs red with holly berries, evergreen table decorations, as well as sprigs of mistletoe hanging high and hidden, but poorly.

Beard insisted Amanda and Jim were guests and had hired in help to cook and serve, but Amanda would not allow the banquet to be prepared except under her supervision. And Jim seemed to feel the same way about the bar. Beard knew he could not stop them working, but he also knew, when he insisted, they would take off their aprons and join his guests. Beard had purchased yams and potatoes by the bushel, hams by the dozen, and enough cornmeal to make bread for a company of infantry, as well as pots of butter and honey. He had also hired a couple of hunters to bring him a dozen of the biggest birds they could kill.

This banquet would be the biggest celebration Central Illinois had ever seen—a celebration of the incredible bounty God had heaped upon them all in the past two decades.

The musicians arrived early, ostensibly to tune their instruments, but with their knowing the bar would be open, he suspected other motives. Charlotte and Amanda were in ceaseless motion. Jim was calmly laying mugs and glasses on the bar and making certain beer kegs and barrels of whiskey were where they could be easily reached. The aromas from the kitchen not only made his mouth water but also made his mind wander to winter celebrations of bounty in the Connecticut Reserve from his youth.

And then the noise and laughter started. His first guests were those with the longest path of travel. The Chandlers' sleigh, pulled by two horses still prancing after pulling all afternoon, slid around the corner and into the livery. It would be far too late for them to return after the party. They would stay for the night.

Big Dan Bell walked in, looking shy and awkward. "Dan," Beard boomed, "I have never seen you in a frock coat. Now stop being sheepish and get yourself a drink. Jim, pour him a mug, not a glass, of whiskey. He looks like a man who needs it."

And soon they were all there, every friend Beard had ever come to love in twenty years. Every one save the fiery Mo McConnel and the calm Enos Marsh. He so wished both were.

As the crowd of revelers grew, so did the warmth of the laughter. The band started to play soft and formal music in the background.

Within an hour, there was not a mood in the room that was not pure joy. Beard stepped up onto an empty chair, stemmed glass in one hand and dinner knife in the other. He struck the glass with the edge of the knife, producing a clear, pure tone that couldn't be ignored. He did it twice more, and all turned silent and looked toward him.

"My dear, dear friends. It is time for dinner. Grab another drink at the bar and then come join me." Beard took his seat in the middle of the table, his back to the fire.

When all had taken their seats and Amanda had all the kitchen help rushing in with platters of food, Beard rose again, but this time not on the chair. Again, he used the empty glass and knife to pause conversation and get almost one hundred souls to turn their eyes to him.

"Friends," he boomed, "I have invited you here so that we may give thanks together for the bounty of this land. My father told me that George Washington declared, even in the midst of war, a day to give thanks and that the year after the war the Congress did so as well. I do not know what has happened to that fine tradition. It seems to have slipped away. But not for us, friends, not for us."

There was a roar of approval from his guests. He stood silent, waiting for it to cease.

"I have been here twenty years. The only one in this room here longer than me is the man who made me welcome, made all of us welcome, our friend Chaubenee." Beard looked down at the big man sitting across the long table from him. He motioned him to rise. Chaubenee did not. He motioned again. Still he did not. "Chaubenee, I will not go on until you rise and receive the thanks and gratitude you deserve for letting this all become true."

The room applauded. Then there was the tap of a foot. And then of others until the demanding chorus got what it wanted. Chaubenee rose and nodded to all.

"I do believe you've turned red, Chaubenee."

The room erupted in laughter, and Chaubenee joined in.

"Since the day this man welcomed me with the enigmatic phrase 'I've been expecting you,' the first words he spoke to me, all has been progress. Hard work, but progress and prosperity. And during this year, 1838, perhaps the most of all. Look around you. Who among us is not finding what it was we came here seeking? And by your individual efforts you have made a community. And such a community. We now have services for three different churches. Children can walk to school, and soon"—he looked at Reverend Horn—"we may have to build a building just for school and let the city hire a full-time teacher."

Horn did not smile, but others in the room gave thunderous applause.

"We have a town. We have a town government. We have the structures to make these decisions, do these things. And we have a county of our own, Cass County, and, by vote of that county, we are the county seat. We will soon need a courthouse."

"You gonna build it, Tom?" a voice shouted from the back.

"I'll make everyone in this room a deal. If Francis agrees with me, and I think he will, we'll contribute the lot."

Arenz said nothing but nodded approval, and the crowd roared.

"And if you all will build the courthouse, I'll build the jail."

Applause filled the room.

"Speaking of which, we may need one. I don't know if you've all heard, but our first grand jury met last week. There were thirty indictments—twenty-seven for keeping a gaming house and two for keeping a house of ill repute." He looked at Reverend Horn again. "You've got a lot of work to do, Reverend, or I'm going to have to spend more money than I'd planned to build a very large jail."

Even the sober Horn chuckled.

"Let me tell you what else we've gotten this year. Thanks to the fine work of Dr. Chandler and the great sacrifice of Francis Arenz, bids to build a corduroy road from here to Springfield are out." He nodded toward tall, thin Charlie Knapp. "May I tell them, Charlie?"

After a nod of approval, Beard continued. "Charlie Knapp's firm has been awarded the contract to provide logs for the twelve miles between here and Bluff Springs. Oh, I forgot to tell. The selected route is through Bluff Springs, right under the Chandlers' home, not through Virginia."

More applause.

"And I have saved the best for last. Francis always has a list of things this town needs next. And he seems to tick them off one at a time. And aside from his newspaper losing too much money, he's always succeeded. The one thing I know he wants for us but hasn't yet managed to get is a bank."

Beard looked down into the deep-set quiet purple eyes of his partner sitting beside him.

"I've got an early Christmas present for you, Francis. I received a letter from Assemblyman General McConnel two days ago. The State of Illinois will be allowing Beardstown a license for a state-chartered bank."

It was the only time Beard had ever seen Francis Arenz startled.

When the applause stopped, Arenz rose to his feet. "You all know Tom and I are partners in this venture of making a prosperous and refined place for all of you to raise your families. But I think you also know we each have our own separate enterprises. And not only that, but we seem to have separate political affiliations. So sometimes he surprises me, as he just did. But sometimes I surprise him as I'm about to."

Now it was Beard who looked cautious.

"Tom, since you laid out the last fifty-seven blocks within the charter of our city, you haven't had enough to keep you busy, just running the ferry and this hotel. So, I've found new work for you."

Every breath was still with anticipation. Neither seemed able to exhale.

"Beardstown will have a US post office as soon as we can build it. And you, Tom Beard, will be its first postmaster."

Again, all stood and applauded and, for one of the very few times in his life, Tom Beard had nothing to say.

* * * *

Tom Beard sat by the window, many of his guests having already gone into the fresh snow that had gently fallen all during their celebration. Charles Chandler had requested a waltz of the band. They were quick to comply. Chandler had taken his wife's hand and the two, looking for all the world like they would be in place at Schönbrunn Palace, waltzed elegantly around the floor of what was otherwise a frontier, riverfront bar.

Beard sipped slowly at the brandy he had learned to enjoy. Life was perfect when he just let it be, and for now he was. Francis Arenz, brandy snifter in hand, walked easily toward them.

"May I join you, Tom?"

"Francis, of course."

"Tom, I don't mean to add gloom to a perfect evening, but I've a question. We can discuss it later, but now may be a good time."

"Shoot."

"What did you have to agree to in order to get the State of Illinois to give a bank charter?"

"Whole bunch of things Mo tells me are conventional. Mostly, we'll have to raise some $20,000 in deposits before we can open, and we'll have to agree to maintain a certain percentage of them and not loan them out. Mostly, that's it."

"Mostly?" Arenz's word came out slowly.

"Mostly. Yes, mostly," Beard responded.

"Tell me the rest. The part you don't want to tell."

Beard exhaled and set his snifter on the table. "The bank has to agree to buy $50,000 worth of bonds in the Meredosia and Jacksonville Railroad Company. But before you complain, payment of the bonds will be guaranteed by the State of Illinois."

The purple eyes sank deep into the brows. "Tom, I'm not worried about their solvency. I'm worried that we are funding a competitor. What is the bromide—selling them the rope they will hang us with?"

Beard removed a cigar from his pocket, bit off the end, lit it, and took a very long time to get it fully fired. "Francis, we are a river town. We are prosperous because we handle freight for the center of the state, mostly Springfield, from the river. The Meredosia and Jacksonville does not threaten that."

"It may, Tom. Meredosia is a better port than we are. It's right across the river from St. Louis. And a boat bound for St. Louis just diverts across the river, and they are sending freight into Illinois."

"Francis, what you say about the port at Meredosia is true. But that line runs to Jacksonville. Nowhere else. We handle no freight going from here to Jacksonville. I truly don't see the worry. Suppose, just suppose, someone in Springfield thinks of bringing freight from Meredosia to Jacksonville by rail, and then Jacksonville to Springfield by wagon. Twice the handling and three kinds of equipment—boat, rail, and wagon. That is just not going to happen."

Arenz nodded agreement. "No, that won't. I agree. But what if they extend that line from Jacksonville to Springfield. What then?"

Beard held the cigar over the floor and let it burn as he pondered, his eyes staring up at the candles flickering on one of the chandeliers. "I've heard nothing of a plan to do that. Have you?"

"No. But I fear it."

Tom puffed at his cigar, head back in his chair, watching the smoke change patterns as it dissolved into the candlelight cast by the chandeliers. But he did not speak.

Finally, it was Francis Arenz who broke the silence. "Do you miss her, Tom?"

Beard continued to puff and did not look down as he spoke. "I wanted to build an empire, Francis. I wanted this more than I wanted her."

Francis seemed to know better than to speak, to just let Tom answer at his own pace. "That's what she wanted, too, you know. To build an empire."

The silence remained peaceful, but it remained.

"The empire Sara wanted did not fit into my plan," Tom finally said, his eyes focused firmly on Francis's. Tom extended his arm and waved it slowly until it had taken in the whole room. "What Sara wanted to build would have created a great deal of money, but would not have been welcomed by all. We wouldn't be celebrating like this if she'd gotten her way."

The silence returned.

Arenz sipped his brandy and spoke again. "So she settled for attention and perhaps adventure instead."

Tom took the cigar from his mouth and ground its glowing end out in the ashtray. He did not look up. "I never ask Dan or Charlotte about her. I have no idea of where she is or exactly what she is doing, but I'd bet a lot of money you're wrong. Sara did not settle for anything. Somewhere she is building an empire of her own design."

CHAPTER 29

JUNE 22, 1839

Beardstown, Cass County, Illinois

Chaubenee sat on his horse, looking at a dozen wagons pulled up beside the largest, and last, of the sepulchral mounds. There were at least thirty-five workmen, shovels in hand, throwing what remained of the mound into the wagons. He recognized only one of the men, a man he'd met only briefly at Beard's Thanksgiving celebration seven months before. His name was Henry Meyer. The big Indian merely sat looking, a far-off expression in his eyes, watching Meyer and his crew profane the sacred.

Meyer looked up and gave the big Indian a friendly wave, said something to one of his men, and turned to walk toward him, a large smile on his face.

"Hello. It's Chaubenee, isn't it? I'm Hank Meyer. Tom Beard introduced us at his big dinner."

Chaubenee looked down at the man, a man of middle height with a sunburned bald head, a bulbous red nose, bloodshot eyes, and a smile displaying two blackening teeth. "Yes. Tom introduced us."

"When you see Tom tell him I'm leveling the last of these mounds. He'll be able to sell the lots as flat land when I'm done." His tone suggested he was doing a favor.

"Do you know this is sacred ground?" Chaubenee asked, looking down.

"Didn't know that. Sacred to whom?"

"Long-ago people."

Meyer's smile was genuine. "Well, I'm grateful for the work they did. They're going to make an elevated base for the two new grain elevators I'm building at the north of town. Enable me to get the grain stored high enough for gravity feed onto the barges. Very helpful."

Chaubenee said nothing and turned to go.

"Oh, Chaubenee. One of my guys found something here Tom might find interesting. Might even want as part of the history of his town."

The friendly man dug into his coat pocket and pulled out something. He handed it up to Chaubenee who extended his hand to accept the offering.

Chaubenee opened his palm and looked into it. It contained a small crude silver cross, a few silver beads, and over one hundred beads of jet. The beads and the cross were all drilled, the remainder of a thin rawhide thread still holding them together.

"You'll see Beard before I will, I'm sure. Give it to him for me and tell him where I found it. May interest him."

Chaubenee put the contents in his pocket and turned, slowly walking his horse away.

On the way back to the hotel he passed dozens of homes, some of split log, some of plank, some of new brick. And all with fine green lawns. He sat erect and did not try stopping the tears that came into his eyes.

CHAPTER 30

FEBRUARY 17, 1840

Beardstown, Cass County, Illinois

Nigel Hoskins did not like Beardstown. He did not like Illinois. In fact, he wasn't certain he liked America. The only city in this godforsaken wilderness he'd vaguely enjoyed was Boston, and even that had been forced upon him. It was his employer, Merchants Trading Bank of London, that had forced it upon him. He had joined the firm immediately upon commencement from Oxford and after six years with the bank, learning his craft, had been shipped by them to what his wife, Victoria, still referred to as "the colonies." Nigel was to be the bank's representative to trading-firm clients in that city. It was a position that other young men may have seen as an opportunity to not only represent a major London financial house in a new venture but to be free of the constraints of superiors as well. But Nigel had seen it as a demotion, being removed, as it were, from the corridors of power. And it was seen by his bride of three years as being removed from society, even civilization.

She worried what sort of education they would get for their two young boys. But they really had no choice, and so they had gone.

Perhaps Nigel's attitude showed in his work. Or perhaps it was his natural hesitance to extend himself personally, or beyond what he saw as his authority, that made it so. Whatever it was, the vast resources of Merchants Trading Bank aside, new clients did not come to the firm in Boston. Loans, profits, and client base did not grow under Nigel's leadership. He could see failure on the horizon, and the thought of dismissal was moved from unthinkable to a daily conversation among the voices in his head.

Then he met Nicholas Biddle, the head of the Bank of the United States. Biddle was, he thought, the most sophisticated and urbane man he had met in his three years in the US. Aside from Biddle's being president of America's only national bank, his dramatic and public disagreements with President Andrew Jackson and his refusal to back down had made him a figure of international reputation.

Hoskins saw in Biddle an opportunity and had eventually suggested his services might be available if Biddle had need of a properly educated and trained international banker. And then the offer came, but when it did, it was not the offer Nigel had hoped, nor expected. It was not with Bank of the United States, which, as Biddle explained, was not the safest place right now for any young banker, the president having publicly stated his intention to kill it. Biddle thought not but also thought it best that if Hoskins were to rise in America, he should come to understand trade west of the Alleghenies, the growth engine of America. He would introduce Hoskins to the West's largest bank, the Bank of St. Louis. There Hoskins would learn "the idiosyncrasies of trade in America. Not the international, oceanic trade but domestic trade in the great American river system," Biddle had said, "and once you learn that and the Bank of the United States has been rechartered and is secure, perhaps there will be a place for you with us." How could he say no?

So off they went to St. Louis, and they hated it even more. Victoria most of all. It was hot, wet, muddy, and diseased. The population was almost entirely male and almost entirely drunk. Any of the women who were not whores were plain and without social graces or sophistication. Only the boys loved it. It was rowdy and free, and they could be the same as well. And they were. Victoria, small, thin, face perpetually pointed into a pout, stood, sweat soaking her clothes and causing her forehead to glisten. "They are turning into little savages."

And Nigel liked it no better. He had ever been large. His natural tendency to corpulence had given way to jowls, a double chin, and protruding belly, and he was only in his early thirties. He pined for the cool weather, even the fog, of London. If the heat and humidity were uncomfortable for his wife, they were, to him, unbearable. And if he had failed to relate to the traders and businessmen in Boston, here they were anathema. He hated them and it showed.

His hope Biddle would pull him off the frontier and back to Boston or Philadelphia crashed with a simple newspaper headline, "Jackson Refuses to Extend Bank's Charter." Failed in London and Boston and now in this pigsty, Hoskins was sliding steadily downward on the pole of professional success, so when the offer came to be president of the newly chartered Beardstown State Bank, he felt he had no other option.

They had given him a new home that they considered large. It was brick, three bedrooms upstairs, and a receiving area, dining room, and study on the first floor. The whole was raised some four feet off the ground to keep the house from flooding in the spring, with a wide staircase leading from the street to a veranda that ran across the width of the house. The kitchen was out the back door.

"It is no more than a cottage," Victoria complained, her lips pursed into their normal pout.

Nigel had towered above her, mopping his flushed face.

His bank building was new and made of imported stone to look impressive. It wasn't. It was small with only two barred teller windows on either side of the lobby. At the rear where the lobby ended there was a short hallway. A large floor-mounted vault was encased behind bars on one side of the hall. On the other side of the hall were two rooms. One was for records. The other, at the end of the hall, was his private office that, in addition to access from the hallway, had a door leading to the alley at the rear of the building.

Nigel Hoskins sat behind his desk, studying his books. His bank was solvent and prosperous. It was his first professional success since coming to this cursed continent. Including the founders' deposits of $20,000, the bank had deposits of $117,211. They held $50,000 in railroad bonds and had $60,111 in loans due. Most of those were to small local businesses, which Nigel hadn't known how to value, but they were loans the founders encouraged him to make. That left a reserve of just over $7,000 in bills and specie currency held in that big iron safe across the hall. That was the 15 percent reserve their charter from the state required. Well, not quite. He held no reserve against the founders' deposits or the $50,000 in railroad bonds. Bond payments were guaranteed by the State of Illinois, so there was no risk involved.

* * * *

Beard sat at his usual table in the window. He was watching the usually unflappable Francis Arenz rush, virtually run, up the hotel steps.

Arenz burst through the door and flew straight to Beard's table, waving a paper in his hand that he threw down on the table. "We're fucked!"

That Beard was stunned showed all over his face. "Francis, I've never heard you swear before, much less that."

"Read it. Yesterday's paper from Springfield," the small dapper man demanded.

Beard hurriedly unfolded the paper and pressed down the front page. The headline screamed out at him: "Governor Signs Bill Extending Meredosia and Jacksonville Railroad to Springfield." Beard's expression didn't change. He looked around the room until he caught Amanda's eye. "Amanda, bring Mr. Arenz a cup of coffee with a shot of brandy. Francis, you're usually the calm one. We've changed roles here."

"Thomas, this will destroy our city."

"Calm, Francis, calm. We have our new road. It will take at least two years to build that line. We'll continue to prosper until then. And who knows what will happen in the meantime. Besides, how are they going to pay for it?"

"It's farther down in the article when you read it. More bonds, and all guaranteed by the state," Arenz answered.

Amanda waddled to them, a steaming mug of coffee in one hand and a shot glass of amber-colored liquid in the other, her white teeth beaming joy and goodwill. "Mr. Arenz, I don't know what your troubles are, but perhaps Gospel wisdom is in order here, 'Let the troubles of the day be sufficient unto themselves.'"

Arenz smiled for the first time since his arrival. "I can always count on you for wisdom, Amanda."

"No," she said. "You count on Matthew, not Amanda," and turned and walked away.

"Francis, she's right. Lots can happen. Any number of ways for this rail extension to fail."

Francis Arenz looked up, and even with the morning light on his face, his eyes showed no purple, just black. "That won't save us, Tom."

Beard turned his chin sideways and pursed his lips into a quizzical frown. "Why not?"

"Our bank holds $50,000 of those bonds. If the railroad fails, our bank fails."

Beard's chin came back square, and his face registered contentment. "Those are guaranteed by the state. They're sure to keep paying no matter what."

CHAPTER 31

AUGUST 5, 1840

Springfield, Sangamon County, Illinois

Governor Thomas Carlin had his Irish up, and when his Irish was up the red widow's peak, which his middle part seemed to emphasize, became a red arrow pointing to his eyes, which were flashing rage.

"McConnel, fix this Goddamn mess you've gotten us, the State of Illinois and me, into. And I want it fixed now."

Thomas Carlin wasn't the only one who had his Irish up, and General Murray McConnel's eyebrows now pointed up as sharply as Carlin's widow's peak pointed down. The two red arrows aimed at each other.

"Don't call this my mess. I didn't authorize the extension of that line to Springfield, and I sure as hell didn't sign the legislation extending the state's guarantee to pay those bonds. Who was it that did those things, Governor?"

Carlin's long jaw and pointed chin came up aimed at McConnel, like a dagger raised to strike. "And who,

General"—he hurled the title like a spear—"is chair of the Committee on Internal Improvements and has been for my entire term? And who, General, promoted the Meredosia and Jacksonville Railroad in the first place? River port to his hometown. Who?"

"And it worked, too. Didn't it, Governor? Jacksonville is the most prosperous city in the state. And the damn bonds were paid regularly by the M&J until someone wanted it extended to a capital that is so new it has no freight save the wide asses of politicians."

The governor turned his back to McConnel and walked to the window running almost to the ceiling of his office and looked out at the moonlight marking a path across the capitol lawn. He killed the remainder of his whiskey, set the glass on the windowsill, and stood, clenched fingers tucked into the small of his back. Without turning he said, in his usual well-controlled tenor voice, "Get that railroad back to work, Mo. We need revenues from them to make those bond payments."

McConnel walked around the governor's large desk and stood beside him by the window, looking at the same fascinating glimmering path across the lawn. "I would if I could, Tom. But neither I, nor you, nor anybody else can bring life into that corpse. They have no money in the bank. They could not afford to buy coal for their boilers, much less pay crews for even a week's labor. The best any financial house could do would be to put gold coins in the eyes of that corpse to pay the way of the Meredosia and Jacksonville Railroad across the river Styx."

Carlin didn't turn, just stood looking out the window.

McConnel put his arm around his friend's shoulders. "There is no money, Tom. And worse yet, there will be no money from the federal government. The president is our friend, but he has no time to help us before he goes. He'll not only be gone in six months . . ."

For the first time since walking to the window Carlin looked at him.

"He'll lose, Tom. Harrison is going to beat him and beat the pants off him in Illinois. We are on our own," McConnel finished.

Carlin looked back out the window and as though addressing the moon said, "Then what will we do?"

"We have to make the bond payments," McConnel responded.

Still looking dreamily outside, the governor said, "You know the budget as well as I. There isn't enough money. There is not going to be enough money."

McConnel took his arm down. "We should have thought of that when we extended the guarantee."

There was a long silence. A cloud slipped in front of the moon, seeming to break its spell. "I asked before: What do we do?"

"We raise all the taxes we can raise. We pray for something to change, because if it does not, we become the first state in the Union ever to declare bankruptcy."

CHAPTER 32

DECEMBER 4, 1840

Beardstown, Cass County, Illinois

The evening was beautiful and serene. The storm had stopped, leaving only a new layer of pure, clean snow behind. Hopefully the last before spring. Wind had ushered the storm clouds south, their passing leaving nothing to impede the light of the nearly full moon allowing the sparkle of the new snow to glitter on every street, building, tree, wagon, and, most of all, the frozen river. All seemed so peaceful that none were left with any sense of work they might have to do. Only a fool would do other than appreciate this gift from a benevolent Creator. Even Jim had stopped work and joined the other three at their usual table by the window.

Francis Arenz stepped away from the table for a moment and returned, a bottle in his hand. "Gentlemen, may I pour us each a shot of Mr. Beard's finest sour mash to toast the evening?"

Beard, extending his empty glass toward Arenz, answered, "You may indeed, Francis; you may indeed. But instead of a toast to the evening, I propose each of us toast to the thing that brings them the most happiness this evening. And we'll start with you, Francis. To what do you toast?"

"Ah," said the small German as he finished pouring into all four glasses, "for me that is easy. As Beardstown's leading Whig, I am brought most happiness by the election of our nation's first Whig president, William Henry Harrison."

"To Harrison," added Jim and Beard.

Chaubenee neither spoke nor lifted his glass.

As the other three glasses came back down to the table, Arenz looked toward Chaubenee, a quizzical expression on his face. "You do not join us?"

The big Indian looked at his companion with an expression of sadness in his eyes. "I mean no offense to my old friend, but I cannot join a toast to your Harrison. He is a bad man."

Arenz's face became even more puzzled. "How do you know that?"

Chaubenee let a small smile show. "I met him once. And in my meeting, he lied. To my face. He is, your new president, not only a liar but a cheat."

Arenz now looked puzzled. "Where? Where did you meet him?"

"At Grouseland, the mansion from which he ruled the Indiana Territory. I fought him many times. He is a brave warrior and a very good one. But I have nothing good to say of his character. I only hope, for the sake of the nation, that he does not govern long. But let me not ruin the mood. Pour another shot for those who just drank and let me propose a toast to what makes me happy tonight," Chaubenee said.

Arenz picked up the bottle and poured another round.

They all raised their glasses as Chaubenee raised his. "I am the only Potawatomi of my generation who will be allowed the privilege of living out his life and dying in the place where he was born. That is in large part to my friend Thomas Beard. It is to him I propose this toast. To Beard."

"To Beard" was the chorus, and they followed.

"Francis, pour again," Beard commanded. "It is my turn."

Arenz did and Beard raised his glass. "I do not toast the failure of the Meredosia and Jacksonville Railroad, but I do toast to the success of the river transportation model. The model on which this city was founded and the prosperous present it has produced. The failure of the M&J has only proved river transportation is not only the way of the past and the present but also the way of the future."

Beard raised his glass higher and looked at each of his companions. "To river rats."

When the glasses were down, it was Arenz who spoke. "This seems to be a night of differences as well as joy. Thomas, I agree our river model has worked. And I agree the M&J has failed. But I don't agree future rail will fail. They failed not for reasons of efficiency but because of bad economics. Rail will be back, and it will not only succeed but will supersede the river trade. Next time, Thomas, we must be part of that, or our city will fail."

Before Beard could respond, Jim, one of his rare smiles on his face, spoke. "Pour again, Mr. Arenz. I have a toast to my own happiness. I will let you two men of commerce battle on a less joyous night."

"You're right, Jim." Arenz picked up the bottle and poured into their glasses again.

Jim picked up his glass and held it high. "I was born a slave. My Amanda was born a slave. Of all the men of my race, in America, only just a few, a very, very few, die free. I will not only be allowed to die free but with a good woman, good work, and good friends. My toast is to a good life. My life."

"To Jim and his life," all exploded.

Jim added with a smile, "I know most whites think slavery is all right, but I'm blessed by the Lord to have run into you few who do not think so."

"Jim, you sure you know what whites think of slavery?" It was Beard who asked.

Jim merely looked at him.

Beard continued. "I've heard the story of the abolitionist who stole you and your old master who came back to reclaim you. Your master would have beat the abolitionist to death, I hear, had Marsh not stopped him. You know there are those who would abolish slavery. Give their lives to do so. You know there are Southerners who would kill, and I suppose die, to keep slavery. I suppose you know that?"

Jim nodded.

"But, Jim, those are not the only thoughts whites have. You know McConnel?"

Again, Jim nodded.

"He hates slavery. He's not really an abolitionist. Oh, he'd like to abolish slavery, but it's not a moral cause with him. He thinks it gives the South an unfair advantage in growing crops. He's a Democrat. But his view is closer to Francis's, the Whigs' view. Most Democrats think more like Illinois's secretary of state, a guy named Douglas, Stephen Douglas. He has a concept he calls 'popular sovereignty,' which says each and every state should decide on its own about that question. And there are a lot of Americans who think for every new slaveholding state, we should let in a free one. Sorta 'you get one; I get one.'"

Jim suddenly looked very concerned. "So could Illinois change its mind and allow slavery?"

Beard picked up the bottle and topped off each of the glasses. "No, Jim, it could not."

"Why are you so sure?"

Beard nodded understanding. "Back in the beginning it was the State of Virginia that owned all the land north of the

Ohio, all the way to Canada and from the Appalachians to the Mississippi. At one point they gave up their claim to it and gave it to the whole of the US. But on one condition. That no state ever made out of any of that land would allow legal slavery."

Arenz abruptly sat forward and thundered, "Virginia did that?"

Beard nodded. "Virginia did that. Slave state Virginia did that. Plantation-dependent Virginia did that. Surprising, isn't it?"

"Stunning," said Arenz.

Beard turned from Arenz to Jim. "Jim, even people who depended on slavery to make themselves rich knew it was wrong. Most still do. I don't know how it's going to happen, but America will work this out."

* * * *

The following morning, the line from the front door of the bank ran halfway down the block. It had started when the bank opened its doors at ten o'clock and had grown since then. And they had all wanted the same thing. They wanted their deposits back. They were all small deposits; none of the founders had asked to cash out. If so much as one of them had, however, the vault would have been drawn dry.

Over the course of the morning cash in the vault had dwindled. Hoskins knew they were down to less than $4,000. He had tried to assure all in line to stay calm, and that the bank still had plenty of money. But there were two things that worried him. He would have to close at three o'clock, and as long as the crowd didn't panic and allowed him to lock the door, he'd be fine—for now. That was one worry. Tomorrow was the other. If this happened again tomorrow, he'd be out of cash. Then what would he do?

Hoskins let himself into the safe and took out cash for each teller. He needed to ensure they all had enough to last until he got back. Then he went into his office and let himself out the back door. Once out, the big man perspiring even in the light spring heat made his way to Francis Arenz's land office.

When he walked inside, there were two people besides Arenz in the office. He struggled to keep his voice calm. When he caught Arenz's eye, he allowed his concern to show.

"Good afternoon, Mr. Arenz. I hope you're well today."

The fact that he'd addressed him as "Mr. Arenz" let Francis know something was wrong. "Gentlemen, this is Mr. Nigel Hoskins, the president of Beardstown State Bank. Presuming our negotiations are successful, you may well need his assistance in a day or two. Will you excuse us for a moment? I'd forgotten Nigel was coming by. We won't be long."

The two men walked into Arenz's office and closed the door.

"Francis, have you been outside today?" Before he could answer, Hoskins continued. "There has been a line outside all day long. Withdrawing. We're down to less than $4,000 on hand."

"You've had almost $14,000 in withdrawals?" Arenz's voice was startled. "Which of the founders has withdrawn?"

"None," Hoskins answered.

"How could you have gone through almost $14,000 in withdrawals from small depositors?"

"We haven't, Francis. There has been some $3,000 withdrawn."

Arenz's deep-set eyes turned to black. "Nigel, we have almost $120,000 in deposits. Reserves should be $18,000. Where are they?"

The big man's face went red and sweat appeared at the folds of the tissue at his neck. "I've not been holding reserves on the founder's money nor against the state bonds. We had $7,000 in reserves this morning."

Arenz's eyes glowed anger, but his face was impassive. "I heard the state was going bankrupt yesterday, but I didn't think it would cause a run on the bank. It is public knowledge that the bank had been required to buy railroad bonds to obtain our charter, but I didn't think our customers would link the two so quickly."

Hoskins continued to sweat profusely and was now wiping his forehead with a pocket handkerchief. "Francis, the queue has been orderly. Normal closing time is in thirty-five minutes. I am concerned they will become disruptive when I attempt to close the doors. I need you to reassure the good citizens of Beardstown that the bank, of which you are a founder and officer, will be open tomorrow so we are able to close."

Arenz rose, took his hat from the hall tree, and said, "Let's go."

As they walked through the lobby he said, "Gentlemen, I fear I've got to go away for an hour. May we continue conversation tomorrow?" And without waiting for an answer walked out the front door.

When they were within a block of the bank, Hoskins turned to avoid the line and approach the bank from the alley.

"No," Arenz said with no other comment. He continued straight, and after they crossed the intersection and reached the waiting line, he stopped to chat with the man in the rear. "Hello, Ernst," he offered to the man, and looked at his watch. "Ernst, the bank closes in twenty-five minutes. Not sure the line will get you there. Might be better if you come back tomorrow. We'll open at ten o'clock."

Saying similar reassuring words to all he knew caused the line to dissipate toward the end. When his watch showed three o'clock, Arenz allowed the next two persons in line to squeeze in and assured all remaining they would open at ten o'clock tomorrow as usual. Then he took the large brass key from his pocket and locked the front door.

When the business of the day was complete and the tellers' cash drawers all reconciled, Hoskins let all his employees out the front door. He made one last cash-withdrawal slip, which he duly recorded, showing his modest savings withdrawn.

* * * *

That night, Jim was sweeping the floor of the now-deserted bar. Chaubenee sat quietly smoking his cigar. Beard and Arenz looked into the reflecting pools that were their drinks.

"We're out of money, Tom. It's the first time since I came to America I've not known what to do." Only the top of his head showed as he spoke. He raised his head slowly, his eyes showing no color but black in the night. "What do we do?"

Beard looked up, pulled his shot glass to his lips, tilted his head, and drained it. His head stayed back for a moment as though he were enjoying the burn of the whiskey going down his throat. When he brought his eyes back down to meet Arenz's, the weariness was gone. They were resolute. "You have done all you can for today. Tomorrow the work is for me. Your work starts again the day after."

"What work?" Arenz asked.

"Beardstown and Cass County will need money. New sources of money. You are the politician, so it will be for you to convince the city council and your fellow bounty-board members to raise them. We must. People will need help for the next couple of years, until this passes. That will be your part."

"Who shall we tax? Who has money?"

"You and I, Francis, and men like us. Property owners and businessmen. A license for each business. Suggest the ferry needs a license to land on this side of the river. Make it three or four times what I pay Schuyler County. That will set an example. Then smaller license fees to all other businesses. And let's tax property. A tax for lot values. Those methods will tax those who still have money."

"Tom, if we tax property, there will be those with no cash. They may go on the county auction list for courthouse sale. You sure we should do that?"

Beard nodded. "You're right. We need the revenue, but we'll have to find a way to stop foreclosures. I'll have to go talk to McConnel. The state may have to help there. But for now, Francis, that is your work. Raise some money."

Arenz hung his head low again and didn't speak for a long time. The small man of great dreams and intellect spoke into his glass. "I'm embarrassed, Tom. So embarrassed. I caused this. My hubris. I wanted this bank, and I forced it and financial failure upon us."

Beard snorted. "You make yourself bigger than you are, Francis. This is not about you. This is all over the state. It was the State of Illinois that wanted too much, not you. Every town in the state will be like us before the month is out."

Arenz raised his head but not his shoulders and looked at him from under his brows. "I've always been the smartest. Others may have failed, but my job was to protect this place, not destroy it. I will retire from public life. I have a few acres down by Indian Creek. A small community of mostly German farmers is gathering there. I will retire to the country."

"Retire if you must, but first you must help me clean up this mess. Only then may you retire."

Arenz nodded as with consent.

"Gentlemen, it has been a very long day. I'm going to bed." Beard rose and walked to the stairs. As he got there he looked to Jim in the bar. "Jim, have the hay wagon hitched before dawn for me tomorrow. And I'll need you to come with me."

Beard rose, took two steps toward the staircase, stopped, and turned back to Jim. "And, Jim, before you go to bed, would you go to Mr. Hoskins's house and tell him to meet me here at six o'clock in the morning."

* * * *

In a low line along the eastern horizon, the black was showing a hint of giving way to the grey of predawn when the wagon pulled out of the stable yard behind the hotel and rolled slowly onto Main Street, Jim at the reins and Tom Beard sitting quietly beside him on the lazy board with a very nervous Nigel Hoskins between them.

"Jim, when you get down to the bank, get the horses up on the boardwalk so the bed of the wagon is pushed against the doors of the bank. I don't want any space between the wagon bed and the bank's front doors."

Jim just nodded. When they reached the end of the block, he demanded the team step up onto the boardwalk and pull the wagon up behind them and then along the walk. When he reached the bank building, Jim slowed the team and forced them to pull the wagon ever closer to the building until he could hear its wood bed scraping along the bank's stone facade.

"Stop just as soon as the front of the wagon passes the doors."

Jim did.

Beard stood and stretched, enjoying the early-morning cool and the sky now beginning to show blue in the east. He stretched one long leg over the seat and stepped onto the wagon boards behind. "Jim, just unhook the team and walk them back to the stable. I'll be here awhile."

As he watched Jim walking the team away, Beard sat down on the wagon bed, his long legs dangling above the street. "Nigel, no reason to sit there by yourself. Might as well come back here and join me."

He sat and he waited. It wouldn't be long.

Just as the yellow curve of the sun rose over the horizon, the first of them arrived. He was a short man with heavy rounded shoulders riding a huge horse that was surely more accustomed to a plow harness than a saddle. Jim studied him coming. As soon as he was close enough to distinguish the face, his name came to Beard. It was Bernwick, Moses Bernwick. A farmer with forty acres just south of town.

"Morning, Moses," Beard called in his most friendly tone.

Bernwick didn't reply until his horse was standing next to Beard, their boots almost touching. "Morning, Tom." Bernwick nodded perfunctorily toward Hoskins. "When's the bank opening today?"

"It's not going to open today, Moses." Beard maintained an almost jovial tone.

"Why not?" It was a bark.

"Moses, I suspect you've come to get your money."

"Yep."

"I imagine that's why everyone will come today. That's why they came yesterday and the day before. Bank's out of money, Moses. That's why it won't open today. That's why Nigel and I are here."

The rider took the leather hat off his head and used the palm of his other hand to scratch what was already an unruly mass of brown, stringy hair. "When will the bank have money, Beard? I want mine back."

"Me too, Moses. Me too. Bank's sound, Moses, just out of cash." Beard heard the sound of horses' hooves and looked up. Two more riders and one buckboard were coming toward him. "Let me hold on just a second until these folks show up. They'll want to know as well."

"Morning, Beard," rolled a deep bass voice from the rider of the horse now close to within ten feet.

"Morning, all," Beard said calmly, waiting for the others to arrive. "I was just explaining to Mr. Bernwick here that the bank won't open today. For the last two days depositors have been taking their money. We ran out at close yesterday."

By now the sun was up, and the light revealed a dozen men and women walking toward him, some quickening their pace as they came. Beard stood so all could see him. "Let me say this to all of you. We're not opening today. We got no money to give out. We've given out all of our cash reserves, but that doesn't mean we're insolvent. Your money is safe. We just have to let some of it come in from loans due. Then you'll get yours back."

A big man sitting aside a tall, well-gaited stallion pulled a revolving pistol from his belt and fired a shot into the air. All heads turned, including Beard's. "I want my money, Beard," he growled. "And I intend to have it. And you, Hoskins"—he pointed the pistol at Nigel's tweed vest—"will open those doors and get it for me."

Hoskins stood saying nothing but with the look on his face of a man about to pee in his pants from fear. Tom rose and stood calmly, arms dangling at his side. "And you'll have it, sir. Can't say when, but as we get payments in, we'll dole them right back out."

The man cocked the pistol and leveled it, now at Beard. "Now, Beard. I want it now."

"Mister, if you're going to shoot me, not much I can do about it. But it won't get you your money any faster, and it may get you hanged."

The pistol didn't move. "Before I decide whether to kill you or not, I got one question for you."

Beard didn't move, stiffen, or speak save the single word "Ask."

"You get your own money out of that safe before it ran dry?"

"I don't know your name, mister, but how much money you got in here you want back?"

"$100." The pistol didn't move.

"That's a considerable sum, sir. I'm a founder. I've got $5,000 in here. So do the three other founders. That's what we put in when the bank was founded. It's still in there. All of it."

The man dropped the hammer, uncocking his revolver. "When I hear you have money, I'll be back for mine." He turned the horse and trotted away.

Nigel Hoskins's legs folded under him as he fell, his plump body making a plopping sound as he landed on the bed of the wagon.

CHAPTER 33

AUGUST 10, 1841

Beardstown, Cass County, Illinois

Tom Beard could not remember having seen Reverend Horn look unkempt. And he was not certain that was the word for how Horn looked just now, standing in the post office door. His black worsted suit and white shirt with Roman collar were clean. And his boots were wiped as well. But even from behind the counter Beard could see the stitches holding the black patch onto the right knee of his trousers. The shirt was clean but very faded, almost yellow from wash and wear. And the boots showed no sign of polish, much less shine. But it was the burlap bag slung over the big man's right shoulder that truly made him appear as if he hadn't had enough to eat in weeks.

"Reverend Horn, are you here for mail? You have some, I believe. Shall I look?"

"Please do, Mr. Beard. Please do."

Beard stepped away from the counter to the wall lined with small pigeonholes behind him. "I was correct, Reverend. There are three letters for you. However, none of them are stamped with prepaid postage, so you'll owe the post office seventy-five cents."

"And that, Mr. Beard, is why I've brought this small sack of sweet corn. Everybody has gone to a barter system. I presume the post office has as well. The good Lord knows my parishioners certainly have." Horn gave out smiles like secrets, but he gave one now. "Donations have not come in this form in almost ten years"—he swung the bag off his shoulder and held it up as though it were on display—"but this is all they have to offer."

Beard looked saddened at the stern holy man's plight. "Reverend, how about I buy that bag of sweet corn? For say seventy-five cents."

Beard reached into his pants pocket and took out seventy-five cents in coinage and handed it to Horn who gave up his sack and another of his infrequent smiles in return. Once Beard had set the bag behind his counter, Horn gave the seventy-five cents back, and Beard delivered the letters.

"Care to come by the hotel tonight and have dinner with me, Reverend? I've got some dang good corn to cook."

Horn frowned, but there was a twinkle in just the corners of his eyes. "Thomas, I once told you that you were on the edge of blasphemy. I see you've not changed." He turned to walk out the door.

"Dinner's on at seven o'clock, Reverend. Amanda always says the place feels right when you are there."

Horn stepped into the doorway and then turned back. "Tell Amanda I send my regards. I won't be able to see her tonight. I need to go pray with a family a few miles out of town. They are losing their farm to taxes for the same reason I had to barter for my letters. No one has money, and the government demands they be paid in the very same cash the government made to disappear. If you could do something about that, it would be a mighty service to all of us."

* * * *

Tom Beard and Murray McConnel sat across the big desk from Governor Thomas Carlin. Introductions made and pleasantries past, McConnel brought them to the business at hand.

"Governor, Tom and I rode up from Edwardsville together in '18. He is a man who has made a city, a prosperous city, from the wilderness. He is a man of prudence, wisdom, and vision. If he were in politics, he'd whup us both." McConnel's grin was received with the same from the governor. "He is living, as we all are, with the currency crisis that is everywhere on the frontier. And he has come to me with a 'fix' for one of our major problems. What he suggests is radical, but I've pondered it and I can't see the flaw. So I bring him to you in hope that you will hear him out and apply your wisdom to his thought."

"Mr. Beard, if Mo McConnel says I should listen to you, then I will. I don't promise to agree, but I'll listen. Fire away."

Beard swallowed once and then moved his face back into its most charming attitude. "Governor, our merchants are doing all right. There is much use of barter instead of cash payments, but they get along and will be standing when the world gets right again. It is our farmers who are in the most trouble. They all have crops that they, too, can barter, but they can't barter their mortgages. So they all get in arrears on mortgage payments and eventually get foreclosed."

"I understand all that, Beard. Nothing you've said is unknown to me," the governor commented.

Beard nodded. "They would be making money if there was money in circulation. And they will be making money, when you get it back in circulation—as we all know you will. So how do we protect our farmers in the short run? That's the question."

"Agreed!" The governor nodded affirmatively.

"Here's my thought. Suppose it were the law that a foreclosure sale can't happen unless the price paid is at least two-thirds of the value. Not much money around now, so those that have been selling have been going very cheap."

"Agreed again," said the governor, "but who is to say what property is worth if not the market?"

Beard's face broke into its usual huge smile. "A committee, Governor. A committee of three. The debtor appoints one; the creditor appoints one; and the county appoints one. Each of those state value, and they take the average."

Governor Carlin paused in deep reflection, rubbing his chin. "So, the debtor will appoint a friend who places the value sky high."

Beard nodded.

"And the creditor will appoint an employee who will say it's worth very little," the governor continued.

Beard nodded.

"And the county, where the farmer votes and has friends who vote, will say it's worth about what the debtor's friend thinks it's worth because the county official is up for election or will be again soon."

"Exactly, Governor!" Beard beamed.

The governor extended his long jaw toward McConnel. "Mo, you know the problem is this is all going to be an unconstitutional intrusion on bankruptcy law."

"Governor," Beard said, pulling his attention back, "how long will it take you to get us through this liquidity crisis?"

"Two years," Governor Carlin answered immediately.

"And, Governor . . ." McConnel's voice pulled the governor back to him. "How long will it take for the banks to mount a legal challenge and get the courts to overturn the law?"

The governor visibly relaxed and eased back into his chair, grinning. "At least three, Mo. At least three. Beard's Two-Thirds law will be passed before summer recess, Mo."

CHAPTER 34

JULY 31, 1846

Indian Creek, Morgan County, Illinois

The heat of the day beat down on Beard and his horse. It had only been a two-hour ride and he'd never forced the beast out of walk, but both horse and rider were soaked with their own sweat. Beard wasn't certain which was higher, the temperature or the humidity. By late afternoon the heat would have pulled enough moisture from the earth and the river to form low clouds. And those clouds would create a little lightning for show and maybe a little rain to make tonight's sleep easier, but now it was just hot.

He wanted to see Arenz, to sit on his veranda with an iced tea. Francis was the only man he knew who had built an icehouse to save the blocks he cut from his creek in the winter and keep enough packed underground to last through the summer.

Horse and rider rose over a low swale and there it was, Arenz's magnificent mansion in the country. "Recluze" he had named it. "Mansion" was perhaps not the right word. The behemoth that Hank Meyer, the grain dealer, had just built—now that was a mansion. Architecturally, Recluze had more the look of gracious country living than the decadent opulence "mansion" suggested. It was framed wood, the foundation raised four feet off the ground. Not that there was any risk of flood this high off the valley floor, but one had to walk up the veranda steps, and that imparted a sense of grace. Or perhaps it was not merely the wide staircase but the covered veranda that encircled the front and both sides of the house that imparted grace. The front of the house was very wide, allowing, as he had previously discovered, for both a large receiving room as well as a huge study, two walls of which were lined with floor-to-ceiling bookshelves requiring a rolling ladder to enable a man to recover anything from the top shelves. The library and the receiving room were on either side of the entry hall. The roof, at a sharper angle than any Beard had ever seen, a "mansard roof" Arenz called it, allowed for three dormer windows across the front of the house, supplying each of the upstairs bedrooms with abundant natural light as well as evening breeze when it was available.

It was just what Francis had said he would want, a quiet place in the country to entertain and to have discussions with friends and colleagues who were always welcome to drop in. Recluze was his Parisian salon and Francis the salon's elder statesman, a role for which he had been preparing his entire life.

The man, standing at the top of the outside stairs waiting for him, was still very dapper in his dress. Even as Beard dismounted, he could see that the black widow's peak had become solid silver in color as had the hair at his temples. But his hair was still full and rich and all the rest still solid black.

"Hello, Francis, my dearest friend. If you feel as well as you look, you are defying age," Beard boomed as he bounded up the steps two at a time.

Arenz reached up to place his hands on the shoulders of the larger man and held him fast. "I have missed you, Thomas. Less than ten miles and you so seldom come to see your old partner and friend."

Beard saw real warmth in the deep-set eyes that twinkled purple in the light of the midday sun.

"Just leave your horse. One of the boys will come around and get him momentarily and lead him to cool shadows and cooler water. Now come in, and let me get you something cool as well."

The two men sat in Arenz's study surrounded by nine-foot-tall walls almost fully lined with books. The table between them had one book lying open, its leather cover showing. Beard reached forward and spun it toward him. The brown leather cover was embossed, in half-inch-tall yellow letters, *Faust* and, below that in somewhat smaller letters, "Johann Wolfgang von Goethe." Beard, careful not to lose the page to which it was opened, looked at the print. He could not read it.

"You still read German, Francis?"

A meek smile came to his friend. "I have spent the last twenty-five years mostly in English. It is pleasing sometimes to read in my native language."

"What is the book?" Beard asked.

"A story about a man who does a deal with the devil. When I was a boy, Goethe wrote the first half. It took twenty-five years for him to come out with this second half. I'm not done yet, but I have the sense that over those twenty-five years his opinions have matured."

"Sometimes, Francis, men's opinions do change." Beard paused for a moment and then added, "But not always."

Arenz laughed. "You, for instance, still believe the river is eternal and railroads an ephemeral fad."

"Ah, don't be so certain, Francis. I may come to your way of thinking before I die." Beard paused. "If I live a very long time."

Over the sound of their laughter came a knock on the study door to which Arenz responded, *"Geben Sie."* A plump young woman in her early twenties, her golden hair braided into pigtails, opened the door with one hand, a small tray of drinks balanced on her other. She crossed the room and placed two tumblers full of ice on the table. She filled each from the pitcher on the tray and then set the pitcher on the table as well. *"Ist das alles, Herr Arenz?"* she asked with a smile.

"Ja, danke," Arenz responded.

She turned and left.

"I work to get the Germans who have gathered here at the creek near me to use English, but it's hard for the new ones."

Beard nodded and took a deep swallow of the lemonade. "Francis, that is wonderful. I'm going to have to encourage someone to open an icehouse in Beardstown. Lord knows there's enough of it to cut in Mascouten Bay." Beard took another drink, drained the tumbler, and poured himself another.

"Francis, the rail drove the state broke and our town into poverty for a few years, but as wealth returns, so do the railroads. But this time the state will not fund them. The Rockford and Rock Island Railroad has discovered another way to fund their expansion."

Arenz merely stared at him, expressionless, the deep-set purple eyes encouraging him to continue.

"They are making the towns finance them."

"How much do they want to extend the rail to you?" Arenz asked.

"They want $150,000."

Arenz whistled. "That is a lot of money."

"What they propose is that we sell bonds. That sound familiar?" He smiled a sardonic smile. "They want $50,000 now and the remaining $100,000 spread over fifteen years."

"Do they say why so much, Tom? It can't possibly cost that much to extend that track from their main line between Rock Island and St. Louis."

"That is the very interesting part. They have to cross the Illinois River. They want us to pay for the railroad bridge."

Arenz nodded. "It's always the river, isn't it?"

"Yes. It always has been. But if they don't cross it in Beardstown, they'll cross it somewhere. Wherever that is will become the center of rail traffic."

Arenz's face beamed. "And all it will cost is more than we have?" He laughed. "No one ever said that railroad men don't know how to squeeze every dollar out of an economy."

"But if they create the economy in the first place, why should they not?" Beard finished the thought.

"Tom, you sound like you've become a convert."

Tom Beard shook his head. "No. I'm forever a river rat. But this is about the town's future. I'll help make it happen, but it will be for someone else to see it through."

Arenz's smile grew large. Larger than Beard had ever seen. "So, Goethe is right; men, even Tom Beard, can change."

Beard reached into his coat pocket and removed a letter. "I've been wanting to talk for months, but this is what motivated me to come now," he said, waving the letter. "It's from Enos Marsh. He writes long, but the summary is he's about as happy as a man can be. By the time he got to Tejas, Sam Houston and his ragtag army of Americans had whupped Santa Anna, and Tejas had become Texas. He settled a little town he called Waterloo. He's always had a good eye to the future, that man. Turns out that the Texans changed the name of the place to a guy they think of as their founder, guy named Stephen Austin. And when they asked President Tyler to let them join the Union and he agreed, they made it their state capital. Enos has gotten rich again. So now he's bored again. Said there were becoming 'too many rules.'"

Both men laughed.

"When he wrote this"—Beard waved the letter again—"the war with Mexico hadn't started, but he saw it coming. He says when it's over, he's going to go west again—California if we get it from Mexico, Oregon if we don't. The man has the soul of a gypsy."

"No, not quite. Enos Marsh has the soul of a pirate. A kind pirate, but a pirate nonetheless," Arenz said, then added, "When you write him back, send him my regards.

"My stomach tells me it's time for dinner now. If they don't have it on yet, we'll have a drink before dinner. You've yet to tell me the news from town. I want to hear all."

The two men rose and walked out of the study and crossed the entry hall where Arenz opened the wide double doors that led to the receiving hall. There could be no other word for it. No matter how many times Beard saw it, he was always struck by the rococo magnificence of the place. It took up half the large main floor, running from the front of the house to the rear along one side of the building. There were two large windows running from window box almost to ceiling, each four feet wide along the veranda, flooding the entire room with light. There were two similar windows along the back wall, but those Arenz kept covered with translucent curtains so the light coming in the rear was more subdued. And, as Arenz had once pointed out to him, they also kept out the view of the stable and barn lot behind. Along the side wall was a fireplace large enough to accommodate two small stone benches inside the hearth.

"For intimacy and warmth in the winter when only three or four souls are engaged," Francis had said.

The ceiling was the same nine-foot height as in the study, but these walls were not covered with books. They were covered with tapestries Arenz had imported from Germany. The ceiling itself was covered with pastel frescoes of sylvan scenes, each of which was about six feet square and encased in relief wooden carving covered in gold leaf. It was a medieval banquet hall on the Illinois frontier. And today that dining hall contained only one small table set for two.

Arenz went to a sideboard, took two lead-crystal, wide-bellied stemmed glasses, and poured two fingers of brandy into each. He handed one glass to Beard and offered his raised up in a toast. "To civilization created from wilderness." The men struck the glasses together, filling the room with the high, clear tone of struck leaded crystal.

"Francis, it seems to me civilization requires women. Why have you never married?" Beard asked.

"Perhaps for the same reason you never remarried. 'We came to a place where land is cheap but women are dear,'[2] and a man can only indulge one obsession at a time. Mine was the same as yours, Thomas."

"Building an empire in the wilderness." Beard seemed to almost conclude the thought.

"It will be a few minutes before she brings in the turtle soup, so update me—newspaper, courthouse, bank, anything newsworthy," Arenz commanded.

"Simple things first, Francis," Beard started. "The boatyard has produced its first stern-wheeler. We had to import the boiler and some of the finishing items like the cabin furniture, the polished wood steering wheel, the single steel rod centering the paddles. But the boat was all made and assembled in Beardstown."

"As you've always dreamed, Tom. As you've always dreamed."

Beard continued. "We have some new institutions—a library society; Freemasons and Odd Fellows have opened

---

2.   Melvin R. Gilmore, diary entry of Jane Mosey Ward in *Prairie Smoke* (St. Paul, MN: Minnesota Historical Society Press, 2002).

local chapters; we have a volunteer bucket brigade. I still worry for our city of more wood than brick or stone, but at least we now have one small pump wagon, a hose, and trained volunteers. And new churches. They have mostly moved out of the community hall you and I built. School is still there, but the Methodists and the Lutherans have built their own churches."

The young woman with golden pigtails walked into the room, a large serving tray raised over her broad shoulder. After setting it down, she removed two bowls and a soup tureen that she placed on the table. The two men stood watching her.

"*Herr Arenz, Abendessen.*" She smiled at him.

"Please, Tom. I'm starved. But I want to hear more of the burgeoning religious life of our community as we eat."

The two men sat alone in the middle of the huge room, Beard feeling a bit overwhelmed, Arenz the king of his domain.

"The soup is delicious. Not sure I knew you could make soup of a turtle, but this is really good," Beard said.

"Finding turtles is easy by this creek. Finding someone who knows how to cook them is hard. I'm glad you enjoyed it. Now tell me of churches."

"Francis, I know the German countries fought a lot of wars for a long time between Catholics and Protestants. I know you're a Lutheran, and I've heard you say men should worship as they will, but I'm not truly sure what you think of Catholics. We now have a congregation of them, and they are building. And the man who started it was, is fascinating."

"Tell me, Tom. Who is he?"

"He came up the river from New Orleans. A few German friends asked me to meet him with them and I agreed. He came striding off the ferry like a man at complete ease and in charge of his own destiny. He was a man wearing the strangest costume."

"Stranger than Horn's?" Arenz asked.

"Similar but very different. It was also black worsted with a white shirt and Roman collar. But that was the end of the similarity. Father Felix, that's how he introduced himself, was not wearing pants and a frock coat. His was almost a dress. Fitted down to the waist like a shirt might and then open, flowing pleated skirt all the way to the ground. And a hat. What a hat. Felt, close fitting at the crown but with a stiff brim that extended out to his shoulders."

"A crow!" Francis said.

Beard looked stunned. "That's exactly what Chaubenee called him. You know him?"

Arenz smiled and shook his head. "No, I don't know Father Felix, but I know the Jesuits. All Germans know the Jesuits. They were the pope's intellectual troops to stop the Reformation, stop the growth of Luther's 'apostasy' in Germany and elsewhere. They are very well educated, bright, and dedicated. It is said that Jesuits have the ability dispute the Bible with either God or Satan. But here, here in North America, the story was a little different. When the French held Canada, the Jesuits were the ones to bring the word of God to the Indians. That is probably how Chaubenee knows them. But when the English kicked the French out, they evicted the Jesuits as well."

Arenz looked back down and directly into Beard's eyes. "No Jesuit has ever done a wicked thing to me. I only know my ancestors feared their very presence." There was a long pause. "But these are not parish priests. What was he doing here?"

"Father Felix said his order was opening a university in St. Louis. He had been invited by Catholics in Beardstown to minister to them. And so he came and, while here, celebrated Mass. I'm not certain what that is aside from a Sunday service where communion is served. And then he did something I've never seen a man of God do, something I couldn't imagine one doing."

"What was that?"

"He pulled $50 out of his own pocket and gave it to the man who had extended the invitation and said, 'This is my contribution to the church I hope you'll build here.'"

"Tom, I'm curious. What was he like personally?"

Beard thought for a moment. "I liked him. He was young and vigorous. And he appeared generous, and his pledge to help was enough to make everyone believe, me included. But the thing I like most was that he was human."

"What do you mean?"

"Do you remember when Hank Meyer dug up the biggest of the sepulchral mounds to raise the foundation of his grain silos?"

Arenz nodded.

"And do you remember that he found a silver cross and a few silver beads and a lot of jet ones strung on a thin piece of rawhide?"

Again, Arenz nodded.

"The night before he left, we all had dinner at the hotel, and Chaubenee gave it to him. The father's face went white, and he, a man as talkative as I am, seemed struck dumb and merely held it in his hands lovingly, just staring at it. He asked Chaubenee where he'd found it, and Chaubenee told him. If it were possible, the man looked even more dumbstruck when Chaubenee explained. Finally, he said, 'Then this place is the spot called the Beautiful Mound Village?' Chaubenee said it was so, and the man wept. He didn't sob; tears just rolled down his cheeks. When he recovered himself, he swallowed once and said, 'This belonged to one of my brothers.' Chaubenee responded, 'I thought it was so, Father. I have been saving it for you.' Not one of us understood, but we knew we were watching something of profound moment."

"Did he tell you what it was, Tom?" Arenz asked.

"None of us asked."

"It is called a rosary. Catholics use them for prayer beads. Most Catholics have them, and most carry them with them daily. Certainly, every priest has one, often worn at their belt. I've known all along that the Mascouten must have buried a French priest in their burial mound. He must have been a man much loved and admired." Neither spoke for a reverent moment. "I'm glad he's gone home to his brothers."

There was a noise at the end of the room as the large young woman walked through the door that was the entry to the dining room from the serving area. "Entrée, Herr Arenz." This time her serving tray contained two plates, each covered with a silvered lid. She placed them before the men and pulled the lids off with a flourish, opening the room to the sweet smell of roast pork loin surrounded by small carrots.

Arenz patted her arm and said, "Danke, Helga."

"My mouth is literally watering," Beard said.

"Then fill it, Tom. Fill it."

For five minutes the only sounds in the room were those made by silverware bouncing into china and the sighs of satisfaction from an especially delicious bite. But when hunger was tamped down, conversation started again.

"Francis, you have not bothered to come to town since the courthouse was built. It is a beautiful structure and there in no small part thanks to you."

"I did nothing, Tom."

"Nothing save give half the land. You and I owned that lot together, you know."

"You were the one who supplied the funds, Tom."

"Don't know where you heard that, Francis, but it's not so. The good citizens of Beardstown chipped in to build that courthouse. All I paid for was the jail." And then he smiled broadly. "When those railroad crews you've always wanted come to town, we're going to need it."

Arenz laughed, then changed the subject. "How close are you to getting the bank back?"

"We managed to keep Hoskins around, but the truth is I don't think he's got anywhere to go. I mistrust his judgment after he decided, on his own, we didn't need the reserves we'd committed to. But to get our bank open again we need Hoskins, or someone like him, so I let the family stay in their house and found things for him to do. In the last four years we've managed to collect enough on the loans the bank made to pay most of our depositors back. It'll take another few years for you and me to get our money back; then perhaps we can go to the state and reopen the charter."

Arenz frowned, and his eyes receded even deeper into his face.

"OK, Francis, here's some good news. But I'm guessing you not already know but probably arranged it. Beardstown has a paper again, and it's a Whig paper."

Arenz beamed. "I might have had a little something to do with that. Maybe." Arenz's widow's peak twinkled silver in the light of the chandelier. It was almost the same color as the teeth he was displaying. "Speaking of Whigs, I may have a bit of insider news I can offer you."

"So, retirement in the country doesn't leave you without other guests?" Beard teased.

"Perhaps you're not the only one." Arenz's face still carried the big smile. "You will remember Abe Lincoln, the young state representative from New Salem who carried the road-construction bill for us?"

"How do you forget a man who looks as disjointed as a starving cow? Of course, I remember him."

"He's going to be the Whig candidate to the US Congress from our district. And he's going to win."

"He may win the seat, but Whigs have a tough time in Beardstown. We always seem split. Your Whigs get half the votes, and Mo's Democrats get half the votes. Never can tell. Got a question about him, Francis."

"Ask."

"Where does he stand on the war with Mexico? It's a popular war around here. Looks like Central Illinois may even send a regiment or two of volunteers. And that's a long walk."

"Just between us, Tom?"

"Promise," Beard said, "just between us."

"He's against it. Thinks it's just a foreign war and maybe to snatch some land. But it won't be an issue."

"Why?" Beard asked.

"Because it's already decided. War's been declared. No one is going to ask him what he thinks between now and November. He'll win."

"Fair 'nough, Francis. Fair 'nough. But if he mouths off about it once he gets to Washington, Illinois's Seventh Congressional District won't send him back for a second term."

* * * *

Someone had forgotten to leave a chamber pot. At least Beard couldn't find one when he woke in the middle of the night needing to pee. He pulled on his trousers, but no boots, and quietly padded down the hall. At the head of the staircase the door to Francis Arenz's bedroom stood ajar, revealing moonlight flooding through the window, and onto Francis's bed where he and Helga were lying beautifully arm in arm. Beard smiled, both surprised and happy, hoping his passing would cause no creaking to wake the contented couple as he stepped gently on the treads downward and then out the back door to find the privy.

CHAPTER 35

SEPTEMBER 8, 1849

Beardstown, Cass County, Illinois

The day was hot but the water flat and easy rowing for the small skiff. Beard thought it a surreal scene as he rowed between the straight lines of trees with brick houses behind, the residents of Beardstown standing on their front porches waving and sending a cheery "Hallowww!" as though he were a float in a marine parade.

"Howdy," Beard shouted back. "Need anything? I've got jugs of water and some dried meat."

"Could use some whiskey!" one friendly voice shouted back.

Beard let his skiff coast forward. "Next trip, George." He waved and went back to his oars.

His skiff rocked to one side, and he looked over just in time to see two hands and the head of Anthony Hoskins appearing over the gunnel. He threw an unruly mass of wet blond hair out of his eyes, and, beaming boyish joy, said, "Hello, Mr. Beard. Nice of you to come visit."

Beard could not help but be infected by his enthusiasm. "What, you've never had anyone row to your house before?"

"Well, it's flooded here before but never this much. Comes up another six inches and our floorboards will be taking water."

"Pull yourself on in here, Anthony, and I'll give you a ride home."

The boy started to pull over the edge as the boat dipped deeply toward him.

"Stop! Stop, stop, stop."

The lad slid back into the water, and the boat righted.

"Let me slide across the bench to the other side for balance." Beard did so as the strapping muscular form of the younger Hoskins boy pulled himself easily into the skiff. Beard started to pull again, this time moving the boat slowly up the Hoskins yard. "You sixteen now, Anthony?"

"Yes, sir. But, Mr. Beard, would you call me Tony? Everyone else does, and I like it."

"Everyone but your mom." Beard chuckled. "She hates it, doesn't she?"

The dripping muscles of young Hoskins, naked save for a pair of short pants, and drying in the summer sun, looked the image of a young riverman. "She's never gotten over being British. I never was," Tony responded as the skiff slid up to the front of the Hoskins house and bounced off the front steps. "Lean a little to your left, Mr. Beard. I'll step by you on your right and tie us up."

"Thanks, Tony."

Big Nigel Hoskins, more corpulent and florid than ever and dressed as though to go to work, up to and including a silk cravat around his fleshy neck, stepped onto the porch. "Welcome to Château Hoskins, Thomas."

Tony had used the bowline to tie the boat to a support post holding up the veranda, and Beard stepped out of the boat just as the thin little Victoria Hoskins stepped out the front door.

"Anthony, you're an embarrassment. Get in here and get some clothes on and stop looking, and acting, like a young savage."

"Yes, Ma." The tall young man smiled back at her.

"And don't call me 'Ma.' That is not a word. It's Mother or ma'am. Now get in here, Anthony."

Tony stepped by her and smiled over his shoulder at Beard.

Victoria Hoskins, looking the picture of embarrassed indignation, said, "Forgive him, Mr. Beard. I do my best, but I fear Illinois has more influence over a young boy than his mother." She then looked up at her husband. "When we take those boys home, they will be a daily mortification to us." And so pronouncing, she turned and departed into the house.

"May I pour you a drink, Thomas?" Hoskins asked. "And would you like to come in?"

"No to either. I'm just making my rounds, seeing that everyone has enough supplies to last out the floodwaters."

"That's good of you, Thomas, but we're well prepared. We have history now, you know." He said it with a smile. "But I've not seen enough of these to know how quickly to expect the water to recede."

Beard turned and looked out into the flooded street. "Water is going down. Probably two weeks more until all can start cleaning up. But the bank is higher. By next week I think you'll be able to get in. Soon as I see the water has receded enough to get you in, I'll row over and collect you."

Hoskins nodded understanding.

"Nigel," Beard continued, "I'm glad you were able to wait out the financial market. We'd not have been able to reopen without you. For that I, and the city, am grateful."

Hoskins looked up and down the flooded street. "I think it's no secret that Victoria hates it here. But Anthony, Tony, and Spencer belong here. Victoria is right in one sense and wrong in another. They would be a daily mortification to us in London. But then they would be mortified by London as well. This is their home." He returned his gaze to Beard. "And mine as well." He looked at Beard for a long while.

It was the longest Beard had ever felt those brown eyes fixed upon him. He knew more was coming and merely waited for Hoskins to make whatever decision was forming in his mind.

"Thomas," he finally started, "I have learned from you and this place. The financial panic taught me much. Loans here are harder to analyze. There is not much history, from businesses that make application for loans, that I may analyze. But there is much greater opportunity for them. I have learned that some will grow hugely with the help of my, our, loan. Some will fail despite them." He paused, forming the words. "The only thing for a banker to do is his best and to have a very prudent reserve."

Beard reached out and in silence patted the big banker's shoulder. He untied the bowline from the porch support post and stepped into the skiff. "Before leaving, Nigel, I'd like to offer a word of advice. You have a privy in the back."

Hoskins nodded.

"So does everyone on this street." Beard pointed up and down the row of houses. "They are all flooded. Don't let your boys swim after a flood."

* * * *

Amanda walked to the end of the hall and knocked on Beard's door. When she didn't get a response, she knocked again. When there was still no response, she took the key out of her apron, unlocked the door, and let herself in. Beard was still lying in bed, covers pulled up to his chin, and apparently sleeping. She walked to the window, threw open the curtains, and let the midmorning sun flood the room. Beard stirred with a low moan.

"Mr. Beard, time to get up, honey." It was more a command than a request.

Beard didn't move. His eyes blinked, but he didn't move.

She turned from the window and walked toward the bed, seeing him for the first time. He was pale and his forehead covered in perspiration. The covers around his chin were wet. "Mr. Beard. Honey, you look terrible. You OK?"

He rolled toward her voice and opened his eyes. His lips formed a very weak smile. "Amanda, I feel awful. Let me sleep a bit."

"Yah, that's how you look, too." She walked to the bed, sat on the edge, and put her hand on his forehead. "You burning up. No wonder you feel bad. How about you take some tea? I'll get it for you."

Beard had closed his eyes again. They fluttered. He spoke again but very weakly. "No. No tea. Nothing. My stomach is a mess. I'd throw it up."

"Anything hurt but your stomach?" she asked.

Again, the weak smile. "All of me hurts. I ache everywhere."

She patted his shoulder, rose, and closed the curtains. "I'll get some wet towels to wipe you. And a dry set of sheets."

Amanda walked out of the room and down the stairs. She turned into the kitchen, collecting a washbasin, towels, and clean sheets from the closet.

Jim was standing by the stove, pouring himself his midmorning cup of coffee.

"Jim, Mr. Beard is sick. Really sick. I'll nurse him best I can, but he needs a doctor. You go get Dr. Chandler an' do it quick as you can."

* * * *

Dr. Chandler shooed Chaubenee and Jim out of the room while he and Amanda tended to Tom Beard. She had cooled him as best she could and tried to keep him on dry sheets, but he sweated them wet almost as soon as she changed them.

After Chandler examined him, the doctor motioned her out of the room and followed. Chaubenee and Jim stood waiting.

"Come on downstairs," Chandler said to all. "We need to talk."

When they were seated, Chandler spoke. "Amanda, you have done everything I would have told you to do. You're keeping him as comfortable as possible and, more than that, keeping him cool. You need to keep that up but even more. Get wet towels on his body as well as his head. Keep him as cool, clean, and comfortable as you can. If the fever breaks, he'll live. If not, we are going to lose our friend and leader."

Chaubenee was the one who spoke it. "Beard is too strong to die. If any man is strong enough to beat this, it will be him."

Chandler looked at the powerful man, real sadness in his eyes. "It is a disease we call typhoid. It usually comes from contaminated water. But it is very strong, Chaubenee. We can't be sure. Aside from Amanda's care, there are two things I think you should do. One of you should go bring Francis Arenz, but the rest should stay with him. And also, now that we have that telegraph wire, you should send a telegram to Murray McConnel. I'd send it to both Springfield and Jacksonville. The presence of his friends will give him strength."

* * * *

They all sat in Beard's window seat as they had so many times before. Chaubenee, General Murray McConnel, Francis Arenz,

Jim, and Amanda, all watching Dr. Charles Chandler walk down the stairs. There were a bottle of brandy and a bottle of corn whiskey sitting on the middle of the table. The doctor poured himself a shot of whiskey before he sat down. All looked at him in rapt silence and anticipation.

"I don't think our friend will make it through the night. He has fooled me many times before and I hope he does again, but he has lost so much fluid and he is still hot. He hasn't got enough water inside to fight the fever. Unless it drops miraculously in the next few hours, Tom Beard will be gone."

Not a word was spoken. Amanda stood and poured for each, and then, what no one had ever seen her do before, she poured a shot of corn whiskey for herself. She sat back down, held her glass up as though examining the color against the light. After considerable study she looked around the table, making eye contact with each until she was looking slowly and steadily into her husband's eyes. "Jim, you and I were born slaves. You are Jim, and I, Amanda. Nothing more. Free people have two names." She looked back around the table again. "Unless one of these gentlemen thinks it's wrong, I think we should have two names as well, and I think our last name should be Beard. Jim and Amanda Beard." There was a long pause. "Do any of you think that is wrong?"

McConnel looked at her steadily, his normally arched eyebrows straight lines across his face. A tear slowly rolled down one cheek. He raised his glass to all, choked once, and said, "To Jim and Amanda Beard." They all raised their glasses.

PART IV

THE NEW FRONTIER

CHAPTER 36

MAY 5, 1858

Cass County Courthouse, Beardstown, Illinois

James McHugh sat in his office, musing about his exceptionally good fortune. That only three years out of law school he had returned, almost triumphantly, to his hometown, appointed not only the youngest state's attorney in Illinois, but also the first in Cass County. No more would violations of the laws of the state be adjudicated in Beardstown by a gaggle of attorneys riding in a circuit from town to town, always one judge and two attorneys, who, upon arrival, decided which of the attorneys would be prosecutor and which defense on a given day. Now he would be the prosecutor of offenses here and, under the laws of the State of Illinois, also the one who decided which offenses were worthy of prosecution.

A light tap on the door brought McHugh's thoughts out of his reverie just in time for him to watch his office door open and see first the tall stovepipe hat leading the way of the bent head and, once that cleared the door and straightened again, the tall, thin, angular-to-the-point-of-awkwardness frame of a bearded man dressed entirely in black—black hat, black beard, black frock coat, black pants, black boots. The only things not black were the white shirt and cravat and the teeth showing from behind a slow, gentle, and very self-assured smile.

"I presume, sir, that you are the new state's attorney, Mr. James McHugh?" The tall man spoke in an easy and almost-kind tone.

McHugh rose to his feet and appraised the man, not certain what to make of him. "I am he," was his response.

The tall man extended a hand, populated with long, bony fingers, at the end of a preternaturally long arm. "I am Abraham Lincoln, Mr. McHugh. I am counsel for Duff Armstrong. I wanted to meet you on neutral ground before we meet in legal conflict tomorrow."

McHugh tried to keep the complete surprise from his face but knew he'd let it show. He reached forward to extend his arm across his desk and looked straight up to peer into the soft large brown eyes of the man who he thought must have been six or seven inches taller than his own five foot, nine inches. That Lincoln had not yet taken his hat off made that feeling most distinct, and that his hand seemed twice the size of his own made him feel almost childish in this man's presence.

He tried to recover his confidence. "Please, Mr. Lincoln, sit down." He motioned to the chair beside the desk.

Lincoln removed his hat with one hand and, at the same time, extended his other arm to the back of the chair, and without need to move his feet, pulled it toward him. Once the chair was in place, he slowly moved himself to a sitting position, his legs not seeming to quite fit.

"Mr. Lincoln, I've heard your name many times. But I'm surprised to see you here."

"Why is that, Mr. McHugh?"

"Since you came back from Washington in '49 . . ." McHugh halted, thinking he was starting this interview in a contentious way.

Lincoln chuckled. "You can say it, Mr. McHugh, since I was the only sitting congressman from Illinois to lose my seat in 1848. I did think the war was ill advised but concede my proposed amendment was an imprudence."

McHugh momentarily stayed mute, the more flustered for the man's candid admission of political error. He forced a smile and continued. "For almost ten years now I thought you'd spent all your time representing various railroads. I didn't know you defended criminals."

Lincoln's nod conveyed an avuncular ease. "When I was young, your age perhaps, I rode circuit. In fact, I rode circuit to Beardstown and often. Some days I would represent the state and some days the defendant. As I suspect you know, it was the custom in those times. But you are right, Mr. McHugh, about one thing."

"What is that, Mr. Lincoln?"

"I don't defend criminals, and I won't be tomorrow either."

McHugh was suddenly put at ease. The battle joined. This, he was good at, and looked forward to. Now he would not only get to convict a murderer but defeat one of the most famous corporate lawyers in the state. He eased back into his chair and ran his hand through his thin brown hair, his fingers combing it as they went. His large white teeth beamed joy as he rocked forward to peer closely into the dark, deep-set eyes of his opponent.

"Ah, Mr. Lincoln, I think by tomorrow evening we will both find that it is not so. You know Armstrong's partner in the beating of the deceased—J. H. Norris is his name—has already been found guilty of the murder. A jury in Mason County found it so. The only reason your client's case has been moved here is that the citizens of Mason County are so angered by his offense that they can't be counted on not to storm the jail and hang the man."

"Yes, I am aware of all that. But the deceased, Mr. Metzker, engaged in two fights that day, did he not? The first with Duff Armstrong after Metzker had grabbed the feet of my peacefully sleeping client and pulled him off a wagon bed and onto the ground. Reasonable cause for any man to fight, I think you would agree. There is sworn testimony of those now-established facts from Norris's trial. What I've come about is to see what your witness list is and to what they will attest." Then Lincoln gave a long pause. "I don't mean to offend, Mr. McHugh, but I understand you are new at your job. So I want to make certain you understand that if you have any testimony you don't reveal to me as Armstrong's defense counsel, that testimony will not be allowed in tomorrow's proceeding."

McHugh did not respond with words but merely pulled open his desk drawer and pulled out two sheets written in a neat and precise hand. "This is my entire witness list and a summary of issues to which my witness will attest. I'm not that new, Mr. Lincoln." McHugh handed both sheets across the desk to Lincoln.

Lincoln accepted the papers, took spectacles from his pocket, put them on, and sat in silence for five minutes, reading. When he was done, he said, "Is this my copy, Mr. McHugh?"

McHugh nodded.

"It is a nice summary, and you have developed your case well, Mr. McHugh. Your sole witness is a Mr. Charles Allen. Tough to refute an eyewitness to the crime."

"It is, Mr. Lincoln. It is. Especially when your codefendant has already been found guilty."

Lincoln rose, collected his hat. Folded the papers and put them in his coat pocket. "You are a thorough professional, Mr. McHugh. And a credit to your office. I look forward to meeting you tomorrow. I've not been in the new courthouse."

McHugh rose with him and offered his hand. "Not so new, Mr. Lincoln. It's been there for over twelve years now. You've been away a long time."

* * * *

"Your witness, Mr. Lincoln," came the slightly nasal, but very satisfied, voice of James McHugh as he turned his back to the judge and his star witness, Charles Allen, and walked to the small table reserved for the prosecution between the rail and the judge's bench.

Lincoln rose in the slow, awkward style that seemed to be necessary to get his limbs and body from a sitting position to an upright one. He walked slowly but purposefully toward the witness box, never taking his soft eyes off Charles Allen. He stopped a respectful distance from him, swung his head to the jury for just a moment and then back to the witness. "Mr. Allen, first I want to thank you for serving the people of Illinois and blind Lady Justice today. I understand you had to travel all the way from Petersburg. Petersburg was my home for a number of years, so I know it took you at least two days to get here and will take you as long to get back. The state needs men with a sense of civic responsibility. Thank you for yours."

Lincoln paused, then continued.

"Now, Mr. Allen, all I'd like to do is confirm that I, and the jury"—Lincoln again turned his face to the twelve and nodded to them—"understood everything you said properly. So will you just repeat a couple of things for me?"

"Yes, sir," responded the young man with the shock of hair bleached the color of cornstalks by the sun.

"Tell me again, please. What time was this fight?"

"Well, sir, it was between nine o'clock and nine thirty at night."

"Could it have been earlier, Mr. Allen?"

"Oh no, sir."

"May I ask how you could be so certain?"

"Well, sir," he said, the words coming with a slow but satisfied smile, "there is a large clock behind the bar where I'd been standing. Just like the one in the schoolhouse in Petersburg. The last I looked at the clock, it was a few minutes after nine o'clock."

"Thank you for that confirmation, Mr. Allen. Another question if I may. How long had you been in the bar?"

"Well, I didn't leave the camp meeting until after dark. So couldn't have been more than an hour or hour and a half."

"And you were drinking beer?"

"Yes, sir."

"How many beers might you have had in that hour and a half?"

The smile disappeared now. "It had been a very hot day. A cold beer was perfect. But only two. I didn't have money to buy more."

"So you'd nursed two beers for an hour and a half?"

"Yes, sir," came a hesitant response.

"And it was when you stepped out from the saloon that you saw the fight?"

"Yes, sir. I walked out the door and stopped in my tracks. There was a fight going on across the street."

"So you watched from in front of the saloon?"

"Yes, sir." The response firmer again.

"Was it directly across the street from you, Mr. Allen?"

"No, sir. It was across the street and maybe two wagon lengths up."

"Mr. Allen, was that street in Havana the same width as those here in Beardstown?"

"Why yes, sir. Same as everywhere."

"Did you ever walk any closer, or did you stay by the saloon door?"

"Never moved, sir. Watched it all from right where I was."

"Let's estimate. Streets here are sixty feet wide. And a wagon is maybe ten feet long. Would you estimate you were eighty feet away?"

Allen's face beamed. "Well, that would be eighty feet on two sides of a triangle. I'd have been looking down the hypotenuse." He paused. "I remember learning that in school." Another pause during which Lincoln gave the young man a smile of encouragement and appreciation of his knowledge. "So maybe seventy feet is more like it."

Lincoln nodded. "So, seventy feet away and an hour and a half after the sun set. That right?"

"Yes, sir. That would be right. Seventy feet and an hour and a half after sunset."

"And you saw three men fighting on the ground, but from the distance and in the dark, you could clearly recognize all their faces. Clearly enough to be certain that it was my client." Lincoln paused and turned to point at a very serious and sad-looking Duff Armstrong.

The witness bolted in. "Oh yes, sir. But like I told Mr. McHugh when he asked, it was almost bright as day. The moon was bright."

"So, the moonlight was that bright?" Lincoln asked.

"Yes, sir, it was. No clouds at all."

"Mr. Allen, do you remember where the moon was?"

There was a long pause. Allen put his hand on a stubble of blond whiskers on his chin and rubbed. "Yes, sir, I do. It was just about where the sun would be at an hour after noon in the summer."

"Thank you, Mr. Allen. Let me confirm what the jury and I have heard before I dismiss you. Some hour and a half after sunset, in a bright moon located about one o'clock in the sky, on a cloudless night and from seventy feet away you saw three men fighting in the dirt with such clarity that you can identify

Mr. Armstrong"—Lincoln again pointed to his client—"as the man striking Mr. Metzker repeatedly on the head with a slang-shot."

"Yes, sir. That is what I said. That is correct."

"Thank you, Mr. Allen. Again, I am grateful for your testimony."

Charles Allen looked at the judge, got the nod he was seeking, rose from the witness chair, and walked to the prosecution's table where he sat with the state's attorney.

Lincoln looked up at the judge. "Your Honor, I have only one witness. May I call him now?"

"Please do, Mr. Lincoln." The judge turned to the bailiff. "Swear in the defense's witness when he's seated."

Lincoln turned to the courtroom. "The defense will call Mr. Isaac Wisdom, newly elected president of the Beardstown Library Committee."

A stooped man, back bent to a curve, wearing a weathered frock coat, his grey hair unruly and unkempt, rose up, his face showing the results of a shave poorly administered sometime within the last few days. He was carrying a large paperbound book under one arm. When he had seated himself in the witness chair, he shifted the large book to his lap in order to free his right hand for the oath. When that was completed, he sat quietly though his face displayed the effort of straightening his spine.

"Your Honor," Lincoln addressed the judge rather than his witness, "I have asked Mr. Wisdom to bring with him the current copy of *The Old Farmer's Almanac*. May I ask you, Judge Harriott, to examine the almanac closely and perhaps to invite Mr. McHugh, the state's attorney, to join you in that examination. I would ask you to confirm whether the volume Mr. Wisdom holds is, or is not, a current and proper edition of that book."

There was a general stir of surprise among the audience and jurors as well as looks of consternation from both the judge and the prosecutor. Judge Harriott nodded to McHugh and beckoned him forward as Wisdom struggled to move the large volume from his lap to the judge's bench. Having completed the task, he sat quietly waiting as the two men pored over the volume. After several minutes and much rustling of pages, the judge dismissed McHugh, who returned to his seat, reached over, and slid the volume back into the librarian's lap.

"Mr. Wisdom, on behalf of both the State of Illinois and the blind goddess Justice, let me express my appreciation for your service here. Mr. Metzker was beaten on the evening of Saturday, August 29, 1857. Would you be so good as to consult the reference manual you brought along and tell me what time moonset was on that date?"

Isaac Wisdom nodded and then thumbed the almanac to the proper page. He looked up at Lincoln as best he could. "Mr. Lincoln, there was no moonset on August 29 of last year. It was a new moon. There was no moon, sir." And he allowed the pages to collapse folded into his lap.

There was a general inhale that amounted to a gasp from everyone in the courtroom, save for Counselor McHugh, whose mouth hung open in horror.

* * * *

"Counselor Lincoln," Judge Harriott intoned, "you may proceed."

With that, Lincoln rose from his chair and began his closing argument:

"Gentlemen of the jury, the state's attorney, the Honorable Mr. James McHugh, has summarized his case for you and done his best to impress upon you that close facial recognition is possible in starlight from seventy feet with three men writhing in the dust between two wagons. And, as is the custom in our country, he will also enjoy a last opportunity to address you and the comments I'm about to make. And those I'm about to make do not reflect much on the facts of the case but the character of my client. When I was a lad of nineteen, I came north from Kentucky and found myself in New Salem with no way to make money for food or shelter save the strength of my arm and the sweat of my brow. But until I could find a job and get some payment, I was unable to provide for my most funda-mental, life-sustaining needs. It was that 'poor friendless boy that Armstrong's parents took into their house.'[3] Could such a kind and Christian couple also be parents who raised a mur-derer? The only thing all the witnesses agree on is that Duff Armstrong got into a fight with Mr. Metzker. Not a proper thing for a boy to do, we would all agree. But the witnesses also agree that Metzker grabbed Duff Armstrong by both ankles, drug him from the bed of his wagon, and dropped him on the ground. Not hard to imagine that most among us would fight in such circumstances. But doing so would make none of us killers. Neither does it make one of Duff Armstrong. Ladies and gentlemen, Ned Armstrong, Duff's father, died earlier this year. Mrs. Armstrong has no one to care for her in her old age save her only son, Duff. Do not miscarry justice twice by find-ing an innocent man guilty and depriving an aging widow of her sole means of support."

* * * *

"Has the jury come to a unanimous verdict?" Judge Harriott asked when they returned in less than an hour.

---

3.   Judith E. Hager, "Mile Eighty-Eight: The History of Frontier Beardstown, 1818-1860" (graduate research thesis, Northern Illinois University, 1965), https://huskiecommons.lib.niu.edu/allgraduate-thesesdissertations/3964.

The jury foreman rose. "We have, Your Honor. We find the defendant not guilty of any charges."

There was joyous pandemonium in the courtroom. Beardstown had never had such a show, and it seemed to all it had been a morality play that had ended happily. Duff Armstrong ran to his tearful mother and threw his arms around her. Lincoln followed closely behind. Once outside, he caught them.

"Duff." He spoke it loudly enough to get the young man to turn away from his mother. Seeing it was Lincoln, he stopped and parted from his mother; and when Lincoln caught them, they both embraced him.

After a moment Lincoln put his hands on the young man's shoulders and looked down into the grateful eyes. "Duff, I want a promise from you."

"Anything, Mr. Lincoln."

"Duff, you did not murder a man, but you were drinking and brawling. Those are not the markers of virtue. Your mother is a widow. Care for her."

"I will, Mr. Lincoln. I will. I swear it."

CHAPTER 37

AUGUST 11, 1858

Beardstown, Cass County, Illinois

The old Indian rode slowly into the stable.

"Chaubenee, your hair is completely silver in the sunlight. You're getting old." It was Jim's slow, easy drawl that greeted him.

Chaubenee slid off his horse and, leading it by the reins, led the beast into a vacant stall. "Same as always," he said, "about ten years older than you. And what is that expression you use? 'The pot calling the kettle black'? But in this case, it's the moon calling the snow white. If I'm silver, that beard of yours is white."

The two old friends embraced.

"And where do I find you off riding to?" Jim asked.

"To you."

"Chaubenee, your house is two blocks. You've been walking here almost every day for thirty years. Why are you riding?"

"You already said it, Jim. I'm over eighty summers now. That walk gets longer and longer."

Jim just nodded. "And why are you coming to me?"

"Thought you might want to join me. I'm going to the town square."

"What's there besides the bandstand?" Jim asked.

"Jim, do I remember that your Amanda reads?"

"She does, a bit."

"Has she been reading the newspaper? The Democrat one. *Beardstown Democrat*, it's called."

"Not so much. She's always been partial to the Whig one Mr. Arenz started all those years ago. Why?"

"Well, did Mr. Arenz's paper tell her that Stephen Douglas, one of Illinois's senators, is speaking in town today?"

"She mentioned it. Why?"

"Ever since I was a boy," Chaubenee said, "whenever leaders spoke, I always listened." His eyes became unfocused and he drifted. "That's how I met Tecumseh. His brother was speaking. Very eloquent, both of them." Then he snapped back. "Anyhow, I'm going to go. Thought you might want to come with me."

"Any special reason I'd be interested?" Jim asked.

"I hear he'll say what he thinks about slavery. Other guy, that lanky stork of a man who defended that Armstrong man last month, he's speaking tomorrow. They'll have different opinions. I wanna hear both. Thought you might as well."

Jim's focus sharpened. "Let me wash up." And he turned to walk to the hotel.

"Bring Amanda," Chaubenee shouted after him.

* * * *

The three sat on a blanket in the midst of a crowd of thousands. It seemed as though half the county's population was looking up at the pudgy man with lots of hair above his round face. He stood behind a podium set up on the edge of the bandstand and was slowly panning the crowd as though trying to size it up before he started.

"Goodness," said Amanda. "I didn't know we'd grown so large."

"I hear there are over ten thousand people in Cass County now. Mr. Beard would be proud, wouldn't he." Jim stated more than asked.

"Friends!" The short man's voice was huge. "I am your native son, and I'm here to ask for your support for another term as your representative to the US Senate."

The crowd roared approval.

Douglas basked in the applause and let it die before he spoke again. "This is not my first time in your town, but the last time I was here it was not much more than one mud street and a few buildings. That was when I volunteered to fight in the Black Hawk War."

Again, a thunderous approval.

"And since then, it is obvious you have prospered"— Douglas let his arm sweep around to all the buildings surrounding the square—"and I hope you will agree that I have helped make it happen. I hope you'll indulge me, but I'd like to remind you of that."

Douglas adjusted his collar, then continued.

"One of my greatest contributions to Illinois, and to the West, has been the opening of the land our beloved Thomas Jefferson bought from the French. Much of the development of that land had been stuck, for political reasons, and all because of the intransigence of politicians from the South over the rules set down when Missouri and Maine came into the Union. But I unblocked that jam with the authorship of the Kansas-Nebraska Act, and now trade flows in abundance through your city. My opponents in this election will be from the newly formed Republican Party. They are a party to destroy unity, to destroy prosperity, to perhaps destroy the Union because they are abolitionist."

There was a general, but not universal, chorus of booing.

And Douglas went on for another two hours. When he was done, those in the crowd, some boisterous and some in quiet contemplation, dispersed to their homes or the saloons.

As Chaubenee and the Beards walked back toward the knoll, it was Jim who asked, "What did he mean early on about 'unblocked that jam'?"

It was Amanda who answered. "You know I try to read the paper after I close the kitchen. I'm not sure I understand but maybe. Right after you freed me, Jim"—she looked at him with a smile that after all their years together still reflected her great admiration—"they let Missouri in as a state. When they did, they drew a line from about where the Ohio runs into the Mississippi all the way west and said there could be no slave-holding states north of that line. Well, it worked then, but since then them damn slave-owing states—" She stopped and looked at Chaubenee. "Forgive me, Chaubenee. You know I don't swear but sometimes."

Chaubenee interrupted with a snort. "Sometimes they're the best words, Amanda."

Amanda still looked chagrined but carried on. "Since then, the slave-owning states have refused to allow more states into the Union because they didn't want to be outnumbered. Senator Douglas's bill did away with that line."

They strolled in silence until they got to the knoll, and as they started up, Chaubenee asked, "I got most of his meaning, but he kept using a term I don't know. 'Popular sovereignty.' Either of you know what that means?"

Again, it was Amanda who spoke. "It's a term they use to mean that each state should be able to vote whether they allow slaves or not."

"So, these new states, Kansas and Nebraska, will vote on whether they allow slavery or not?"

Amanda nodded affirmatively.

"And that's why," Chaubenee asked, "they are calling it 'Bleeding Kansas'? The whites are killing each other over how to vote."

Amanda nodded again. Jim smiled a huge smile.

"Why are you happy, honey?" Amanda asked.

"I'm glad they care that much."

"Come on inside and let me get all of us a cold lemonade." She laughed. "Unless you men want something stronger."

Chaubenee and Jim sat in the usual front-window table. Amanda balanced a platter over her shoulder. It looked heavy with the three glasses and the pitcher of lemonade. She set it down, poured for all, and joined them.

Chaubenee took a long pull at the cool drink. "How's it been for you two since Mr. Arenz died, what, two years ago now?"

"About the same," Jim answered. "His brother has taken over and not changed much."

"But it will soon," Amanda answered.

Jim studied his glass.

Chaubenee's expression was inquiring. "What's changing?"

Amanda looked at Jim for a moment and then answered. "Since they opened the new Park Hotel, just off the square, we've lost our place as the finest hotel north of St. Louis. We don't have as much business as we used to. Mr. Arenz's brother is putting this up for sale. Who knows what happens then?"

The studied silence around the table was broken by Chaubenee. "My place gets awfully quiet and way too big. You two have worked hard for a long time. Why don't you both move in with me?" Then Chaubenee smiled. "I promise, Amanda—I'm less work than this hotel."

Chaubenee rose quickly, knowing it was something they would not discuss in front of him. "Let's all go together tomorrow and listen to this Lincoln fellow."

* * * *

The next day, they sat again, listening with the thousands. Lincoln was so different from Douglas. Tall as Douglas was short, thin as Douglas was thick, amusing as Douglas was serious, warm as Douglas was sober, ugly as Douglas was ordinary. They could not have been more different save for two things. They were both sons of the frontier and both politicians. Within moments Lincoln made that clear.

"Gentlemen, ladies. My name is Abraham Lincoln. I have been around your city almost from its beginning. I rassled a man for a campsite here once. I lost."

The crowd laughed loudly at this self-deprecating humor.

"I have ridden circuit court here. I sponsored the bill that brought in your first road from Springfield. I represented you in the US Congress. I was here less than three months ago defending the innocence of a falsely accused man. So, I can think of no better place to make this announcement. Today I commence my campaign to become your next US senator."

The crowd applauded and whistled approval.

"There are a few things I'd like to tell you about why I am doing this. But I want to start with one clear statement. I will run as a Republican. I know Stephen Douglas was here yesterday speaking to you, and I know what he has to say about the Republican Party. He says it is a party of Northerners and a party of abolitionists. The party is neither, and I am certainly not an abolitionist.

"Slavery is an institution in America. I don't like the institution, but it is an institution that will fail and disappear. It will do so if we, as a nation, follow a path that will naturally take it there."

And Lincoln went on for another two hours.

As the Beards and Chaubenee made their way back, it was Jim who spoke first. "Mr. Lincoln is wrong, I think."

"About what?" Chaubenee asked.

"He thinks, at least he wants us to believe he thinks, that slavery will fail on its own. It won't."

"Why do you say that, Jim?" Amanda asked.

"Americans, white Americans, are killing one another over whether just one state, Kansas, will have slaves or not. You think they will not kill each other over whether the entire nation should have slaves or not?"

The three strolled in somber silence. Chaubenee stopped for a moment, his breath seeming to come in short gasps.

"Honey, you all right?"

"I'm fine, Amanda, just old. Very old." As he pulled air into his huge chest, Chaubenee looked up into the bright summer sun. "I have always liked the warmth of the sun, even in the heat of the summer." He paused and looked down at the ground. "I will hate being in the cold soil."

Then he looked back up, taking in Jim and Amanda, a smile now brightening his face. "When the time comes, and it will soon, bury me in a place where the sun shines upon my grave."

CHAPTER 38

APRIL 24, 1859

Beardstown, Cass County, Illinois

Nigel Hoskins's coat was hanging on the back of his chair. He had one elbow on the table with his forehead propped in his hand. His newly acquired reading glasses were perched on his nose and, while they made the letters on the printed contract clearer, they were not comfortable on his face. He couldn't concentrate on the document without peering down at it, and every time he peered down, the glasses slipped farther down his nose and the letters went fuzzy. "Bloody hell," he muttered.

James McHugh sat across the table, as calmly as though at prayer, waiting for the banker to finish reading.

"Jim," he finally said, "I think I have it all, and it appears to be just as you said it would. The Rockford and Rock Island will extend their main line from Rock Island to cross the river here, at Beardstown, and extend from here to Springfield and then down to St. Louis. Further, they will place their round-house here for turning trains back to their points of origin, and they will build a shop for repair of both cars and engines. They will promise to commence construction required to fulfill the contract within two years and be completed and operational within four. In exchange for that, we give them $150,000, which will be distributed as $50,000 upon execution of the contract, the remaining $100,000 paid out over fifteen years from bonds the City of Beardstown will issue."

He sat up straight and looked down into McHugh's brown eyes that were contemplating him with interest. "You and I are clear. As executor of Francis Arenz's will, I am authorized to provide, from his estate, the sum of $50,000 directly to the R&RI when, but only when, as per the terms of his will, I am presented with a fully executed contract."

McHugh never lost eye contact and merely nodded.

"This document appears to be exactly as you, the city's representative, said it would be. Those terms are consistent with the will. There is, however, one term in the contract that is not a term with which I am familiar. And it seems to be of moment. So I need to call on your legal wisdom to help me understand."

McHugh's steely expression never changed. "If I can, Nigel."

"The term is 'force majeure.' It is their one excuse for neither starting nor finishing their work on time and not being in violation of the terms of the contract."

McHugh was an expressionless statue. "It means acts of God or civil insurrection. That is things completely beyond their control. Perhaps an earthquake or a tornado. Or a war. That's about it."

Hoskins nodded. "Then you may tell the city that the document is acceptable to the Arenz estate, which, when presented with a fully executed original of this document, will release a check of $50,000 made to the railroad."

"Good," said McHugh. "I was certain you would agree."

Hoskins rose and stepped from the table to a sideboard where he picked up two crystal glasses and a cut-crystal decanter half-filled with auburn liquid. He poured two fingers of the liquid into each glass and returned to the table where he sat back down, pushing one of the glasses toward McHugh.

"James, this is worth celebrating. The city needs this. To the future!" He hoisted his glass.

McHugh did the same. They knocked them together and then both men downed the draft in one long swallow.

"James, I must say this is a bit odd."

"How's that?" McHugh responded.

"For as long as I've been here, this city has been driven by founders. This is the first city initiative with none of them here to celebrate."

McHugh nodded. "Francis Arenz two years ago and Chaubenee two months ago. They are the last, and they are gone."

CHAPTER 39

APRIL 21, 1865

Beardstown, Cass County, Illinois

Hannibal Percy stood as tall and straight as his sixty-five years would allow, his right forearm bent at the elbow and extended forward, the palm of Vivienne de Villiere lying gently upon it. In three decades as a riverboat captain, he'd never had such a beautiful woman onboard. In her mid-to-late twenties, Miss de Villiere was tall, almost his height, and slender. Her jet-black hair was dressed pulled into a bun at the nape of her neck and coiled around with a precisely woven braid. The almost-alabaster color of her skin made the jet of her hair more prominent. Her cheekbones were pronounced enough to move a small shadow across her cheeks as she turned into the noonday sun. But most striking of all were her eyes, their grey, seemed to him, the color of a still winter morning. The one flaw on her face was the nose. It was narrow but a touch too long for her face. The flaw imparted to the face a haughty grandeur.

The dress completed her commanding appearance. Cinched tight at her narrow waist, it buttoned up the front to her neck and was covered from the shoulders by a short cape. The sleeves appeared from under the cape and bloused out wider as they fell down her forearms. A full ten inches wide, their fall revealed a cascade of lace undersleeves buttoned tight at the wrist. Festooned with flounces, the maroon taffeta skirt billowed out over a crinoline petticoat.

Percy walked her, the first to be debarked when the gangplank was released, to the six-passenger surrey, pulled by matching white geldings and positioned at the front of the ramp of the *Illinois Queen II*.

"Miss de Villiere, it has been my pleasure to captain you on your journey. I do hope when you return, I will also enjoy the pleasure of seeing you back," Percy said as they reached the step to the rear seat of the surrey.

"My captain," she responded, offering a soft but controlled smile and speaking slowly in the easy, pleasant accent of the Deep South, "much as I have enjoyed your company and the grandeur of your boat, if fortune smiles upon me, this little city"—she nodded up the bank to the brick buildings above—"will be the end of my journey."

Percy could not help himself. He bowed from the waist as she released his arm and stepped beside the largest man Percy had ever seen. The man, Heracles by name, was at least six and a half feet tall and must have weighed 250 pounds. And it was all muscle. His waist was no bigger than a normal man's, but it seemed as if even the tailor could not get enough cloth into that coat to keep the arms and chest from wanting to bulge out of it. As though his mere size were not formidable enough, his shaved head made him look like some antique palace guard trained not to speak but to kill. The head was glistening with perspiration in the spring sun, and perhaps it was no more

than the effect of the sunlight's refraction, but Heracles's dark
black head glowed an iridescent purple.

Miss de Villiere nodded to her guard. Without a word, he
put his hands on her waist and, with apparently no more effort
than Percy would have extended to pick up a glass, raised and
set her in the rear seat of the surrey. He then walked around the
front of the horses and stepped up and seated himself on the
front bench next to the driver, his bald head bulging upward
against the canvas covering of the surrey.

Percy's eyes turned to the driver, a small, quick white man,
black wavy hair grown long over his shirt collar but covered on
top with a smart, new bowler hat. Somehow his very presence
had reminded Percy of a ferret. The pistol showed because, as
Percy had noticed on their trip, it was his habit to wear a white
linen shirt under a waistcoat but with no frock coat above. And
he always wore garters to hold up his sleeves.

The boat was pulled tight to the dock and the gangplank
released. As they pulled forward, Miss de Villiere turned her
head over the rear of her seat and said, "But when you're back,
Captain Percy, please feel free to call on me. You, I will always
receive." She did not wave.

The other face in the back seat of the surrey turned to
him as well. It was the milk-chocolate-colored face of Miss de
Villiere's maid. The black woman had been as tall as her mistress
and perhaps as thin but with the strength of muscles showing
in her shoulders and arms. Her face gave away little save that
her normal expression was haughty. Her accent had been of
Jamaica with a lyrical quality Percy enjoyed. But he knew if
the life of slavery was hard in America, it was much harder in
the Caribbean. It made him wonder where that haughty quality came from. She always dressed in flowered-print dresses
and a floral-print cloth tied around her head. All the hair that
showed beneath was silver, a color that didn't match the face

that appeared to belong to a woman of something less than fifty.

* * * *

The moment René pulled the surrey to a halt in front of the Park Hotel, Heracles was out of the seat and moving around in front of the horses. He stopped beside the rear steps and extended the back of his hand, sturdy as any railing. His mistress placed hers on top of it and stepped down onto the boardwalk.

"Heracles, see the trunks get up to the room, and René, you see to the horses and surrey in the livery. Mavis, stay with me." She turned to the hotel whose front doors opened as if by magic before her. Mavis, a half step behind carrying a tapestried valise, followed her across the lobby to the front desk. Every eye in the lobby had turned to watch.

"My name is de Villiere. My agent wired from St. Louis for a two-bedroom suite with a sitting room," she announced to the young clerk behind the desk.

Before the desk clerk could respond, a middle-aged man dressed in a waistcoat with a silk cravat at his throat, and pulling on a frock coat as he approached, moved the young man to one side and stepped before her. "I'll handle this, Ben. Welcome, Mrs. de Villiere. I'm Jerome Schmidt. I'm the manager here."

She looked coolly at him, no hint of either a smile or a frown on her face. "It's Miss de Villiere, and thank you for your welcome."

Schmidt allowed a smile to cross his face. "Miss de Villiere, we got the wire, but it neglected to say how long you'll be staying at the Park."

"Perhaps indefinitely. Perhaps only a few days. I'm uncertain as yet."

"We can accommodate either but will hope for the former. Do you have bags?"

"My man is outside waiting for assistance. It will be more than one trip. He'll need them watched outside."

"I'll send help immediately. If you'll follow me, I'll show you your rooms."

"Mr. Schmidt, was it?"

"Yes."

"Mr. Schmidt, I also have a man outside with my horses and surrey. He'll need to be directed to your livery and then shown to our rooms as well."

"Certainly, Miss de Villiere. If you'll follow me."

Jerome Schmidt threw open the doors to his best suite with a flourish. He'd not intended to put them here, but upon seeing her, he'd instantly changed his mind. If the governor did show up, he'd just have to take second best. The doors opened into a medium-sized room with a desk, a large couch, and a small divan as well as a coffee table between them. There was an Oriental rug on the floor. The floor-to-ceiling curtains, when he opened them, revealed a small balcony with a wrought-iron table and two matching chairs. He was proud of this room.

She viewed it all with casual indifference. "Let's look at the bedrooms now." It was a command.

Schmidt took her first to the smaller of the two. It also had a window onto the street, but the interior was small and the furnishings consisted of an armoire, an end table, two beds, and a small wingback chair.

"Let's see the other, Mr. Schmidt."

The two women followed him quietly across the sitting room, their silence making him nervous. He opened the door to the master bedroom, hoping for some sense of appreciation. None was forthcoming. The room contained a canopied four-poster master bed, a large armoire, a divan, and French doors leading to a balcony fitted similarly to the one beside it servicing the front room. The balcony also offered a view of the town square and bandstand.

"This will be adequate, Mr. Schmidt," she said in her slow drawl, "but you will need to replace the divan with a small bed."

"Of course, Miss de Villiere," he responded instantly.

She looked at him, allowing her nostrils to flare just a touch. "And I will need a tub and hot water brought in an hour."

"Of course," he stammered.

"Thank you, Mr. Schmidt. That will be all." She dismissed him.

* * * *

Three hours later the four of them sat together in the common room. Mavis had combed out Vivienne's hair, and it hung around her shoulders and down the middle of her back, covering the silk dressing robe she wore. "There are some things we need to do and quickly. Mavis, I want you to get the papers from the last week of the *Beardstown Democrat*, I believe it's called. Only paper they have."

Mavis had removed her headscarf. As she nodded understanding, her heavy but short silver hair moved with her.

"I'll spend my afternoon and evening doing research.

"René, I know Illinois is a free state, but we picked this town because it voted against Lincoln in both '60 and again last year. There will be some Southern sentiment here. But until we learn the place, I don't want you, Mavis, or you, Heracles, out alone. I don't want trouble of any sort. Trouble could ruin everything. So, René, you go with her.

"When you two get back, René, I want you and Heracles to exercise the horses, but exercise with a purpose."

"What purpose?" René asked in his thick, mumbling Cajun accent.

Vivienne smiled. "That's my René. Always on point. I need to know everything about this place. It's only about ten thousand people. By the end of the day tomorrow you'll have ridden every street in town. Before I go out, I want to know what's around me, what the neighborhoods are like, what the businesses are, where the restaurants are. I want to know how these people live and why. You two men are, as always, my eyes and ears. I need to know.

"Heracles, you stay with me until René and Mavis get back. Then you go out. It's four o'clock now. If Mavis gets to the newspaper office and back in half an hour, you'll have maybe two hours of daylight. And when you come back, bring us all some dinner.

"Go on now. I'll nap while you're gone."

※ ※ ※ ※

"I do wish they had some chicory in this coffee. It tastes weak as tea," Vivienne complained to the breakfast table.

"Honey, when you get me a kitchen, you know I'll fix that." Mavis smiled.

"Good morning, Miss de Villiere. Is our hotel to your satisfaction so far?" Jerome Schmidt inquired.

"Good morning, Mr. Schmidt. And thank you for asking. Aside from our fondness for Southern cooking, we have only one complaint."

"What is that?" he asked, a look of contrition already forming on his angular face.

"I would be grateful for sheets with a higher thread count if you have them."

Contrition turned to exasperation. "I will look into it, Miss de Villiere." Schmidt turned and walked away.

"I see you've got him right where you want him," René offered with the biggest smile of the morning.

"Where she wants all men, you mean," Mavis offered without smiling.

But Vivienne did.

She looked at René with a look he understood before she spoke. It would be today's expectations. "Today, I want you two to finish learning the town, but I want something more. I want you to find a spot where we can build if I decide to stay. Out of town, but just. I want it close but don't want the neighbors to see the building. And I want it on an easily traveled road and with a very pleasant view. No less than ten acres. See what you can find. In the meantime, I have other business to attend to."

* * * *

James McHugh looked up, upon hearing the light tap on his door, just in time to see his secretary slide in sideways into the door he'd barely opened. He didn't like being interrupted when he was writing, and Todd knew it but had a conspiratorial smile on his face he wasn't even trying to hide. "A Miss Vivienne de Villiere here to see you."

"Does she have an appointment? No, she doesn't." His nasal tone made the words sound like condemnation. "I have no appointments this morning. Tell her to make one."

"You want to see her, boss." The voice was one of total self-assurance.

It got his attention. "What does she want?"

"She wouldn't say." The tone was the same and the smile even bigger.

"So, she doesn't have an appointment; she won't say what it's about; and you think I want to see her?" He was more mystified now than angry.

"That's right," Todd responded. "You want to see her." He said no more.

McHugh put his pen on his desk. "Send her in."

One minute later, he was looking up at the most beautiful face he had ever seen, smiling down at him. McHugh prided himself at keeping his emotions off his face, but he failed this time and knew it.

"Good morning, Counselor. Thank you for allowing me to interrupt what I know must be your busy schedule." The voice was like warm oil being poured over him. Then the warm oil extended its hand.

And the warmth of it burned, but this time McHugh maintained himself. "You're welcome, of course, Mrs. . . ."

"It's Miss, Mr. McHugh. Miss Vivienne de Villiere."

"It is a state's attorney's job to serve, Miss de Villiere. That's what I'm here for." He found her eyes at exactly the height of his. But hers were magic. He knew it and she knew it. But it was magic he could—and would—resist.

"Please have a seat, Miss de Villiere." After she accepted his invitation, he continued. "How may I serve you, Miss de Villiere?"

"Actually, sir," she emphasized the "sir," "I'm here to attempt to be helpful to you."

Now he let the surprise show. "How is that, Miss de Villiere?"

"It comes to me that your term of state's attorney is almost up, and that in Illinois yours is not an appointed job, as it is in my home state."

McHugh merely nodded.

"And I have come to make a small contribution to your reelection campaign." She reached into her bag and pulled out a little purse that she set on his desk.

McHugh did not reach for it. "Now that is a surprise, Miss de Villiere. A pleasant surprise but very unexpected. May I inquire why you are doing this?"

"Yes. Of course, you may. It is a very reasonable question. A complete stranger walks in and makes a campaign contribution; the question is almost de rigueur. There are several reasons really. In my home, civic responsibility was the first among duties. My father preached that to me often. I am, thanks to his parenting, of civic inclination. Also, I hope to open a business here, make Beardstown my home. This would be my first small step here in fulfilling those duties. And I have read the papers of your city and believe your administration of all to be reasonable and wise."

McHugh studied her intently for a moment, making no attempt to hide his inquiry of her eyes and expression. She showed nothing save what she intended him to see, and he knew it.

"Wisely and nobly spoken, Miss de Villiere. May I inquire why you chose Beardstown for your new home?"

"Yes, I'd like you to know. Two reasons really. First, as you know without asking, I am a Southerner. As soon as Vicksburg fell and the river opened, I came north. I will make my home and my life away from the sounds and scenes of battle. But as a Southerner, I know there are places where I may not be welcome, or at least places where I will be more welcome than in others. And I find that your Cass County voted for Stephen Douglas, a Democrat, as did all of the Southern states in 1860. Also, your county voted for George McClellan and his peace overtures to the South in 1864. It is not that I'm political; I'm not. I merely wish to be welcomed."

McHugh studied the beauty before him ever more closely as he listened. When she finished, he remained silent for a moment. "There is far more to you, Miss de Villiere, than first meets the eye. You are a very studied woman."

She smiled the most winning of her smiles. "I will take that as a compliment, Mr. McHugh."

"You said there were two reasons. What is the other?"

"My business is one, which, to be successful, requires a city with some wealth. Yours is such a city."

McHugh laughed.

Now it was her turn to control what her face showed. She succeeded and said, "What have I said to amuse you, Counselor?"

He regained his composure and smiled politely toward her. "Forgive me, Miss de Villiere, but you consider what you see wealth? The war has been very hard on us. For our wealth we depend on river trade, which has almost entirely stopped. All shipyards along the river were turned to building for General Grant and Admiral Porter. And our outlet to the world is New Orleans. Trade that has been cut off entirely. What you see outside my office is a very poor version of Beardstown."

For the first time in the conversation Vivienne de Villiere allowed her face to show emotion she did not intend. She leaned forward in her chair. "Mr. McHugh, may I speak candidly?"

"Please, I'd like to hear candor from you."

"On my way here this morning, I walked by a bakery, the smell of warm baked bread wafting out its open door. I walked by a dress shop with women's parasols and bonnets on display. You have wealth indeed. Far more than you seem to know. Ten months ago, I was living in a cave dug into the side of a clay hill to keep from being killed by the shells thrown by the same Admiral Porter who you complain deprived you of your ability to replace old or blown-up boats like the *Illinois Queen*, on which I arrived just yesterday. What was inconvenience to you and disrupted your ability to create wealth ruined mine entirely. You have wealth here, sir. I am here just to start over and hope to earn a piece of it and continue my life with some small sense of grace." She sat back in her chair, her face drained of expression.

McHugh spoke not at all, merely studying both her and his own reaction to her.

Her face molded back into the mask of control she conventionally wore. Once certain she was again in control, she said, "My sincere apologies, Mr. McHugh. That was unworthy of me. Please accept my apology."

For the first time McHugh felt a humanness in her, and it eased in him his need to be in full control. He leaned toward her and, looking over the purse she had put on his desk, spoke. "The fault is mine, Miss de Villiere. I knew almost nothing of you when you came to me, but one of the things I did know was that you were from the South. It was callow of me to allow myself to be so totally blind to what your existence must have been like. What it was that caused you to wander so far, and so completely alone, to a land of not just strangers but enemies. You have courage, Miss de Villiere; I must give you that. I must honor that. Accept my apology for not doing so earlier."

They sat momentarily in silence. She rose with that heart-crushing smile on her face and extended her hand. "Good morning, Mr. McHugh. Again, my name is Vivienne de Villiere. Thank you for making time in your busy schedule to meet me."

He reached over and took her hand, recognizing her smile for what it was. "You're right. A fresh start."

And they both indulged in a small laugh.

"There is one thing you've not told me that I'd like to know before you leave," he said.

"What is that, Mr. McHugh?" Her smile seemed genuine.

"What is this business you bring to Beardstown that is to allow you to continue your life 'with some small sense of grace'?"

"Ah, commerce," she responded. "That is something I'd hoped to discuss with you. It will be a slightly long telling if you'll indulge me."

"Gladly."

"Then just let me share some thoughts with you. Mr. McHugh, I come from a world of grace. Civilized people with time and interest to enjoy long, slow discussion, to eat well, to dance. To enjoy one another. I would like to create that society in Illinois rather than spend the remainder of my life pining for the one I have lost."

"Miss de Villiere, I fear you will not find that here. We are agrarian, it's true, but without slave labor, our holdings are small, each worked by one man and his family. Maybe one hired hand. I think creating that society here is a dream not to come true." McHugh's tone was almost chiding.

"Oh, that I understand, Mr. McHugh. But there are other ways to create that same height of civilization."

"How?"

"Mr. McHugh, you seem more sophisticated than I was prepared for. Have you ever been to France?"

He chuckled. "New York is as close as I've been. I went to school in Connecticut. Lots of vacation days in New York."

"I've not been there, but let me describe what I've seen in Paris, and you tell me if New York is the same. The Parisians gather in homes for what they call salons. They spend afternoons and evenings discussing literature, sometimes with musicians playing. The food is fabulous and the conversation lively and witty." She looked at him with a smile containing a hint of sex appeal. "The women are beautiful. It is life they are living, Mr. McHugh. I plan to create a space like that for Beardstown. For the men of Beardstown to enjoy." Her smile was now triumphant.

"Miss de Villiere, that would be wonderful. What city would not like such a place? But you said, if my memory serves, that you were here to earn a small piece of our wealth. How does creating such a 'salon'—that was your word—bring you wealth?"

Her smile became almost conspiratorial. "You are right, Mr. McHugh. I do not have the wealth to offer the city such a place without some compensation. But it is a place I know how to create, that I may have been born to create. If such a place were available, a lovely and gracious architectural setting, perhaps with gardens, certainly with music, a piano I'm thinking, a marvelous dinner by a great cook served well—cooks from the South do marvelous things, you know, unusual things— the best whiskeys and brandy, fine Madeira wine for the older gentlemen, good cigars of the best Cuban tobacco, perhaps a billiards table, and beautiful women dressed in the height of fashion with whom to laugh away the evening, what do you think the businessmen in Beardstown would pay for such an evening?"

He was smiling now, a smile of understanding. She had just revealed it, in the most refined, elegant, and almost-magical way he could have imagined. And he thought she was right. She may have been born to create this. "I'm uncertain, Miss de Villiere, that I personally would ever be a patron of such a 'salon,' but I think you may have picked your market well. I think there are many prosperous gentlemen here who perhaps have to travel long distances now to find such places or perhaps have never done so and can only imagine the experience. I think you would find Beardstown accommodating."

This time her grey eyes joined her sensuous lips in the smile. "Oh, I'm so glad you agree. Then I think I will stay.

"Mr. McHugh, when I first arrived you asked what you could do for me. At the time, I thought of nothing, but after our conversation, there is something you could do, if you will."

McHugh was suddenly back on guard, and his countenance showed he was. "What is that, Miss de Villiere?" he asked with great caution, even hesitation.

Her lips maintained the smile, but her eyes were no longer part of the duet. "Like any business, I will need a banking relationship. Could I impose upon you for such an introduction?"

McHugh pondered for just a moment. "Come back to see me tomorrow after lunch. I'll know then."

Vivienne de Villiere rose and again extended her hand. "Thank you, Mr. McHugh. I have enjoyed our conversation. I hope you have as well."

He accepted her hand, walked around the desk, opened the door to his office, and watched her cross the outer office and depart. He stood staring at the outer door as it closed. When it did, he looked down to see Todd's face beaming what he would have normally considered an inappropriately familiar smile. "Todd, what does de rigueur mean?"

* * * *

"This steak is as tough as an old boot," René complained.

"You don't want it, I'll eat it." The low rumble sounded more like a foghorn than a voice.

"You want another, you may have another, Heracles. René is just being irksome."

"Because he's René," Mavis added.

"Bet a cup of hot, black chicory coffee would change his mood. It would certainly change mine."

"I see we've all been cooped up together just a touch too long. This may last awhile, so let's all stay on our best behavior," Vivienne scolded, and then, looking directly at René, added, "René!"

"Sorry, Miss de Villiere," René mumbled.

Mavis looked at the cool, beautiful presence that had been beside her for over twenty-five years. "How long, honey? 'Cause I'm not used to the books constantly showing declining balances. They been doin' that for well over two years now."

Vivienne gave her a smile that showed no concern at all. "I'll have the answer to that question by this time tomorrow." Then with a manner of casual indifference she looked across the dining room to a rigid Jerome Schmidt standing in the corner and beckoned him.

Schmidt scurried to her summons and was surprised to be greeted with a smile. A first from her. It worried him as much as it pleased him.

"Mr. Schmidt," she said, her smile lingering, "would you be so kind as to ask our waiter to bring Heracles another of those delicious steaks.

"But before you go, a question if I may.

"Do you know Mr. McHugh, your state's attorney?"

"Oh yes, ma'am. Very well."

"Is Mr. McHugh a God-fearing man?" The smile seemed genuine.

"Oh yes, ma'am. Very much so."

"You seem very certain, Mr. Schmidt. How is that?"

"Well, ma'am, we go to the same church. I see him and his family every Sunday."

"So, Mr. McHugh is active in the church."

"Oh yes, ma'am. In fact, the church is discussing building a school of our own. For our children. James, Mr. McHugh, is head of the committee looking into it."

"What a fine man. How lovely. What church is it you and he attend, Mr. Schmidt?"

"St. John's Lutheran, ma'am. Fine church. If you stay in Beardstown, we'd love to see you join us some Sunday. Services are at 11:00 a.m."

"All of us, Mr. Schmidt?" she asked, making a small motion with her extended index finger to make a circle of all at the table.

Schmidt stood silent for a moment, flushed, and swallowed. "Some of the churches in town take an abolitionist view to the congregation. Ours tends to vote more Democratic."

"Thank you, Mr. Schmidt." She dismissed him. As he walked away, she said with a perky tone, "Don't forget Heracles's steak."

* * * *

"Good afternoon . . . Todd, is it?" she said as she collapsed her parasol. "Mr. McHugh is expecting me this time."

The secretary came up from his desk and stood to greet her. "Good afternoon, Miss de Villiere. I will tell him you're here." He turned, tapped lightly on the inner door before opening it, and after an exchange too quiet for her to overhear, turned back to her. "Please do step in." He held the door open long after she had passed.

"Thank you, Todd. That will be all," came the nasal command.

"Please do sit down, Miss de Villiere." He waited for her to adjust her skirts into the chair. "I have been able to arrange the meeting you requested. Nigel Hoskins, the president of our local bank, will make time for you late in the afternoon."

She rewarded McHugh with a smile, a reward that she knew he would appreciate. She also knew that he would not let his expression reflect that appreciation. "Thank you, Mr. McHugh. I am grateful."

"I trust you will forgive me, but I felt it necessary to share portions of our conversation with Mr. Hoskins."

She gave a small nod, but her grey eyes were cool.

"The bank closes at three o'clock. He will see you at three thirty."

Neither the eyes nor the expression changed. "The entry will be unlocked?"

"No, they lock its front doors promptly at three o'clock. He has asked that you come to the back of the bank. There is an alley with a rear door."

Vivienne sat silent, her eyes gone cold. She had never in her life found herself directed to the rear door, to the alley. The realization of the life she was choosing came with a stark suddenness. Until this moment it had all been nothing more than a plan. Now it was real.

McHugh studied her face calmly. The display of cold emotion dissolved into a small, calculated smile. She was back in control.

"I will have my carriage at the alley door at three thirty. Thank you for arranging it, Mr. McHugh. Before I go, there is one other thing with which I'd appreciate your help."

"What is that, Miss de Villiere?"

She reached into her bag and again produced a small silk purse that she held in her lap. "I understand a church in town, St. John's Lutheran I believe, is making plans for a church school."

McHugh momentarily lost control of his composure, a look of surprise flashing onto his face. "It has not yet become a plan. It is only at a state of contemplation at the moment. Why do you ask?"

"Has the contemplation gotten so far as to estimate costs for this structure?"

"Not in specifics, but the cost of building a small house runs about $500. That would be a reasonable approximation for cost."

She raised the purse from her lap and, leaning forward, held it toward him. "Perhaps this would be enough to move the contemplation to the planning stage?" She held the purse halfway across the desk.

McHugh studied her for a moment and then reached his hand toward hers. When it got to the middle, he turned it palm up.

She dropped the purse into his open palm.

"Are you a Lutheran, Miss de Villiere?"

"No, I am merely civic minded, as I told you, but I do have an especial interest in education."

He sat back into his chair. "Shall I put the donation in your name?"

"Mr. McHugh, I have come to rely on you already in the conduct of my affairs in Beardstown. I will rely on your discretion in this matter as well. Perhaps your minister would think it inappropriate for a woman attending Mass at St. Alexis's to be making such a contribution. And perhaps the good father at St. Alexis's would agree. Feel free to make the appellation as 'anonymous' or any other way you see fit. As long as you know there is a civic-minded businesswoman now in your town, that's all that matters to me."

He watched as she rose, brushed her skirts straight behind her, picked up her bag and her parasol, and started to turn away. She stopped suddenly, her face the picture of composed ease.

"One other question, Mr. McHugh. Does your role as state's attorney allow you to maintain any private clients?"

He rose as he spoke. "My job with the state keeps me very busy, but I manage to maintain a few."

"Would you be willing to add me to that list? I will need legal assistance with the details of setting up my life and business here."

He was willing to let a genuine smile show. "The door to my business will always open to you, Miss de Villiere."

She allowed her lips to rise slightly at the corners. "And mine to you as well, Mr. McHugh."

He walked her to the front door, which he opened, and watched as she stepped out, opened her parasol, and stepped directly into the surrey sitting at the curb.

"René, I have two hours before my next appointment. Let's drive out and let me look at the land you think might do for our home."

* * * *

There was only one door at the rear of the bank building. René pulled the surrey up close enough that she had to take only one step in the muddy alley before knocking.

Nigel Hoskins's heart jumped. He was almost sixty now, but if James McHugh's description was even close, this was a woman he wanted to meet. He opened the door to a vision whose beauty was suffused in the glow of pink light transfused through her parasol. The grey eyes steadily looking at him, seeming to take all of him in, made his heart jump again and caused a jolt of adrenaline that rushed all the way down his belly and into his groin. He couldn't help but smile. "Please do come in, Miss, Miss de Villiere, is it?"

He stepped back and made room for her, his eye falling on the new and spotlessly clean surrey sitting next to his door and the small man with black hair flowing behind his bowler studying him from above.

"Forgive my receiving you in the rear. My day, today, was fully scheduled. When James McHugh suggested I see you, this was the only time available. We lock the front at three o'clock sharp, so this was the only way. I hope you understand. Please have a seat."

As she folded herself into the leather padded armchair in front of his desk, he noticed for the first time that in addition to the parasol, she was carrying a small tapestried valise that appeared heavy enough that she chose to set it on the floor beside her rather than in her lap.

"Of course, I understand, Mr. Hoskins." She favored him with a smile that would have won the heart of a Roman centurion. "I am grateful you could meet with me under any circumstance."

"I am pleased to do so and be of assistance. How may I, and the Beardstown State Bank, help?"

"I am new here. I hope to make Beardstown my home. Perhaps, just perhaps"—her grey eyes twinkled at him—"with your help I will be able to. And the first thing I will need is a safe place for this." She pulled the valise from the floor and then, using two hands, lifted it up to his desk. "I am tired of carrying it."

"And what is 'it,' Miss de Villiere?"

"Please"—she nodded toward the bag—"open it."

Hoskins pushed his bulk up from his chair, leaned forward, and unsnapped the valise. He peered, then stared, and finally reached into the bag, removed a handful of gold coins, and let them fall through his fingers and back into the bag. "Double eagles," he observed.

"You'll find there are 250 of them."

Hoskins sat back down. "Miss de Villiere, your voice betrays your origins. You are a Southerner. McHugh tells me from Vicksburg. May I know how a woman from war-ravaged Vicksburg obtains $5,000 in gold? I know the question is impertinent, but if we are to develop a banking relationship, it is a thing I should know."

Her smile was reassuring. "I will have no financial secrets from you, Mr. Hoskins. It was not I who obtained them but my father. He was the owner of a proud, beautiful, and prosperous plantation called Panther's Leap. The Pouncing Kitty, we laughingly called it. When Grant managed to cross the Mississippi, or perhaps properly said when the incompetent General Pemberton allowed him to cross, my father knew it was over. With the loss of Vicksburg, he knew the war itself would be over soon. The South would be cut in half, and there would no longer be any hope. . . ." She stopped and gave him a conspiratorial smile. "If, as you say, our voices betray our origins, then you are British."

Hoskins smiled accommodatingly.

"And Daddy knew that once that happened, there was no longer hope that your nation would intervene and break the blockade of our ports. Our cotton would never get to your mills, and so no guns would come back in return. He sold everything that week—the land, the field hands, the horses. He sold it truly cheap, and the buyers thought they were getting a steal. But he got something and, in the end, they got nothing. The only things he did not sell were two domestic staff and two horses. What you see in that bag is the sum of value created by three generations of the lives of de Villieres. And it needs a secure place to rest."

Nigel Hoskins sat, his hands folded across his belly, studying her. His fascination with both her beauty and story was not quite enough to overcome thirty years of dealing with frontiersmen with great stories. There were riches in some of those dreams but irrationality in even more. "Your father, Miss de Villiere. Is he here with you as well?"

Vivienne de Villiere gave a small chuckle. "My father, for all his wisdom and foresight, was a believer in the Southern way of life. Or perhaps he was so attached to the grace and beauty of his plantation that he simply did not have the strength to rebuild. He took the two horses, very good horses, and went off to find General Forrest's cavalry. I suspect, knowing Father, he found them. I doubt I will ever find his grave."

"And he left you and your mother to fend for yourselves?"

"I never knew my mother, Mr. Hoskins. She died when I was very young. I was raised by a Jamaican slave. The head of our household staff. Very smart woman. Taught me all I know about business."

Hoskins looked startled. "What would a Caribbean know of business, Miss de Villiere? Much less a slave."

"Why, Mr. Hoskins, I'm surprised at you. America's first banker, Mr. Hamilton, learned all he knew of business in the Caribbean before he ever came to America," she said with a teasing smile.

"Miss de Villiere, your correction makes me blush, I fear, but Alexander Hamilton was not a slave."

"No. No, he wasn't. But the system is very different in the Caribbean, and slaves must learn business or die."

The big British banker sounded curious. "Inform me."

She nodded and assumed an expression of sobriety—a teacher's expression. "At Panther's Leap, we cared for our slaves. It was not out of kindness, I suppose, but we perceived doing so as in our own interest. We wanted them healthy and strong, just like expensive horses. And perhaps even happy, as it tended to make their work easier mentally. We fed them, housed them, nursed them, and called a doctor if an illness was beyond our ability to cure. That is not the system in Jamaica, or the rest of the Caribbean, as Mavis taught me. There, the life of a slave is much harder, and cheaper. They are worked dawn until dusk and then must care for themselves and their families if they have them. To do so they are given small plots of land on which they grow yams or plantains or perhaps exotic fruits. But just as man can't live by bread alone, neither can he live by yams alone. So the slaves develop markets of their own to swap or even sell to one another. They get good at it or die. Mavis was very good at it. Kept all my father's accounts for years. Keeps mine as well."

"She reads and writes?" Hoskins showed real surprise.

"Poorly. But she is skilled with arithmetic."

Hoskins nodded with a new light of understanding coming to his eyes. "But my question remains. Your father left you to fend for yourself?"

"I suppose you could look at it that way, Mr. Hoskins. But neither he nor I did so. He had raised me to take care of myself. To thrive in the world. That our whole world had changed was beyond our ability to control. But he knew my ability to control any world in which I found myself would be enough. And he left me the money you see before you. And he left me the important members of the house staff. That was enough. That will be enough."

"This Mavis. He left her with you?"

"Yes."

"And she still is?"

"Yes."

"You said, 'House staff.' That implies others."

"There is one other. Heracles. He was our majordomo. Huge man, Heracles. Very quiet but formidable. Even the biggest of our field hands feared Heracles."

"Do you not mean Hercules?" Hoskins inquired gently.

She offered a soft smile of understanding. "I fear Daddy's Greek was better than his Latin."

"Do they know Illinois is a free state? Now that you are in Illinois, will they stay with you?"

"Oh yes. They both know. They also know of Dred Scott." She looked at him almost cutely. "I think, Mr. Hoskins, you would be amazed at the things the house staff of rich plantations visited by well-read and sophisticated people come to know. But they will stay with me. We are the only family each of us has left."

"And the small man driving your surrey? I did not see him well, but he looks white."

"Your eyes told you true. His name is René. He is French. Cajun, as we call them in my part of the world."

"Is he part of your staff as well?"

"He is and will stay with me as well, if that is your question. René is family."

"Related by blood?"

"No. He comes from what we in Mississippi call 'poor white trash.' Orphaned very young as far as we knew. Grew up living by his wits and his fists on the streets of Vicksburg. Constantly in trouble with the law and constantly beat up, as he was small. But he seemed not to have the ability to back down. He was off to reform school, not a place to be in Mississippi, when my father took him in. My father liked that he was very smart and had great courage. He was no more than eight then. René became devoted to my father. Would have slept at the foot of his bed, had Father let him."

"Then why did your father not take him along to join General Forrest? Is it not conventional for cavalry officers to have private retainers in the South?"

"It is. And René wanted to go. He very much wanted to go. But Daddy said I would need him more than he would. Made René swear to keep trouble from my door."

Hoskins leaned back, tilted his head up as though studying the detail of his copper ceiling.

Vivienne said nothing. There was nothing more of her past he needed to know. He would speak next, and then she would know.

"Miss de Villiere, I learned my trade in London, as your ear has told you. But I have been a banker on the frontier of America for over thirty years. Banking is different here. Banking relationships are based less on books and history than on trust and imagination. I find it helps me judge these things if I understand the person, and not just the business. That is why I have inquired so much of you and your history. You have been candid with me or, if not candid, then you are a very good storyteller." He smiled at her.

She let her face remain impassive.

"And I have learned of you what I need to know personally. But now I need to know about your business and what business arrangement it is you would propose."

Vivienne stayed deep in her chair. Her face remained circumspect. "Not complicated really, Mr. Hoskins. I have $5,000 in specie that I will deposit with your bank. Aside from living expenses, I will need to withdraw from those funds money to buy a piece of property on which to build my home. René has found a suitable piece about a mile east of town just off the road leading to Chandlerville. It sits high enough to avoid any floods and offers a beautiful view of the bay. On that property I will construct my home and furnish it. I would propose to buy the land, offer the land to you as collateral, and finance construction with a loan from you."

She stopped and looked at him and offered the warmest and most intimate of stares, her grey eyes seeming to pull him into her. She spoke in almost a whisper. "Has James, Mr. McHugh, told you of the business, the world I will create in my home?"

Hard as he tried not to, Hoskins found himself being pulled into her vision of a world he had not even contemplated since he left London, a world of beauty and charm and wit and sophistication and sensuality and yes, sex. But not sex as a perfunctory body function. Sex of slow, easy, beautiful, lustful fantasy. And he saw it all in those grey eyes. "Yes. Yes, he has. In some detail."

"Then I will not belabor you with it save to say, the world I will create will be the richness of the world into which I was born, and offered not at the cost of a lifetime of labor, but merely at the cost of an evening's entertainment."

Hoskins snapped himself back to this world, this room, this bank. "Have you figured out what this . . ." He paused, then continued. "*Home* will cost."

"Perhaps you could help me there. Let me tell you what the building is."

Hoskins nodded agreement.

"Most of the new construction here I see is brick."

"Yes. We have our own brickyard. For five years now. It has made brick construction so much less expensive," Hoskins explained.

"What I see is a three-story brick house with a very wide veranda facing down to the road and the bay. The ground floor will open to a large sitting room with a bar along one wall and the remainder filled with couches and sofas, small tables around, and a very large fireplace along one wall. Behind that will be two rooms. One a library large enough for a billiards table in the middle. The other a kitchen of commercial size. The second story will contain bedrooms. I'm thinking six. Then the third story, which will simply be below the roof, with dormer windows, will be a storage area and some smaller bedrooms for staff. There will be a stable behind. The grounds leading up from the road will be a park. Many trees but grass and flower beds maintained as well. I'd like construction to leave any large trees in place. We'll put bench seats here and there. It will be a place to stroll. What will that cost, Mr. Hoskins?"

He pondered for just a moment. "The most expensive house we've had built here was milled boards instead of brick and had much decorative wrought iron. It was about the same size, perhaps a bit smaller. The reported cost was $24,000. That's a good starting point."

"Let's call it $25,000. There will be some additional open-ing costs to stock the bar and pantry, that sort of thing. Let's say the loan is $27,000."

Hoskins looked stern again. "That is a great deal of money, Miss de Villiere. A great deal."

"Mr. Hoskins, I've never been to London, but I've been to Paris. I presume the salons in London are the same. In the years you have been on the frontier, have you not longed for the salons of London in your youth? The founders of this city were men of vision and courage. This is your chance, Mr. Hoskins. Your chance to match their courage with your own. To bring something to the frontier that not even they had the vision to imagine."

She went completely silent and held his gaze. There was no more to say. The sound of a word from her now would do no more than puncture the balloon that was the vision she had implanted rising in his mind. She remained silent.

His reverie broke open and a very wide smile with it. "Miss de Villiere, this house you will build, this salon, is so grand it will require a name."

She let her smile match his. "I think, Mr. Hoskins, you just named it. It shall be 'Le Salon.'"

* * * *

They had finished dinner; the dishes had been removed; the decanter of brandy and the cigars she had ordered had been sent up. Wrapped in her long robe, Vivienne sat on the couch, her feet tucked under her, a snifter of brandy in one hand and a cigar in the other.

"We have celebrated now, but it's not a victory. It just means we are able to begin. Mavis, you and Heracles and I have a house to build, and we have very little time in which to do it, less than a year. Land to be purchased—I think I can get McHugh to convince whoever owns that land to sell it. We have plans to draw and construction to complete. Every day we waste is a day we lose money.

"And you, René"—she pointed her cigar toward him— "have the hardest job of all, but only you can do it. And if you fail, we all fail."

He leaned forward across the table, set his drink down, and said nothing, all of his concentration focused on her.

"René, you have to go home. Getting there should be easy. The war will be over soon, and the river is open now. You may have to bribe your way onto a supply boat, as we did to get out, but you can do that."

"Easy as stealing a hot apple pie cooling on a windowsill." His dark eyes flashed with excitement. "What do I do when I get there?"

"You find four or five girls."

René laughed. "That's even easier."

"No, it's not, René. It may be very hard."

The abruptness in her voice stopped his laughter instantly.

"René, you know all the girls I grew up with. Those my age, a few years older, a few years younger. It's those girls you must find, René. Who knows where they will be? They won't be at home. They won't have homes. But you need to find them. When you do, you bring them back with you."

She had never seen René look befuddled in her entire life. It made her laugh. "You say to them that I send my regards. You say I worry about them. You say I've found safety and even grace. Use that word, René, 'grace.' You say I've sent you to find them and to offer them shelter and protection. That I've sent you to save them. Before you say anything other than I send them my regards, though, you find out if they are single. You don't say anything more to married women. Just my regards."

"How about widows?" he asked. "There may be a lot of war widows."

"You are clever, René. Widows are even better. But no children. If they have them or are pregnant, you say no more than I send my regards. And no matter what, you don't tell them anything about what's planned here. Just I've found sanctuary and I want them to join me.

"I want four or five, René. Not fewer than three nor more than five. If you can find the Beaulieu girls, I'd especially like that. And the Gartland girl, the younger one. The two older sisters are bitches; the younger was the most beautiful of us all, difficult sometimes but so beautiful. They would be the best of the lot."

René's grin became salacious.

"Stop that, René," Mavis barked.

"And René, when you come back try not to stop in St. Louis. I don't want those girls there. Try to get a boat upriver from Alton if you can."

"Damn," René said, disappointed.

"Oh, René, you get to see St. Louis, but on the way to Vicksburg, not on the way back. There's something you need to do there."

Suddenly René looked skeptical.

"Oh, you'll like it. You need to buy two things and have them shipped for arrival before the river freezes."

"What?" He was still skeptical.

Vivienne could not contain her grin. "First, a billiards table."

René gave an approving nod.

"And second, a piano," she added.

René dropped his brandy snifter with a splintering crash and dove across the table, wrapped her in a hug, and kissed her cheek.

"See, honey," Mavis said. "You get to do the only thing you'd rather do than fight. You get to be the piano player in a whorehouse."

* * * *

One week later, the two men watched as the light breeze dissolved the blue-grey smoke of their cigars into the green flashes of the spring foliage above.

"James, this is a very good cigar," Nigel Hoskins complimented his friend. "Where did it come from, if I may inquire?"

"Is good, isn't it?" McHugh responded. "It's from here. Rolled by a new little shop on Fourth Street, called 'Curly's Cigars.'"

"Curly's, eh?"

"Bit of a joke. He's bald as a billiards ball. He's just back. Discharged from the 114th after a cannonball took his leg off above the knee. Seemed in oddly good spirits about it. Said, 'Well, Mr. McHugh, I've found work that can support me without having to stand up.' He's learned to roll a good cigar, hasn't he?"

"He has indeed." Hoskins exhaled a long stream of blue-grey smoke and watched as it diffused above him. "Your brother's in the 114th, isn't he, James? This Curly have any report on him?"

"He did, Nigel. He did. Said young Albert had moved from a know-nothing, politically appointed, second lieutenant to a damn competent company commander. Be home soon now, I'm hoping."

"From your lips to God's ears, James. To God's ears. It is a shame Mr. Lincoln won't be alive to see it."

"It is, I agree. Heard that Booth, the assassin, was killed or perhaps burned alive in a barn, but one way or the other, all of him that came out was cinders." McHugh seemed pleased as he said it.

"James, I've lived in America most of my life, but I'm still a foreigner. I see it with less passion than were I born to it, but it seems to me, Cass County is an odd mix of attitudes about all this."

McHugh was looking up into the trees, watching his smoke dissipate, seemingly lost in thought. When he looked back down, his expression was one of sharp attention. "I'd love to hear how you see us, all these folks you've lived with this long."

"Illinois has always been a free state, and almost everybody I know would have it no other way. But you seemed to want it all left alone. It wasn't worth dying or killing over. Since I've been here, county elections have always been close—Whigs versus Democrats and too close to call. Then the Whigs fell apart because the Northern Whigs wanted the growth of slavery controlled by the federal government and the Southern Whigs wanted that growth controlled by the citizens of each state. They both blew away in the same wind that brought us the Republicans. So now it's Republicans versus Democrats.

In '60, Cass County voted for the Democrat who carried the South. Passions were high in the country. And they were high here. More than one such argument around here settled with fists. But passions or no, this county sent over three hundred fifty men to fight and die for the Union. The Union has won the war, James. That's clear. Everyone but Jefferson Davis seems to know it's over. So the Union will survive, but, James, if Beardstown is in any way representative of the rest of the country, this won't solve the question of slavery in America."

McHugh had listened patiently to Nigel Hoskins's analysis. Listened to every word. He studied on them as he rolled the cigar in his mouth.

"You are a more thoughtful man than I, Nigel. Perhaps it's just an advantage of maturity. Or perhaps, as you say, the perspective of a man whose roots are not here even though his life is. Or perhaps your Oxford education, or merely that by nature you are more thoughtful than I. I'm not certain of any of those things. But what I am certain of, Nigel, is that it will soon be over. And unless my brother is killed by the last shot fired, he will be home soon. And that when the war is done, it will force that damn railroad to stop using that Goddamn 'force majeure' clause and fulfill its obligations. And then prosperity will come back to us, Nigel. It *will* return."

McHugh stopped speaking and concentrated on the last of his cigar for a moment. Then he rose, tossed the stub into the grass.

"Nigel, I gotta go to work. You should, too. But don't forget to start buying your cigars from Curly. He served under my brother, and he gave his leg so you and I could have this chat. What was it Mr. Lincoln said, 'All gave some; some gave all.' Well, Curly gave some."

CHAPTER 40

MARCH 28, 1866

Beardstown, Cass County, Illinois

Heracles sat quietly on the front seat of the surrey watching the paddle wheeler turn sharply out of the current, then cut power entirely and drift slowly to landing. The steam whistle of the mighty boat gave one last proud blast announcing its presence as it drifted softly against the dock and crew members made her fast. Before the crisp nip of spring air blew the dark smoke away from the stack, the smoke contrasted sharply with the chunks of white ice not yet melted and floating lazily with the current. He could see René surrounded by a gaggle of women, the faded colors of their dresses trying, but failing, to be gay in the spring air. He strode smartly from the end of the dock up the bank, the women trudging more stolidly behind.

Heracles's almost-always passive face showed no expression, but he could not help but observe the wilted state of René's covey. He'd known them all since they were young, he presumed, but recognized none. Only one carried a parasol, and even before he stepped down to get the luggage, he could see it was patched. All save one of the five wore gloves, and even those showed darning of old tears. But it was the dresses that told more of the story than their other garments. Not only was the cloth of each faded by the sun, but it also drooped flat and low against their hips; the excess of cloth, no longer held up by crinoline or steel hoops, dragged in the mud before and behind each like a besmirched train. Only their hair appeared normal, each head dressed fully and properly as though to assure the world that they were proper young women even if their circumstances had become meager.

"Ladies," René barked, "two of you hop up front and the other three in the back while Heracles and I strap on the bags."

Heracles stepped down from the surrey and started back toward the steamboat.

"Heracles, you do not remember me?" The question came with a saddened smile from a thin young woman with dark hair and a complexion the color of lightest amber. She was standing shoulder to shoulder with another woman, perhaps a year younger, who shared her coloring.

"I remember you, Miss Beaulieu. May I help you up?"

"Thank you, Heracles. I would appreciate that."

He held his hand toward her, palm down. She put one hand on the surrey rail and the other on the back of his. As he raised his arm she rose with the ease and grace of a cobweb drifting into the breeze.

As she slid to the middle of the rear seat, Heracles looked at her younger sister and still holding his hand in place said, "Miss Beaulieu."

The younger girl repeated her sister's motion but with not quite the same grace.

There were surprisingly few bags. No trunks at all and only eight valises for the five women and René. After René strapped the last of them on, he pulled himself up until the toes of each of his feet were firmly on the luggage rack, his hands holding firmly to the support members of the surrey's canvas top.

"OK, Heracles. Let's take these ladies to their new home."

Heracles lifted himself up and while still standing on the step looked down at the two ladies in the front seat, his embarrassment showing. "Ladies, you will need to move as far to your right as you possibly can."

After a moment's shuffling, the woman closest to him with a mass of black curls said, "That's as far as we can go. You'll just have to slide in." There was a hint of a smile on her thin face.

Heracles forced his way down, looking straight ahead as though his failure to see her would somehow make it not true that they sat with their thighs crushed against one another. He unwrapped the reins from the buggy whip. Once he had them all firmly in his huge right hand, he took the buggy whip out of its stand, and popped it in the air between the heads of the matched team. They started at a trot up the bank and then rolled past the Beard Hotel and down the main street of town as every head on both sides of Main Street turned to make a full study of the newly arrived Southern ladies.

They rode silently until Heracles turned the surrey left on the last street in town and moved them along what within three blocks became a country lane.

"Heracles." A voice from the rear seat of the surrey came easily and spoke with authority. "You did the Beaulieu sisters the honor of remembering them, but I don't think you recognize me, do you?"

Without turning his head to look, he answered, "No, ma'am, I do not."

"My name is Louise Gartland. I was a bit younger than your mistress and not around Panther's Leap that often. But any of us had to see the size of you only once and hear your name to remember it and you."

Heracles neither turned to her nor spoke.

"Will you tell me of Illinois while we ride?"

"I know little to tell, Miss Gartland, save of the house we have been building for you. Sometimes I come to town on errands, but mostly I carry out Mavis's instructions and train the new staff in preparation," he rumbled slowly.

"Ah yes, Mavis. Formidable Mavis. She is hard to ignore.

"You just said, 'Train the new staff in preparation.' Preparation for what?"

Heracles didn't speak. Shortly he used the length of his whip to point to a large brick house flirting through the trees several hundred yards from the road. "Miss de Villiere will answer."

The surrey drove up the white gravel lane that curved through the park. He pulled to a stop on the circulation, before a wide staircase leading to a large double-wide front door. Vivienne de Villiere was standing before the door, her bright-yellow dress brilliant in the spring sun. A step behind and to her right stood the commanding figure of the grey-haired Jamaican. Heracles drew to a stop, stepped out of the surrey, and handed the reins to a blond livery-clad young man who, if anyone had bothered to look at him, would have blushed in mortification at being so conspicuously dressed.

Heracles turned to get the bags but, looking up, saw Louise Gartland standing motionless above the surrey's top step, her arm extended toward him. He stopped and offered the back of his hand, which she leaned into as she stepped down. She was the last of all the women scampering up the steps toward Vivienne. But once they got there, they all stopped and not a sound was made. No giggles, no laughter, no kisses—just expressions of stark realization that they were no longer equals. She had saved them. They were hers. All save the last, who walked slowly up the steps, the women before her parting like cabinet doors, until Louise Gartland stood face to face with

Vivienne de Villiere. She put her hands on Vivienne's shoulders and pulled her close enough to kiss her on each cheek.

"You are our savior, Vivienne. Thank you." She stepped back.

And then they all seemed to descend upon their hostess, giggling and laughing and crying.

Louise stepped behind the gaggle and to Mavis. "It has been a long time, Mavis. Do you remember me? I was much younger four years ago. Much younger."

Mavis looked at her with unrestrained study. "Younger perhaps but no less forceful, even then."

Vivienne escorted them all through the large front doors and the cloakroom and into the expanse of the sitting room beyond. She led them all to a large leather-covered sofa and matching divan extending at a right angle from one end of the sofa. On the polished maple table between them were six crystal glasses and a bottle of claret. As soon as they were seated, she poured for each, took one in her hand, and invited them to do the same. "I know you have a hundred questions, but now is not the moment. Now, only a small toast." She lifted her glass. "To a life of refinement, culture, and ease," she said. "Join me."

And each did.

"We are all genteel ladies, and we will act as such. We will talk over dinner. It is early spring, but Heracles has managed to procure some quail and one large goose that was too lazy to fly farther south last winter."

They laughed with her.

"You will remember the care and skill with which Mavis ran a kitchen."

"And the rest of your house as well, as I recall," offered a voice.

And all laughed again.

"Well, tonight you'll get the best dinner you've had since Grant crossed into Mississippi. But before then there are things for you to do. Mavis will lead you down the hall behind you and up the stairs. On the next floor each of you will find your rooms. And the moment you open the door you will find a brass tub filled with steaming water."

There was a collective moan.

"Soak. Bathe yourselves. And when you are done, look into the armoire. You will dress like ladies. The dresses may not fit perfectly, but we can fix that later. You will also find an open bottle of claret. Don't let it go to waste. Tonight is a night for celebrations. To celebrate a new start. Dinner will be served in two hours.

"Mavis, would you show the ladies to their rooms."

"Ladies, if you will just bring your glasses and follow me," Mavis commanded.

Mavis was the only black woman any of them had ever heard dare use that tone.

* * * *

The music of the piano hung lightly at the edge of conversation, but the waltz gave a sense of elegance and festivity that had been absent from their lives for a very long time.

"Wherever did René learn to play Strauss?" Esther Beaulieu asked. Before Vivienne could answer she added, "Robert and I used to waltz to that very tune." Her face took on a wistful, faraway expression.

"René learned it the same way he learns all his music. He heard it. He can't read music. He just has this gift," Vivienne answered absently. Then she turned to Esther and was overwhelmed with the sadness covering her face. "Esther, what has happened? Shall I have René stop?"

A small tear ran down the side of the older Beaulieu girl's face. She dabbed at it with her napkin. "No. No, it is beautiful. It just brings back memories."

Vivienne studied the face made oddly beautiful in its sadness and said nothing, waiting for Esther to say more.

"Vivienne, did you know Robert and I married?"

"I remember only that you were engaged. What a beautiful couple. The toast of us all."

Esther dabbed her cheek dry. "We married quickly. No ceremony, just our local church. All had changed. Robert was off to war." The smile turned from sad to impish in an instant. "I suppose the truth is we wanted just one night together before he went off." She leaned closer to Vivienne and spoke in a tone so low it was almost a whisper, but the smile continued. "It was wonderful, Vivienne." She sat back upright in her chair. "I'm so glad we did. It turned out it was our only chance. At least I had that to remember him by."

"What's happened to him, Esther?"

"He didn't last two weeks. Was killed in Jackson before the Yankees even got to Vicksburg."

Vivienne slid her chair a few inches to her left and put her arm around Esther.

"What are you two whispering about over there?" The question came from across the table. It was Barbara Carson who spoke. "Whatever it is, please share. There are only six of us here, and it is a festive evening."

Barbara Carson was a big girl with large hips and breasts and red hair that seemed to highlight her pale skin and make her blue eyes flash joy to the world. Oddly, her face showed none of the flesh of her body. She was all high cheekbones and square jawed. Very pretty, in a Nordic sort of way, Vivienne had always thought.

"You are right, my dear Barbara, no private conversations tonight, so I will say it out loud. You are all thinner than I supposed. You especially, Barbara. I had those dresses cut from memory, and I remember you as having large breasts that seemed to entice every man in the room. And now I've had the tailor leave far too much room in the bodice of your evening gown. I'll have to get her over here to remove some of that material."

Barbara laughed a hearty, almost coarse, laugh. "No, you won't. Give me two months of Mavis's kitchen and I'll be back to forcing every gentleman I meet to struggle to maintain eye contact with me."

The six of them all laughed along with her, the excess of claret moving them as much as Barbara's wit.

Two young women in their early teens approached the table from the kitchen and, still displaying the awkwardness of uncertainty, began to clear the remains of the feast. They filled their serving platters, then hoisted them above their shoulders and turned back to the kitchen.

"Vivienne," called Louise Gartland from the middle of the round table.

Vivienne turned her attention to Louise and was taken, as ever she had been, with the woman's still-almost-girlish beauty. She was black Irish, that wonderful blend of genes created when thousands of Spanish sailors washed up on the Atlantic coast of Ireland struggling to get home after Drake and his fleet of small English ships inexplicably destroyed the Spanish Armada come to conquer Elizabeth's England. Her hair was dark brown, almost black, her complexion olive. The parts of the face were all slightly exaggerated. The eyes were large and steadily brown. The nose long and straight as was her jaw. The mouth large with full lips parted to display perfect teeth. Only her ears were too small for her head. It was a face whose parts should not have worked, but they did. It was a face of power and beauty.

"Yes, Louise," Vivienne answered.

"I've wanted to ask you about the house. Your whole life, your father had given you free rein over the décor of Panther's Leap. What was it you teasingly called it—'Pouncing Kitty'?"

Vivienne nodded, and the ladies high on spirits giggled.

"And you had made that place oh so feminine. We were all jealous. The rich fabric of the wallpaper in every room, the moldings at the floor and the ceilings. The richness of the pastel curtains and silk fabric on every piece of furniture."

The others all nodded agreement.

"You see, Vivienne." Louise moved her hand around the table. "We all remember. But this. This is so different. So male. All the furniture is leather and the walls covered in wainscoting and the floors dark wood and Bokhara rugs. And behind this huge room a billiards room and a card room. So unlike you, Vivienne. What's gotten into you?"

Vivienne's face broke into a satisfied smile. "Louise, I'm glad you asked. There is much I want to tell all of you, and your question is a very good place to start. But first let the girls serve dessert—when is the last time you had chocolate cake?"

There was a chorus of approval.

"With it we'll have something René brought with him from home. Something I've missed terribly—chicoried coffee. You'll find the coffee in Illinois is so flavorless, but tonight it will all be as it was at home. As soon as these girls bring us dessert and coffee, I'll tell all."

Five minutes later, the cake and rich, sharp coffee were served. Mavis had shuttled the servers out of the room, leaving them to clean up in the kitchen and assuring them she'd attend to anything more the ladies needed. Vivienne sipped her coffee and, after a deep sigh of satisfaction, stood up.

"Ladies, Louise has asked a very insightful question, and I'd like to answer it. You all know my father sold Panther's Leap just before the end. Sold the land, the equipment, the field hands. Sold all but the house staff." She paused. "Actually, all besides Mavis and Heracles. I suspect there were lots of conversations, maybe even at your dinner tables, about what a fool old Claude de Villiere had become for selling out so very cheaply. But he got something, and that was more than any of your fathers got. He left me the money, and I used it to get me—to get all of us—here. I picked this place for several reasons. First among them is that Beardstown, like Vicksburg, is a river port and soon to be a railroad center. It is, and will be, a prosperous place, and unlike many other places in the North, Southerners are welcome here. But lastly, and perhaps most important to me, to us"—she looked around the table and made eye contact with each—"there is something we can offer here that they need but do not have. There is no culture here. There is no charm here. There is no sophistication here. And that, ladies, we have in abundance. And those qualities will create for us a refined life to live."

Each and every pair of eyes looked at her with intensity. She had their attention. She was capturing their imaginations.

"I have named this grand house. And no, I did not name it 'Pouncing Kitty.'"

There were giggles.

"I've named it 'Le Salon.' It is from here that we, the six of us, will bring culture, sophistication, and charm to this prosperous, but vulgar, place. Here, men of wealth will be able to find conversation of politics and wisdom. They will find it along with a fine meal and very good whiskey and wine and cigars of the finest tobacco. They will find the recreation of gentlemen, billiards, or a hand of cards. And they will find all of that wrapped in the charm of women worthy to bring it to them. That will be your part. Ladies of a finer society, here to make gentlemen of men who brought civilization, but not culture, to the frontier. We are needed here, ladies."

There was the small patter of politely clapping hands.

"Now, let me bring the honesty of my situation to you. When my father exited society, he left me a valise containing $5,000 in gold. All he had. To create this"—Vivienne pointed up and pirouetted—"cost me five times that. I have developed a banking relationship here and borrowed deeply. I am, dear friends of my youth, deeply in debt."

She remained absolutely silent, letting the impact of her words soak deeply into the understanding of these once-pampered souls.

"I have sent René to rescue you and offered you shelter and my protection. But I can only protect and shelter you as long as the bank is paid. And I must work to do that. And so must you."

There was a hard silence. It was Louise Gartland who broke it. "What would you have us do, Vivienne?"

Vivienne nodded recognition of the question. "Men will pay for what we offer not just because we are all young and beautiful. They will pay because they hunger for the lives we have lived. They will pay us to teach them a better way to be. They will pay for drinks and dinner and cigars." Vivienne paused again. "They will pay for *everything* we offer."

Louise was looking skeptical. "How will it work, Vivienne?" Her tone was very controlled.

"Each of you will earn one-third of every dollar your guests spend. I will pay for your wardrobe and food. You will pay me back for that and rent for your rooms from your earnings. What is left over will be yours."

There was a long silence around the table, each of the five dark into the shelter of her own thoughts.

It was Judith Harrelson who spoke it. Judith was a very tall and very thin woman of extraordinary grace in her carriage. She was also the only blonde among the group. She was known to be quiet and sometimes thought of as slow. "Vivienne, are you expecting us to prostitute ourselves?"

There was a sharp inhale around the table, but no one spoke.

Vivienne's face was expressionless as she let time pass. Before speaking she looked at each. "No one here will be asked to do anything she does not wish to do." She let that soak in completely. "If you have a gentleman you wish to entertain for the evening, that will be entirely your affair. And if you do, you will not have to sully yourselves about money. But of what is added to his bill upon departure, half will be yours."

Vivienne stood entirely still, making no attempt to avoid any who wished to speak or confront her. None did. "There are a few details about this you may wish to hear. I've asked Mavis to address you on administrative details. Mavis." She beckoned.

The tall, muscular black woman with grey hair stepped forward. "Ladies, I want to speak to some things that I'm thinking are on your mind." The mellifluous cadence of her voice brought them to her. "Most of you know I've managed the household of the de Villieres for over ten years. You may not know I managed all of the finances of Panther's Pounce, not just the household but the land as well. Numbers were a gift to me. I'm good with them. I will manage this house as well. I have done some figuring, and I think each of you may be able to get by with income from food and drink. If you are good at cards, you may do even better. But it is the details of the . . . *upgraded* services I'd like to discuss. First, I ask you to remember when going to your rooms earlier, you will have noticed there was no grand staircase from this main room. The staircase was down the hall. That was intentional to allow complete discretion. You may also have noticed that there were long ropes with tassels on the end hanging from each of the four posts on your bed."

Several heads nodded acknowledgment.

"Those are not just decoration. They are bellpulls. Some of you ladies may know that even the most loving of gentlemen sometimes wish from a lady things she does not wish to offer. Especially when the gentleman in question is drunk."

There were small giggles from several of the women.

"If you allow a gentleman into your room and he misbehaves, merely pull the cord. A bell will ring beside the piano, where René will generally be found, and behind the bar, where Heracles will be most of the time. They will stop whatever they are doing and come to you immediately."

Eyes were wide, perhaps with excitement, perhaps not.

"Lastly, there is beside each of your beds a small table with a drawer in the front. If you pull it open, you will find a supply of 'French letters.' The house staff will keep them supplied."

She paused and looked at the young women's tentative expressions. "I have known most of you since you were girls. You know me for what I am. You know me to be honest and straightforward. I am also at your service anytime I can be useful."

Mavis made a small curtsy and stepped away.

Vivienne stepped to her place. "My dear friends, you are all I have left of my life. And it is the same for you, or you would not have come with René when he invited you. We are as sisters. I know I have told you much and perhaps asked you much. You may wish to sleep on all of this. I will depart now and leave you to talk among yourselves and think in the quiet of your own rooms. If there are things to discuss, let us leave them to the morning light." She turned, walked across the room, and disappeared down the hall.

They all sat in momentary silence. It was Judith who finally spoke. "Ladies, welcome to our new home—the Pouncing Pussy."

* * * *

Vivienne was up early. She was sitting looking east out the library window, watching the sun slowly rise over the trees and fill the sky with light and the day with warmth. She was wearing a long robe and sitting in a wingback chair, her legs crossed and a cup of that marvelous coffee René had brought back with him, when she heard footsteps behind her. She turned to see the beautiful face of Louise Gartland, her long straight hair falling down and softening the power in the face. She was wearing the faded and mended dress she had arrived in less than fifteen hours earlier. In her hand, she held a carpetbag with sides bulging.

Vivienne did not uncross her legs or rise, but she did smile. It was a slow, sad smile. "Louise, come in. Let me get you a cup of hot coffee and some breakfast."

Louise crossed the room and approached the low coffee table. She dropped the valise, which landed with a soft plop, and eased herself into the chair. Her voice was very gentle, almost resigned. "No thank you, Vivienne. You've already done more for me than I can repay. More than anyone else I knew could or would have done. I'm grateful enough."

Vivienne, still sitting deep in her chair, said, "But you're leaving me."

"Yes, I'm leaving you."

"Was it what Mavis said?"

"Perhaps."

"Are you a virgin, Louise?" As she asked it, she uncrossed her legs and leaned forward to set her cup on the coffee table.

"Vivienne, the war changed everything. We all did things we would never have considered before the war. And we did them gladly. We all knew the world might end the next day. It made every night a last night. No, I'm not a virgin. Not nearly, anymore."

"But it bothers you?"

"Sex? No, not at all. In fact, I've become fond of it and admit there is a thrill the first time with every man. No, it's not sex."

Vivienne leaned forward again and poured a refill from the sterling pot before her. "Then what?"

"What you are doing here is wonderful, Vivienne. I believed every word you said last night. You are risking all to create a world we once knew, not only for yourself, or your rescued friends, but as an offering to a world that needs it." She paused. "Whether that world knows it or not."

For the first time Vivienne let expression show on her face. She was genuinely curious. "What, then?"

"Vivienne, if there were some way to live this life you offer for free, I would. But I will not be sold into it. I can never think of myself as being an object to be bought. That's all. No more. I am free. I will stay that way."

"Louise, do you remember what I said? None of you is obligated to any act at Le Salon."

There was a light knock on the door. One of the young staff being trained stepped in. "May I get you anything, ma'am?"

"Yes," Vivienne answered. "Bring me some toast and honey, and bring Miss Gartland a coffee cup and the biggest breakfast you can put together."

"No, Vivienne."

Vivienne gave her the full benefit of her most winning smile. "Yes, Louise. You're going to need it." Then she looked at the young girl by the door. "Do as I told you." She looked back at Louise. This time the smile was not winning but soft and sad. "Can you answer my question?"

"Yes."

"Will you?"

"If I stay here, I will get by. I am good at cards." She offered a grin. "But one night I will have had a glass too many of claret. Some man will be charming. A man perhaps who has been trying to seduce me for weeks or maybe months. It may even be that he will be handsome. We will end up in my bed, and I will enjoy myself, perhaps a great deal.

"The next morning, he will be gone, or go after breakfast, and, as you said, there will be no sullying talk of money.

Mavis will take care of all of that. But at the end of the month there will be just a little more money in my reckoning than I expected. And I will know I have sold myself. The only time for me to stop it, Vivienne, is now."

Vivienne de Villiere looked out the east window to the morning sun, now too bright above the clouds, too bright to look at directly. She looked back down at her articulate and thoughtful friend. "Louise, we all sell ourselves. If not with me, how do you propose to sell yourself?"

The door opened, and the server came in with a large tray loaded with another pot and porcelain cup as well as a covered serving dish.

"Just put it on the coffee table here," Vivienne instructed.

She did, poured a cup of steaming black coffee, and removed the cover from the plate, revealing biscuits covered in gravy, two eggs, and three strips of thick bacon.

Louise looked at it and, when she heard the door shut, looked up. "I think I will stay in this town. Home would make me sad, and I liked your logic of this place. I'm probably far more educated than most of these frontier things. Maybe a job teaching school until I find some man to whom I wish to give myself."

Vivienne poured herself another cup of coffee and looked up to see Louise slowly chewing, a satisfied look on her face. "Will you stay here today? I may be able to find you that job for you. We open tonight. If I've not secured your position by then, just stay upstairs in your room. Will that work?"

Louise poured another cup of coffee. "Vivienne, however will I repay you all you have done for me?"

"Be my friend. No matter what, Louise, be my friend."

* * * *

"Good morning, Todd. Do you think you could arrange for Mr. McHugh to see me?"

He knew by now that this particular smile of Vivienne de Villiere's was entirely impersonal and designed merely to win him, or any other man, to her way. But Todd didn't really care that he was being manipulated. From her he enjoyed it. "No one is with him now, Miss de Villiere. Let me see." He tapped lightly on the inner door and slipped in, only to return momentarily. "He will see you, Miss de Villiere. It is always nice to see you."

"Thank you, Todd." This smile was playful.

"Good morning, Mr. McHugh. Thank you for making time."

"Your smile is a nice break from my morning's work, Miss de Villiere. Please sit down."

She pulled her skirts away from her sides and forward as she sank into the chair. "This morning, Mr. McHugh, my visit is only partially business."

"Really?"

"I've come to deliver an invitation," she announced. "Tonight will be the opening of Le Salon. Many of the city's better citizens will be there. I hope you can join us."

Again, he shook his head. "It has been my pleasure to have helped you get started, and I'm pleased with your civic spirit. But I've told you before, yours is not an establishment for me."

She looked at him unblinking but with no hint of disapproval or rebuke on her face. "Then there is one other thing I wanted to ask about. It's that 'civic spirit' interest."

"What's that?" His skeptical look returned.

"St. John's new school. I hear it is almost complete."

"Yes, just a few weeks to tighten up the roof."

"Have you found a teacher?" she asked.

Now he genuinely looked skeptical. "No."

"Then I would like to introduce you to a friend. Highly educated. Speaks French. Toured Europe. Reads the classics and isn't a bad musician either."

"And where did you find such a woman?"

"Ah, Mr. McHugh. That is standard education for Southern women. Would you like to meet her? She is a friend from my childhood. She arrived yesterday and is looking for work."

McHugh sat back deeply into his chair, running a pencil through his fingers. "She won't be working for you?"

Vivienne shook her head. "No, she won't be working for me."

"Then I would like to meet her, yes."

"Her name is Louise Gartland. I'll schedule something with Todd. I'd be very surprised if you, and the church, don't find her acceptable." Vivienne rose to go. When she reached the door, she stopped and turned to face him. "Mr. McHugh, you will be missed this evening. I know you feel no need for the society of Le Salon. But one thing to remember. All men, no matter the resources with which they surround themselves, at some point in life find they are inadequate. When that day comes, and it will, my door will always open to you, James."

CHAPTER 41

MAY 9, 1868

Beardstown, Cass County, Illinois

Sam Hitchcock was a big man, tall, broad shouldered, but even in middle age his hips and waist were boyishly thin. His boots with tall heels worn under his dungarees betrayed his western origin. He wore a vest over his white cotton shirt, his badge pinned on it. Outside the office his wavy chestnut hair was covered with a wide-brimmed Stetson, and his Navy Colt hung low on his right hip, but here, sitting behind his desk in the jail, he kept both in front of him, the Stetson lying with its crown up and the gun belt, as always, positioned so the handle faced toward him. He was an affable and easy man, quick with a smile but woe to the man who either set his hat crown down or called him "Sammy."

He looked up as the door opened and a dapper James McHugh stepped through, removing his bowler as he came. "Hello, boss." Hitchcock smiled up.

"Sheriff, I keep telling you, I'm not your boss. You work for the county, same as me."

"Well, James, I do keep sending campaign contributions to Mo McConnel in hope the old man still has enough federal connections to get me appointed marshal, but so far it hasn't helped. If it ever does, I'll stop calling you 'boss,' but until then, every time you walk in that door it's to deliver an order, from you or one of your grand juries, to arrest somebody for something. What little chore have you got for me this morning? And do you have time for a cup of my bad coffee while we talk about it?"

Even the normally sober McHugh couldn't help but be charmed by this big man who preferred words to his fist or gun but seemed very adept with all three. "If it's free, I'll take it."

Hitchcock rose and stepped to the wood-fired stove with the pot warming on top, picked a tin cup off the shelf, filled it, and handed it to McHugh. "What do you need?"

McHugh nodded his head toward the cells showing down the hall. "Full house this morning," he observed.

"And every Sunday morning for the last three months. Ever since the city finalized the easements for the railroad to start laying track, I've had cells full of drunken railroad laborers every payday evening," the sheriff responded.

"You never knew our founders, did you, Sam?"

"McConnel, yes, but the others were dead before I got here."

McHugh sipped his coffee, aimed his mouth to the floor, and spat grounds off the tip of his tongue. "I'd seen them, even met them, when I was a boy. But my father told me that Beard and Arenz had a very different opinion about the railroad. Arenz saw it as the future and necessary for the prosperity of the town. Beard was a 'river rat.' He used to say, 'Beardstown is a place where land is cheap and women are dear. Whole lot more men here than women. And single men do what single men do. They drink too much; they gamble; and they fight.'

But Beard didn't mind that. He said they might be rowdy, but they were part of the community—invested—and they were just blowing off steam, but they were interested in the future and cared what was good for their town. He dreaded the coming of the railroad. Said they'd bring in a lot of single men, but those men would be nothing but trouble. They would not give a damn one way or the other about the damage they did."

Now it was Hitchcock's turn to nod down the row of cells. "Beard built this jail, didn't he?"

McHugh nodded.

"He seemed to see the future. It's full of railroad men. None of our own—just what did Beard call them?"

"Itinerant laborers," McHugh filled in. "And they are, and we've got to protect our citizens from them and them from each other."

"I'm doing my best, boss. Doing my best."

"I understand that," McHugh said. "Heard you had to call the doc last night to get two of them stitched up. That right?"

"Yeah, mostly just black eyes and bloodied noses back there. By now they're best pals again. But doc needed to pull a slug out of one's shoulder."

"You know who shot him?"

"Yeah, bouncer at some cheap dive that sells diluted whiskey and runs a couple of whores in a crib upstairs. Little guy but very tough."

McHugh arched an eyebrow. "Prostitution's illegal, Sam."

Now it was Sam Hitchcock's turn to arch an eyebrow. "And you know we look the other way. It's an outlet for all those boys back there. If we close the cribs down, they won't have much to do and they'll all be trying to kill one another. We'll have more trouble on our hands, not less."

McHugh set his coffee cup on the desk, a small smile on his face. "I know that, Sam. Not suggesting otherwise, but I want that bouncer gone before he does kill someone. You know his name?"

"Funny name. Earp. Wyatt Earp, I believe," Hitchcock said.

McHugh looked back to the cells. "You usually let them out when they've slept it off, don't you?"

"That's right."

"Don't do it just yet. Go arrest that bouncer. Earp was it? And throw him in a cell with a few of those boys in it. Maybe even the one Doc had to stitch up. Don't let them kill him, but let them have a little revenge. Then let the crews out, but keep Earp until an hour before sunset and tell him not to let the sun set on his ass in this town."

Hitchcock said nothing, just nodded understanding.

"And, Sam," McHugh added. "Little man is quick to draw that gun, you said. Take a couple of deputies with you. If I lose you, I'll want it to be to a federal marshal's star, not a marble slab."

* * * *

Sam Hitchcock stood in front of Walden's Hotel, counting down from one hundred. He'd had his two deputies unpin the badges from their lapels before they entered. Their instructions were to walk to the back of the bar and sit, order a beer if the bartender came to them. He wanted to make certain they were behind Earp when he confronted him. At zero, Hitchcock walked in.

Walden's Hotel was small, dark, smelled of stale beer and barf, and if it had any rooms to rent, they only came from taking one of the girls to them. As he opened the door, the noon-light behind him revealed only three seemingly hungover men at the bar, a bartender, his two deputies sitting quietly in the rear, and a small man standing, the sole of one boot pushed into the wall behind him. It was to this man that Hitchcock walked.

"You Earp?" he asked.

The small man brought his foot to the floor and shifted his weight so he faced Hitchcock directly. "Yeah, what's it to you?"

The three recovering drunks at the bar and the bartender all turned to the sound of sharp voices.

"You shot a man last night."

"That's my job," he said, dropping his right hand low to his side.

Hitchcock's eyes stared unblinking into Earp's face. "You seen the star yet, Earp?"

Earp glanced down. His expression changed to one of surprise.

"And my job, Mr. Earp, is to see you don't." There was silence in the room. "You'll be coming with me. And you'll be coming without the gun. You can give it to me or leave it at the bar. Your choice." In his peripheral vision, Hitchcock saw the bartender reach below the bar. Without taking his eyes off Earp, Hitchcock nodded and saw motion in the back of the room as his deputies rose. "Bartender, you reach for that shotgun, you're dead. And you, Mr. Earp, will very slowly raise your right hand to your lapel. Then you will reach with your left hand to your gun belt and unbuckle it."

There was silence in which a mouse running across the floor could have been heard.

"Sheriff, that's my brother. I was here last night and will witness he did nothing wrong. That big railroad thug pulled a gun first." The voice came from the bartender.

Hitchcock didn't answer. His eyes never left Earp's. The silence was filled by the sharp click of a pistol hammer pulled back and then another, followed by the rough voice of one of Hitchcock's deputies.

"Brother, hands on the bar. Now! If they come up any way but empty, you're a dead man."

Wyatt Earp smiled a slow bitter smile. The next sound was the sound of his leather holster hitting the floor.

"Now, Mr. Earp, turn facing the wall and put both hands behind your back. Billy," he shouted to his deputy, "keep your gun on that bartender. Mike, come over here and snap a pair of cuffs on Mr. Earp."

When the cuffs were securely on, Hitchcock turned to the bartender. "Brother, what's your name?"

"Virgil, Virgil Earp," came the response in a surly tone.

"Virgil, take your left hand off the bar and reach down there and come up with that shotgun. And when you pull it up, I want you to put it on the bar."

The hand slowly went down and came back up holding a double-barreled shotgun, its barrels sawed off to less than a foot in length.

"Thank you, Virgil," Hitchcock said in a very friendly voice. He stepped to the bar, picked up the gun, broke open the breech, and pulled shells out of both barrels. He held up the shells and examined them. "Buckshot, Virgil. You're a killer. You'll find your shotgun lying outside the door."

With the handcuffed Wyatt Earp before them, Hitchcock and Deputy Mike walked out. Billy followed slowly, walking backward, his pistol still raised.

CHAPTER 42

OCTOBER 13, 1868

*Le Salon, Chandlerville Road,
Beardstown, Cass County, Illinois*

"Ladies, everyone get another cup of coffee or tea and take a seat. You know I like to get these meetings to start on time."

They were all there—Ellen and Esther, the dark-haired, light-amber-skinned Beaulieu girls; tall, thin, graceful Judith Harrelson; curvaceous, redheaded Barbara Carson—greeting the morning as they always did, wrapped in silk dressing gowns, hair down and lounging in the overstuffed sofas that made up the living room. Vivienne was, as usual, already dressed and in a daytime gown and Mavis, in one corner, hovering over all like a mother hawk at the nest.

"Let's start out with new information for the book."

"Gary Connish has gotten himself inducted into the Masons and is very happy about it, but his wife is not. She thinks it will cause him to spend even more time away from home. I'm guessing it will be an excuse to spend even more time here." Ellen's comment was met with a chorus of giggles.

Barbara unwrapped herself from the back of the over-stuffed chair, yawned, sipped again at her tea, and offered, "It appears Isaac Metz has found religion. Or perhaps his wife has, but they are joining the German Lutheran Church."

The silence following went on long enough that Vivienne prodded. "That's all the news on jobs, friendships, social clubs, churches, and politics worth recording?"

Judith, ever languid but precise in her movements, set her cup down and moved forward in her chair. "Vivienne, I heard something odd. Maybe worth reporting. Do you remember that dark, thirtyish, and oh-so-handsome young man who was here last night? I don't think he'd ever been here before. He devoted his evening to me and talked quite a bit toward the end. He's from Chicago. With the Chicago, Burlington and Quincy Railroad. But he came in alone, not with any of the Rockford and Rock Island men. He'd been sent here to see how the R&RI was doing on finishing the track and the round-house. He said the CB&Q was buying the R&RI, but no one knew. Then he shut up immediately like he'd slipped."

She picked the cup back up and took another sip. "I knew you'd want to know more, so I got him another drink or two. Later in the evening he said it was true. His line was, 'Deal has been agreed at the top. I'm just here to make sure we'll get what we're paying for.'

"I gave him a little kiss, and he shut up again."

This last met with more giggles.

"Thank you, Judith. That news will buy us more goodwill at least.

"That it?" She looked around the room, and none of them offered more news.

A pretty, young, blond girl of perhaps sixteen came in through the kitchen door, carrying a tray with the aroma of warm buns wafting from a basket. She moved around the room, offering them to each of the women.

"Ladies, I have a specific question." Vivienne stood as she spoke. "Business has been slow for the last month. Some nights we only host two or three gentlemen. Business in town is booming in anticipation of the railroad opening. Why are we not seeing our business boom, too? You all know we all prosper or fail together. We can hope it's just short term and business will go back to normal and even pick up." She paused for a moment. "But my beloved daddy used to tell me, 'Hope is not a strategy.' We do need to figure this out."

No one spoke a word. "OK, then that's all for today, but keep an ear tuned on that one. We need to know.

"Judith, if you have a moment, would you step back into the office with me?"

The morning meeting broke up, and Vivienne and Judith walked back to her office.

"Have a seat, Judith," Vivienne offered, pointing to the sofa, and sat at one end herself. "Judith, do you think your young man will return?"

"I know he was taken with his evening. That's not it. But I'm not at all certain he was here more than a day. He may have already left for Chicago. Why?"

"Because that may be the most money-making tip Le Salon has ever received—maybe."

Judith, sitting erect, brought herself even more so until she was sitting as tall as she possibly could. "How so, Vivienne?"

"If CB&Q is buying the Rockford and is keeping it quiet, there is a reason. Both of those railroads trade their stock. One or both will rise on this news."

"Which one?" Judith asked.

Vivienne shook her head. "I don't know, but I know someone who does. And if he does, I may give him a little of my own money to invest. It was you who discovered the secret.

You should get something out of this as well. If I put some of my money in, would you like me to add some of yours as well?"

"Yes. Thank you, Vivienne. But do you really think this news is that important?"

There was a light knock on the door, and then it opened to reveal the same pretty, young blonde who had delivered the warm rolls at the meeting. She was holding the same basket. "Miss de Villiere, I came to see if you wanted a roll."

"Thank you, Nancy, but no."

Nancy didn't move. "And to see if I could talk to you for a moment." A long pause and then, "Alone."

Vivienne looked at Judith who nodded and rose. As she turned to walk, she said, "Thank you, Vivienne. I'm interested."

Young Nancy stepped aside and let Miss Harrelson walk by. Judith shut the door behind her. Nancy stood holding the tray, frozen in place.

"What is it, Nancy?"

She hesitated a moment and then blurted, "May I work for you, Miss de Villiere?"

Vivienne's smile revealed her confusion. "Why, you do work for me, Nancy."

The young girl set the basket on the desk, looked back at her, and said, "As one of your ladies?"

Vivienne sat silently for a long moment. She patted the sofa beside her and said, "Come sit beside me, Nancy."

The young woman did. As she turned to sit, she did so very slowly and, in imitation of what she'd seen since she had been at Le Salon, brushed her skirts from behind her and sat down very slowly, her back as straight as she could make it.

"Nancy, you have worked here for three years now. Tell me what you see."

Nancy, still very erect, turned her head toward Vivienne without moving her shoulders. She shook her loose hair and let it settle behind her. "Miss de Villiere, what I see are very cultured women engaged in discourse with powerful men. They listen to the men and then almost always have something relevant to say. They meet them as equals. They are studied in politics and culture. They are charming and seem fearless. That is what I see."

Vivienne studied her as she never had. This girl, whom she'd known since she was a child, was blooming into a young woman. She would be a very pretty young woman if she were shown the way. And that she had been watching and paying attention and learning was clear both from the studied way she was comporting herself and the way she spoke. "Do you think you could be those things, Nancy?"

"I am studying everything I see here, Miss de Villiere. I'm learning politics. I read the paper every day and try to understand both sides of each issue, not to argue but to discuss. Culture is harder. I have no access to Shakespeare or Milton or any understanding of art. But I am smart, Miss de Villiere, and if you'll let me have access to your library, I'll learn." She paused. "On my own time, of course."

Vivienne went very slowly. "Nancy, you are what would have been known in my home as a downstairs maid. Do you know anything about what happens upstairs?"

Nancy was eager to respond. "Only in theory, ma'am. I'm a farm girl, and I've watched animals all my life." She stopped. "But somehow, I think there must be more to it than I've learned from them."

Vivienne sat quietly for a moment. "All right, Nancy, I will think on it. And yes, you may have access to the library in the daytime before guests arrive."

"Thank you, Miss de Villiere. I am grateful. Before I go, may I tell you one other thing I have seen here?"

"Of course, my dear."

"I've seen the value of information. And I have some information you want but no one else seems to know."

Vivienne allowed her bemused curiosity to show on her face. "What is that, Nancy?"

"I know why business has slowed."

Bemused was instantly replaced with unabashed curiosity. "Tell me, then."

"There is a boat tied on the river south of town. Customers go there."

Vivienne's expression changed again. This time it was somewhat patronizing. "Oh, my dear, those aren't our customers. The gentlemen who come here are not men to go to some flatboat crib."

Nancy shook her head so violently that her blond tresses thrashed back and forth across her nose. "It's not a flatboat, Miss de Villiere. It's one of Admiral Porter's old boats that has been completely refitted. There are below deck a bar, a dance floor, and a piano player. The private rooms, I'm told, are very posh."

Again, her expression changed dramatically. The original shock faded into understanding. "Do you know who's running it?"

"I don't know their names. But it's two brothers. They used to work at a dive in town called Walden's. Sheriff Hitchcock had one beat up and thrown out of town last spring. The other followed. I've heard they bought the boat in Peoria."

"Thank you, Nancy. I am grateful for the information. It is useful. Very useful. And it does show me you have learned well. Use the library. We will talk more."

Nancy stood. "Thank you, Miss de Villiere. I'll make certain your faith in me is worthwhile." She walked to the door.

"Nancy," came the voice behind her.

She turned. "Yes, ma'am."

"Are you a virgin?"

She blushed. "Yes, ma'am."

"Stay that way. I'll find a man who is anything but an animal to show you those wonderful things you haven't yet learned."

* * *

"James, I have a piece of news that I think may be of interest to you. I heard just this morning and thought that you would not only be interested but urgently so."

"Now how, beautiful Miss de Villiere, could I not be interested after such an introduction?" he said as he held her chair while she seated herself. As he walked around to his side of the desk, she scolded him.

"And how, James, besides forcing the use of your first name, will I ever get you to call me Vivienne? Is it truly so hard to say after these several years?"

He smiled an honest, open smile. "OK, you win. Vivienne it is. But only in the office."

Her smile in return was teasing. "I promise. Only your office or Le Salon."

His smile toned down. "You are persistent. Now what is this urgent news?"

"The Chicago, Burlington and Quincy is buying the R&RI Railroad."

He looked at her speechless, his mouth slightly open and jaw slightly forward. "How do you know that?"

Her expression went back from teasing to self-contained. "James, you can't ask me that save to say that in my business I hear many things that are not said elsewhere."

"But can I rely on it?"

"There was a young CB&Q executive in town yesterday. He had been sent here to find the state of construction 'to make sure we'll get what we're paying for.'

"James, I know it is so, but what I don't know is what to do with that information."

"I do, Miss de V . . . Vivienne. I know, if it is true."

"I cannot prove it's true, but I do know men well, and I do know that when they are a little drunk and a little weak, they say two kinds of things. Brags or facts. I know the difference. Perhaps I can persuade you." She reached into her bag and pulled out a leather purse that she laid on his desk. "I ask that you put this wherever you put your own money on this news."

James McHugh sat looking at the purse for a moment and then reached out and took it. "All right, Vivienne, I will."

"Good." She gave him a satisfied smile. "I have one other small item to discuss. This to discuss with the state's attorney."

McHugh's expression went back to the one of cool contemplation with which he usually greeted her visits. "The state's attorney is listening."

"You know I am civic minded and interested in the well-being of the community."

Now his smile became bemused as he knew this would be all about self-interest.

"News has come to my ears that there is, moored on the river south of town, one of Admiral Porter's old gunboats being run as a house of prostitution. I did not think such disregard for public morality was allowed here."

McHugh smiled like the cat who ate the canary.

"James, would you take it more seriously if you knew that the scum pimping these poor girls had been arrested and then thrown out of town by Sheriff Hitchcock earlier this year?"

The smile became a scowl. "Who?"

"Two brothers with a very odd last name. Burp or something like that."

The smile returned. "Madam, the state's attorney thanks you for doing your civic duty and assures you the miscreants will be dealt with."

"Thank you, Mr. McHugh." She rose to go.

He watched her rise, straighten her skirts, drape her parasol over her arm, and leave. Her hand on the door handle, she turned to look at him, her expression now sincere.

"James, I do look forward to the evening you see fit to come visit me at Le Salon."

CHAPTER 43

FEBRUARY 9, 1869

Le Salon, Chandlerville Road, Beardstown, Cass County, Illinois

The cold, dark night grew even colder and darker as the few lights of the city disappeared behind him. He rode with his neck pulled in low below his greatcoat, one gloved hand on the reins and the other in his pocket. The horse, seeming to want to get wherever it was his master was taking him, and wherever it was to get into a barn and out of the cold. But James McHugh was in no hurry. He was pensive and somewhat melancholy, his soul almost as dark as the night; he wasn't sure he should be doing this at all, but he felt the need to do something, and he was drawn, pulled to the place. Off to his right a light twinkled through the trees and then a few more, and finally warmth glowed through the dark. Two small, low carriage lamps marked the entrance. He pulled the reins to the right, and his mount easily turned up the lane, prancing, sensing journey's end.

As James approached the great house, he was met by a young boy bundled against the cold in an expensive great-coat of his own. He dismounted and handed the reins to the lad, watching him disappear with his horse around the side of the house. James rose up the steps slowly, one at a time. In response to his single drop of the large brass knocker, the door was opened by the largest man he had ever seen. The man was so black that, in the night, almost the only things visible were his teeth and the whites of his eyes and his shirt. But huge as the man was, even more noticeable was his dress. The only thing McHugh had ever seen like it was a news-paper illustration. The pants were black as was the jacket, which was cut square at the hips. Its long satin lapels almost gleaming, even in the dark. A white shirt, held together with shiny mother-of-pearl stud buttons, filled the space between the lapels. The collar of the shirt ran up the neck, the tips folded over. Below the collar was a black bow tie. McHugh was stunned to silence.

"Good evening, sir." The voice was a rumble. "Please step in and allow me to take your coat and gloves and show you to the bar."

"You're Heracles." McHugh recovered himself. "She's men-tioned you." And then stepping forward and shrugging out of his coat, he said, "And yes, thank you. And would you tell Miss de Villiere that James McHugh has accepted her invitation?"

Heracles hung the coat with the others on a rack along the wall and then opened the door into the main salon. A large fire roared in the fireplace. There were two groups of men around the room. One was a group of only two sitting on a couch facing one another. Between them was a woman, tall even sitting, the grace of her carriage requiring no motion to display itself. Her evening dress covered her shoulders but was cut down in the front and squared off above her small breasts. Her blond hair was pulled back off her thin face and gathered in a short braid circled into a bun at the nape of her neck. The table before them housed two crystal tumblers, both half-full of amber liquid, and a stemmed glass containing a reddish liquid. There was also a brass ashtray holding two large and lit cigars, the sweet aroma of their tobacco drifting across the room. Both men looked up and nodded a welcome. One offered, "Hello, James. Good place to be on a cold night."

Not wishing to engage them, McHugh responded by rubbing his cold hands together and said, "A whiskey will warm that out of me, Rupert," and continued to follow Heracles across the room.

The second group was of three men shoved close together around a small serving table and engaged in a lively discussion. A buxom redhead sitting with them said something at which they all laughed uproariously. None of them bothered to look up as he passed.

"René, I believe Mr. McHugh would like a whiskey. Please do seat yourself, sir," the huge man rumbled again. "I'll tell Miss de Villiere you're here."

The small man with the flowing black hair looked over from behind the bar. "How would you like your whiskey, Mr. McHugh?"

McHugh responded, "Neat, please—two fingers."

A crystal tumbler and bottle appeared almost instantly. "Mr. McHugh, I'm going to leave you the bottle as I'm also charged with entertainment here and need to step away." René pointed to the piano sitting in the space across the room from the roaring fire. "This weather calls for something reassuring, I think."

McHugh sat staring into his whiskey as though it might provide some vision of the future, as the room filled with a soft lullaby. He felt her before he saw her.

"James." It came as softly as the lullaby.

He turned to look up into placid grey eyes that seemed to invite him in.

She reached out to the bottle beside his drink and refilled his almost-empty tumbler. "James, I'm sitting in the library with a friend of yours. Come join us."

Much as he wanted to be here this evening, to be in her company, he was fearful of being alone with this woman in this place. He didn't know who his friend was, and he didn't care. Their presence would relieve all sense of temptation he felt when he looked into those eyes.

"I'd like that very much. Lead on." He picked up the drink and turned to follow the rustle of silk ruffles on the train below the large ribbon across the back of her dress, large, but not large enough to hide the slow, undulating sway of her hips.

The doors to the library were open. He was stunned by what he saw as he stepped between them. The billiards table, which took up the center of the room, was handsome, but the stunning part was what surrounded it. Two walls of the room were finished with bookshelves floor to ceiling, a rolling ladder allowing access to the top shelves. In one corner were a small sofa and a wingback chair each finished in tanned leather, brass tacks decorating the places the leather covering was attached to the frame. A small glass coffee table completed the seating group. The tall, corpulent frame of Nigel Hoskins filled the winged chair almost to overflowing.

"James, you will forgive me if I don't stand. I fear our mutual friend Vivienne may have indulged me too much to easily rise." His brown eyes flashed humor; the warmth of his smile pushed his bushy eyebrows up toward his hairline.

James was glad it was him, and his feeling showed. "Nigel, if you put on another ten pounds, you'll not be able to get out of that chair drunk or sober."

Hoskins's only response was a chuckle that confirmed McHugh's point by making his jowls jiggle.

Vivienne pulled her skirts forward and slid onto the sofa in the corner nearest Hoskins. McHugh took the remaining seat on the sofa.

"We have her surrounded," Hoskins observed. "Now tell me, my friend, what brings you out here on a cold and dreary night? I thought you avoided all higher culture."

"Nigel asks my very question. I, too, would like to know. What is the occasion that brings this, your maiden visit to Le Salon?"

McHugh leaned forward, picked up his glass, took a long pull, swallowed, set the glass back down, and smiled a pensive smile. "Nigel, you've been here since I was a boy. Who would you consider the founders of this town?"

Hoskins's lips pursed together, and his eyebrows knit in concentration. "Let's see. Certainly, Tom Beard. And a banker cannot leave out his money partner. Marsh, was it? What was his Christian name? Not sure I know."

"Enos," McHugh offered.

"Yes, that's it. Enos. And I know he was a latecomer, but I'd include Francis Arenz on my list. And the old Indian. Chaubenee, was that it?"

"Yes, they would be on my list, but there is one other you're forgetting, Nigel. Perhaps you never met him."

"You're right; you're right. The lad who rode up here with Beard and helped build the first cabin and then went on to fly very high. McConnel. General Murray McConnel."

"That your whole list?" McHugh asked.

Hoskins remained pensive. "Yes. Yes, that's my list. Those five. What about them?"

Sadness flushed McHugh's face. "They're all gone."

Hoskins set his drink down. "No, no. The general's gone to Jacksonville, but he's still with us."

McHugh shook his head. "No. He's gone. The wire came in this afternoon."

"James, I'm sorry. Is that what has you bothered? He's an old man. Must be seventy or more. Didn't know you were that close to him, James. I'm sorry, but we all get old and die. I'm starting to feel it myself. What did the general die of?"

"Heart failure, I believe."

"Common enough in old men and very quick at least."

"Yes," McHugh agreed, "very quick. Especially in his case. Induced by a .45 slug."

"What?" Hoskins sat straight upright, and Vivienne lost her look of interested composure. "Who? Why?" Hoskins asked.

"Wire didn't say, Nigel. Just that he was shot in his office. We'll find out more tomorrow or soon after."

"James, I'm sorry. No wonder you're down," the soft voice of Vivienne offered. Her eyes offering shelter as well.

"Vivienne, it's not Mo McConnel. No matter how he died. That old man led one hell of a life. Did far more and built far more than any of us. I'd gladly trade my adventures for his."

"Then what?" she asked.

"He's the last of them. The era is past. There is no more frontier. At least not here. The moments of life and death, pure victory or pure defeat, man against the wilderness. Those are all gone. It just made me sad knowing all of them, and the time they represent, are gone. Gone forever."

They sat quietly for a moment. Hoskins for the first time pulled his bulk forward out of the depths of his large chair. "James, you're wrong."

McHugh looked startled. "Wrong about what?"

"Oh, not wrong about the founders all having passed. That's true enough. But look what they have created. What they have left us. They came into the wilderness just fifty years ago. Correct?"

"Yes," McHugh said, and nodded. "Beard and McConnel arrived here with the first snow in the fall of 1818. That was just months over a half century ago."

"And they created a small city. A prosperous city. They planted the seed of civilization and then nurtured it and watched it grow. They have bequeathed some ten thousand souls comfort, safety, and all the amenities of modern life. And something else as well. They have created a place of culture. Look around you, James. What do you see?"

Hoskins stopped talking. McHugh sat still. "No, James, look around. Tell me what you see."

McHugh panned the room. "Well, I see books. Lots of books."

Hoskins looked at Vivienne. "What books are they, Vivienne?"

"Mostly, they are literature in English and German. There is Faust up there, book by Goethe, in German, and the play by Marlowe in English. I think I've got everything Shakespeare ever wrote up there as well. Lots of contemporary novels— Brontë and Austen; women do write, you know. Some Dickens and Scott. I try to have what men may want to read. We've got a lot of political and philosophical things as well. Full set of *The Federalist Papers* if you're interested. Hobbes, Locke, that sort of thing."

"Any ancient wisdom?" Hoskins prodded.

"Oh yes. What I can find of Aristotle. I've always admired the Stoics, so you'll find Marcus Aurelius and Seneca."

"In Latin?" Hoskins continued to prod.

She flushed with a bit of embarrassment. "Well, Dante is in Latin if that counts."

"And Greek?" Hoskins wouldn't stop.

"I brought only two books north with me, both of those in Greek. The rest are new. But my father loved Homer, and I've got both the *Iliad* and the *Odyssey*. But I admit you won't find them here. I keep those in my room."

Hoskins looked back at McHugh. "Tell me what else you see here. Let me prompt. Beside you."

McHugh turned to his right and smiled at the beautiful woman beside him. He turned back to Hoskins. "I see in this room, and the other, beautiful women. In fact, beside me is a gorgeous woman dressed for the evening in a style I've never seen. I'm presuming it is the newest fashion." He turned back to her. "Is it, Vivienne?"

"It is, sir." She smiled mischievously. "And while we are discussing style, did you notice Heracles's suit when you came in?"

"I did," Hoskins interjected. "He is as sartorially splendid as the Prince of Wales."

"Why, Nigel." Vivienne gave him a look of complete approval. "You do keep up."

He smiled charmingly. "They require it to maintain my British citizenship, you know. I believe Edward did away with tails as evening wear just three years ago. A 'tuxedo' it's called."

"Nigel, you get a drink on the house," she said, and blew him a kiss.

Pleased with himself, Hoskins looked back at McHugh. "Before I stop quizzing, also tell me what you hear."

For the first time McHugh smiled as though enjoying the game. "Well, Nigel, aside from the 'oh-so-proper' accent of yours, it is the music of Brahms."

"Why, James." She beamed. "There is more to you than a mere country lawyer. You get a drink on the house as well. And since you're close enough, I won't have to blow this to you." She bent to her left, twisted her head, and kissed his cheek.

Nigel's boomed laughter filled the room. "James, I do believe you are blushing." He paused for a moment and then picked up his glass. "Now that our hostess and I have jollied you out of your uncalled-for melancholy, allow me to propose a toast." He held his glass toward them and said, "To the men who created Beardstown and brought culture and wealth to the wilderness. To Thomas Beard's town."

And they chorused after him.

"TO BEARDSTOWN!"

HISTORICAL NOTES

1. Chaubenee (also found in the literature as Shabbona) was the most accepted and revered of the Indian natives by the white migrants to Illinois. He is buried, and his grave marked with a large stone, in Evergreen Cemetery, Morris, Illinois.
2. General Murray McConnel was shot and killed in his office in Jacksonville, Illinois, on February 9, 1869. I have been unable to find the cause of his murder, but the local papers used the word "assassinated," which suggests it was of political motive.
3. I have been unable to find any history of Enos Marsh after he sold his holdings in Beardstown. There are internet postings on gravestones for Enoch/Enos Marsh, but none match his dates closely enough to make me certain they are for the Enos Marsh who was a founder of Beardstown.
4. Sara Bell and Tom Beard had three children, a fact that I have left out of this novel as I could find no way to make them useful to the narrative. I find no records of Sara Bell subsequent to Tom Beard divorcing her on grounds of infidelity. I do, however, find record of one of Tom Beard's sons killed in a gunfight in the American West in the 1870s and the record of

one granddaughter living in New York at the end of
the 19th century.

5. The German village that formed on Indian Creek
    some eleven miles south of Beardstown named itself
    Arenzville, Illinois, in honor of Francis Arenz.

6. Since *Beardstown* is a work of fiction, I do not feel a
    strict obligation to precise historicity in the novel, but
    I do feel an obligation to the narrative of the history.
    The one place I have egregiously warped facts to suit
    the purpose is in presenting Jefferson Davis as a par-
    ticipant in the Black Hawk War. After being gradu-
    ated from West Point in 1828, Davis was assigned to
    duty at Fort Crawford in Prairie du Chien, Wisconsin.
    While that puts him within the area of conflict, there
    is no evidence he fought in any engagement in that
    war or was ever in Beardstown, Illinois, though he did
    command the escort detail that took Black Hawk to
    prison at Jefferson Barracks in St. Louis at the end of
    the war.

    I hope you will forgive my indulgence, but I sim-
    ply could not resist the temptation to put Jefferson
    Davis and Abraham Lincoln in such close contact so
    early in their careers.

SNEAK PEEK FROM AMERICAN PIED PIPER

~ *The* ~
AMERICAN TRILOGY
BOOK 3

"In Italy, for thirty years under the Borgias, they had warfare, terror, murder, and bloodshed, but they produced Michelangelo, Leonardo da Vinci, and the Renaissance. In Switzerland, they had brotherly love, they had five hundred years of democracy and peace, and what did that produce? The cuckoo clock."

—spoken by Harry Lime as played by Orson Welles in *The Third Man* in 1949

The line is said to have been written by Welles.

CHAPTER 1

OCTOBER 1906

Mokane, Missouri

The huge birds rose in a far-reaching, slow upward spiral, their long black necks and heads extended stiff as tree branches before their fat grey-brown bodies, the brilliant white triangles, formed from the backs of their heads to the bottoms of their necks, evoked the image of the chinstrap below some palace guard's black beaver hat. *But what it really is, is a perfect target.*

Cunningham had fired both barrels as soon as the flock of Canada geese rose from the quiet eddy downstream. He had missed both times. Sam Clark rose slowly from the blind, all six feet of him standing straight and tall and all two hundred pounds poised, a granite statue, holding the big 10 gauge pointed straight up into the sky. It didn't matter that they saw him now. *After Cunningham's shots they know we're here. That's why they started the long, slow spiral. They think they'll gain elevation enough to get above our range before they level out. Smart as they are beautiful and tasty. But today, they're wrong.*

As the lead bird leveled out the others rose to him forming their flying V to head upriver.

"Sam, even you will never reach them now."

Without moving, the statue answered, "Bet you twenty-five cents, Mr. Cunningham."

"You're on, son."

Over the steady honking of the flock came the tremendous roar of the big, long-barreled shotgun. A second later they watched as the lead bird's head snapped up into an impossible angle, and then the bird tumbled, with no glide at all, body rolling over head again and again, his fall ending in a large splash into the Missouri River.

The rust-brown dog, with curls waving down the length of his back, sat at the front of the blind, the same statue his master had been save that the tip of his pink tongue jerked in and out of his mouth, steadily drooling saliva. Clark said not a word but leaned down low enough for the motion of his hand to show in his dog's peripheral vision; palm flat and finger held rigidly together, he swung his arm in an arch from his hips to his waist. The dog bolted from sitting into the air, a vision of leaping perfection, his hind legs extended behind, his front legs tight up against his chest, only his paws hanging down and his head extended as far forward from his body as his neck would allow. The leap pulled him two feet off the ground and landed him five feet into the river with a splash. He didn't head to the floating body of the goose but swam as directly out into the current as he was able until he was as far from the shore as the goose. Only then did he then turn his head upstream and dog paddle easily until the drifting trophy floated into his mouth. He turned and headed to shore, the current pushing him downstream as he went.

"I believe you owe me twenty-five cents, Mr. Cunningham," Sam said.

Cunningham had long since risen from his camp stool to admire everything he had just seen—the majesty of the bird, the not-to-be-believed skill of the shot, and the perfection of the training of the retriever. "Nobody can shoot flyers that high. I wouldn't have thought even you could do it, Sam," Cunningham said, looking into the light brown eyes of Sam Clark. He saw a man of no more than twenty, but he was a man. There was no boy in his face anymore. His mass of light brown hair was almost as wavy as his dog's. The face was wide and the jaw square. The ears were rounded and lay unobtrusively against the side of his face. Only his nose, which was long and straight but a bit too thick, saved him from being handsome. His lips were neither thick nor thin, but something about them and the flare of his nostrils, even in this small moment of glory while acting as guide to his father's boss and manager of the entire line of the Missouri, Kansas, and Eastern Railroad, showed a hint of cruelty, or perhaps just arrogance. C. C. Cunningham reached into his pocket, took out a quarter, and flipped it into the air. Sam looked once, extended his hand palm up, and allowed the falling coin to drop into it.

"How do you do it?"

Sam smiled now. It was smile that softened his face and made him look a touch humble. "I've been doing it long as I can remember. Shotgun shells are not cheap and what hard-earned money I ever got was from running a trapline. This time of year, furs aren't worth much yet, so even if I bother to set the trapline, I don't earn much. Not enough to buy a lot of extra ammunition; that's for certain. So best not to miss, always has been really. Also, I'm prepared a bit differently than you or others." He held the shotgun before him and snapped open the breach. A huge shell popped out. "It's a ten gauge, so a bit more giddyup than your twelve. And I had in double-aught shot. Pretty small pattern but it will reach a long way."

"Why did you let them get so high? You could have reached them as they circled downriver before they leveled out, but you didn't. Why?" Cunningham smiled now. "You just showing off or egging me into betting that quarter?"

There was a crunching sound in the brush on the down-river side of the blind. The Chesapeake Bay retriever came crashing through, the goose in his mouth seeming almost as big as he, its head dragging the ground on one side of the dog's mouth, its feet on the other. He sat down on Sam's left side.

Sam bent down until his hand was under the goose, under but not touching. "Give, Teddy," he commanded softly.

The beast dropped the goose into Sam's hand and then stood and shook violently throwing water everywhere.

Sam used his other hand to scratch behind the dog's ears. "Good dog." Sam straightened up, shifting the goose so he held it by the neck just below its mangled head, the black tip of the tail still touching the ground. Sam finally answered the question, "Mr. Cunningham I'm pleased to take your money, and it pleases me to be better with highflyers than most, but that wasn't the reason. The reason I let it go so long, sir, was your pleasure."

Cunningham cocked his head to one side looking up at Sam with a quizzical, almost skeptical, expression on his face.

"How long have I known you now, Mr. Cunningham? Maybe eight years?"

"Sounds right," Cunningham answered.

"And you always like to have dinner your last night with something we've hunted and Dad has cooked. That right?"

Cunningham nodded.

"You and I have never hunted birds on the Missouri before, so you didn't know, but the problem isn't finding them. The problem is retrieving them from that current." He pointed to

the river. "Teddy is the first Chessy I've ever owned. He's unbe-
lievably strong, and that curly coat of his keeps him warm long
after labs have given up. Aside from the fact that he likes to
fight a bit too much he's the best dog I've ever owned. But even
Teddy can't swim against the current of the Missouri. Only way
he was going to retrieve your dinner was if I shot it upstream
so he could let it float back to him. As it was, he was pushed
a quarter mile downstream before he could get back to shore.

"So, it was for your dinner, Sir." Sam held the goose up
between them. "That's why I had to wait."

Cunningham beamed a big smile. "I always have liked you,
son. Enjoyed watching you grow.

"Now I've got to get cleaned up and return to work. Let's
get back the hotel before I burn much more daylight."

The two men and the dog walked away from the river into
the tree cover above the bank. The leaves were turning golden.
The morning sun even revealed a few flashes of red color in the
canopy above. Enough of the leaves had fallen to make a soft
crunching sound underfoot. The big palomino stallion and the
smaller black mare stood where they had left them, tied to two
small hickory trees. By the time Sam tied the goose behind
his saddle Cunningham was already up on the palomino. The
big stallion snickered and nudged Sam's butt as he mounted.
Sam, halfway up, stood in one stirrup, reached behind him,
and scratched the white blaze down the middle of the otherwise golden face.

"I see the big guy likes you," Cunningham observed.

"I often ride him. But the stable belongs to your railroad.
I figured he's yours. You should have him when you're here."

The two walked their horses slowly through the woods to
the dirt road that ran along the bluff between Mokane and the
bridge across the river at Jefferson City.

"Sam, you've been out of school for a couple of years now. Ever think about going to work for the railroad?" Cunningham inquired.

Sam gave a small laugh. "Mr. Cunningham, railroads name themselves for towns—Chicago, Burlington, Quincy, Rockford, St. Louis. It's a very long list. I was born and raised in the only town named for a railroad not the other way around. Mokane - Missouri, MO, Kansas, KAN, and Eastern, E. MOKANE. Mokane, Missouri. My father has cooked in the railroad hotel my whole life. Of course, I've thought of working for the railroad."

"What would you like to do?"

Sam stretched forward across the saddle pommel, twisted over it until he was looking at Cunningham. "Drive one."

Now it was Cunningham's turn to laugh, "Sam, everyone wants to drive one. Those jobs are damn hard to come by. Seldom come along. How about working for us in the hotel?"

Sam sank back into his saddle looking down along the row of grass growing between the two dirt tracks that defined the road. "Mr. Cunningham, I already work in the hotel. You know that. I serve you dinner every night."

"Oh, I was thinking of something full time. Maybe manage it."

"Thanks, but no, Mr. Cunningham. I've watched my dad as long as I can remember. You've given him a good job. It pays enough for him to get all three of us kids though school, well fed and clothed, and we all get to live in the hotel and use the stable. But no. Thanks, but no. I don't see a future here, Mr. Cunningham."

"Fair 'nough." Cunningham nodded. "How about we get you a job in the shop. Teach you pipe fitting and toolmaking and maybe even boilermaking. Good money, there."

"It's not that I'm not grateful, Mr. Cunningham. I am. It's kind of you to think of me. But that's just not me to work in a shop. I'm an outdoor guy. Being the engineer, driving a train, watching the world go by, seeing places. That suits me."

Cunningham pulled back on his reins and stopped the palomino. Sam followed his lead. The two sat facing one another in the shade of the tree-canopied lane. "Sam, you're a good lad and will be a good man. I'd like to help you. Like to have you with us. But an engineer's job just isn't in the cards even if I wanted to. We just don't need any and don't know when we will."

Sam nodded and started back down the lane.

"What will you do, Sam?"

"Probably, what I am. Trapping fur has always made me some money and soon as it gets colder and fur grows longer it will again. But now I'm old enough, I've found lots of your passengers like to stop here and pay me to guide them hunting. I think that may be a life for me."

The stable was in sight. The two men rode in. Cunningham dismounted and handed Sam the reins of his horse. "Think about it, Sam. I'll be here all day and tonight. I leave in the morning on the 10:12 to Jeff City. Let me know if you change your mind.

"Now I'm going to clean up and get off to the depot and my work. Have the palomino rubbed and fed. I'll be ready to go in an hour." He walked out of the barn and into the light.

Sam shouted at Cunningham's back as he left. "We'll have your goose ready for dinner, sir."

* * * *

Sam used his left hand to push open the swinging doors that separated the kitchen from the dining room. That C. C. Cunningham sat alone, no one else in the room, seemed to heighten the eerie sense the flickering light from the gas lamps along the walls imparted. Sam held the serving tray high over his shoulder as he walked to the middle of the room. He sat the tray on a small serving table next to Cunningham's round table. *The man looks the picture of contemporary refinement.* He was dressed in a three-piece sack suit, the white of his shirt showing only at the cuffs and the collar, his wide silk necktie covering up almost all the shirt not covered by his five-button vest. The gold watch chain looped between his vest pockets shimmering even in the low light.

Cunningham saw him looking at it and pulled a large gold watch from one of his vest pockets and held it up by the chain. It became a swinging gold pendulum. "Ball Standard. Only kind a railroad man will have."

Sam lifted the cover off the soup bowl on the serving tray and placed the bowl in front of Cunningham as the railroad baron put the watch back into his vest pocket. "You always seem to like Dad's turtle soup, so I got one and Dad simmered it all day. Hope you enjoy it. Goose will be ready in ten minutes."

Cunningham nodded. Sam collected the tray from serving table, again hoisted it above his shoulder and returned to the kitchen just in time to see his father take the goose from the oven and start cutting the delicious smelling entrée.

"Sam, just five minutes to finish the vegetables and butter the potato, and it will be ready for you."

Sam looked across the kitchen at his father, working so rapidly to pull it all together. He looked small and old. *Why has he accepted this as his lot?* Sam stood by the half swinging doors and watched the back of Cunningham's head as he slowly spooned up his soup.

The front door burst open and allowed in a blast of cold air and a stranger. The stranger looked bedraggled, cold, and very thin. It was a thinness not of athleticism or asceticism but starvation. His face was hidden behind a leather hat that looked as worn as he. The stranger shut the door and removed his hat, almost reverentially. It revealed a face gaunt enough to match the body. The cheekbones looked skeletally pronounced. The eyes were sunken so deep that Sam could not make out the color, but even from where he was, he could see they penetrated all they touched with a hellish flame. The man, the beast, whatever it was, walked with a measured pace, unbuttoning his threadbare coat as he came. When the last button parted, the coat fell open to reveal Levi's as worn as the coat and a pistol as powerful as his eyes. The holster hung low from his hip. The gun barrel was so long it extended out the bottom of the holster. He walked steadily toward Cunningham who sat watching him come.

When he reached Cunningham, the stranger carefully laid his hat on the table and said, "You're C. C. Cunningham." It was a statement not a question.

Cunningham appraised the apparition before him carefully. "I am. I don't believe we've met."

"Oh, I know you, Mr. Cunningham, but no reason you'd remember me. I was twelve years old and part of a crowd on the courthouse steps in Fresno when last I saw you. You were the station chief for Central Pacific there."

Cunningham's words came out with forced joviality. "I was a very young man. Probably twenty-five. My first major assignment with any railroad."

"My parents bought eighty acres from the Central Pacific in 1876. Bought it cheap because there was nothing there, and, until the railroad, no way to get crops to market even if there was. But the Central Pacific helped them get a mortgage and promised the new rail would make them prosper. And they did; everyone did, as you remember, Mr. Cunningham. Everyone did until you upped freight rates so high there was no profit left."

Cunningham started to rise.

The long Colt Peacemaker came out of the holster and was leveled at Cunningham's chest. "The day I saw you, Mr.

Cunningham, was in 1882. You were on the courthouse steps. The bank had foreclosed on the mortgage, and the farm my parents worked themselves almost to the grave to make prosperous was being sold. We went to buy it back knowing none of the neighbors would bid against us. But you did. You were surrounded by a pack of gunslingers to protect you from my parents and the other farmers. You bought our farm for past taxes and mortgage arears. Daddy died the year after and momma a couple later. I was fifteen when she died. That was twenty years ago. I been lookin' for you ever since."

Sam stepped back from the kitchen door, grabbed a serving tray, and threw the plate of goose on it.

"Sam, stop it's not ready," his father called after as Sam hoisted the tray to his shoulder and boldly threw open the door to the dining room.

The Colt muzzle came around until it was pointed at his chest. The bore got ever bigger as Sam got ever closer.

"No place for you here, son." The man's eyes said more than the words.

Sam kept coming. "Mister, I see you have business with Mr. Cunningham. That's between you and him. I have business with Mr. Cunningham as well, and I intend to do mine just as you intend to do yours." He sat the tray down on the serving table and slid the plate of steaming goose in front of his guest. "I hope you'll find it as you like it, Mr. Cunningham." He reached back to the serving tray, picked it up, and made a motion as if to raise it to his shoulder.

The edge of the tray slammed into the stranger's Adam's apple with a viciousness that drove him backward even as he dropped. Sam took one step toward the fallen man and kicked him between the legs. The only sound was the crunch of bone as the man grabbed at his groin, his throat unable to breathe or scream. Sam picked up the fallen pistol tucked it into his belt, grabbed one of the injured man's wrists and drug him across the floor and out the front door.

He was back inside in less than two minutes, the gun belt thrown over his shoulder. "I've tied him to one of the posts on the porch. I'll let you decide what to do with him."

Sam stopped and gave an amused smile. "I'm sorry about your goose. Pa wanted me to wait to bring it until he had the vegetables ready, but I thought you'd prefer it now."

A still stunned C. C. Cunningham sat arms and legs akimbo and just nodded.

Five minutes later Sam came back from the kitchen, this time with the vegetables, a hot cup of coffee, a bottle of brandy, and a leaded crystal tumbler. "Thought you might want this, Mr. Cunningham," Sam offered.

Cunningham smiled, his face showing its usual composure. "Sam, would you do two things for me?"

"Of course, sir."

"Take that fellow to the sheriff and tell him what happened. Also tell him I don't want him to do anything just now. I'll be in, in the morning, to discuss it."

"And the other?"

"Train's at 10:12 a.m. Tell the sheriff I'll be in at about nine thirty. Have the surrey ready and out front at eight thirty."

"Mr. Cunningham, it will only take you fifteen minutes to get there."

"Sam, I want you to drive me. We have some things to talk about."

* * * *

Sam sat in the surrey, watching Cunningham walk out of the Mokane Missouri Railroad Hotel. Cunningham, as usual, was dressed nattily. Tweed three-piece sack suit, with well-polished lace-up boots. The derby he perpetually wore covering a receding hairline. Cunningham was a small man with a small frame, but his waist was beginning to bulge. The wire-rimmed glasses he wore gave him a scholarly look that the fierceness in his black eyes betrayed. He may have had a small man's complex but C. C. Cunningham was a very hard man and wanted it to show.

He walked around the surrey and got in beside Sam. "Turn around and drive down by the river. We have time, and I want to talk."

Sam did as instructed and drove out of the little town of Mokane. Within five minutes they were back along the dirt track that wound through the fall woods.

"Sam, do you know who Andrew Carnegie is?"

Sam thought for a moment. "Steel guy? Right?"

"That's right. Do you know who J. P. Morgan is? John Pierpont Morgan?"

Sam thought again. "Can't say I do. He from around here?"

"No, Sam. He's from New York. He's a banker, a financier, he would call himself."

"Why do you ask, Mr. Cunningham?"

"Ever heard of Gary, Indiana?"

"Can't say I have," Sam responded.

"No reason you should. It's brand-new, a town Carnegie and Morgan are building."

"Where?"

"Right at the bottom tip of Lake Michigan, Sam. Just across the line from Illinois."

"Odd name for a new town," Sam offered.

Cunningham gave a snort. "It is indeed. Elbert Gary is Morgan's attorney and one of his business partners. They've named it for him."

"Why are you telling me all this, Mr. Cunningham?"

"Morgan, Carnegie, and Gary are building the largest steel mill in the country and putting it in this new place. They say they'll have four blast furnaces and employ five thousand people.

"You know what it takes to make steel, Sam?"

"No, sir."

"It takes two things. It takes iron ore and coal. Lots of iron ore and lots of coal. And you know what those two have in common?"

"No, sir."

"They are heavy as hell and really expensive to move. And you know what they don't have in common?"

"No, sir."

"Nowhere in America are iron ore mines and coal mines close together. So, to make steel, one or both really expensive and hard to move things have to be moved."

"Know where there's lots of iron ore, Sam?"

This time Sam just shook his head.

"Bunch of low mountains called the Gogebic Range right where Michigan and Wisconsin and Minnesota all come together at the far west end of Lake Superior.

"Know where there's lots of coal, Sam?"

Sam's broad face opened into a tooth-displaying smile as he looked over at his companion. "That one I got. Southern Illinois and northern Kentucky got more coal than they know what to do with."

"Bingo," Cunningham responded.

"And can you guess how they get them together?"

Sam smile became small and self-satisfied. "They run boats full of the iron as close as they can get it to the coal, say the bottom end of Lake Michigan, and then they run railcars of coal up from southern Illinois to the same place. This Gary, Indiana place."

"You are clever, Sam. Now let's keep going. Do you know the rail carrier dominant from northern to southern Illinois?"

"Not sure, but I'd guess the Chicago, Burlington and Quincy."

"Bingo, again."

"Now, Sam, you grew up with rail, so this next part is going to be easy. Will they drive those engines the length of the state and then return them with empty cars?"

"Nope. Too far for the crews. They'll uncouple the cars from the engine somewhere halfway, hook them to a new engine with a new crew, and let them take it to the terminus. That crew may even bring the empties back with it and allow the crew returning south to take the empties with them for refill."

Cunningham looked over at the young driver, a real smile of satisfaction on his face. "You've learned more about running a railroad than you know about hotels, young man. When the CB&Q bought the Rockford, Rock Island, and St. Louis they inherited a small roundhouse and shop at a town in the middle of the state called Beardstown. U.S. Steel, that's what Carnegie and Morgan are naming this this venture, will open the first furnace in two years. CB&Q has that long to expand that Beardstown operation. Part of that expansion is new equipment and crews." Cunningham stopped his speech and turned to look closely at young Clark. He wanted to see his response when he said what he'd been leading up to. "It's your chance to become an engineer, to drive a train, if that's what you really want to do, Sam."

Sam Clark kept his eyes fixed on the road as he brought the surrey to a complete stop. Only then did he turn toward Cunningham and let his joy show in his expression. "You tell me what to do, Mr. Cunningham, and I'll do it. And be forever grateful."

Cunningham's smile was genuine. "First, turn this thing around. I've got a nine thirty appointment with the sheriff, and you need to get me there on time. I'll tell you what to do as we ride."

Sam swung the horse around and slapped the leather of the reins along its back and gave an enthusiastic click, click, a sound made with his tongue fixed firmly in one cheek. The horse understood and broke into a trot.

"I have three letters for you, Sam. I'll get them out of my valise when you drop me. The first is to a man named George Grainger. You'll find him at CB&Q's offices in Beardstown. It is a letter recommending he hire you and get you trained as an engineer. The letter is sealed, Sam. Don't open it. It's for Grainger, not you."

"Yes, sir."

"George and I have been friendly competitors for years. I respect him and I flatter myself the feeling is mutual. I can't guarantee he'll hire you, but I'm hopeful. I'll wire him you're coming.

"Second letter is to a tailor in Beardstown. Guy named Lorenz Adler. He used to be in Jacksonville. He's made me suits and is very good. He's German so it's pronounced like there's a t in front of the z. Comes out very much like Lawrence. I called him Larry once. I recommend you don't. See him and get a suit before you go to Grainger's office."

"Mr. Cunningham, I don't have money for a suit."

"The letter takes care of that, Sam. I'm buying you the suit."

"Can't let you do that, Mr. Cunningham. I'll never be able to pay you back."

Cunningham laughed from his belly. "Oh, yes you will. I forgot to tell you, but this Beardstown place is just below a thing called the Sangamon Slough. It forms where the Sangamon River flows into the Illinois. Forms the slough and the Mascouten Bay. They make the best duck and goose hunting on the Mississippi flyway. You owe me free guide services the rest of your life."

Sam's cheeks flushed pink. "Thank you, Mr. Cunningham. Don't know how I'll ever repay you."

"Sam, I believe I'm the one who owes you a debt I'll never be able to repay."

There was a moment of embarrassed silence between the two men.

"Sam, take the ferry across the Mississippi at Alton. From there just follow the Illinois River. Beardstown is at mile eighty-eight. You'll find a rooming house there. If you take that Chessy of yours the rooming house will let him stay. Should be no problem. You'll also find a livery for your horse. Then have Adler make you the suit. Shouldn't take him more than two days to make. Only then go see Grainger. After that we'll keep our fingers crossed."

"Thanks, Mr. Cunningham. But I won't be needing the horse. I'll walk."

"No. No. You won't walk. It's probably two hundred miles. I'll not have you freezing your ass off before you even get there. And Indian summer here or not, by the time you walk that far it may be winter. I told you I had three letters. One is to you. It's a gift from the Mokane Kansas and Eastern Railroad. Take the palomino. He's yours."

ABOUT THE AUTHOR

Foster lives and writes overlooking R.A.T. Beach in Torrance, California. He is the author of the five-star reviewed *Alpha Male*, the Pushcart Prize–nominated *Non-Semper Fidelis*, and *A Panther Crosses Over*, the first book in the American Trilogy series.